The Road to Deer Run

Elaine Marie Cooper

iUniverse, Inc.
New York Bloomington

The Road to Deer Run

iUniverse books may be ordered through booksellers or by contacting:

iUniverse
1663 Liberty Drive
Bloomington, IN 47403
www.iuniverse.com
1-800-Authors (1-800-288-4677)

Because of the dynamic nature of the Internet, any Web addresses or links contained in this book may have changed since publication and may no longer be valid. The views expressed in this work are solely those of the author and do not necessarily reflect the views of the publisher, and the publisher hereby disclaims any responsibility for them.

ISBN: 978-1-4502-1919-8 (sc)
ISBN: 978-1-4502-1916-7 (dj)
ISBN: 978-1-4502-1918-1 (ebk)

Library of Congress Control Number: 2010903561

Printed in the United States of America

iUniverse rev. date: 3/29/2010

This book is dedicated to the memory of my daughter,

BETHANY JEANNE COOPER

December 12, 1978 – October 20, 2003

In a family of writers, her creative star shone the brightest

Acknowledgments

There are so many that have contributed advice, technical expertise, and enthusiasm for this novel. I could not have accomplished this lengthy effort without you.

First and foremost, I acknowledge the support and patient efforts of my editor-husband and soul-mate, Steve. Your understanding of the written word and your tireless efforts to support this undertaking have been so appreciated, and your humor has been a welcome relief from the strain of editing! Thank you for believing that this work could really be accomplished. It could not have been without your love, support, and understanding.

I also wish to say thanks to Dave Toht, editor at Greenleaf Publishing, Inc. Your enthusiasm for the idea behind this story and your technical know-how have been instrumental in helping this project become a reality. I thank you for being so encouraging.

A special thanks to Krista Hill, David Bernardi, and all the editors at iUniverse who helped make this novel a more polished read. I really appreciate your vision.

To Elaine Germano, Certified Nurse Midwife, DrPH, FACNM, of the American College of Nurse-Midwives, I say a hearty "thank you." Your expertise in midwifery gave credibility to an eighteenth-century scenario. Bravo to you, brave midwives!

To Katie Leporte for her wonderful cover design—you captured the feeling of the story with the beauty of your art. Thank you from the bottom of my heart.

Elaine Marie Cooper

To my faithful and enthusiastic first-draft readers—my niece Julie, my sisters Christine and Mary, and my daughters-in-law Kristen and Jenni—a huge "thank you" does not seem sufficient. How could I have kept on this long journey without you? Your constant prodding ("Where are the next chapters?") and your infectious interest kept me going. You are all a blessing to me.

To my mom, Lucy Prince Mueller, whose great, great, great grandparents were the inspiration for this story. Thank you for your excitement about this project that brings life to our family's history.

To my sons, Benjamin and Nathaniel, thank you for bravely plodding your way through a "chick book." You two are the joy of my life and I love you both more than you will ever know.

No acknowledgment would be complete without thanking the two very special grandparents of mine from the eighteenth century, Daniel Prince and Mary "Polly" Packard. They are the inspiration for this story. Their love overcame the difficulties brought on by being on opposing sides during a time of war. Theirs was the ultimate example of a courageous and romantic love story.

I also owe a debt of gratitude to Karen Kingsbury. Although we are not directly acquainted, her wonderful fiction has inspired me and shown me the impact a novel can have in one's Christian walk.

And special thanks as always to my Lord and Savior Jesus Christ, from whom all blessings flow.

Prelude
Ode to a Soldier

Soldier boy, so far from home,
Walking paths that are unknown.
"Will I live or will I die?"
The soldier boy's lonely cry.

I trained to fire my musket gun,
To shoot so straight at someone's son.
But when I saw his face turn gray,
I longed to be so far away.

This path is full of fear and strife,
My next turn may just end my life.
So let's be cautious in our zeal,
Cause death's dark door is very real.

Soldier boy, so far from home,
Walking paths that are unknown.
"Will I live or will I die?"
Only God can hear his cry.

From the diary of Mary Thomsen

Chapter One

Daniel

The road never ended.

Nor did the thoughts that haunted the young British lieutenant night and day.

How did I ever get to this place? he wondered. Only twenty-two years of age, he felt as ancient as the granite stones lining the dirt highway.

This war had long ceased being an adventure. He had seen enough bloodshed, starvation, and disease to last his entire lifetime. Only last night, he held one of the regimental soldiers as he gasped his last breath, one more victim of the food shortage. The lad was only seventeen, the same age as the lieutenant's brother had been. He would never forget the young man's bones poking through his clothing.

"Lieutenant, sir." Another soldier's greeting interrupted his thoughts.

"Yes, Smythe." The lieutenant glanced sideways at the thin-faced recruit with terror in his eyes.

"How much longer, sir ... 'til we get to Boston, that is?" Smythe asked anxiously.

Lieutenant Lowe tried to appear encouraging, but he didn't know what to say. After all, they were prisoners of war. Although the Continental Army had stated that the prisoners would be put on ships to return to England (as long as they never took up arms against the colonies again), the British lieutenant knew better. There was no way the colonial rebels would allow them so easy an escape. The "Lobsters," as the King's soldiers were called by the colonial rabble, would be confined to a putrid camp where disease would rage and death would soon follow.

But this poor soldier looked for any hope he could hang onto, no matter how slim. Without hope, Lieutenant Lowe knew the young man would not survive.

"I do not know the distance, Smythe," said the officer. "It is a long way to the boats … and it is a long way home. But you are still strong, and you will make it."

"Thank you, sir." The younger man fell behind his lieutenant once again in the ragged line of prisoners.

Daniel Lowe breathed in a shallow breath of frigid air and tried desperately to ignore the mounting pain in his left leg. He held little hope for his own survival. While attempting to save his regiment, he gave away enough of his allotted food to seriously jeopardize his own health. Not that the weevil-infested sea biscuits were sufficient for even one man. His muscular frame shrank from weeks of deprivation and miles of forced marching. His filthy and tattered uniform hung loosely on him. And then there was that wound.

That last battle near Saratoga brought his first encounter with rebel lead. The ball found its home, shearing a large hole in his thigh muscle. He treated the injury as best he could without clean water and bandages.

As Daniel glanced down at his leg now, he sickened at the sight of green pus draining through the old bandage. As each step became more excruciating, he knew his limb was in serious trouble.

"Move along you wretches," yelled a colonial guard to the slow-moving prisoners. They were being marched to Boston, still a patriot stronghold. The Continentals had no time to pamper these wounded and exhausted troops, remnants of the army of British General John Burgoyne. It was late October after all, and the chill in the air promised an early winter.

Snow flurries dusted a thin layer on the bare oak and hickory trees along the dirt road. The stark outlines of gnarled branches and the dead leaves surrounding every tree trunk only added to the grim and lifeless scene as hundreds of men dragged their legs forward one step at a time.

The freezing wind whistled through the creaking tree limbs, eliciting painful groans from the poorly-clad soldiers.

Daniel's long hair was coming undone from the ties that usually held it neatly in place. Each gust of wintry air whipped the strands into his eyes, stinging sharply each time. Despite the discomfort, the weary officer had neither the strength nor inclination to retie his hair back in place.

Why bother? he thought.

The enticing smell from nearby hearths beckoned at the prisoners' nostrils. The intense hunger of the men played vividly on each face as the scents of unobtainable bread and roast venison only heightened their sense of hopelessness. Daniel glanced at the eyes of his fellow soldiers. Most of them were filled with tears from the cold wind as well as from despair. He waged the same battle of disheartenment.

This is a death march to be sure, thought the young lieutenant.

The excruciating pain in his limb was overwhelming. Nausea welled up in Daniel's stomach as he forced himself to put one foot in front of the other. But he knew he couldn't keep up much longer. He devised a plan. At some point, he would slip away into the thick woods along the highway.

Better to crawl under a tree to die than fall on the road and be shot by some impatient guard.

The famished army of prisoners were trudging through a local town when the lieutenant saw a chance for escape. Several youngsters from the village threw rocks at the British soldiers while shouting, "Dirty Lobsters!"

As the bellowing voices of the angry colonists distracted the guards, Daniel sprang for the woods, the pain in his leg temporarily overshadowed by the fear of being caught. His heart raced. His lungs sucked in deep pockets of cold air that fairly choked him. In his frantic escape, he lost all sense of time.

"Prisoner escaping!" shouted the guards, but he kept running. He threw off his red uniform—it would only be a target for a Continental marksman. Without his coat, the cold air gripped his torso. But he didn't stop. The sound of musket fire and the whistling of lead forced his legs to move faster than he thought possible. But he wasn't thinking about his actions. He responded to a visceral desire to survive.

His race ended in an abrupt and anguished halt as his leg gave way. Falling on the ground, he dragged himself behind some thick berry bushes that were long since void of fruit. The thorns dug into his chapped hands, but he hardly noticed the pain because his leg screamed for attention.

Then suddenly and for a brief moment, he sensed something had changed. He forced himself to lie still. All was quiet.

The musket fire has ceased, he thought. *They've stopped their pursuit.*

Despite Daniel's relief, the throbbing pain in his limb reached a crescendo. Nausea thrust him into spasms of heaving, but there was nothing in his stomach to expel.

As the retching ceased he laid on his back in complete surrender. He stared at the cold gray sky through the trees overhead and hoped for one last glimpse of life, but even the forest birds had hidden themselves from his sight.

It doesn't matter, he reasoned. After all, he deserved all of this. And nothing could change all that had occurred in these last months of war. Nothing could erase his many transgressions.

Now, all he had to do was close his eyes and let the inevitable shadow of death completely darken his already blackened soul. All was lost anyway. His war, his troops, his health, and, worst of all, those he loved.

As he believed his life was slowly ebbing away, Daniel Lowe held little hope of reaching heaven. But he couldn't take this hell on earth. He closed his eyes and waited for the reckoning of his Maker.

Chapter Two

Mary

She stared into the fire for what seemed like hours. In fact, it had only been a few moments.

That's how time had become for Mary Thomsen. Barely nineteen, the young farmwoman should have been contemplating a hope-filled future. Instead, she struggled with a sense of despair following recent events. Standing in front of the long fireplace did little to comfort her body or spirit.

Ever since her brother Asa was killed in battle, Mary had faced the reality of war in a sickening and personal way. She wrestled with thoughts of what her younger brother probably endured in those last moments of his life. Had his death come in an instant so that he did not suffer? Or had he lain there for minutes or even hours in pain, knowing the end was near?

Tears filled her eyes.

Dear, sweet Asa, she thought. Only sixteen, he loved music as much as he loved life. It was his gift on the fife that awakened his patriotic fervor and drew him to join the cause of liberty. He wanted to lead Continental soldiers to victory through his melodies.

"No one will aim their musket at a fifer," said Asa the day he signed on. "They have better targets to attend to."

He was always the optimist, Mary thought.

But in the midst of an explosive battlefield, no amount of hope could keep the barrage of lead balls from finding their mark on Asa's body. Even his fife, which their older brother James returned home after that last battle, was scarred from musket fire. It was a bittersweet reminder of his short life. It now rested on a brick above the fireplace. Mary touched the instrument lovingly with her fingers, imagining the sweet sounds Asa's lips could bring from the whittled wood.

"Mary." Her mother's voice caught her attention away from the hearth.

"Yes, Mother," she said flatly. Her voice had taken on a monotone timber in these last few weeks.

"Why don't you and Sarah go aleafing while there's still enough light of day? We want to have a good supply for the bread-making this winter."

Widow Thomsen wanted desperately to rally the spirits of her older daughter. Mary and Asa had been best of friends, sharing a love of music that seemed to stir from within them both. It seemed now as if the melodies had left Mary's heart forever, much as Asa's breath had left his body. The widow hoped that any diversion would brighten the spirits of her despondent daughter.

Sarah's childish voice spoke up in protest to Widow Thomsen's request.

"Please, Mother. I do not wish to go out in the cold. I am so tired of winter already," said six-year-old Sarah as she huddled by the fire.

Widow Thomsen looked at her youngest child with tenderness. Born just eight months after her father's sudden death, the blond-haired girl was a gift from heaven. She brought life and laughter to nearly every situation and spread her loving smile to friend and stranger alike.

Mary wished that she could capture into her soul some of the warmth emanating from Sarah. But the older sister was empty, alone, and as cold as the winter ice on their pond.

The older daughter stared at her only living parent in wonderment. Despite so much heartache in her life, Widow Thomsen was as steadfast in her faith as the stalwart cliffs not far from their farm—never changing through any raging storm.

Mary often heard her mother quote the verse, "The Lord giveth, and the Lord taketh away. Blessed be the name of the Lord." She knew that her mother grieved greatly over this most recent loss. Although her parent cried easily at the mention of Asa, Mary also saw that the widow's belief in a loving God never wavered.

She was far less sure of God's concern for their welfare than her mother was. The older daughter's faith in a caring Creator was shaken to the core. How could a God who truly loved them have allowed so unfair a death?

Why did he take Asa away?

She forced her thoughts back to the moment at hand, and her sibling's concern.

"Let Sarah stay indoors near the fire, Mother," Mary said. "I can gather enough oak leaves and sticks myself. There is no sense in both of us facing the wind and cold."

Sarah raced to her big sister and hugged her heartily.

"Thank you, Mary. I am the most blessed of sisters."

A small smile spread across Mary's lips.

"It is I who am the blessed one, to have a beam of sunlight living right inside our home on this cold wintry day," she replied. Although her words were forced, the sentiment was true enough. Mary hugged her sister tightly as she fought back the tears that flooded her emotions so frequently these days. Her head often ached from crying.

The outdoor air might be refreshing, she told herself as she put on her gray cape.

"Here is a blanket to gather the leaves in, Mary," her mother said, tucking the woolen piece under her daughter's arms. "Do not be gone too long. The storm may become severe."

"I shall hurry."

The frozen air hit her bare face as she left the farmhouse. She gathered her hooded cape closer around her neck. Although the painful cold numbed her skin, Mary knew that the real dullness she sensed was in her wounded soul.

She forced her legs to plow through the frenzied wind. The swirling movement of the wintry air reflected the agitation in her mind.

As she headed deeply into the woods on their farmland, Mary's thoughts wandered from Asa and then to her father, now long gone from a drowning accident. Just as quickly, her mind turned to her older brother James, still fighting in the War of Revolution. They hadn't heard from James since he had returned Asa's body home some three months ago. What if he, too, was dead? It could be months or years before they knew. Or would they ever hear word of him again?

The only thing that Mary Thomsen was certain of was that she hated this war and she hated death. Would she ever know joy again? Would she ever feel safe? Would she ever feel alive?

As she walked farther amongst the thick trees, Mary searched for the dry oak leaves that would cushion the bread dough in the Thomsens' oven.

She was so engrossed in her task that the sudden sound of musket fire in the distance made her heart skip a beat. Instinctively, the young woman dropped to the ground to take cover.

Unhurt but frightened, she huddled close to the earth. Mary clung to the blanket and tried not to give way to panic.

I must keep my senses about me, she thought.

Her whole body shook with fear. Soon the woods were quiet once again and the only sound that filled her ears was her own breathing, which came in rapid spurts.

Mary waited until her breath slowed before she dared look up. Standing gingerly, she hugged the blanket tightly. Her whole body stiffened from the cold and from sheer terror.

Should I run home? Should I keep going?

As the frightened farmwoman tried to decide her next move, she sensed something different in the woods.

There was a presence.

Chapter Three

Samaritan

She smelled him before she saw him.

Mary knew that someone was nearby but she could not see a soul. The wind carried the scent to her person, as if beckoning her to follow her senses. The odor was unmistakably that of infection. Perhaps even death.

Frightened but curious, Mary pursued the source. She went several yards before the smell became stronger, leading her to a thick grove of berry patch. As she carefully parted the twisted branches, what she saw made her gasp in fear. There lay the body of a man.

He wasn't moving. His clothing, face, and hands were smeared with dirt and old leaves. A week's growth of scraggly beard and his unkempt long hair added to the unsettling sight. His breeches were torn over his left thigh, exposing a large bandage soaked with brown and green stains.

Was he dead? She could not tell if the man's chest was rising. Dare she run away and leave the poor soul? What if there was any breath left in his body? What if someone had found her brother Asa like that, and did not at least sit with him 'til he died? Even a stranger can bring some comfort to a dying human.

Can I abandon this poor wretched person?

She knew she could not.

Using the blanket to protect her hands, she spread the prickly branches aside and drew closer to the body. The stench of illness filled the small clearing where the man lay and Mary fought the nausea that gripped her.

Then an alarming realization hit her as she surveyed the man's attire more carefully. He was a King's soldier. Even without his scarlet uniform, his finely woven breeches and waistcoat gave away who he was. And to Mary, he was the enemy. He had probably fallen out of the line of prisoners that she had heard were coming through town.

He is one of Burgoyne's troops, she thought with a shiver.

"Dear Lord," she whispered. "What shall I do?"

Her mind went to the story of the Good Samaritan. In that tale, the only person who would help a beaten stranger was a Samaritan, the victim's sworn enemy. She had never imagined that she would be faced with a similar scenario. And she had never understood before now how difficult a choice the rescuer had made. But although the Samaritan may have wrestled with the decision, he had chosen the right course.

Can I make the same choice? she wondered with fear.

She knew that she must, for her heart would not let her abandon this man.

But was he still alive?

With trepidation, she gently placed her hand on the man's chest.

Mary's touch awakened Daniel Lowe. The dazed soldier's eyes opened wide in alarm, and he grabbed her arms and cried out. As he gripped her limbs with all his meager strength, his senses seemed to clear as he stared into her face.

Mary was seized with fear. The pressure on her arms was almost unbearable.

"Please, sir," she begged. "Let me go. I mean you no harm." She was so terrified that the words barely came out. Mary had heard frightening accounts of the King's soldiers attacking colonial women. The thought filled her with horror.

Despite his apparent confusion, Daniel released his firm grip. He rubbed his eyes as if to clear his thoughts.

"What is your name, sir?" she asked.

Daniel stared at her in disbelief. "Such kindness, miss—I've not heard that in so long." He paused a moment before answering. "My name is Lieu...Lowe. Daniel Lowe."

Mary's fears calmed as his expression softened, and she realized the man was confused but did not intend to harm her. She looked at him carefully. She remembered her mother telling her to look into a person's eyes and you could read his soul. And Daniel Lowe's eyes were filled with many things—fear and pain for certain, but another quality also. Gentleness. It seemed ironic to her, considering his occupation. "I am Mary Thomsen. I live not far from here."

Daniel stared at the young woman.

"Where am I?" he finally asked, the words coming forth with difficulty.

"You are near the village of Deer Run in the colony of Massachusetts, sir."

The British soldier tried to lift his leg to a more comfortable position. The effort made him wince in pain.

The young woman looked at the source of his discomfort and noted the discolored bandage. It was soaked in a putrid liquid, undoubtedly the source of the smell. She was certain that the dressing had not been changed in quite some time. The thought of such neglect—even towards the enemy—outraged Mary.

"Sir, did they not attend to your wound?"

"Once," he said. "Many days ago."

He shook his head in bewilderment. "Why do I hear compassion in your voice, miss? Surely you must know who I am...I must be dreaming..." His eyes widened. "Good gawd, miss! Did I hurt you?" he asked anxiously. "I was having a nightmare—I thought you were someone else. Please tell me I did not injure you."

"I am unharmed, sir." She looked at the bedraggled man. He was weak and probably starving. His wound was causing him terrible pain. "I think it is you who needs some assistance," she said.

The snow was falling more heavily and the wind increasing in intensity. Mary knew that she needed to move this man to shelter or he would not survive the night. But where?

Bringing him to her home was impossible. Her mother would never help a soldier of the Crown. As Christian a woman as her mother was, Widow Thomsen still reeled from her son's death. She would consider any King's soldier to be responsible for the murder of her child.

11

Then Mary remembered the English wigwam. The remnants of an earlier settler's first home, the wigwam had been patterned after the structures built by Native Americans. Although she hadn't been to the shelter made from bark and branches in several years, she hoped it would provide enough protection for this soldier. When she and Asa played there as children, Mary never imagined that it would ever serve as more than a playhouse in the woods. It would now be transformed into an infirmary.

"Mr. Lowe, we need to find suitable protection for you or you will die from this cold. I know a shelter not more than fifty rods from here. I shall help you get there."

"Why are you helping me, miss? Do you not know who I am?" he asked incredulously.

"I know that you are a person in dire straits, sir. I am not here to decide who lives or dies, but to help a wounded person who will surely die without my assistance. Do you think you can get to your feet?"

"I shall try, miss."

The weakened soldier crawled out from under the thick shrubs while Mary used the blanket to hold back the thorny branches. It took all his remaining strength plus Mary's strong arms to help him to his feet. He cried out in pain when he bore weight on his left leg. Mary encouraged him with her words to keep him upright and moving.

"Sir, we can do this together. Lean on my shoulder."

Walking was a painfully slow process. Every step brought a gasp from Daniel as sharp pain seared through his limb.

Mary held her arm around his left side to support his efforts. She was appalled to discover that his bony ribs protruded from underneath his waistcoat.

Did the Continental guards treat their prisoners with such cruelty? she wondered.

Mary's lean shoulders strained beneath his right arm.

"Miss," he gasped, "I fear your strength will give out."

"Do not fear, sir. These shoulders have borne many a burden," she said with difficulty. "And you are not the heaviest I have carried."

They were both quiet for a long time as they concentrated on the effort at hand. She was breathing as hard as he was, and the cold air made the struggle even greater.

The crude structure appeared in the distance.

"We are nearly there," Mary gasped between breaths.

Although the wigwam was in remarkably sound condition for its age, some of the bark strips attached to the branches were askew. But this shelter would have to do. Neither one of them had the strength to go on.

They both struggled through the open door and fell upon the earthen floor. When she was able to catch her breath, she looked over at the weary man staring at her. His dark hair and his face were covered with sweat. His deep-set eyes glistened from the freezing air and from the incessant physical suffering.

Despite his agony, he managed to quietly say, "Thank you, miss."

She looked down at the woolen blanket still grasped under one arm.

"Let me put this over you to keep you warm," Mary said.

Before she laid the cover over his thigh, she took a good look at his bandage. The sight made her ill and frightened all at the same time.

Mary was thankful that she and Asa had brought several armfuls of hay to the wigwam from their barn many years ago. The siblings would sit for hours on the comfortable piles of straw and make up songs. She now used the old stalks to help insulate Daniel from the cold.

"Mr. Lowe, I must get some medicinals and change this bandage for you." The young woman looked at the putrid cloth and tried not to imagine what lay beneath. "I cannot tell my mother that you are here, but I shall manage to bring the supplies that you need. Before I depart, I shall bring you some snow to quench your thirst."

Mary stepped outside of the wigwam and scooped up a handful of the powdery substance. She hurried back inside and helped support his head. The bristly edges of his beard scraped against her hand as he devoured the frozen liquid from her cupped fingers.

"Do not swallow too much, sir, or it will chill you," she cautioned. "I shall bring you some warmer liquid when I return."

He grabbed her arm once again. This time it was with gentleness.

"Miss, I do not know what to say, I…"

He started to say more but she placed her hand over his and whispered.

"Hush, sir. Please save your strength." She felt his rough hands and for the first time noticed that they were covered with dried blood. "I shall bring some slippery elm for these wounds, sir. I shall sally forth lest the darkness set in."

When she stood up, Mary realized that her long brown curls were coming undone from her linen cap, loosened from the effort of helping Daniel to the shelter. She grabbed at the wayward locks and tucked them back inside her cap, suddenly self-conscious in front of this stranger. Her face burned a little as her eyes met his.

"I shall not tarry at home for long, sir."

Daniel stared at his angel of mercy as she slipped out the doorway. He lay back on the soft bed of straw and breathed in deeply.

"I hope she returns," he whispered under his breath. He closed his eyes in utter exhaustion.

Chapter Four

Lies

Mary's heart was racing as she ran back to the Thomsen farm, her mind whirling with conflict.

What shall I tell my mother? she wondered. Widow Thomsen would undoubtedly be suspicious. How could Mary explain the medicines, rum, and bandages that she would need to help Daniel Lowe? More worrisome, how would the young woman explain that she was helping a King's soldier? She was still mired in these thoughts when she arrived at the farmhouse door.

Breathless, Mary thrust the door open. She stood there and gasped for air, her face reddened from cold and exertion.

Widow Thomsen's eyes opened wide with concern.

"Good Lord, child, what has happened to you?" the widow asked, fearing something dreadful had occurred. "I should never have sent you out into the woods by yourself." In these troubled times, one could never feel safe anywhere.

"Nothing has happened to me, Mother," Mary answered. "I … I found a dog. But he's wounded terribly. I must bring him some supplies. I think he may have been shot and the wound is festering and horrible." Mary hated herself for lying, but she went on. "I think he may die without help." At least this last part was true.

"A dog? Mary, he may carry contagion to you. Hydrophobia is rampant in the woods and dogs can bite if they are in pain."

"Mother, he is as gentle as can be, but suffering terribly. Please allow me to dress his wound," she said, fighting back guilt.

Widow Thomsen looked carefully at Mary. There was life in her daughter's eyes that had not been there just two hours ago. It was as though the dog had given her a new sense of purpose and joy. It had been a long time since Mary had seemed her usual self. How could Widow Thomsen deny her daughter this diversion from her pain over losing Asa?

"All right, Mary," she consented. "But let me go with you to assist."

"No, Mother," she shouted with far too much energy. She bit her lower lip. "I am sorry. It is just that … I do not wish you to have to take Sarah into the cold. Just show me how to tend the wound and I can manage."

She hoped that she had not given herself away. Her mother looked closely at her again.

At last she said, somewhat proudly, "You are becoming quite the young woman, Mary. It was not that long ago that looking at a small bleed would send you into a faint. You have come a long way, have you not?"

"Yes, Mother," she said. Her cheeks were still red from the cold. But they also burned with shame from this blatant lie to the woman she loved the most in the world.

Mary gathered the supplies while Widow Thomsen explained how to treat the infection. The daughter prayed in her heart that someday her mother would understand—and forgive her.

Mary faced the outdoors with a new sense of purpose. She ignored the biting wind as best she could and hurried along the familiar, well-trodden path.

The extra blanket that her mother had used to hold the supplies would provide another layer of warmth for the British soldier. But even with two woolen blankets and the old straw, keeping her patient from freezing was going to be difficult. It was certainly not safe to make a fire in the wigwam. Any passerby would discover this makeshift infirmary in an instant from the smoke billowing out the stone chimney.

But as she trudged through the new-fallen snow, there was an even more pressing concern. Was Daniel Lowe still alive?

The worried Samaritan was startled out of her troubled thoughts when she saw a rider approaching on horseback.

"Good Lord," she whispered under her breath. It had not occurred to her that Continental soldiers might be looking for an escaped prisoner.

What was I thinking? What will I say?

"Good day, miss," the young corporal greeted her as he tipped his tricornered hat.

"Good day, sir," she said, smiling brightly despite her racing heart.

Could this soldier see the fear in her eyes?

"You wouldn't have perhaps seen anyone in these woods hereabout, would you?" the soldier asked. "Specifically in a red coat, miss."

"A red coat?" She feigned a shocked expression. "Why, no sir. Should I be concerned?"

Her heart was fairly bursting with anxiety as she piled one lie upon another.

Am I the same Mary Thomsen who believes lying is a sin? she wondered. *What is happening to me?*

Still, she could not forget the desperation of Daniel Lowe. She realized that her compassion took precedence over her conviction that hiding the truth was wrong.

"I should say so, miss," the corporal stated emphatically. "Several of Burgoyne's men have disappeared between New York and Boston—on their way to prisoner-of-war camp, I hear. I wouldn't mess with any of them if I were you, miss. They don't treat our ladies like ladies, if you know what I mean."

Mary swallowed hard.

"I shall remember that, sir. I shall just finish taking these supplies to our neighbors and then hasten home."

"Let me accompany you for your safety, miss," the soldier said dutifully.

The blood drained from her face. Before she could reply, they both heard a shout in the distance.

The corporal looked towards the voice.

"I am sorry, miss, but one of my men is calling. He may have found one of them Lobsterbacks." Just as he began riding away, he turned

17

and warned, "You need to get yourself home as soon as possible." Fortunately, he was heading away from Daniel's hideout.

Light of head now, the young woman sat on a large rock for a moment to collect her thoughts.

What am I doing? she thought. Could she be guilty of treason? Lying to a soldier in wartime—a soldier on her own side? And hiding the enemy? What would her brother James say? All these thoughts and more raced through her troubled mind.

She suddenly felt more alone than she had in her entire life.

Mary wept. And then she prayed desperately for wisdom. And that's when she felt the comforting presence of her God, not condoning her lies but encouraging her to go on. Emboldening her to go forward and bring comfort and help to a wounded man.

With new resolve, she wiped away her tears with the back of her hands. Then she stood up from the rock and pressed on toward the wigwam.

Chapter Five

Wounds

Daniel was sure the woman would not return, and he did not blame her.

The soldier knew that she would put herself at great risk to help the enemy. But once she thought it through, his angel of mercy would change her mind, he reasoned.

Or perhaps her mother would find out the truth. A parent would never allow her daughter to come back. In fact, the mother might report him to the rebels.

Daniel sighed in despair. Hopelessness was returning. He closed his eyes, nausea and pain his only companions.

No sooner had he withdrawn into his dark thoughts than he heard the hinges of the fragile door rattle. When he finally dared open his eyes, Mary was leaning over him.

"You are alive?" she whispered, more question than fact. "I was not certain you would still be breathing."

"You came back."

"I told you I would, sir," Mary answered. She did not add that she had almost lost heart in her promise, nearly letting fear overtake her. As she unfolded the medical supplies from the blanket, Mary glanced at the gaunt and wounded soldier. She knew now that she made the right choice when she returned to the wigwam. One look at Daniel Lowe was enough to soften the most hardened patriot heart.

"I brought you some rum to ease your pain," Mary said. She had adopted an air of self-assurance, as if she had nursed many a wounded man. In fact, she had never before tended a patient on her own.

Why did I not pay more attention to my mother's nursing care? she reprimanded herself silently.

With the village doctor needed on the battlefield, Widow Thomsen often assisted the local townsfolk with their injuries and illnesses. Many midwives, such as the widow, provided nursing care. She had an assortment of medicines that were purchased a few years ago at the apothecary in Boston.

Mary recalled her mother saying, "It is only wise to be prepared, in case a war begins." The midwife's voice was filled with sadness and resignation.

The younger woman sometimes assisted her mother in cleaning wounds. But as soon as the blood flowed, Mary's face would blanch. The widow would then excuse her daughter from further duress by sending her on an errand. Widow Thomsen would smile at the patient at such times.

"My Mary's not got the strongest constitution when it comes to nursing," the midwife would explain.

Because Mary missed out on so many learning opportunities, she was now ill prepared for the task at hand. She berated herself for not fighting fear and nausea while her mother was trying to train her.

Now the only hope for this man is an inexperienced and weak farm girl, she thought with dismay.

Dear God, she prayed silently, *give me the skills and strength that I need to help him.*

Mary held Daniel's head up and brought the flask of rum to his lips. He took several gulps and then gasped as the burning alcohol seized at his insides.

He coughed a few times and fell back down onto the pillow of hay.

Daniel stared at Mary, misunderstanding the fear in her eyes.

"You needn't worry, miss. I'll not let on that you have helped me."

"I am not concerned about that, sir. I only fear that I will not be of sufficient help to you. Your wound looks quite poorly. But I shall do the best I can," she said, trying to sound brave.

She wrapped a cloth around a sturdy stick so he could bite down when the pain became unbearable.

"Let's allow the rum to settle in before I start," she said. Mary wanted the alcohol to achieve its peak effect before she started removing that horrid bandage. Anger surged through her again as she questioned the justice of the guards who ignored so obvious an infection.

Mary sensed Daniel's gaze.

"What did you tell your mother, miss?" he asked.

The young woman looked down at her hands and bit her lip slightly, a nervous habit she had had since she was a child.

Mary confessed, "I … I told her I had found a dog with a wound."

"A dog." Daniel laughed weakly. "I see what you must think of me and the other 'Lobsters'."

He turned away and stared at an array of old cobwebs strung across the straw-lined ceiling.

Mary furrowed her eyebrows and frowned.

"Sir, it was not meant as an affront. I did not know what to tell her. That was the only explanation I could think of to convince her that I needed these supplies. I told her the rum was to clean the dog's wound."

Daniel looked over at her and his eyes softened once again.

"I am sorry, miss. After all you've done for me already, I've no right to question you."

There was silence for a few moments, when Daniel spoke.

"You have never mentioned your father, miss. Is he away at war?"

Mary looked at her hands again.

"No, sir. He died when I was but twelve. We had a terrible flood that year and he drowned in the river."

"I am truly sorry, miss."

Mary continued on.

"My brothers went to war. But Asa…" She struggled to complete her thoughts. "Asa was killed in battle. He was only the fifer…" She could not go on. Tears flowed down her cheeks. She sobbed, "He was my best friend in the world."

Now it was Daniel who struggled to control his own tears.

"What idiot would shoot at a fifer?" he mumbled to himself.

21

Mary looked up at him with cold eyes and said tersely, "An idiot King's soldier, sir."

Daniel's countenance fell, and she immediately regretted her harsh words.

"Sir, I am sorry. My words are born of a depth of sadness that I have never encountered before. Please forgive me," she said as she wiped tears away from her cheeks.

The young soldier looked at her with understanding.

"There is nothing to forgive, miss. Please do not distress yourself further."

Mary noticed that Daniel's words were beginning to slur. It was time to put aside her sadness and concentrate on dressing his wound.

She set up her supplies next to his leg and laid them out on the blanket. They included the rum, a cloth napkin filled with lint, dried balsam apple leaves soaked in vinegar, and strips of clean linen.

"Dear Lord, please help me," she whispered in prayer.

Daniel's eyes had been closing but he opened them up wide at the sound of her voice.

"What, miss?" he asked. There was some confusion in his voice.

"I need for you to help me by staying as still as possible," Mary said close to his ear. "I will lift the blanket now and remove the old bandage."

Mary was again assaulted by the overpowering odor of infection. The green pus completely soaked the aged bandage, which must have been applied a week or more ago. The edges of the cloth that covered his entire thigh were dried out.

Removing this bandage was going to be difficult for her and painful for him. Mary shivered at the thought but pushed away her fears. Bracing herself she resolved, once and for all, to handle this like the nurse she needed to be.

"Mr. Lowe, put this stick between your teeth and bite down on it when you feel the need," Mary instructed.

His eyes told her that he trusted her implicitly. She hoped that his trust was not misplaced.

With all the confidence she could muster, she untied the outer wrap encircling the bandage around his upper leg. She tore away at the edges of his tattered breeches. To reach the entire wound, Mary widened the hole in his clothing. Hiding her alarm at the extent of infection, she poured rum onto her patient's thigh to loosen the cloth. Daniel winced when the strong alcohol soaked through the pus-covered material and reached the raw, inflamed wound underneath.

As she carefully removed part of the old dressing, Mary noted with horror that the blood and infectious matter had become one with the cloth. The sickening bandage was stuck hard. She poured more rum onto the wound and gingerly tugged at the edges of the linen. Still, it did not budge.

Daniel slowly pushed himself onto his elbows and stared at his leg. His face turned white.

"Miss, you must pull with all your might to tear the dressing off," he instructed.

Mary shivered uncontrollably.

"Mr. Lowe, the bandage is fastened to the wound. If I tear it away quickly, you may bleed a great deal. And the pain ..." She looked at him earnestly. "The pain could be unbearable."

Daniel had fear in his eyes.

"I know this, Miss Thomsen. But it is the only way." He laid back and put the stick in his mouth. He closed his eyes tightly and clung to the earthen floor with his trembling hands.

For a moment her muscles seized with tension, then Mary grasped the edges of the bandage with both hands.

Give me strength, dear God, she prayed in her heart. With all her power, she tore away the wretched cloth from the bed of inflammation.

An anguished cry broke forth from Daniel's clenched mouth. Mary had never heard such a dreadful sound in her life.

She struggled to control her tears while pressing a clean cloth over the wound to stop the bleeding. The gaping injury with a cavernous center covered half of Daniel's upper thigh.

"I am so sorry, Mr. Lowe," she muttered as her mouth trembled.

Daniel's whole body was shuddering in pain. Mary looked at his deathly pale face. Rivulets of tears were rolling down his cheeks, leaving trails on his dirty skin. He clenched the stick in his mouth with such force that she feared he would bite through the thin branch.

"Please, Mr. Lowe, hang on," she half whispered.

Once the bleeding had slowed down, Mary prepared the packing of lint soaked in the solution of vinegar and balsam apple leaves. Her hands were completely covered with the soldier's blood, but she hardly noticed. She was consumed with finishing her task.

She deftly packed the deep wound with the pledget of soaked lint. It took more than she thought so she prepared more packing and filled the bloody crater. Once that was done, she applied clean linen. A thin strip wrapped around his thigh kept the dressing in place.

With the task complete, she wiped the sweat and tears from her face. Streaks of Daniel's blood smudged her forehead and cheeks.

Mary picked up the old bandage and was horrified to see small pieces of duck cloth from his breeches. This meant that the heavy canvaslike remnants had embedded into his leg when struck by the lead ball.

No wonder it would not heal, she thought, realizing why the infection was spreading.

"Mr. Lowe, I know why…" She suddenly stopped. "Mr. Lowe?"

Daniel lay silently on the earthen floor, not moving. His face was so pale, and in the dim light of the wigwam, she could not tell if he was breathing.

Her tears came again.

"Dear God," she cried. "Has there not been enough death? Please have mercy on this poor man. Please, Lord, let him live."

She stayed on her knees next to Daniel, closed her eyes, and put her hands on the back of her head. The young woman was wracked with heartache and sadness. Then someone touched her.

Her head sprang up and she saw Daniel's eyes upon her.

"Were you praying for me?" he asked weakly. His hand was gently squeezing her arm.

Mary was too relieved to be self-conscious about her entreaties to her Maker.

"Yes," she whispered gratefully, breathing more easily.

"Why?" said the young soldier who looked at her incredulously. He noticed the blood on her face and tried to wipe it off with his fingers.

"You are wearing my blood," he said, his words slurring as he spoke.

Mary smiled at him. She placed his hand back on his chest and remembered how those wounds from the thorny bushes had prompted her to bring the slippery elm. This old Indian remedy from the elm tree bark had several medicinal uses, and was especially soothing for abrasions.

She made a paste out of the crushed bark and water and then gently spread it over his hands. He smiled warmly.

"You have a soft touch, miss."

"It is the slippery elm that is soft, sir."

"No, miss. It is your heart that is soft." He spoke slowly, the rum taking its full effect. He stared up at her leaning over him as she covered him with the blankets.

"You have a lovely neck, miss," he said as he reached up to touch her skin.

Mary rolled her eyes and gently placed his hand back under the blankets.

"And you, sir, are speaking from the spirits you imbibed," she said, smiling at his ridiculous but handsome grin.

As he fell into a deep slumber, Mary whispered close to his ear, "I shall return in the morning."

She used the rum and what was left of the flask of water to clean Daniel's blood from her face and hands. The numerous red streaks bore testimony to her mission of mercy, a mission that many might consider an act of betrayal in this heated war.

Mary started to leave the wigwam, then turned and looked once more at her slumbering patient. She whispered a prayer of gratitude as she closed the door behind her.

Chapter Six

Fever

Fatigue came upon Mary as she trudged the long path home.

As long as she was caring for Daniel, her adrenaline had energized her. Now however, she was nearly overcome with exhaustion.

Mary was grateful for the wind that followed the snowfall—it would hide the tracks that might lead searchers to Daniel—but it's powerful force made her return home even more tiring.

By the time she reached her destination, Mary was dizzy and weak.

"What took so long, Mary?" her mother asked, her voice filled with worry. "I thought you'd been hurt."

"The wound was very bad, Mother," she replied with difficulty, yawning as she answered. "It took longer than I thought, but it has been tended to."

"Where did you leave the dog?"

"In the old wigwam." Mary yawned. "I am going to prepare for bed, Mother."

"But Mary, you need some supper after being out in the cold."

Mary was too tired to answer. After disappearing into her bedroom, she slowly removed her gown and linen petticoats. Crawling into bed wearing her nightshift, the exhausted Samaritan curled up on her feather-filled mattress. She was too weary to pull the quilts over herself and shivered before closing her eyes.

When her mother checked on her, the daughter was already fast asleep. Widow Thomsen gazed at her tenderly and covered her with several quilts.

"Dear Lord, please watch over Mary with your tender mercies."

The older woman stoked the logs in the small fireplace and gently stroked her daughter's hair before slipping out the bedroom door.

***

Mary awoke with a start before dawn the next day. She immediately thought of Daniel in the wigwam and wondered how he was doing.

Quickly dressing in her knitted stockings, she put numerous layers of petticoats over her nightshift to keep out the cold. These garments were then covered by a wool gown.

She made as little noise as possible as she stepped into the main room, where her mother and Sarah shared the big bed.

Mary made every effort not to awaken them as she gathered a flask of water and more slippery elm. Besides being useful for wounds, the tonic made from the elm tree bark would serve as a soothing balm for Daniel's stomach. The drink would provide nourishment while preparing his digestion for more substantial foods. Mary learned from her mother the art of gently coaxing a starving stomach back to normal eating. She was relieved that she had paid attention to at least some of Widow Thomsen's nursing lessons.

Slipping out the door of the farmhouse, she was besieged by the powerful wind. But the cold air was not the only sensation Mary felt on this late October morning. There was a surge of emotions that she had heretofore never experienced. There was excitement and fear—and something else. It was an unfamiliar stirring in her very core at the thought of seeing her patient again.

Even as she sorted through these feelings, the situation caused her concern.

How long can I keep the truth from my mother? she wondered. *How long can I keep Daniel hidden? And with winter nearly upon us, how will he survive out here in the woods?*

Although the abandoned wigwam still had a fireplace, burning logs would signal Daniel's whereabouts to any passerby.

Because of these worries and the lack of a recent meal, Mary's head throbbed.

When she finally came to the wigwam door and stepped inside, she stopped suddenly and gasped. Daniel was still alive, but he was shivering and covered with sweat. Mary placed her hand on his forehead. His body was ablaze with the heat of a fever.

"Mr. Lowe," she said with a hint of panic in her voice. "How long have you been suffering from fever?"

Daniel struggled to push the words out between the shudders from his body.

"I do not know, miss," he gasped. "Awhile, I think."

"Can you sip some water, sir?" Mary said, trying to sound calm.

"I can try."

Mary helped him get his head and shoulders up as she held the flask for him. He was too weak to consume more than just a few sips. His head fell back onto the bed of hay. His dark eyes looked more sunken than before and his gaunt cheeks were fiery red. His breaths came rapidly and with obvious struggle.

He needs more than water, Mary thought with alarm.

This sickness was beyond her knowledge of care. A fearful realization crept into her thoughts. The time had come to reveal the truth to her mother. Widow Thomsen would surely know which medicine to use. But what would her grieving mother say about helping an enemy soldier? Mary tried not to panic. Somehow, she had to convince her mother that helping Daniel Lowe was the right thing to do—the Christian thing.

Mary prayed silently.

Dear Lord, please convince my mother, even if I cannot.

She took in a deep breath.

"Mr. Lowe," she said as evenly as she could, "I need to get you some help. You are quite ill."

"Miss Thomsen … who will you tell?" Daniel spoke in short bursts, his eyes filled with fear.

Mary placed her hand on his.

"I shall only tell someone I trust. Please do not fear. I must get you more help than I have to offer. But do be assured, sir, I shall not desert you."

Daniel looked at her with sadness.

"Please come back."

"I shall," she said. She fought back the tears that stung at her eyes. She turned to look at him once more before leaving the wigwam. "I shall come back."

Daniel closed his eyes. He was grateful for Mary's help, yet terrified of another rebel knowing his whereabouts. He knew now that he could trust this woman with compassion in her eyes. But who else would help the enemy? The wounded soldier wanted to run, but his body was too ill to move. All he could do was moan in pain and fight the fearful thoughts that assaulted his mind.

Sleep came, but with nightmares worse than ever. He envisioned pained cries from his troops as they were gunned down by fervent rebel soldiers.

Then there were the terrifying shrieks of wounded comrades still very much alive but too weak to crawl off the battlefield. Wolves tore at their flesh in the night, and anyone who tried to rescue them from this horrible death was himself struck down by enemy marksmen.

But the worst dream—the one that recurred every night—was of his younger brother Oliver taking his last breath. Inevitably, the fevered soldier woke up screaming his brother's name. It would only take a moment for Daniel to realize that the nightmare had been real. Oliver was truly gone and Daniel was responsible.

If only I had not shouted his name, the lieutenant chided himself. That painful memory filled him with immeasurable sadness and guilt. Exhausted and gravely ill, he closed his eyes once again.

Will this unending saga of pain ever end? he wondered hopelessly.

***

Mary ran all the way back home. When she flung the farmhouse door open, Widow Thomsen, who had only recently awakened, looked up in surprise as her daughter burst in, gasping for breath.

"I thought you were still in bed," the mother said.

"Mother, I have something to tell you."

The daughter now had her mother's full attention. Mary looked over to be sure that Sarah was in a sound sleep. She whispered just in case the girl should awaken.

"I have lied to you, Mother, and I beg you to forgive me." Her lips trembled with remorse.

"Lied to me?" Widow Thomsen sat on a chair in dismay.

"Yes, Mother." Tears streamed from Mary's eyes. "I am so sorry. It is not a dog I am caring for in the wigwam. It is an injured man."

Widow Thomsen's mouth dropped open in astonishment.

"Why would you lie about a man needing help, my dear? And why did you not let me tend to his wound? I do not understand."

"I did not think you would want to help him, Mother." Mary's tears turned into sobs now. She took a fitful breath but kept her voice low. "He is a British soldier," she whispered with difficulty.

There it was. She had spoken the truth of the matter that might change their relationship forever.

The look on Widow Thomsen's face became stone cold.

"Come with me, Mary," she said, grabbing her shawl from the hook on the cabin wall.

The older woman walked briskly out to the barn. Mary followed at a short distance, dreading the unpleasant encounter that she knew was inevitable.

Once inside, Widow Thomsen whipped around to face her daughter. The older woman did not hold back on her anger now that they were out of earshot of the still-sleeping Sarah.

"Mary, have you gone absolutely mad?" her mother said, seething with rage. "What are you thinking? Helping the enemy, putting all our lives at risk?"

"Mother, it is not like that," Mary pleaded.

"Not like what, Mary? Not like we are at war? Not like the British haven't already killed one of your brothers? Not like you are helping the very enemy that shot him?"

Mary had never seen her mother so angry. The daughter tried to regain her composure so she could respond, but the angry words were like arrows shooting at her from every side.

"Mother, please listen to me," she begged.

"Listen to what?" her mother continued. "Listen to how you are comforting the enemy, the very person who may be responsible for your brother's demise? How could you?" Widow Thomsen wept.

"Mother, how could you encourage me to help a dog but object to me helping a sick and injured human being?" Mary asked slowly. The passion in her voice surprised even herself.

Now it was her mother's turn to receive the sting of her daughter's words.

"Mother, this soldier could be dying. He is in terrible pain. He was on his way to prison camp, where you know he would not have survived. I have tried to help him, tending his wound and bringing him water. But now he has a terrible fever and needs help beyond what I can give him. I need your help, Mother. *He* needs your help."

Widow Thomsen looked unconvinced.

"What would you have wanted someone to do for Asa if they had found him after he had been wounded," Mary continued. "Would you not have wanted a Samaritan to see to his wounds? To bring him comfort?"

There was silence for a long moment. The only sound in the chilly barn was Susannah the cow bellowing her displeasure at not yet being milked. Mary's words had stung deeply, because they were the truth— even if Widow Thomsen did not want to hear it.

Several moments passed before her mother finally replied.

"All right, Mary. I shall bring him some medicine and water," she said flatly.

"Thank you, Mother." The young woman squeezed her parent's shoulder in gratitude. "I was not expecting this terrible dilemma either. But once I came upon him in the woods faring so poorly, I could not turn my back on him. You will see what I mean."

Widow Thomsen appeared doubtful.

"I will do my part, Mary. Please do not expect my heart to be in it. Stay at the farm with Sarah, while I take some Peruvian bark to the man. Do you know his name?"

"Lowe. Daniel Lowe," Mary replied. "Thank you, Mother."

Widow Thomsen looked pointedly at her daughter before she turned to go back to the farm to gather the medicines.

"I shall be back before long."

With both hope and trepidation, Mary watched her mother leave for the wigwam.

"Please God," she whispered, "let her see him through your eyes."

31

The older woman forced herself to walk towards the aged structure, which she had not visited in many years. The last time she had come to the wigwam was to seek solace after her husband drowned in the river. She fought back tears at the memory of her husband's death.

"Lord," she prayed as she walked, "I miss my husband so, especially at such times of uncertainty. He would have known what to do." She wiped the tears from her face. "Lord, please show me what to do."

When she reached the wigwam, she stopped and took a deep breath, then opened the fragile door.

Daniel heard her enter but was too weak to respond. He looked at the older woman with fear.

Widow Thomsen gazed at the soldier lying under the blankets. He was emaciated and feverish and certainly appeared to be dying. She took in a deep breath and spoke to her enemy.

"Mr. Lowe, my daughter Mary has told me about your illness and I have come to bring you some medicine," the widow said without emotion.

The look in her eye told him that she did not share the same compassion towards him that her daughter had. The thought occurred to him that this woman might give him poison rather than medicine. Offering him a drink that would end his life would certainly be understandable. This war had brought out the worst in many a man and woman on both sides of the battlefront. He knew that much for certain.

"What is it?" he asked weakly.

"It is called Peruvian bark, Mr. Lowe. It has been blended with wine to make it easier to ingest." She looked at him and surmised his concern. "You think I mean to harm you, do you not? That is not the case, sir. But I will confess that I am only here because my daughter has seen fit to take you under her wing. I do not profess to share her great concern for you. But because Mary has convinced me of your need—which is obvious, sir—I shall do what I can to help you."

"Thank you, madam," Daniel replied with difficulty.

She helped him lift his head and instructed him to swallow several gulps.

"There, Mr. Lowe. That should help with your fever. That is all I can do for you."

Widow Thomsen did not bother to check his wound, since Mary had already changed the dressing less than a day before.

"I shall come back later with more medicine and water. You seem to have enough blankets for now."

She turned and left the wigwam without looking back.

"I am certain he will be dead by morning," she mumbled to herself. The experienced nurse did not have a hint of regret in her voice.

***

Mary and Sarah were preparing the evening meal that would simmer over the fire all day. But Mary's thoughts were not on the vegetables she was washing. She was concerned about her mother's coldness towards Daniel. Mary had never seen such bitterness in her parent before and it frightened her.

What would her mother say to him? What would she do? Widow Thomsen had always been the epitome of compassion as long as Mary could remember. But where had her mother's heart of mercy gone?

"Why is mother taking so long, Mary?" Sarah asked. "I thought she would be here by now. She promised to show me how to cut out the pumpkin."

"She will be here soon, I am sure," Mary answered. "I can show you how to do the pumpkin if you like."

Just then the door opened and Mary looked up with anticipation.

Widow Thomsen looked at her. "The task is done," she said.

Mary looked at her in confusion, wanting more details.

"That is all? No further news of the situation?" She cast a glance at Sarah. She could not divulge too much in front of her sister.

Her mother looked at her again but gave no hint of compassion.

"I doubt that the *dog* will survive the night."

The daughter stared at her in disbelief, fighting back the anger that welled in her heart towards her mother.

"Then I shall stay with him to bring comfort whilst he lives," she seethed.

Mary put aside the vegetables for the dinner and quickly gathered more medicines, water, and another blanket for Daniel.

"Mary, this endeavor is futile," her mother protested.

Her daughter glared at her for a moment.

33

"It is never futile to show compassion, Mother." Mary hurriedly put on her cape and left.

As she returned to the makeshift infirmary, she stifled back tears. She cried not only for Daniel's sake but for the deep outrage that stirred in her heart towards her mother.

How can Mother be so merciless? she thought. She wondered if they would ever feel close again.

When she opened the door to the wigwam, Mary's eyes sought Daniel's. He stared at her in relief and swallowed hard.

"You've come back," he said. He shivered from the fever.

"I told you I would, Mr. Lowe. I always keep my promises," Mary said softly.

She brought out a piece of linen cloth left over from an old shirt. She poured water on it and began to dab the coolness on his face and forehead.

"That should help your fever lessen. I have brought more of the Peruvian bark for you as well."

Daniel appeared relieved.

"Thank you for all your help, miss," he said. "I do not deserve all your provision." He stopped to catch his breath. "I do not take your kindness for granted. And I know how ill I am ... this may be my last chance to tell you ... how grateful I am for your tenderness ..."

Using so many words caused him to speak in fits and starts, and he struggled to get them out.

"You do not need to speak, Mr. Lowe. Save your strength for healing."

Her voice had a melodious quality that seemed to mesmerize him. He was too weak to remember that it was not proper to stare at a woman with such unabashed admiration.

Blood rushed to Mary's cheeks when she noticed his glances. She tried to concentrate on tending to his illness. If her mother was right and he would not survive the night, then Mary determined to stay with him to the end. She prayed under her breath that her mother was wrong.

The minutes passed slowly. Several times an hour, Mary encouraged Daniel to drink sips of water. She gave him a few gulps of the medicinal wine and brought the extra blanket up around his shivering shoulders.

But mostly she prayed. Without God's help, she knew there really was no hope for Daniel Lowe.

As the sun sank lower on the horizon, cold enveloped the thin wigwam walls. Her patient was in and out of delirium, and his nurse tried not to despair. Daniel was shaking so from fever that his teeth chattered. Soon Mary began shivering uncontrollably from the cold.

The young woman drew closer to Daniel. She cradled his head in her lap, the blankets surrounding them both. The chill in her hands was a soothing comfort for his fever, while the heat raging in his body provided the warmth that she needed.

In any other time or place, their closeness would have been extremely improper. But at this moment, their survival depended upon ignoring protocol.

Chapter Seven

Repentance

The day drew to a frigid close as Widow Thomsen and Sarah finished eating their stew.

"Where is Mary, Mother?" Sarah asked, bewildered by the empty chair at the table. "I miss her. Are you not worried?"

Sarah was confused by the strangeness of the day. Mary was always there for supper and her mother was usually more talkative. Clearly something was amiss. Even a six-year-old could sense that.

"She'll be back in due time," her mother replied. "Her patient needs her, apparently."

"Do you suppose the dog will recover? I'd so love to have a dog," Sarah said hopefully.

"I do not think so, dear. He is badly injured. Not everyone can survive their injuries."

Sarah looked down at her wooden bowl.

"I know that, Mother," she said sadly.

Widow Thomsen recognized that mournful look. Asa had come to his sister's mind again. Tears began to brim at the girl's eyelids, and the older woman regretted her careless words.

"Sarah, let us clean off the table and read from the Bible for awhile," her mother said, trying to change the subject. Asa's death still lingered in their every waking moment. It was a struggle for them all to keep their spirits from being cast into gloom.

The child wiped at her eyes and said with quivering lips, "All right."

The two made quick work of the cleanup. Sarah climbed into her mother's lap while Widow Thomsen sat in the large chair by the fire. This was the wooden seat her husband had used for so many years. Many stories had been read to the children at the Thomsen home in this very setting. The mother opened up to her favorite book of Proverbs.

"Let us see what God's word has to say to us in the Good Book, Sarah. We can always glean much wisdom from these pages, can we not?" The widow's eyebrows furrowed. "I could certainly use some discernment now," she whispered under her breath.

She began to read from Proverbs 25. She liked to read the chapter that coincided with that day of the month. The familiar phrases came easily until she reached the twenty-first verse. "'If thine enemy be hungry, give him bread to eat; and if he be thirsty, give him water to drink.'" The words made her stop short.

"Go on, Mother," Sarah encouraged.

"I think perhaps I missed yesterday's reading. Let us go back to chapter 24," the widow replied. "There now, let us begin again," she said, satisfied that Sarah had accepted her explanation.

The reading went smoothly once again until she reached verse 10. "'If thou faint in the day of adversity, thy strength is small.'" Widow Thomsen paused for a few seconds, then went on. "'If thou forbear to deliver them that are drawn unto death, and those that are ready to be slain; If thou sayest, Behold, we knew it not; doth not he that pondereth the heart consider it? and he that keepeth thy soul, doth not he know it? And shall not he render to every man according to his works?'"

Widow Thomsen slowly put her Bible down and placed one hand over her mouth. Her lips began to tremble.

"'Those being drawn to death.'" She repeated the words slowly, then looked at her younger daughter. "Sarah, please sit in the chair a moment whilst I pray in the other room."

The young girl got off her mother's lap.

Widow Thomsen walked into Mary's room and closed the door. She stared for several moments at the fire in the hearth. And then she prayed.

"Lord, I know well that this man has been injured and is starving. He was most certainly on the road towards death in the prison camp. He could even have died along the way. And there is no manner in which I can come before you to claim that I knew it not. Mary has clearly brought the matter to my attention." Tears welled in her eyes. "I know this bitterness in my heart toward the British troops has obscured my obligation to forgive." She paused a moment as her mouth quivered. "I am so ashamed of the hardness in my heart towards someone in such desperate need." She wiped the tears from her cheeks. "Please Lord, forgive me," she whispered.

The widow stood a moment longer and then turned with resolve. When she came back into the main room, Sarah saw that her mother had been crying.

"Mother, what is wrong?" the child asked in alarm.

"Nothing that I cannot make right. Sarah, come with me. Mary and I need your help."

***

Mary fought the drowsiness that could overtake her as she and Daniel struggled to stay alive in the wigwam.

The young woman knew of many unfortunate victims that had succumbed to the effects of a freezing night without a fire. The shivering Samaritan had glanced several times throughout the evening at the cold and empty fireplace. She longed to set some logs ablaze for warmth, but it would not be safe.

"Your hands are getting cold, miss," Daniel said to her. His fever had broken and his thoughts had cleared. Her fingers had been lying on his cheeks and with the heat of his face now diminished, he felt the increasing chill in her skin. "You must go back to your warm home," he said with urgency in his voice, as he saw her eyelids struggle to stay open.

"I just need to close my eyes for a moment," she said dreamily, leaning against the bark wall. She thought she would just rest for a short while. She did not realize that she was drifting into a dangerous slumber.

"Miss Thomsen," he said more loudly as he squeezed her long fingers with his. "Please do not tarry any longer."

Mary did not answer him, and he gently grabbed her face.

Her eyes opened slowly. "What ... what are you doing?" she asked. Her voice was filled with irritation at this intrusion into such a comforting calm. *Perhaps if I just close my eyes, the disturbance will cease...*

"I am trying to keep you awake, miss." Daniel's voice became louder and filled with alarm. "You must go home where you can be warm."

Mary's eyes opened wider. She looked down at Daniel and became more aware of her surroundings. Then she remembered her mother's lack of concern for Daniel's well being. She resolved once again to be there for this suffering man.

"I shall not leave you as long as you need help," she said.

He left his hand on her cheek and spoke with gentleness.

"I cannot have my nurse die for my sake. Please go."

While Daniel attempted to lift his head from her lap so that she could leave, they both heard a sound outside. Footsteps were approaching.

Mary instinctively held her patient closer, as though her actions could prevent someone from abducting him. Her heart skipped a beat. She feared the worst.

Had they been discovered by soldiers looking for escaped prisoners? Mary's throat went dry and her breathing quickened. Her eyes widened as she stared at the door.

Her terror turned to astonishment as her mother and little sister came through the doorway. Mary's sleepiness was replaced by renewed energy and relief. Yet many questions remained hanging in the freezing wigwam air.

"Mother, why are you here with Sarah?" Mary asked in bewilderment. *Why would she involve my sister in this dangerous secret?* she wondered. *Why are they both here now? Darkness has already fallen. What is my mother thinking?*

"I shall explain it all later, Mary. I told Sarah that we found a young soldier who is hurt and we need to rescue him. Right now we need to get you both back to the warm fire at home."

Daniel and Mary looked at each other, unable to comprehend the change in her mother's attitude.

Sarah stared at the freezing couple.

"Mary, why do you embrace that man?" she asked incredulously.

"To keep him warm, silly child," Mary's mother answered impatiently. Then she looked straight at Mary. "That *is* why you are holding him, is it not?"

"Yes, Mother, it should be obvious we are both freezing." Mary shivered even more as she and Daniel struggled to their feet. Her stiff limbs ached with each movement. She tried to hide her own discomfort as she and her mother helped the soldier sit upright.

Daniel needed the strength of both women to get to the farmhouse. He moaned in pain as each step put pressure on his left leg. More than once, he begged to stop so he could find relief from the incessant throbbing.

"Mr. Lowe, I know this is terribly painful for you, but we must hurry," said the widow. "There may still be troops out and about. We will be at our home soon."

The thought of a warm fire was enough to give Daniel strength to go on. He still had no idea what had changed the mind of Widow Thomsen.

Mary was grateful that much of the snow had melted in the daytime. The young woman would not have to worry about leaving footprints that might give away their secret. She was still contemplating the incredible change in her mother's heart when their home finally appeared. They arrived none too soon, as Mary's meager stamina was fading.

The warmth from the fire as they entered the farmhouse was a healing balm to the entire group, but especially to Mary and Daniel. The women assisted their patient into Mary's room, which would serve as his infirmary. Mary and Sarah both struggled to remove the soldier's boots before easing him into the bed.

"I have never seen boots like this before," Sarah said in bewilderment.

"Sarah, please put them by the fire and make no mention of the boots," Widow Thomsen said sharply to the girl.

"Yes, Mother."

The nausea that had recently plagued Daniel returned. The dizzying sensation overwhelmed him as his pale face contorted into a pained expression.

"Mr. Lowe…" Widow Thomsen started to say, but she could see the young soldier was about to vomit.

The long walk combined with his pain and illness had been too much for the weak man. As the widow grabbed a basin and held it under his chin, Mary held his head. When the retching ceased, Mary helped him lay his head back on the pillow.

"I am sorry," he said weakly.

"There is nothing to be sorry about, Mr. Lowe," Mary said softly. The young woman's face was as white as a sheet. Widow Thomsen saw her daughter's complexion and feared she might faint.

"Mary, why do you not get some food? You must be starving. I shall tend to Mr. Lowe."

Mary did not have the strength to argue. She slowly got up. "I shall see you in the morning, Mr. Lowe."

Their eyes met as she left the room. Daniel wished he could say something that would reflect his deep admiration for this young woman. He wanted to tell this angel with the green eyes that he would never forget that she had not deserted him in his desperation. But while the words were silent, his eyes expressed his gratitude to her.

Sarah stared at Daniel from the doorway, intrigued by this stranger staying in their house. She had seen him becoming ill while her mother and sister helped him. The two women had often been at her side when she was sick. While her mother took the basin out of the room to clean it, the girl approached his bedside.

"I am sorry you are ill, Mr. Lowe," Sarah said. "I hate it when I feel poorly like that." The child reached out with her small hand and placed it upon his. "I shall pray that you feel better soon."

Daniel looked at her closely for the first time. The child was a miniature version of Mary, although Sarah's hair was lighter in color and her eyes a rich brown.

"Thank you, little miss," Daniel said to her with a weak smile. "What is your name?"

"My name is Sarah Thomsen," she stated matter-of-factly. "I am six years old and I can help my mother and Mary cook now."

"It is pleasant to meet you, Miss Sarah Thomsen," Daniel said, amused by the child's boldness and charm.

"Do you have any sisters?" Sarah asked.

Darkness fell over Daniel's countenance. "I used to."

"Used to? What happened?"

41

"She died of smallpox when she was but seven," Daniel said with difficulty.

Before Sarah could speak further, her mother returned with the clean basin. She had heard the conversation between her child and Daniel.

"Sarah, please let Mr. Lowe rest now. Your talking will wear him out," Widow Thomsen said. She escorted the girl towards the other room.

Sarah gave one last glance at the patient before giving him a smile.

"Good night, sir."

"Good night, little miss," he replied.

"Forgive my talkative child. I fear the lack of men in our home at the moment has her curiosity aroused when she finally sees one."

"There is nothing to forgive, ma'am. Both your daughters are charming and kind."

"They are a gift to me, Mr. Lowe, of that I am sure. Now, let me look at that wound of yours."

***

Sarah approached Mary at the table near the main fireplace. The older sister was trying to stay awake long enough to eat some stew.

"Mary," Sarah said with a grin on her face. "The man called me 'little miss.'" She giggled and ran off to play with her doll.

Mary smiled as she took a few bites of sweet potatoes and carrots. She knew that she would not be awake for long. She pulled herself up from her chair and went to lie down on the bed that she would now be sharing with her mother and sister. So tired was she that she did not even bother to remove her gown or petticoats. She pulled the layers of handmade quilts up around her chin and sighed deeply.

As she drifted off to sleep, her thoughts dwelt on two things from this day. First, the remarkable change of heart in her mother—it could only be explained by divine intervention.

Even more extraordinary, and puzzling, was the memory of Daniel Lowe's hand touching her face.

Chapter Eight

Coat

The scent of lavender slowly infused Daniel's senses.

He was standing in a field of the purple flowers in England. The countryside breeze caressed his face and the bright sunshine warmed his body. He slowly stretched his arms out, taking in the sensations that brought healing to his mind and soul. A smile crossed his face as he realized he was home.

"How are you this morning, Mr. Lowe?" The voice startled him out of his dream. He felt the quilted covers on the rustic bed and remembered where he was.

He slowly opened both eyes and looked at his surroundings. Mary Thomsen was stoking the flames in the small fireplace that kept this side room comfortable through the winter. Daniel looked at the stone wall that housed the burning embers. The tall structure towered upwards past the ceiling. The chimney had been built large enough to accommodate two fireplaces, one in each room. It was certainly a necessity in this frigid climate.

Mary leaned in towards the fire. Her long fingers wrapped around each log that she carefully added to the growing blaze. She deftly turned the hot coals with an iron stoker, coaxing more warmth with each move of her arm. Whenever a scorching ash escaped from the hearth, she used the iron tool to put the spark back in the stone enclosure.

Daniel studied her face in the glow of the fire. The burning embers illuminated the room in this early morning dawn, highlighting her high cheekbones and full lips. Her cheeks, which had been so pale the night before, glowed brightly from the warmth. Her gray wool gown narrowed at her slender waist and gathered in flowing folds to the floor. The wounded soldier found it difficult to pull his eyes away from her.

And that heady scent of lavender—why could he still smell those springtime petals that filled him with memories of home? He realized then that the scent was coming from the bedding.

Mary finished stirring the logs.

"How are you, sir?"

She looked at him more intently now. Her hair—at least the locks that were not hidden beneath a linen cap—glowed a chestnut brown in the light of the fire.

"I think I am better, miss," he said, swallowing with difficulty.

"You are still very pale. I am sure you must be quite famished. Let me get you something that will settle well in your stomach," Mary said.

Daniel was not feeling any hunger. Lack of nourishment and the illness had conspired against him, taking away all desire for food.

"I am not craving any victuals, miss," he said honestly.

"Well then, sir. We have the right medicinal to help. I shall bring it to you promptly." Mary gave him a warm smile and disappeared out the door.

On her way into the main room, she made as little noise as possible. She did not want to disturb her mother and sister. Widow Thomsen and Sarah were exhausted from the previous night's adventure.

Mary brought down the jar that held the slippery elm powder. She sprinkled a small amount into a tankard and poured warm water from the large kettle heating in the fireplace. Lastly, she crushed some sweet cinnamon into the brew to add more flavor. Anything to help perk Daniel's appetite.

She brought the warm liquid to her patient. Daniel tried to appear enthusiastic about the drink, but he was unsure whether he could tolerate anything. With his stomach being unstable these last few days, he was not anxious to be ill again—especially not in front of Mary.

Mary could see his hesitation but reassured him.

"Do not fear, Mr. Lowe. This brew will settle quite well when nothing else will."

She set the pewter tankard on the small log table next to the bed and helped Daniel to an upright position with feather pillows.

The comfort of these soft surroundings was healing in and of itself, Daniel thought. He slowly took the tankard from Mary and gingerly sipped the drink.

"It has a sweet flavor to it," Daniel said with surprise.

"I think it tastes like maple," Mary said. "It is quite soothing as well. You will feel much improved soon."

As he slowly drank, Mary observed his large fingers wrap around the circumference of the tankard. His grip belied his current weakness. Pulling the cup away from his face, he wiped some of the liquid from his beard. His fingers patted his cheeks and a look of embarrassment crossed his countenance.

He hurriedly took a few more sips, and returned the drinking vessel to Mary.

"I think that is all I can manage for now. Thank you, miss. You and your family have been far kinder to me than I deserve. I do not know how to reimburse you."

"Mr. Lowe, there will be no talk of repayment," Mary said adamantly. She gave him a shy smile, which he returned.

"That is only the second time I have seen you smile," Mary said.

Daniel's face became serious.

"Second time? When was the first?"

"It was when you were quite out of your head from the spirits I gave you," Mary said teasingly. She straightened out the quilts on his bed as she spoke.

Daniel's face became red.

"I ... umm ... I hope I did not speak in an unsuitable manner," he stammered. "I really do not remember..."

Mary smiled, recalling his fascination with her neck. But she knew this information would likely embarrass her now-sober patient.

"Mr. Lowe," Mary said reassuringly, "you were always a gentleman in both your words and actions. You've no cause to be concerned."

Daniel's shoulders relaxed and he breathed out slowly.

"I very much appreciated the spirits, miss. And I very much appreciated you dressing my wound. I am sure I would not still be here without your kindness."

"It was difficult," she said, more serious now. "I have never seen such a wound. It gave me no pleasure to put you through such horrible pain. I thought I had killed you." She looked down at the quilts, remembering the agonizing ordeal.

"If I had died, miss, it would not have been your doing. Without your help, I have no doubt that I would be with my Maker. You were remarkably brave."

She looked up at Daniel to see him staring at her with admiration.

"I am not so brave, Mr. Lowe. I am truly frightened most of the time these days. If it were not for my trust in God, I would just want to hide under the quilts all day and night—not that blankets would protect me from the evil that surrounds us."

She stared thoughtfully out the window. The sun was rising behind the bare branches of distant trees.

Daniel stared at her quizzically.

"Your demeanor is so assured, miss. I never would have imagined that you were frightened all the time."

"And I never imagined that I would be having a friendly conversation with a soldier who wears a red coat," she said.

Hearing those words, Daniel's eyes grew wide.

"My coat," he said, sitting bolt upright in the bed. The movement caused him to wince with excruciating pain.

"Your coat?" Mary said. "Please lay back down, Mr. Lowe. You will cause your wound to bleed unnecessarily."

She gently pushed his tense shoulders back onto the pillows.

"Now then, tell me about your coat."

The soldier was in obvious distress. He stammered over his words as he tried to convey the story.

"I threw it down," he said. "When I escaped from the guards, I ran into the woods and threw it on the ground. I knew the bright red would make a fine target for some rebel fellow intent on firing ball at me, so I tore it off and let it go … I know not where."

Daniel stared wide-eyed at Mary, who did not seem to understand the implication.

"Do you not see, miss? If they find the coat on your land, it will lead the rebels here. They will know you have helped me." He grabbed at her arm to emphasize the enormity of the danger.

Mary's eyes now widened as she grasped the great peril she and her family were in if someone found his scarlet garment.

"I shall go and find it," she said with determination. "How far from the dense thicket were you when you tore it off?"

"I know not. It may have been several hundred rods closer to the road. I am not certain."

"I will find your coat, Mr. Lowe. I know our land well and I shall find it."

Daniel grabbed her hand, his dark eyes full of concern.

"Please, miss, if anyone sees you with it, do not admit to knowing who I am. Tell them anything, but do not endanger yourself or your family."

"I shall be safe in God's hands. And he will give me the words to say, should I need to speak at all. Please rest now. I shall return in due time."

He released her hand and watched her go towards the door. She turned to look at him. Courage and fortitude emanated from her youthful countenance. She gave a reassuring smile to her patient before she slipped out the door.

Daniel lay back down, drew in a deep breath, and exhaled slowly. He had never met anyone like this colonial woman before. The young lieutenant usually kept his emotions well guarded. But Mary Thomsen's simple beauty and kindness had completely disarmed him.

***

Mary silently approached her mother's side of the bed in the main room. She whispered so as not to disturb Sarah.

"Mother, please wake up," Mary said. "I must speak with you."

Widow Thomsen opened her eyes and saw the earnest look in her daughter's face. "What is it Mary? Is Mr. Lowe ill again?"

"No, Mother. I have given him some elm tea and it seems to be helping. I must go and find something in the woods. He dropped it and I must locate this piece of clothing."

She did not want to be too specific, as Sarah might be listening to their conversation.

Her mother gave her a look that said she understood. Widow Thomsen had noted the lack of the red uniform the night before.

"Look sharp for strangers," was all Mary's mother said to her.

The young woman fastened her hooded cloak and went out into the chilly morning air.

It was early dawn and many stars were still visible in the sky. While the light increased with each moment, Mary's anxiety grew as well.

How will I ever locate Daniel's coat in such a huge expanse of land? She quietly prayed an earnest plea for guidance as she forged ahead into the thick woods once more.

***

Widow Thomsen rose wearily from the comfort of the warm quilts. She wished that today of all days she could stay beneath the soft coverlets that were a refuge from the cold. The previous day had been exhausting. The normally energetic woman struggled to put on her woolen gown and petticoat over her shift. No time for sleeping in today. The widow headed toward the fireplace.

She stirred the corn gruel that had been simmering over the fire all night. The warmth of the flames reached out to her with a soothing touch that both energized and comforted her.

The repentant woman knew that her task today was to begin making amends to Daniel Lowe.

She poured warm water into a fresh basin and gathered some bayberry soap. From a chest of drawers not far from the large bed, she took out something that had long lain untouched—some of her late husband's clothing.

As she approached the door to the small bedroom, Widow Thomsen prayed that the young soldier would find it in his heart to forgive her.

Daniel was already awake, still fretting about his discarded uniform.

"Mr. Lowe," said the widow, "I hope that you slept well."

She placed the basin of steaming water, the linens, and the hard soap on the table and lay the clothing on the bed.

"I have brought you some new attire, sir. If anyone sees you wearing your uniform breeches and waistcoat, they will surely know who you are. You must dress like a colonist if you are to remain undetected."

Daniel stared at the woman in surprise.

"Widow Thomsen, why have you decided to help me? I am very grateful to you but … I do not understand…"

Speaking deliberately, the widow said, "Mister Lowe, please forgive my sordid demeanor yesterday. It was completely heartless of me and I am very ashamed of my attitude. It was cruel and completely unchristian."

The young soldier could only stare at her in utter amazement.

"I do not know what to say," he stammered. "I did not blame you for hating me. I know about your son, and I am terribly sorry."

Widow Thomsen averted her eyes for a moment and then returned her gaze to meet his.

"Even if you had been the one who killed my son, it would still be my Christian duty to forgive you. And yesterday, the Lord gave me some words from the Good Book to set my soul on the straight path. I repented of my sin and I ask you to forgive me for my hatred."

The pain in her eyes was palpable, and Daniel knew he must respond.

"I feel that I have no cause to find fault with you, Widow Thomsen. I am eternally indebted to you."

"We shall say no more about it, then. You are a guest in our home until you are fully recovered. Then you can decide what you will do about your future."

My future? Now there is a mystery.

When he escaped from the group of prisoners on that long dirt road, he never imagined that he would even survive to face the days ahead. Now, not only was his destiny uncertain, but he had involved innocent women in a dangerous mission. They were providing haven to an enemy soldier. This was not what he had planned at all.

Widow Thomsen interrupted his thoughts.

"God brought you to us for a reason, Mr. Lowe. I do not pretend to understand what his plans are for you, but I trust that he will reveal as much to you in due time."

"God?" Daniel said, trying to hide his anger. "What would God have to do with me being here? I have completely interrupted your lives with my problems, causing all of you discomfort and endangering your very existence. Why would you think that all this has anything to do with God?" His eyes blazed with emotion.

"God has his doing in every part of our lives, Mr. Lowe, whether we realize it or not." She looked at the disillusioned soldier with understanding. She did not press the discussion any further. "Let me help you get cleaned up, sir. I can wash your back for you if you can manage the rest," said the widow.

Daniel was still pondering her words as he unbuttoned his waistcoat and shirt. He rolled onto his side and felt the soothing warmth of the water on his back and the gentle scrubbing of the soap-covered linen. He could not remember the last time his back had been clean. He closed his eyes as his limbs relaxed.

Widow Thomsen smothered a gasp at the sight of the man's ribs. They stood out from his shrunken flesh, evidence that he had starved for weeks. She also noted several deep marks in the skin on his back. They were scars that she recognized well.

"You have had the smallpox, Mr. Lowe."

Daniel's eyes snapped open. "Yes. Many years ago."

The widow did not ask, but she assumed that it was the same outbreak during which his young sister had died.

"Well, I am glad that you survived it," she said.

Daniel rolled onto his back after she had dried him off. Widow Thomsen handed him the cloth with soap on it.

"You can refresh yourself with a washing as best you are able, Mr. Lowe. When you are done, please change into this clean clothing. We will have to hide your current attire."

"Thank you, madam," he said. Daniel hesitated to make any further requests of this kind woman, but he recalled his bristly facial hair earlier that morning. "I hate to impose upon you further, but … is there a razor available that I may use?"

The widow looked at the beard and smiled.

"I suppose we can find a suitable instrument to smooth out that face for you."

He looked at her with gratitude. Widow Thomsen went to the next room and came back with the shaving instrument.

"It belonged to my husband," she said as she gave him the wooden handle that contained the folded blade inside.

Daniel looked at the woman. He understood how difficult this moment must be for her.

"I am grateful for this valuable tool. I shall treat it with great care," Daniel said.

Widow Thomsen nodded and put her head down as she exited the room. "Let me know if you have need of anything else."

Daniel placed the linen into the warm water in the basin. He carefully applied the bayberry soap to the cloth. At first he moved it slowly back and forth across his face and neck. The more he tried to clean himself, the faster his elbows moved as he scrubbed away at the dirt.

But it was not soil that he was really trying to remove. In his frantic efforts to wash away the dirt, he hoped he could somehow wash away the memories of war.

***

Mary had been searching for the scarlet garment for what seemed like an hour. Everywhere she looked, she found only piles of old leaves and branches. Every glimmer of possibility turned futile, time and time again.

Until now.

At first she thought it was one more false hope. Then the light glistening off one of the coat's silver buttons proved this was the treasure she was searching for—the coat that could betray her family.

She picked it up. Her fingers touched the fine wool that had been sewn into the uniform of the British enemy. She shivered slightly as her hands smoothed over the shiny braiding that decorated his lieutenant's attire.

Such beautiful decoration for such an inglorious occupation.

When she was a small child, she had watched the troops in Boston in just such apparel. She had observed them in awe, admiring their finely made uniforms, feeling somehow protected by their presence in Massachusetts.

How things had sadly changed.

These same defenders of her freedom had turned against her and her fellow citizens. Innocent women and children had experienced the frightening wrath of the King's soldiers. The fight for independence from the tyrant King George had turned into a nightmare.

Mary's tears fell onto the coat, which was blackened by gunpowder. She held it close to her face. At first she smelled only the scent of war, but then another scent emerged. It was the fragrance of her friend, the scent of Daniel.

The young woman put aside her troubled thoughts. She had committed herself to recovering this coat, and this she had done. But it suddenly occurred to her that she had a new problem. How would she hide this bulky piece of clothing during her walk home? It was too large to tuck beneath her cloak. It would be far too visible, and the bright scarlet color would give away her secret to any passerby.

Almost instantly, she came up with the only solution that made sense.

The coat will be my unborn child, she decided.

Mary carefully folded the coat inside out so that the freezing buttons would not touch her skin. She was wearing several petticoats to protect her from the cold, so she took the one closest to her skin and wrapped it around the jacket, scooping it into a bundle. She tied the thin linen material around her waist to support her "baby."

It was not perfect, but most passersby would not look so closely at a pregnant woman's belly. It would not be deemed proper.

Mary remembered the waddling walk of many of her mother's patients. She began to imitate the awkward motion, retracing her steps back home. She held tightly onto Daniel's coat to keep it from moving.

She had gone several hundred yards when the moment she dreaded occurred. A Continental soldier on the lookout for wandering prisoners was perusing the outskirts of the Thomsen property on horseback. Mary exhaled in relief when she realized it was not the same fellow from two days before. Otherwise, she could only imagine his suspicion at her sudden impending birth.

"Good day, madam," said the young soldier seriously. "Rather a long way from home for a lady in your condition, eh?"

"Hello, sir," she replied with a smile. "My midwife tells me that long walks are a suitable exercise at such a time."

She was shocked at being referred to as "madam," but she hid her surprise.

"Well, madam, please be aware that we're lookin' for some enemy soldiers 'round here. They may be wounded. They may be dead. Just watch yourself that you don't stumble over no bodies."

"I shall, sir. Thank you for the warning," Mary answered, still smiling and holding onto her bundle.

As she wrapped one hand across her stomach, she felt the coat begin to loosen ever so slightly. The weight of it was making it difficult to keep everything in place, despite the tight knot in the petticoat.

The bundle suddenly moved even more, now more obviously. She grabbed the coat quickly with both hands. She knew she had a strained look on her face.

"Active little one. Must be a boy," she said.

The soldier looked with surprise at the woman's belly. He was not sure what had just occurred, but he was too embarrassed to question the woman. Female matters were alien to this unmarried man. He shifted uncomfortably in his saddle.

"Fare thee well, madam," the soldier said, riding off in haste.

She waved at him with one hand until he was out of sight. She turned back towards her home and gave a huge sigh of relief. She realized now that her heart was racing and her forehead perspiring. The soldier probably assumed she was sweating from her pregnancy.

With the rider now out of sight, she retied the loosened knot in her undercoat. She gave the tie an extra tug to ensure there would be no premature delivery before she arrived home. She waddled faster this time, anxious for this charade to be over.

Dear Lord, do not let me run into anyone I know.

As she reached the farmhouse entry, she was breathing so rapidly that she could barely speak. Her throat was as dry as cotton and she could not wait to drink something.

When Mary opened the door, her mother and Sarah were facing the fireplace. Widow Thomsen turned to look at her, but Sarah was otherwise occupied and not aware of Mary's presence.

Widow Thomsen's face was filled with shock when she saw Mary's "belly." It would have seemed laughable were it not so critical that Sarah not see her sister's appearance. Mary motioned for the widow to distract Sarah, so she could quickly slip into Daniel's infirmary.

As the young woman closed the door to Daniel's room, the British soldier and his angel of mercy faced another. It was difficult to know which of the two was more shocked: Mary at the sight of a clean-shaven Daniel in her father's colonial clothing, or Daniel seeing Mary apparently ready to give birth. When the astonishment faded, they both struggled not to burst out laughing.

"Mr. Lowe, please avert your eyes," Mary said. She covered her mouth tightly to smother the giggles that kept arising in her throat.

Daniel continued to stare at her unexpected appearance. Mary's cheeks burned with embarrassment.

"Mr. Lowe, please turn away," she said more pointedly as her laughter faded. He looked up and then turned his back to her.

"I apologize, miss," he said, ashamed of his lingering gaze. "I was just so dumbfounded … I could not fathom the situation."

Mary undid the knot in her petticoat and pulled out the scarlet garment. She pulled down the layers of her clothing and smoothed them back into place.

"Here, Mr. Lowe," she said as she triumphantly held out the lost treasure. "I have your coat for you."

Daniel turned away from the wall and faced Mary. Drawing in a deep breath, she took a long look at the man's features for the first time. Shaving that rugged beard had revealed another hidden treasure— Daniel's handsome face.

Looking at his coat as if seeing it for the first time, his face contorted with emotion at the sight of the scarlet material and the smell of gunpowder. He took the uniform out of her extended arms and looked up at her from the bed.

"Thank you," he whispered. Tears were fighting their way to the brim of his eyes.

Mary realized that this was a difficult moment for the escaped prisoner and she did not wish to embarrass him.

"I need to quench my thirst," she said truthfully. "I shall return in a few moments."

The young woman left the room, while Daniel looked upon his uniform. Mary could not imagine the thoughts that were going through his mind.

Daniel kept staring at the red coat, the material reawakening images of battle after battle. There were a few bloody stains on the scarlet material, which stood out blackly against the dyed wool. Some of the blood was his own. Some was that of his fellow soldiers. And some belonged to his brother, Oliver.

It was all a painful reminder of the last several months.

As he wiped the tears away with the coat, a familiar thought stirred in his mind. This battered uniform that evoked sadness in his heart now exuded the soothing scent of lavender flowers. This time it was the lining of his coat, which had been touching Mary's perfumed skin.

It was the aroma of home.

Chapter Nine

Conflict

A loud knocking at the door of the farmhouse woke Mary with a start.

Who would be coming to their home this early?

She inched her way out from under the quilts and set her feet on the cold wooden floor. She shivered as she pulled a shawl over her shift and went to answer.

"Miss Thomsen, we need your mother to come quickly!" It was young Richard Beal. The boy was perhaps nine or ten years old, with a puff of red hair on his head and large blue eyes that always seemed to look surprised. He was a sweet and sensible boy. It was no wonder that his mother entrusted him to fetch the midwife.

"Of course, Richard. I shall wake her promptly," Mary answered, trying not to yawn.

"Do you suppose your sister could come to keep me company, miss?" the boy asked hopefully. "I might need some help around the house watching the little ones while my mother is occupied."

"I suppose so, young man, but I shall have to ask our mother. Hurry along and tell your mother that Widow Thomsen will make haste to your home," Mary said with a smile. She knew that Richard had a fancy for little Sarah and he would make any excuse to visit with the girl. It did not matter to Richard that Sarah was not much older than "the little ones."

Mary closed the door. Far too much cold air had filled their home during the conversation. She hurried over to the fireplace to warm her hands.

"I heard young Richard at the door, Mary," Widow Thomsen said sleepily from bed. "I shall gather my things."

"The lad would like Sarah to go along, Mother," Mary replied.

Widow Thomsen rolled her eyes as she put on her woolen clothing.

"That boy will keep the gray hairs coming on my head if he keeps pining the way he does." She paused briefly and thought about the boy's request. "It would be a good diversion for Sarah to get away for the day, however."

"Thank you, Mother!" Sarah's voice piped up. She had been listening in, hoping that her mother would agree to let her go. "I shall be ready in no time."

The widow gathered her supplies, including wine, in case Martha Beal's supply of the drink had run low. She would not want the woman to bear a child without the help of some spirits.

"Put your cape on, Sarah, for it will be a very cold walk to their home without it," her mother reminded her.

Mary packed some bread, cheese, and apples.

"Here is some food for you both, Mother. This chilled air will make you hungry."

Widow Thomsen leaned over towards Sarah.

"Now remember, we must not speak of Mr. Lowe. It is our secret. Remember what can happen to disobedient children, Sarah."

The girl swallowed hard.

"They get put in the stocks in the middle of town?" she asked nervously.

"It could happen, young lady. So remember to obey," her mother said.

"I shall," answered Sarah.

"I almost forgot," the widow said turning towards Mary. "The wound. Can you change Mr. Lowe's dressing, Mary? It has to be done every day."

"Of course I shall, Mother. Now go. Everything will be fine," she said, hurrying the two on their way. It would not do for Mistress Beal to deliver her babe unattended.

It had been nearly three weeks since the women had brought Mr. Lowe to their home. Although his wound was healing, it was going to be a long and painful process.

"Such a wound can take weeks or months," Widow Thomsen had said. Her mother had also told Mary in private that Mr. Lowe might always walk with a limp. Neither woman had divulged that fact to Daniel Lowe. No reason to hamper his recovery with difficult news.

The scarlet coat that caused such a stir just a few weeks earlier was now securely hidden in the barn toolbox.

Mary slowly walked back to the fireplace and stirred the burning coals. She added more wood to the embers, then stretched her arms out with difficulty. She sat down on her father's old chair next to the fire and felt the smooth wood beneath her fingers.

The touch reminded Mary of moments long ago when her small hands would glide over the newly finished wood while her father would read *Aesop's Fables*. The memory brought tears to her now grown-up eyes.

She made an effort not to reminisce about those she had once loved, now gone to eternity. This sadness only added to her physical pain. Her whole body ached from the pig killing of yesterday.

The annual slaughter of farm animals in November provided much of the family's supply of winter meat. The heavy labor of chopping pork for sausages with a spade—normally done by the men—had to be performed by Mary and her mother. The larger pieces of pork were salted and stored in barrels or hung in the smokehouse. Every chunk of lard was saved for cooking and soap making. The daylong event was never a pleasant task. Every muscle in her body was in discomfort from the work.

With great effort, the young farmwoman rose from the chair to begin her day. She strode toward the chest of drawers and pulled out the petticoats and woolen gown that would complete her dress. Shivering from the cold, she slipped on her knitted stockings and tied the ribbons at the top of each so they would not slip down. She pinned up her hair tightly and set her cap in place. Lastly she picked up the bottle of lavender water. The fragrant liquid would be smoothed underneath her nose and onto her arms to curb the stench of infection while changing the bandage, a nursing strategy that her mother taught her.

But while her attire was ready for the day's work, she was not. She longed to lie back down on the bed and close her eyes just for a moment. And then she remembered Mr. Lowe. He would need her help.

Mary ladled out some warm cider for the patient and walked to the bedroom door. She gently knocked.

"Mr. Lowe?" She called to him softly in case he was not awake.

"Yes, come in," he called back. He was already awake, having heard the boy at the door.

As always, Daniel appeared pleased to see Mary. When she walked into the room, her fatigue from the long workday yesterday was evident in her stooped shoulders and labored steps.

"Here is your cider, sir," Mary said, handing him the tankard. The scent of spring flowers wafted from her hands towards his eager nostrils. The enticing aroma elicited a long stare from Daniel towards the young woman.

She had dark circles under her eyes this morning and lacked her usual vitality.

"Thank you," he said, taking the cup from her hand. "Please do not trouble yourself for my sake. I know you are weary."

Mary stifled a yawn.

"My mother worked just as hard as I did yesterday, and she has gone to help Missus Beal deliver her baby. I think I can manage bringing you something to eat and drink," she said, smiling. "I also need to change the dressing on your wound today." Mary was not looking forward to that task, but she tried not to let her apprehension show.

"My wound is much improved," Daniel reassured her. "It is not as wretched as when you first tended to it."

"Mother says it is healing quite well. Would you like me to change your bandages now or later?"

Before Daniel could answer, Mary's attention was drawn to the window by a distant movement on the road leading to their home. A solitary soldier wearing the deerskin hunting shirt of his unit was approaching. At first she did not recognize the bearded man, but she certainly knew that swaggering gait.

"Josiah!" she said in alarm.

Josiah Grant was a friend of her brother James and was in the same company of Minutemen. His appearance was most unexpected.

"Mr. Lowe, stay still and make no sound. And stay away from the window!"

She ran towards the front door, grabbing her cape as she went. She opened the door and closed it behind her before the patriot could knock.

"Josiah, how good to see you!" she said uneasily.

The weary soldier was visibly refreshed at the sight of Mary. He took off his tricornered hat and bowed to the young woman. His eyes scanned her form up and down with a familiarity that made Mary ill at ease.

"You have become quite the lovely woman, Mary. Can we not go inside where it's warm?" he asked, taking her hand.

"No," she answered, startled by his attentive demeanor. "My mother is acting as midwife today so there is no one home. It would not be proper. Come, let us walk. What news of James?" She was anxious for some word about her older brother.

He was leading her closer to the window in the room where Daniel lay. She faced the house so that Josiah would be looking towards her— and away from the British soldier.

"James is well," he replied. "He sends his greetings and will come home when he can. I received news that my mother was ill and so I came home as soon as I could to visit her."

Mary noticed his blanket roll still strapped across his chest. The rest of his military equipment was also intact, as though he had just come from his field of duty.

"But you have not been home yet?" Mary asked.

Josiah placed his musket barrel-side up against the house. He took her hands and closed the distance between them. His penetrating look made her feel most uncomfortable.

"I wanted to see you first, Mary. I was hoping you had changed your mind."

Josiah had made his strong feelings for her known before he went to war, but she had rejected him then. Her affections for him remained, as always, sisterly.

But his passion toward her had apparently grown with time. He drew her closer toward himself. Mary became tense with fear as his breathing quickened.

"Josiah, I…" Mary started to reiterate her lack of romantic feelings for him, but he interrupted her. The look in his eyes terrified her. Josiah drew her body against his own and began to caress her.

"Mary, every night in the camps, I can think of no one but you. Your hair, your eyes … I can practically taste your lips on mine." As he said these words, he tried to experience the taste firsthand.

Without thinking, Mary drew back her hand and slapped his face as hard as she could.

Josiah glared at her with raw anger and grabbed her arms painfully.

"What kind of way is that to greet a soldier returnin' from war? I could force myself on you, you know, and you could do nothin' 'bout it."

"Is that what you want, Josiah?" Mary said with a chill in her voice. "To ravage a woman like the British troops do? Is that what the war has taught you?" She shook so hard that her words came in fits and starts.

The colonial soldier released his iron grip on her arms. He stared at her with fury and humiliation. Without another word, he stalked off towards his home.

Mary turned her back on him, her face reddened with anger. Her relationship with Josiah, a friend since childhood, would never be the same. Tears forced their way to her eyes.

War changes people, she thought.

She stepped into the farmhouse and dried her eyes so that Daniel would not see her tears. When she felt somewhat composed, she reentered his room to begin the dressing change—but the patient was not in the bed.

"Mr. Lowe?" she called with uncertainty.

"I am over here," he said from the floor on the opposite side of the bed. Daniel was trying to get up again, but pain had incapacitated him. "Are you all right?"

"I am. But you are not. What happened?" she asked, as she put her arm around him. She helped him back up to the bed. He fell onto the quilts, sweat pouring from his forehead.

"Is that b…" he seethed, barely halting before he lost himself to anger and offense. "I mean, is that bloke, gone?"

Mary looked at him in surprise.

"You heard Josiah speaking to me?" she asked. How greatly embarrassing! "I am so ashamed…" Her voice trailed off as tears stung her eyelids once again. She looked down at the floor, too humiliated to meet his eyes.

"Did he hurt you?" he asked in a rage. "I wanted to cut his throat."

"No, I am unhurt," she said, looking up in surprise. Her arms did still ache from Josiah's forceful grip, but she saw no need to further inflame Daniel. She wanted to explain the situation to him lest he misunderstood. She did not know why, but this was important to her.

"Josiah and my brother James grew up together. Josiah asked me before he left for war if I would wait for him. I said then that he was like one of my brothers—nothing more." Mary looked down and said through quivering lips, "I guess he did not believe me."

The British soldier looked at her intently.

"I wanted to go to your assistance, but I could not bear weight on my leg," he said with frustration. "That's when I fell."

Mary looked up at Daniel. She could see the humiliation in his eyes.

"You are getting stronger all the time. In due time you will be able to walk again," she said. With a whisper she added, "Thank you for trying to help me."

Daniel was still furious. His hands were closed in a tight grip as he stared down the road for any sign of the unwelcome guest.

"I shall go and get the medicinals for your wound, Mr. Lowe," Mary said. She left the room. She needed to put this incident behind her lest she feel completely enveloped by fear. It was one thing to dread the enemy, but to be terrified by one of her own? The thought was too much to comprehend.

She returned to the infirmary with the clean linen bandages and the balsam apple solution.

"May I remove the quilt, Mr. Lowe, so I can reach your wound?" Mary asked.

Her soft voice soothed the anger in his spirit, and he looked at her with a slight smile.

"You are always so polite, miss. The nurses in the camp would have just torn off the blanket without thinking twice."

Mary looked at him and smiled.

"I am afraid I am not so forward." When she removed the blanket, she saw there was fresh blood on the bandage. "Mr. Lowe, you opened your wound when you fell."

Mary untied the strip of linen holding the bandage in place and remembered with dread the first time she had changed this dressing.

Dear Lord, do not let me feel ill this time.

When she pulled at the bandage after dousing it with some wine, it came up easily, packing and all.

"That was much easier this time," she said, relieved.

The young woman prepared the pledget of lint with apples in vinegar and placed it gently into the wound. The open crater was shrinking in size, much to Mary's relief.

Daniel was very quiet and she looked up to see if he was all right. He was staring at the ceiling, a pained expression on his face.

"Forgive me, Mr. Lowe. I did not offer you any spirits for your pain." She was appalled that she had forgotten so basic a care.

"Do not worry, Miss Thomsen. I would not have accepted such an offer today."

"Are you certain? I can get you something even now," she said.

"I am quite certain," he said. He tried to relax his grip on the bedding so as not to give away the extent of his discomfort. However, the woman noticed that his hands were knotted in tension. She gently touched one.

"I am sorry," she said. It was then that she noticed the old shirt that had belonged to her father. The faded linen shirtsleeve barely covered Daniel's forearm.

"It looks like your arms are a bit longer than my father's were," she said, tying the fresh linen over the dressing. Mary covered his legs with the quilt and looked at Daniel. "Perhaps I can add more material to the shirt for a better fit," she offered.

"Thank you, miss. Was your father a very tall man?"

"Every man is tall when you are a girl of twelve. I know not how tall he really was. My mother says that James is about his size. My brother is a good bit taller than I am."

"I am sorry that your father is gone," Daniel said.

Gazing out the window, she said, "I miss him a great deal. He was a good man, and always so kind. He could make me laugh even when things were not going well. I suppose though, that were he still alive, he might not have abided helping an enemy soldier. I remember how upset he was about the massacre in Boston. That happened only months before he drowned in the river."

Her thoughts wandered to the distant past, remembering her father's anger at the British soldiers who fired into the crowd.

"Massacre?" Daniel replied angrily. "I read the account as a lad in England. It was no massacre. The soldiers fired in self-defense!"

Mary's eyes narrowed as she looked at him with indignation.

"There were young boys killed that day, Mr. Lowe. Are not the troops trained to restrain their arms unless there is good cause?"

"There was good cause, miss." Daniel was now using his officer's voice. "The crowd provoked those men, harmed them even. One of your own lawyers from Massachusetts defended them and your fellow citizens acquitted those soldiers. They had a right to defend themselves."

"Tell that to the boys' mothers, Mr. Lowe. Tell that to the citizens of Massachusetts, who have been shackled by the King's men with tax upon tax. Many cannot support their families and our rights have been stripped away one at a time."

Anger filled Mary's green eyes, and she tightened her grip on the linens she was holding.

"The King thinks we must pay extra for the 'right' to be defended during the French War. Would he have taxed your family in England for being defended from an enemy?"

Daniel started to make an argument for King and country, but Mary interrupted.

"The King wants the benefit of our labor without giving us the rights of citizenship. How does that make us anymore than the King's slaves? I suppose you think as little of us colonists as the Crown does," she said with fire.

Mary headed for the open doorway before turning once more to Daniel. Her eyes blazed with anger as she faced him.

"Perhaps you would prefer some Tory trollop to be your nurse."

She whipped around and stomped from the room shutting the door hard. As she leaned against the wood, she realized how vile her language sounded, and she was filled with shame. She covered her mouth with her hand.

What must Daniel think of me?

The young woman slowly and remorsefully returned to the infirmary. Daniel was sitting in the bed, his mouth open in disbelief.

"I cannot believe that I used such an odious word, Mr. Lowe," Mary said deliberately. "Can you please forgive me?" She looked toward the floor.

Daniel's anger was replaced by amusement.

"I ... I was surprised that you knew the word, miss," he said teasingly.

The woman still stared at the floor.

"I heard my brother and his friends use it once. I had to ask James what it meant," she confessed.

Daniel smiled at her tender honesty.

"Miss Thomsen, you are forgiven," he replied. "But only if you forgive me for my impertinence."

She continued to look downward when Daniel put out his hand to her.

"Friends?" he asked her gently.

Mary slowly looked up at his gesture of peace. She put her hand out to meet his and placed her long fingers into his large grip.

"Friends," she said, and gave him an embarrassed smile.

Daniel held onto her hand for a long while.

Finally she whispered, "I really must go, Mr. Lowe."

He released her fingers with a look of regret on his face.

A moment passed in silence.

"You called him Josiah," Daniel said.

Mary looked up with surprise.

"What?" she asked, confused by his statement.

"You called James' friend by his Christian name," Daniel stated.

"Well, I have known him since I was very small. He is ... was ... like another brother," she said. "I cannot imagine calling him by a more formal title."

"I see," Daniel replied.

Mary looked at him and a smile crossed her lips.

"Perhaps one day I shall call you by your Christian name, Mr. Lowe." She turned and gave him another broad smile before leaving.

Daniel watched her leave, desperately hoping that day would come.

Chapter Ten

Nightmares

The night of the incident with Josiah Grant, Daniel's nightmares returned.

He had experienced a few blissful weeks of restful nights as he healed and regained his strength. But the rage over what happened to Mary rekindled the anger, fear, and terrible memories once again. And the demons visited his mind in full force during what should have been a restful sleep.

"Oliver, no!" he screamed out loud in the middle of the darkness.

Mary sat bolt upright in bed. Her heart was racing and her breathing quickened to the point where she believed she might faint. She looked over at the empty bed and saw that her mother and Sarah still had not returned from Missus Beal's birthing.

She threw off the blankets and grabbed her shawl.

Was someone in Daniel's room? What if Josiah had returned? He could be attacking Daniel at this very moment. The very thought made her ill. She instinctively grabbed a large kitchen knife and trembled as she walked toward his room. She heard Daniel scream again and forced herself with shaking hands to open the door. There was no one in the room with the wounded soldier, but he was yelling as though surrounded by enemies. And he kept screaming over and over for Oliver to take cover.

Mary's throat was so dry she could hardly speak but she resolutely walked over to his bedside.

"Mr. Lowe." She could barely hear her own voice, so frightened was she. "Mr. Lowe," she said somewhat louder.

Daniel's eyes were wide open and his face was contorted in fear. He continued to yell at the invisible ghosts from his memories. She put the knife out of his sight and placed one hand on his arm.

"Mr. Lowe, it is I, Mary Thomsen. You are in our home and you are safe."

She gently stroked his arm and spoke again.

"No one is harming you, Mr. Lowe. Please rest."

Daniel slowly drifted back to sleep. His terrible memories returned to the dark places in his mind where they hid. They could reemerge any moment in the still hours of any given night.

Mary continued to stroke his arm. She began to weep for this man, so far from home and all alone.

It seems so unfair Dear God, she prayed in her heart. *He has been through so much pain in body and mind. Why does he have to suffer so? What is your purpose in all this?*

The thought occurred to Mary, deep in her spirit, that God's son had suffered the worst of pain when he died. And God had a definite purpose in that suffering. Mary understood in her heart that the Creator was doing his work in Daniel, molding him into the man that God was designing. Mary needed to trust in God's plan.

She squeezed Daniel's arm one last time. Then she retrieved the kitchen knife from under his bed, and returned to her bed in the next room. As her tear-stained face dried, she fell into a deep slumber and did not awaken until dawn.

Widow Thomsen and Sarah were still not home when Mary began her daytime chores. She prayed that everything was well with Missus Beal and the new baby. The knife from the previous night's occurrence still lay on the long wooden table. It was a chilling reminder of the terror that had come in the darkness.

Mary approached Daniel's closed doorway and knocked gently. There was no answer.

Opening the door as quietly as she could, she placed some warm cider near his bedside for when he awoke. She looked at him so peacefully sound asleep—a far cry from just a few hours ago. She smiled at his disheveled shoulder-length hair lying across the pillow, making a mental note to bring him one of Asa's leather hair ties.

As she carefully walked back to the door, she heard his voice behind her.

"Miss Thomsen," he said sleepily.

Mary turned towards him apologetically.

"I am so sorry, Mr. Lowe. I did not wish to disturb you. I was afraid I would be occupied in the barn and I wanted you to have something to drink when you awoke."

"It is quite all right, miss," the soldier replied.

She went back toward the bed and picked up the tankard to hand it to him. He drank the warm liquid heartily.

"It is good to see you drinking and eating," Mary said. "If you are ready for some corn gruel, I can bring it to you now."

Daniel took a few more gulps of the cider.

"That sounds very good. Your porridge tastes like hasty pudding from back home."

"I am afraid our dish is not so 'hasty.' It has to cook over a low fire all night long."

She looked at him shyly. "I have something to give you," she said. "Would you think it offensive if I gave you something that belonged to Asa?"

Daniel looked at her warmly.

"I would be honored."

She hurried out of the room and went to the special wooden box that held Asa's belongings. Mary searched through his books and clothes before finding the object of her search—the pouch that held the leather hair ties. Mary fingered the long soft strands of calfskin, holding them close to her face. She looked at them for a long moment before returning to Daniel.

"Here, Mr. Lowe. I thought you might want these for your hair." Mary handed them to the young soldier, who took them gratefully.

"I must look a sight, miss, with my disheveled appearance."

"On the contrary, sir. You look very handsome since you shaved your face," Mary said. "I am sorry, sir. I did not mean to imply that you looked badly before … I mean…" She stopped herself before she completely misspoke.

Daniel smiled.

"You have most certainly seen me at my worst, miss. Thank you kindly for these hair ties. I shall always consider them a precious gift since they were worn by your brother." He smoothed his fingers through his dark brown hair before tying the leather strands into a knot that held his locks in place.

The young woman envisioned Asa wearing these same strips of leather in his light brown hair, and she grew quiet.

Daniel broke her contemplative silence.

"I remember you telling me in the wigwam that he was your best friend."

"Yes," she replied, staring for a moment at the floor.

When she looked up again, Mary found it difficult not to gaze at Daniel. When she had first met the young soldier, he was a gaunt and scraggly man in need of food and shaving. Now he was gaining strength and vitality that shone through in his rich brown eyes. They highlighted the strong angular features of his lean, fine-looking face.

She took in a deep breath and said, "I shall go get the gruel, sir."

She returned promptly with the hot cereal that she had sprinkled with cinnamon. Daniel ate the porridge hungrily. He looked up at her when his bowl was empty.

"Thank you, miss. For everything."

The woman began to speak but stopped herself.

"What is it, miss? There is something you wish to say?" Daniel asked curiously.

"Might I ask you a personal question, Mr. Lowe?"

"You may."

"Who is Oliver?" she asked.

Daniel's face grew white and he looked toward the window. Mary knew immediately she had touched upon a topic perhaps too painful to discuss.

"I regret now that I have brought it up, sir. Please do not feel compelled to tell me." She turned to leave the room, but he called after her.

"Wait," he said in earnest. He looked deeply vulnerable. "How do you know the name, miss?" He looked at her in earnest.

She paused and then said, "You called out his name in the night."

A pained expression filled his eyes as he looked fully into hers. "Did I frighten you, miss?"

"Yes," she said in a whisper. "I thought someone, perhaps Josiah, was hurting you. When I realized you were alone, I knew it was a dream—a terrible nightmare. I spoke to you, but you were unable to answer me. You finally drifted off to sleep."

The two sat without speaking for what seemed an eternity. Finally, Daniel broke the silence.

"Oliver was my younger brother," he stated flatly. "He was killed near Saratoga."

"I am so sorry, sir," Mary replied in astonishment. "I had no idea you had someone from your family with you in battle. I am sure it was a comfort to him to have you nearby."

"I doubt it, miss," he replied bitterly. "My brother hated me for the last several weeks of his life."

Mary stared at the soldier in utter confusion.

"Hated you? I cannot imagine why."

"Please, miss. I answered your question, but please do not delve further. It is too difficult..." Daniel's voice broke off.

Mary paused a moment, then said, "I am so very sorry to have stirred up your sad memories, sir. I shall not be so bold in my inquiries in future."

Daniel stared at her with many emotions at play in his mind.

"You were not too bold." He could barely get the words out. "I would just like to put it all behind me, once and for all."

"We shall let your memories rest, sir," Mary replied.

When she reached over to reclaim his empty bowl, the sleeves of her shift slipped upward, exposing her forearms.

"What is this?" Daniel demanded. Purple bruises in the form of large fingers enveloped Mary's limbs. The woman winced in discomfort at the pressure of Daniel examining her arms. He drew her arms closer to get a better look at the injury. His aggressive action caused her to sit on the edge of the bed, stifling a cry.

71

"That bloody blaggart," Daniel exclaimed in anger. "How dare he put his wretched hands on you like that."

Mary did not know how to respond. She was so humiliated by the incident, remembering the ugly words and the pain of Josiah's grip. But mostly reliving the fear every time she laid eyes on those bruises. And now this friend, Daniel Lowe, had seen the evidence of her indignity. The young woman was mortified.

Daniel saw the look of despair on her face and suppressed his anger.

"Miss," he said more gently now, "I do not mean to frighten you with my harsh words. I am so angered that he hurt you this way. This vexes me so."

He looked at Mary, gently stroking her arms as if trying to erase the misdeed of the colonial soldier.

She looked down at the quilts on the bed, not wanting to meet Daniel's intent gaze.

"I … I never thought that Josiah Grant was a man of good character," she said, her voice growing a little distant. "All the other girls growing up in our village thought he was so handsome. But I did not trust his eyes. They say you can look into someone's soul through their eyes, you know."

The British soldier listened patiently as she spoke. He swallowed with difficulty and then dared to ask a bold question.

"And what do you see in my eyes, miss?" he asked.

Mary's gaze met his. Her face was filled with distress, but she felt comforted in his presence. "I see pain and fear. But mostly," she said almost in a whisper, "I see kindness."

She stood up from the bed.

"Thank you, Mr. Lowe." And then she was gone from the room.

Daniel was filled with an overwhelming desire to go after her—take her in his arms and tell her that the nightmares would all be over forever—but he could not.

But there was something he could do—everything necessary to recover from this wound. He would work with all his might to strengthen his leg. He would once again be the strong man that could protect this woman from further harm.

For Daniel Lowe did not ever wish to be found falling on the floor again when Mary Thomsen needed him.

Chapter Eleven

Siblings

When Widow Thomsen returned that same day, her eyes were drawn immediately to the bruises on Mary's arms.

It took a rapid explanation on the young woman's part to convince her mother that the marks had not come from Daniel's hands. The parent was enraged to learn that it was caused by one of their own townsfolk.

"Josiah Grant will never be allowed near this home again," the widow declared, and Mary knew that her mother would keep that vow to her grave. The older woman was skilled at using the shotgun left from her late husband and was quite capable of carrying out that promise with force, if necessary.

Her mother's demeanor towards Daniel became more positive after the incident with Josiah. It was obvious that Widow Thomsen worried about the long absence from home when Missus Beal was in her lengthy labor. Mary saw the relief in the midwife's expression when she began to trust the stranger under their roof.

"When you are stronger," Widow Thomsen said to Daniel that afternoon, "we would like to invite you to join us at table for the evening meal."

Daniel stared at the older woman with surprise.

"I am grateful, ma'am, for your kind offer. But I feel I have already accepted far too much hospitality from you—far more than I deserve."

"It is not charity I am offering to you, young man. I am sure that once you are able to help out, you will make yourself quite useful. When you are well, you will begin earning your keep."

"Thank you," he said with relief. It was not his nature to accept charity.

"Perhaps you would like a book to read while you are recovering," the widow offered.

"I would greatly appreciate the diversion," Daniel replied.

"Our reading material is limited but I am sure I can find something to suit your interest."

She left the room and returned shortly with a large book. The heavy volume was filled with both text and ink drawings.

"This is one of our family favorites," the widow said. "I hope you will find it pleasing."

"*Pilgrim's Progress*, by John Bunyan," Daniel read aloud. He looked up at the older woman. "I have never read it, although I have heard the title. Thank you, madam."

"You are quite welcome, Mr. Lowe. Now if you will excuse me." The widow left the room.

Daniel carefully opened the front pages and saw an inscription written in a child's handwriting. "Asa Thomsen, received on December 12, in the year of Our Lord 1769."

"Asa's book," he said in a whisper. He carefully turned the pages, reading the words that had fed the mind of Mary's younger brother many years before. Daniel was moved by the thought of this brother and son who was loved by his family. This young man who loved music—and who died in a terrible war.

Daniel forced these thoughts to the back of his mind as he read the opening words of Bunyan:

"As I walked through the wilderness of this world, I lighted on a certain place, where was a Den; and I laid me down in that place to sleep: and as I slept I dreamed a Dream…"

So intrigued was Daniel by these words that he read long into the evening. At last, he could keep his eyes open no more.

***

During the next two weeks, the Thomsen women were hard at work catching up on the autumnal rituals.

The candle-making could not be delayed any longer. The women scurried to set up two large kettles over the fire, each pot containing water and beef tallow provided by a neighbor. The candle rods were strung with the long wicks for dipping into the hot kettles. The coated wicks were then set to dry on long poles across two chairs. The candles slowly grew in size as they were alternately dipped and dried.

It was an all-day event. The women transformed the bare wicks into the source of light that would provide illumination through the long winter nights.

Mary and Widow Thomsen spent another day making candles from the waxy fruit of a bayberry bush. These sweetly scented green candles were Mary's favorite. She was grateful for Aunt Prudence, who faithfully brought these berries every year from her home in Bridgewater.

When the candles were complete, the Thomsens set upon making the materials needed for clothing. While Mary spun flax fibers on the spinning wheel to be readied for weaving, Widow Thomsen carded wool from a neighbor's sheep into tufts ready to spin into yarn. The women worked long into the evenings, until they both fought to keep their eyes open.

While the Thomsens were preparing for winter, Daniel was preparing to strengthen his leg. The injured soldier tried not to despair at the sight of the raw, pitted scar that covered much of his upper thigh. Part of the muscle appeared to be lost forever. He wondered if he could ever regain the use of his limb. Regardless of its appearance, Daniel was determined to work with the muscles that were left. He resolved that he would indeed walk again.

In between readings from Bunyan's book, Daniel spent hours each day working his way into a standing position. At first he could only manage a few moments of bearing his own weight. But as his strength and balance grew, he soon managed long periods of remaining upright.

One day, he decided to take his first steps by himself. This new skill was more difficult than he imagined, and he clutched the edges of the bed to keep from falling.

At that moment, Mary walked into the room with hot soup for him. She quickly placed the bowl on the small bedside table and helped him back onto the mattress.

"Mr. Lowe, we can find you a walking device that you can lean on. I did not know you felt ready to get up and walk about. My mother and I have been so busy. We should have realized your need."

"I do not want a crutch, miss," he replied stubbornly. "I want to carry my own weight."

Mary looked at him with amusement.

"There is a reason that the Bible says 'Pride goeth before a fall,' Mr. Lowe. And your vanity will surely bring you down—right onto the cold floor. Please, let us find you a crutch. With all my brothers' youthful foibles and falls, I am certain we have something in the barn that will suit your needs."

"All right, then," he said. "I shall accept your advice. Not that I want to."

"That is quite clear," Mary answered, bemused.

Daniel looked up at her with a defeated grin. Then he smiled more broadly as he saw her disheveled appearance. Her long hair was coming undone from her cap—a frequent occurrence when she was hard at work—and there were splotches of candle wax across her apron.

Seeing his gaze, Mary became self-conscious.

"I suppose that vanity is not my current dilemma. I should have improved my appearance before bringing you your soup," she said.

Handing him the bowl and spoon, she tried to keep their eyes from meeting.

"Miss Thomsen," Daniel said. When she finally returned his gaze, he continued. "Your appearance is always pleasing to my eyes. Thank you kindly for the soup."

"You are welcome, sir," she replied, and slipped out the door.

Daniel stared after her for several moments. And he smiled at the thought of her arms around him as she helped him back onto the bed.

***

The weeks of hard work were paying off. The finished candles were stacked in a box in the corner. The wool was ready for spinning and the flax prepared for weaving. And Daniel Lowe was strong enough to walk on his crutch out to the main room to share the evening meal.

It was a time to celebrate these accomplishments great and small.

"I must say, Mr. Lowe, it is God's miracle that you are doing so well," Widow Thomsen said.

Her hands were on her cheeks in astonishment as she watched the man struggle toward the big chair by the fire. Daniel was out of breath by the time he reached his destination. He sat in the same wooden seat that was used by Mr. Thomsen so long ago.

The young soldier was pleased despite his exhaustion. He had not walked this far since that first journey to their home.

"It is hard to believe that I used to walk long distances with ease," he said.

"And you shall walk as well again," Mary said.

Young Sarah was excited to see Daniel in the reading chair.

"Would you like me to bring you a book to read, Mr. Lowe? May I sit on your lap for reading time?" the girl asked.

As the words came out of her mouth, she started to climb onto Daniel's wounded leg. Both women gasped and shouted "No!" at the same moment. Mary grabbed her younger sister just before the girl put her weight on his lap. "Thank you," Daniel said gratefully to Mary.

"Mr. Lowe still needs to heal, Sarah. You cannot sit on his lap until he is fully recovered. And only if he says it is all right," Mary said with a stern look at her little sister.

Sarah gave a scowl, then strode angrily over to the fireplace to play with her doll. She had been in a foul mood all day and she did not like being disciplined by her older sister.

Daniel noticed the girl's displeasure and tried to ease her ill temper.

"Little miss, I shall be happy to read you a book if you sit in the chair beside me."

The young girl was so excited by the offer that she was not careful enough near the open fire. Daniel was the first to notice Sarah's apron catch the flame. Without thinking about his leg, he leaped to his feet to smother the kindled linen with his bare hands.

Sarah began to scream and Mary and her mother rushed over to assist. The little girl threw her arms around Daniel's neck and began to cry. He held her tightly for a moment, realizing how closely this family had come to yet another tragedy. The thought filled him with both terror and relief.

"Thank you, Mr. Lowe," Sarah said between sobs. And then the sobbing became more intense as she looked at his face and said, "I miss Asa."

Daniel held her again and said, "I know. I miss my brother as well."

Sarah looked at the man with surprise.

"Was he killed in the war, too?"

Daniel swallowed with difficulty.

"Yes, little miss. He was."

The young girl twisted her face in hatred.

"Was he killed by a dirty Lobster, too?" she asked Daniel, disdain filling her voice.

"Sarah!" Mary said with horror.

"That will be enough hateful talk from you, young lady," said Widow Thomsen.

"But Richard Beal says—"

"I do not care what that young boy says. That is hateful talk. It has no place in a Christian home," her mother said sternly.

Widow Thomsen took Sarah from Daniel's arms and carried the frightened child to the bed. She held the small girl in her embrace and rocked her slowly. It was as though she were a young babe in her arms once again. "I am sorry," she whispered to Daniel, her eyes full of sadness.

Daniel stood there in shock, not knowing what to say. He looked like a beaten man who had suddenly aged ten years.

Mary put her hand on his arm. She wished that she could wipe away the last several moments of time.

"I … I think I shall retire for the night," Daniel said. He grabbed the crutch and slowly made his way back to his room, his shoulders slumped in defeat.

Mary followed him back to his room and closed the door behind her. Daniel limped over to the window, struggling to catch his breath.

"How do I open this?" he asked, breathing far too fast. "I need some air."

Hurriedly moving to the double-hung window, she pushed the lower frame upward and propped it open with a piece of wood. Daniel leaned on the sloping sill, taking in deep breaths of the freezing night air.

Mary waited until he seemed calmer before daring to speak.

"Sarah is just a child, Mr. Lowe. She does not understand. Please forgive her words so unwittingly spoken." She paused, then added, "Sarah cares for you very much."

Daniel looked up at Mary from the open window.

"She would not care for me if she knew who I was," he said.

The young woman waited a moment before daring to speak.

"I know who you are, and I care for you," she said.

"I do not know why, miss." He suddenly realized that she was shivering from the cold air and he turned to close the window. He grabbed one of the quilts off of his bed and placed it around her shoulders.

He carefully sat on the edge of his bed and took in a long, deep breath. Mary sat down a few inches away from the man and looked directly at his face.

"Tell me about your brother," Mary said to him quietly. "Tell me what happened to Oliver."

Daniel stared into Mary's green eyes. She returned the gaze and he could feel the compassion emanating from her. It was the same kindness that he had felt in her presence from the first day he had met her. But now there was something more—a tender friendship that had grown between them, an alliance that transcended allegiance to any country or cause. At this moment, Daniel realized that he could trust Mary with anything, even his very life. He could certainly trust her with the truth.

The story of Oliver unfolded slowly at first, like a small crack in a huge dam. But once the pressure of the distress had become too much for the edifice to bear, the tale poured out like a raging flood.

"Oliver was just seventeen when my father bought him a commission in the King's Army," Daniel said. "I was one of the lieutenants, and my brother and several other ensigns were a part of the Twenty-first Regiment under Burgoyne. On the voyage across the Atlantic, Oliver became friends with a cocky ensign called Gray. I knew this blaggart was trouble from the start.

"When I spoke with Oliver about Gray, he told me I could stop playing the part of older brother. He was in the army now and he did not need me to look after him. I told him it had nothing to do with being family; it had to do with choices and falling in with the wrong company. He scoffed at my attempts to reason with him."

Daniel paused and took a deep breath.

"The real trouble began when we were running low on victuals in the countryside of New York. Our regiment split into companies and I was officer in charge at one farmhouse. We were told to obtain supplies of food from the barns—nothing more.

"Gray ... Gray decided that he wanted more than victuals when he observed a young woman at the farmhouse. He started for the home where he had seen her run inside. 'Anyone else like some female company?' the idiot declared to the entire unit. Several recruits were more than willing to go along with the wayward ensign.

"I yelled for him to halt and return to the orders at hand. I loaded my Brown Bess with powder and ball. Gray ignored my demand, and I ordered him again. I shouted, 'Halt or be shot.' Oliver could see that I was serious and yelled for Gray to stop as well. When Gray kept proceeding to the farmhouse, unbuttoning his shirt as he went ... I ... I shot him. As he lay on the ground bleeding to death, all the others stood stock still. The look on their faces was utter disbelief. No one said a word. And Oliver ... Oliver looked at me with such hatred in his eyes. I shall never forget his anger."

Mary's eyes were wide with terror. She was trembling now, but not from the cold.

Daniel had been staring out the window but turned now to look at her.

"You must think me as cold-blooded as Oliver did."

"How could you think that?" she asked, holding back the tears and shaking her head in disbelief. "You were protecting that innocent woman at the farm ..." She stopped, considering what would have taken place without Daniel's intervention.

Daniel stared again out the window.

"After that day, Oliver never spoke to me again. Until the battle at Freeman's farm, that is. Our unit was holding the right flank in battle but we were standing in the woods where we were open to surprise

81

attack. I was getting ready to order another line of fire when I glanced over to my right and saw an insurgent rushing straight at Oliver with his bayonet. I yelled at my brother to take cover, but in so doing he turned to face a barrage of enemy balls. He was hit several times in the chest.

"I ran to him immediately. That's when a lead ball hit my own leg and I fell next to him on the field. I pulled him to me and held him as he was dying. 'I am sorry,' he kept saying. 'You were right, I am so sorry.' And then he was gone. He died with his eyes still open, and I had to close them for the last time."

Daniel was sobbing now. Mary's cheeks were also moist with tears, and she took Daniel's hand.

"I am so sorry," she said.

Daniel wiped away his tears and continued.

"Then the strangest thing happened. A rebel soldier came at me with his bayonet held high. I knew it was going to be my demise as well, so I closed my eyes to wait for the end. But … it did not come. I opened up my eyes, and he was gone."

"What happened?" Mary asked, incredulous.

"I know not," Daniel said, shaking his head. "I suppose it was not my day to meet my Maker."

He stared at the clear December night sky, lost in the sight of thousands of stars pulsating in the darkness.

They sat quietly for a few moments. They were both overwhelmed by the contrast of the beauty of creation against the ugly tales of war.

Mary finally broke the silence, her voice thick from crying.

"You must realize that Oliver loved you. He knew you had made the right decision when you stopped Ensign Gray at that farm. That is what he was trying to tell you before … he died."

"I had not thought so—until now. My father does not know about Oliver. The last words he spoke to me in England were 'Look after your brother, Daniel. See that he is safe.' I am sure I have disappointed him completely."

"Many men fall in war, Daniel Lowe. Only God decides who walks off the battlefield."

Her words caught his attention and he stared long and hard at Mary.

"You called me Daniel," he said.

Mary seemed surprised by the revelation.

"I suppose I did."

"May I call you Mary?"

"I suppose you may. But not when my mother is nearby."

Daniel could not help but smile as he wiped the rest of the tears from his eyes.

"It is settled then," he said.

"Yes, it is settled," she replied with a smile.

She stood up from the edge of his bed and removed the quilt from her shoulders.

"I must go," she said.

Daniel held tightly to her hand.

"I wish you could stay," was all he said.

Mary wanted to stay with all of her heart. She prayed for the strength to resist the temptation.

"I cannot," she said. As he released her hand, Mary looked at him thoughtfully. "You must feel very alone here, so far from home."

Daniel stared at her for a long while before answering.

"Not when I am with you, Mary."

She walked toward the door, glancing back briefly.

"Good night, Daniel."

"Good night, Mary."

As Mary climbed into her bed, her mother's voice spoke gently out of the darkness to her older daughter. "Do not set your heart on Mr. Lowe, Mary. One day, he will return to his home. I do not want you to bear any hurt."

Mary did not say anything.

Her tears began to flow again, not just for the brothers lost in battle but at the thought that Daniel might return home one day. Then she would never see him again.

Chapter Twelve

Thanksgiving

The group at the Thomsen supper table was startled out of its languor by a bold knocking at the door.

"Hurry to your room, Daniel!" Mary exclaimed.

The women paused long enough to remind Sarah once again not to disclose the soldier's presence.

Widow Thomsen opened the wooden door and saw a courier carrying a parchment. His tricornered hat was covered with fine flakes of snow and his shoulders were shivering beneath his overcoat. The man's horse was several yards back, grazing on a patch of dead grass sticking up from the snow.

"Excuse me, madam. A dispatch from the Continental Congress. May I come in and read its contents to your household?" the visitor asked, his eyes weary.

"Of course, sir," Widow Thomsen said. "Do come in out of the cold."

The courier turned his head for a moment and coughed several times.

"Excuse me, madam," he said. "Bit of a chill in my bones tonight."

"Have a seat, sir. Let me get you a warm beverage," the widow said kindly.

She served him some hot cider and the women looked expectantly at the man. Mary finally could not contain her curiosity.

"What news from the Congress, sir?" she asked.

"Ah yes. The Thanksgiving Proclamation," the courier said. He opened the rolled up paper and began to read:

"Forasmuch as it is the indispensable Duty of all Men to adore the superintending Providence of Almighty God…"

It was a letter to acknowledge and to celebrate the victory of the Continental troops over the British at Saratoga. Daniel listened through the wall to the proclamation.

"It is therefore recommended to the legislative or executive powers of these UNITED STATES to set apart THURSDAY, the eighteenth Day of December next, for solemn THANKSGIVING and Praise: That at one Time and with one Voice, the good people may express the grateful Feelings of their Hearts, and consecrate themselves to the Service of their Divine Benefactor…"

Daniel sat down quietly on his bed and rubbed his forehead with his hand. He continued to listen to the courier extolling praise for the providence of Almighty God for the success in "the Prosecution of a just and necessary War."

Daniel stared out the frosty windowpanes, lost in conflicting thoughts.

He knew that the Thomsen women would want to celebrate this victory. Although Daniel was beginning to understand the colonists' quest for freedom, it did not change his own impassioned memories about his army's horrible defeat. For this family to commemorate the conquest caused him great distress. For the wounded soldier, Saratoga was a dreadful memory. But how could he express his struggle in the midst of their triumph?

As the visitor in the next room finished reading the proclamation, Daniel heard the man cough violently. Widow Thomsen offered the courier more cider before he would proceed on to the next farm. When the dispatcher was finally finished and the front door closed behind him, Mary walked into Daniel's room.

"Are you all right?" she asked.

Daniel turned his head towards the woman. The look on her face told him that she understood the conflict going on in his mind. She knew that the courier's resounding voice would have easily carried the message from Congress straight through the wooden walls to Daniel's ears.

He smiled with his mouth, but it did not reach his eyes.

"Yes, Mary, I am well enough. It is not surprising that your Congress has proclaimed a day of celebration. It was definitely a victory for the colonies. We were overwhelmed in battle," he said, looking out the window again. "It is amazing that more of us were not killed."

"I do not know what to say, Daniel. I have so many confused feelings. Of course, I am relieved and excited that our troops have been victorious. But my heart aches for your loss as well." Mary looked down at the floor. "And it is my great comfort that you were not lost in battle." She looked up at the soldier, the turmoil evident in her countenance.

Daniel looked at her for a long moment.

"There was a time not long ago when I did not care if I lived or died," the soldier said, remembering his desperation and pain. "On your day of Thanksgiving, I shall be grateful for my life—and for you."

"I shall always be thankful for you, Daniel Lowe," Mary said, tears welling in her eyes. "And I pray that you never despair so again."

As she turned to leave the room, she had an anguished look on her face. She stared at his fine features reflected in the light of the fireplace and tried to maintain her composure.

"Good night, Daniel," she said, almost in a whisper.

"Good night, Mary," he said to her, wishing that she would stay longer.

Even the calming scent of her lavender water could not quell the anxiety in his mind. He too was struggling with his feelings for her. The uncertainty about his future besieged his thoughts. The British soldier was beginning to wonder just how committed he was to King and country and fighting for what appeared to be a lost cause.

He could never forget the outrageous horror of the frequent attacks on women and children during the campaign across New York. And Burgoyne—"Gentleman Johnny," as his men liked to call him—seemed at times to be more interested in visiting his lady friend than seeing to the safety and well-being of his troops. These events and more had been a frequent source of consternation to the youthful lieutenant. He realized that he had started his career with a naive belief in what it meant to be a gentleman officer.

Daniel was also surprised by the fervor with which the committed insurgents fought for colonial freedom. Were they so wrong in their quest for justice?

And then there was Mary. Just thinking about leaving her to return to his homeland filled him with such sadness. It was more disheartening than his deepest feelings of despair on the road to Deer Run. Yet how would he find a way to stay here in Massachusetts? How would the village accept him as one of their own once they realized who he was? And would they persecute her for being associated with a King's soldier?

These thoughts filled his heart with sorrow. He lay down on his pillow and closed his eyes, hoping desperately that sleep would give him a respite from his heavy concerns.

***

The next morning was a flurry of activity. Thanksgiving celebration was only three days away, and Mary and Widow Thomsen were beginning the preparations for the feast. The actual day of the eighteenth would be spent at the meetinghouse in prayer. But the day before would be filled with the best bounty from their stores of food grown throughout the year. And of course, everyone hoped there would be fresh turkey, caught in the turkey pen.

When Daniel appeared in the main room from his night's rest, Sarah ran over to him.

"Mr. Lowe, did you hear we are having a Thanksgiving supper?" she asked excitedly.

"I did indeed, little miss." Daniel smiled at the lively six-year-old, then turned to her mother. "Is there anything that I can do to help, madam?"

Widow Thomsen looked up from her task of bread-making.

"I cannot think of anything specific at the moment, Mr. Lowe. I cannot assign you too unwieldy a task, since you are still recovering. However, I know that tomorrow you can help with cleaning the vegetables."

"I can do that, I am sure," Daniel said, feeling a pang of frustration at his still limited strength. "If you think of anything else that I can do, please allow me to assist you as well."

Mary was mixing the ingredients for a celebration cake. She was so engrossed in her baking that she was unaware that bits of the mixture were on her face. The flour gave her a ghostly glow. Daniel smiled at his industrious friend, who took more care in her work than in her appearance.

All at once, Mary stopped her busy stirring and her mouth dropped open.

"Good Lord," she exclaimed. "I forgot Susannah!"

"Oh Mary, that is why I heard her bellowing a moment ago from the barn," her mother said anxiously. "The poor cow must be miserable. But I am much too busy kneading this dough to stop and milk her. Can you do it?"

"I just started adding the butter to the sugar..." Mary began. All at once, both women looked at Daniel with expectation in their eyes.

"I can do it," he exclaimed with confidence. He had never done it before, but he wasn't about to let that stop him.

Mary and Widow Thomsen looked doubtful, but they were so consumed with their need to cook that they were willing to trust him with the task.

"I shall show you where everything is, Mr. Lowe," Mary said, careful not to call him by his Christian name within earshot of her mother.

The young woman picked up a buckskin coat from a wooden hook on the wall and handed it to Daniel. "You will need this in the cold."

"Was this your father's?" Daniel asked her, feeling the softness of the deer hide as he put his arms through the sleeves.

"No. You have outgrown my father's clothing with your healthy appetite," Mary teased him. "This belongs to James."

Mary put on her woolen cape and placed the hood over her hair to ward off the cold wind. They set out the front door for the barn.

There were a few inches of fresh snow on the ground, but the sun shone brightly. The reflection of light off the white landscape caused Daniel to squint.

"This is the first time I have been out of doors since I arrived here," Daniel said. He tried to take some longer strides with his impaired leg. He found this new gait difficult to perfect and occasionally came close to falling. Mary patiently kept pace with his awkward movements.

"It must give you a sense of liberty to escape the confines of the farmhouse," Mary said. "I would feel like a prisoner if I had been closed up in a house as long as you have been."

"I was a prisoner," Daniel said. "Being in your home is nothing like that experience. But breathing in this fresh air—it is invigorating to the spirit to be sure."

As his eyes adjusted more to the brightness, Daniel looked at Mary. He took her arm to make her stop.

"Wait," he said. "If I may be so bold." He wiped the flour off her face. "There. We do not want your lovely skin hiding behind the sweet cake."

"I always do that," she said, blushing hotly. "Mother says I need to cook more neatly."

"Well, if you did cook without wearing the food, I would have no reason to touch your face."

The sudden passion in his gaze startled her. He was standing so close that his buckskin coat touched her cape. Now that Daniel could stand up straight, she was surprised at how tall he was. He gazed down at her with his warm brown eyes—filled with more than just friendship now—causing her heart to race with excitement and turmoil. She swallowed and forced herself to remember her mother's words of caution.

"We had best get to the barn," she said.

The soldier reluctantly followed her to the wooden structure. When they opened the door to the shelter, they were greeted with the loud bellowing of the unhappy bovine.

"I am so sorry, Susannah," Mary said. "I did not mean to forget you this morning."

The cow glanced over her shoulder at the newcomer while Mary handed the milk bucket to Daniel.

"Here you are, sir," she said. She set the small stool next to the animal. "This should give you room to extend your leg out while you do the milking."

Mary started back to the farmhouse. She wanted to avoid being alone with Daniel.

"Wait," he said, trying not to get anxious. "What ... what do I do?"

"Do not tell me you have never milked a cow before, Daniel?" Mary asked with surprise.

"I have never even *seen* a cow being milked before," he admitted, clearly embarrassed.

Mary was incredulous. "So, who did the milking at your house, Mr. Lowe?" she teased.

Daniel turned red in the face. "The servants did."

Mary's eyes grew wide. "You never mentioned that you had servants back at your home, Daniel."

"Well, you never asked, Mary," he replied pointedly.

Mary smiled at this new revelation. "Well, it is never too late to learn. Watch what I do."

The young woman pulled the stool closer to Susannah and blew her breath over her hands.

"You always want to warm up your hands before touching her skin," Mary instructed.

"Always sound advice, I am sure," Daniel said, listening intently.

Mary deftly grabbed at the teats hanging from the cow's udder.

"You use a squeezing and tugging motion alternating back and forth, like this."

The milk began to flow easily.

"There," Mary said standing up from the stool. "Now you try it."

Daniel moved the stool farther away from Susannah to accommodate his longer legs. He rubbed his hands together back and forth, and sat awkwardly on the small stool.

"Susannah does not know you. You might try talking gently to her," Mary suggested.

Daniel turned and looked at Mary. Her suggestion sounded ludicrous.

"Talk to a cow?" he asked in amazement. "You cannot be serious."

"But I am. Animals have feelings. She will cooperate with you far better if you treat her gently."

The lieutenant looked at her smugly.

"I am sure I can get her to give me some milk. I do not need to speak gently to a cow," he said, shaking his head slowly.

Mary pursed her lips and said, "Well then, I shall leave you to your task." She left the barn to return to the farmhouse.

Daniel grabbed at the cow's underside with more fervor than technique. When no milk came forth, he applied more strength and less patience. His frustration grew and he became more angry when not even a drop appeared in the bucket.

"Blasted cow! Give me some milk!" he yelled at Susannah.

When Mary was partway back to the farmhouse, she could hear Susannah bellow loudly and then the bucket being kicked over. A string of curses flowed out of Daniel's mouth.

Mary stopped in her path and shook her head.

"Try being kind to her, Daniel," she said under her breath before proceeding back to the house.

Daniel hoped that no one had heard his foul language. He paused in his endeavor. Perhaps Mary knew what she was talking about.

"All right, Susannah," he said, his voice soft and calm. "Let us try this again. Please, can you give me some milk?"

The young man eased up his fervent grip on the unhappy cow and tried to imitate Mary's technique. Before long, the warm liquid began to squirt into the bucket and Daniel breathed a sigh of relief.

Before he knew it, the bucket was brimming with the fruit of his—and Susannah's—labors.

Daniel awkwardly pushed himself to his feet and leaned over to pick up the bucket. The motion brought him closer to the animal's face.

"Thank you, Susannah," he said, staring into her large brown eyes. The cow just glanced at him, slowly chewing the hay that was in front of her.

The Thomsen women were very impressed with the amount of milk that Daniel had collected.

"Susannah must like you," Sarah said in amazement. "She never gives us that much milk."

Mary waited until her mother and Sarah were busy reading from the Bible together. She looked at Daniel, who was standing next to her at the table while she worked.

"So, did your colorful language convince the cow to be so generous?" Mary asked, keeping her voice low.

Daniel's face became red and he looked away.

"So you were listening in on our private conversation?"

"I could not help but hear," Mary said, raising her eyes and smiling tightly.

"I have been found guilty," Daniel said sheepishly. "I shall try to guard my tongue in future. Please forgive my foul outburst."

Mary smiled.

"You are forgiven." She glanced at the full bucket of milk. "It looks like Susannah has forgiven you as well."

***

The day before Thanksgiving arrived with the smells of a mouth-watering feast. Sarah was in charge of twisting the twine tightly that held the wild turkey cooking over the fire. She had to watch carefully for when it had completely untwisted itself. Once it stopped moving, she had to spin the fowl once again. The smell of the slow-cooking bird was enticing everyone's appetite.

The six-year-old was happily educating Daniel on the art of trapping wild turkeys.

"So you place some corn in a line leading up to the opening for the turkey pen," Sarah explained. "The bird does not know he is heading for a trap. The next thing you know, the turkey is caught in the dug-out pen—and mother is looking for the axe!"

"That is very clever," Daniel said. "And not a shot has to be fired."

"Unless the turkey refuses to be caught by hand," Sarah said. "Then Mother gets her fowling piece to shoot him."

"Ah," said Daniel, amused.

Mary reached for the bread pell, a long handled shovel for removing the baked bread from the layer of oak leaves deep in the oven. When she brought out the crisp corn and rye bread, everyone inhaled deeply of the aroma.

"That smells worthy of a royal feast," said the young soldier enthusiastically.

"Or of a humble Massachusetts meal," Mary said happily. Her cheeks were bright red from the fire's heat and Daniel noticed how the color enhanced her beauty. As she removed her white apron, the red wool of her gown enveloped her in such a manner as to bring a long, admiring stare from Daniel.

Out of the corner of her eye, Widow Thomsen caught Daniel's gaze towards her daughter. The mother's expression showed more than a little concern. "I must address this situation with Daniel as soon as possible," the widow muttered under her breath.

"Mr. Lowe," she said more loudly, "would you be so kind as to set out the linen tablecloth and napkins for us? This is a special occasion worthy of decorating our table board." She held out the cloth pieces toward Daniel.

"I would be happy to make myself useful," he replied, taking the linens. He awkwardly unfolded each piece and set them out as best he could. "I hope I am doing this right."

"You are doing a fine job, Mr. Lowe," Mary said. "Although I am assuming you have not set too many a table in your lifetime?"

"You are most correct, Miss Thomsen. Like many of my experiences here in Massachusetts, it is quite new to me," Daniel replied. He laughed at his clumsy attempts to set everything out neatly.

Everyone was relieved when the widow declared that Thanksgiving supper was ready. As the group of four sat down at the table, Widow Thomsen led them in a prayer of thanks.

"Dear Heavenly Father," she began, "we are your humble servants who have come this day to give you thanks for the victory you have afforded our troops in our struggle for freedom." She went on to pray for the safety of the colonial soldiers, especially for James and those who fought side-by-side with her son.

"And Lord," she continued, "we are grateful for your merciful favor upon Mr. Lowe, that you would bring him back from the brink of eternity and provide your blessed healing upon him. For this we are thankful, Dear Heavenly Lord. Amen."

"Amen," Mary and Sarah echoed.

"Amen," Daniel said softly.

Everyone's eyes widened at the vast array of choices. There were sweet potatoes roasted in the ashes, peas, turnips, and carrots cooked in a kettle, several different kinds of beans, freshly baked bread, and of course, the fresh turkey. Daniel could not ingest enough of the women's hearthside endeavors.

"Save room for the celebration cake, Mr. Lowe," Mary said, laughing. She enjoyed seeing this formerly gaunt man recover to become such an enthusiastic eater.

"Do not fret, Miss Thomsen. I shall gladly make room for your cake," he said.

"Well, I am so relieved that Missus Stearns did not begin her travail before I could partake of this Thanksgiving bounty," said the widow. The woman sat back from the table, obviously satiated. "She should be sending for me any day now."

"The husbands come home from war," Sarah interjected, "and nine months later they are calling for the midwife. That is what mother always says." Sarah innocently resumed eating her cake, wiping crumbs off of her blue woolen bodice.

Mary's eyes opened wide with embarrassment.

Widow Thomsen looked at her younger daughter and said tersely, "That is what we say in the company of females only, Miss Sarah."

"I am sorry, Mr. Lowe," the girl said, now self-conscious. "I did not realize that men did not know this was the way of it."

Everyone stifled a laugh and Daniel nearly choked on his piece of cake, so amused was he by this exchange.

"That is quite all right, little miss. I am grateful to be informed of the 'way of it,'" he said. He stole a glance over towards Mary, who was turning a bright shade of scarlet. "Your cake is delightful," he praised the young woman.

"Thank you, sir," she said, grateful for the change of discussion.

"So, Mr. Lowe," the widow asked, "do you have any family back at your home … up north." She gave a sideways glance toward Sarah so that he would understand that this was how they described his place of origin.

"I have a father and older brother, ma'am. That is all," he answered. "My mother died many years ago when my sister Polly was born. I was but seven."

"I am sorry, sir. So you have no wife or lady friend waiting for you?" Widow Thomsen asked. Mary glanced pointedly at her mother for her boldness delving into this subject.

"Oh no, Widow Thomsen. I had an understanding with a young lady about two years ago. She decided that she did not want to wait for me to return from war. She took up with an older man who was quite wealthy. I heard that they married, but then she ran off with a younger man after only two months. I am quite grateful that I did not become allied with such a fickle woman." He gave a nervous laugh.

All three Thomsen females sat with their mouths open in astonishment. Sarah was the first to speak.

"That is a sin," she gasped. "Leaving your husband for another man."

Daniel gave a half smile.

"I suppose it is, little miss. I am glad that I was spared the hurt and humiliation."

The young soldier became self-conscious about this embarrassing revelation. He felt Mary's hand touch his ever so briefly under the table.

She somehow always knows when I need encouragement, he thought.

"So, tell me about your family. When did they come to the colonies?" Daniel asked, anxious to change the subject.

"We have been here since the first boat," Sarah responded proudly.

"The first boat?" Daniel looked surprised. "You mean the *Mayflower*?"

"Yes, " Widow Thomsen said. "My great, great grandparents were on board that vessel. John Alden was the cooper on the Mayflower, one of the hired men. Priscilla Mullins was just a young woman traveling with her family to the New World. Sadly, Priscilla's entire family died within that first year at Plymouth. Young Priscilla was left on her own. One of the families took her in to live with them."

Mary continued the telling of the oft-spoken tale.

"Half of the group of just over one hundred colonists died that first year. It is only God's provision that any of them were saved at all," she said. "Some of the native Indians helped teach the survivors how to live in the new land. We still plant our corn according to the Indian ways."

"John Alden," the widow added, "was the only hired man on board who stayed behind here in Plymouth. The rest of the crew set sail back to England. John had to learn how to become a farmer in the New World, just like the rest of the colonists."

"The man must have been quite taken with Miss Mullins to have given up his life back home," Daniel said, looking at Mary. She looked down at her hands in her lap.

Sarah gave a deep sigh, caught up in the romance of the story.

"He was smitten with her beauty," the girl said. She then whispered to Daniel, as though she were sharing a deeply guarded secret, "That is what my Great Grandmother Sarah said. I am named after her."

"You do not say?" he whispered back. Daniel stared at Mary again, well imagining the young John Alden being smitten with the beautiful Priscilla.

"Well then, enough talk of family," Widow Thomsen said. "Let us clean up the table and sit by the fire for some reading."

The contented group slowly stirred from their seats at the table at the widow's prompting.

Daniel helped to cover the leftover food with linen cloths before limping over to the chair near the fire.

Mary and Sarah huddled together on the bricks near the fire with a warm quilt covering their shivering shoulders. The lengthy sitting at table had made them realize how cold it was outside.

Widow Thomsen handed *Aesop's Fables* to Daniel to read to the group. As he began to recite from the book, the tales of foxes and frogs and lions danced in the minds of Mary and Sarah. So satiated and sleepy were the two Thomsen daughters that they were soon fast asleep, propped against each other in the glow of the fire.

Daniel looked over at the two and smiled.

"I believe that I have lost part of my audience," he said to Widow Thomsen.

"I believe so," she replied. The woman stared into the fire and then looked at Daniel.

"Mr. Lowe," she began finally, "these words are difficult to say. But let me be direct, sir. I know that my Mary is drawn to you and that you appear to be setting your eyes upon her as well. You seem to be a fine man, but I am concerned that Mary might get hurt in this matter. We are at war, sir, and I do not want your feelings or Mary's to put you both at risk."

Daniel swallowed hard at these words. At length he replied.

"Widow Thomsen, I shall never do anything to endanger Mary or any of your family. Please believe me when I say that I would rather die than put any of you in harm's way."

Widow Thomsen looked long and hard at Daniel.

"I believe you mean that, Mr. Lowe. Mary has borne much hurt in this last year. I could not bear to see her so despondent again." She paused. "Nor could I bear the thought of her risking her life."

Daniel's heart sank at the widow's words. The struggle in his mind and emotions was evident in his tortured countenance. After a few moments, he spoke with great difficulty.

"Nor could I, ma'am. And ... I will do my best not to reveal my affection for her."

"Thank you, sir," she replied with pain in her eyes. "I know that this is difficult for you both."

"Yes," Daniel said. "If you will excuse me, madam, I think it is time for me to retire for the evening." He stood up and placed the book on the chair.

"Good night, sir," she said.

"Good night, Widow Thomsen."

Daniel slowly limped back to his room. When he shut the door, the reality of the woman's words hit him with their full force. He stretched across the bed and covered his eyes with his hands, as hot tears rolled down onto his pillow.

How he would hold back his affection for Mary, he could not imagine. But he had promised her mother that he would.

Chapter Thirteen

Influenza

The next morning, it was obvious that something was very wrong with Sarah.

Usually full of energy upon awakening, the young girl had stayed in bed without attempting to move.

"My head hurts, Mother," Sarah said weakly.

The widow hurried to the child's bedside and felt her crimson face.

"You are burning with fever," her mother said. "Let me make you some tea, Sarah."

The girl began to cough painfully. They had heard that same harsh sound coming from the courier a week before.

Widow Thomsen had fear in her eyes.

"The dispatcher must have been carrying contagion with him. None of us should go to the meetinghouse today. We shall have to pray here at home."

The mother walked over to the cabinet of herbs and teas and pulled down the jar with hyssop leaves. A small amount was spooned into a pewter cup and warm water from the kettle was added. This brew was known to help fight respiratory illnesses, but Widow Thomsen knew this was no ordinary cold.

"This grippe takes a powerful hold upon a body," the mother said quietly to Mary. The widow's lips were trembling as she fought back tears.

Mary saw the rising panic in her mother. The older daughter gently touched her arm.

"Sarah will recover, Mother. She is strong. Why do we not say a quiet prayer for her?" Mary said. She was trying to be encouraging, even though she herself was concerned.

The two women lifted Sarah's health up to their Heavenly Father. They prayed for strength and healing for the small child. Mary also asked for comfort for her Mother in this time of trial. No sooner had they finished the prayer than there was a loud knock at the door.

"I shall get it, Mother. Take the tea to Sarah," Mary said. When she opened the door, Mary saw the anxious face of young Nathaniel Stearns.

"Please, miss," said the handsome thirteen-year-old, shivering in the fresh falling snow. "My mother ... well, the baby is coming. Can the midwife come quickly?"

Mary's heart went out to Nathaniel. He had been carrying a man's work at home since his father went to war with the other Minutemen. The patriot's son was trying to be brave, but it was obvious that his burden was heavy. The impending birth seemed to be causing the young man even greater distress.

"My mother will be there very soon. Please do not fear," Mary said, tenderness in her voice. "Do you wish to come in to warm yourself?"

"Oh no, miss, I'd best get back to Mother. I shall tell her the midwife is coming with haste." With that, Nathaniel left as swiftly as he had come.

Widow Thomsen was with Sarah and was obviously distraught.

"Of all the times to be called away," the mother said, once again fighting back the tears.

"Mother," Mary said, "you know that I will look after Sarah. We do not want Missus Stearns delivering her little one alone. We certainly do not want poor Nathaniel to have to assist her."

Widow Thomsen had to smile at the thought. The image of a nervous Nathaniel helping his mother through her labor brought both laughter and compassion to the older woman's face. Mary was relieved to see her mother's expression brighten.

"Thank you, Mary," Widow Thomsen said. "I know that you can look after Sarah. It is just difficult to leave one's child when she is ill."

The widow looked down at Sarah and smoothed the girl's long hair, which lay across the linen-covered pillow.

"I shall return as soon as the Stearns' baby is birthed, Sarah. It should not take long. Mary will give you the best of nursing care while I am gone. She will tend to your every need. Please rest, little one, and be well." Widow Thomsen gave Sarah a tender kiss, then left her bedside.

Sarah looked like she was about to cry, so Mary went to her side.

"Let me help you with your tea, Sarah, and then I shall read to you if you like. You can close your eyes and rest—no chores today," Mary said, hoping to put a smile on the girl's face.

Mary watched her mother gather her supplies and her woolen cape.

"It is beginning to snow outside, Mother. Please be careful," the older daughter cautioned.

Widow Thomsen brightened as the words were spoken.

"How often have I said those very words to you, Mary? I shall look sharp for any storm. And I know you will take good care of Sarah."

The widow left the warmth of the farmhouse, trudging bravely against the freezing December wind.

The older daughter turned her attention back to Sarah. "Let's try two more sips of Mother's tea, shall we?" Mary encouraged.

The door to Daniel's room opened and the young soldier emerged with dark circles under his eyes. He looked far more tired than usual. When he saw Sarah in the bed looking poorly, he gave Mary a questioning look.

"Is Sarah ill?" he asked.

"Yes," Mary replied. "She appears to have the grippe and she is burning with fever. It so happens that Missus Stearns is in travail, so my mother has had to go to assist her. I told my mother that I would nurse Sarah."

"What can I do to help?" Daniel asked, looking at the child lying so still in the bed. Sarah's cheeks were a bright red, a stark contrast to her normally fair skin.

"You could gather some snow from outside to help cool her fever, Daniel." The young woman noticed the look of fatigue on his face.

When he returned with the basin of snow from outdoors, Mary scooped some of the white flakes onto a piece of linen and placed it on the girl's forehead. The older sister looked intently at Daniel.

"Are you not well?" she asked. "You look weary this morning." Mary was worried that he might also be coming down with the contagion.

Daniel tried to avoid her scrutiny.

"I am well enough. I did not sleep soundly … that is all," he said coolly. He avoided meeting the young woman's eyes, lest his affection for her be evident.

Mary bit her lower lip. She did not understand this sudden change in his demeanor. The way he had looked at her yesterday—the passion in his glances—had made her hope that perhaps he would not go back to England. But now, his seeming indifference towards her caused her heart to skip a beat.

Maybe he does not care after all, she thought. Perhaps he had just been caught up in the festive spirit of the large meal and the heady wine her mother had served. Perhaps he was thinking fondly of his former lady friend. How could such a simple colonial woman as herself compare with a lady of fine clothing and finer skills? She silently chided herself for thinking that she could be the object of his serious intentions. Mary felt the tears begin to well in her eyes.

I am a foolish farm girl, she thought to herself. Her thoughts were suddenly interrupted by the small voice of Sarah.

"Mary, would you sing to me?"

"Sing to you?" Mary asked in surprise. "I have not sung in many months, Sarah. I am not sure that I remember any songs."

Though trying to appear lighthearted, Mary's heart was, in truth, quite heavy. Not only was her sister very ill, but Widow Thomsen was not here to be her nurse. And as far as Mary could ascertain, Daniel did not have feelings of affection for her. Mary was more likely to cry than to sing.

"Please, Mary," the child asked again. "You never sing like you used to. I miss it. Your songs will help me feel better."

Mary looked at her frail sister and held back her tears. How could she ignore such a simple request?

"All right," Mary consented. "But only because you asked so sweetly."

Sarah's eyes lit up in anticipation.

"Could you sing 'Aylesbury'?" Sarah asked before coughing several times again. "It is one of my favorites."

"I shall see if I can recall the words," Mary said.

The older sister tenderly stroked the girl's blond hair across her forehead. It was with just such a comforting touch that Mary had been soothing Sarah since she was a baby.

Mary started to sing the words of the favorite hymn.

"The Lord my shepherd is, I shall be well supplied,
Since he is mine and I am his, what can I want beside?

He leads me to the place where heavenly pasture grows,
Where living waters gently pass, and full salvation flows.

If e'er I go astray, he doth my soul reclaim,
And guides me in his own right way, for his most holy name.

While he affords his aid, I cannot yield to fear;
Though I should walk through death's dark shade, my shepherd's
with me there."

When Mary sang the last verse, she could hold back her tears no longer. Sarah had drifted off into a fitful slumber, and Mary continued to stroke the child's forehead.

Daniel was sitting by the fireside, staring in wonder at Mary. Her voice had taken him by complete surprise. He had been mesmerized not just by the words of the song but also by the soothing sound of her voice. His desire for Mary was both exhilarating and troubling. After all, he had made a promise to Widow Thomsen. The young soldier swallowed with difficulty and then finally spoke.

"That was beautiful," Daniel said, looking at the young woman across the room.

Mary looked up at him in surprise. "Thank you, Daniel," was all she was able to say. She wiped the tears away from her eyes.

"I ... I've never heard that song before," he said. "I walked through death's dark shade when I was in the woods, but I do not think there was a shepherd there with me. There was an angel, though," he said with emotion. "I opened my eyes and I saw your countenance staring at me with compassion."

Mary looked up at him. "There was a shepherd with you, Daniel," Mary said tenderly. "But I am not an angel … just one of God's earthly helpers. I believe that the shepherd sent me to you."

Daniel listened to her words thoughtfully.

"Perhaps you are right. But I do not understand why the shepherd would pay me any mind. I have not served him nor acknowledged him, nor afforded him a place in my life. Why should he concern himself with my well-being?"

The young woman looked at him intently.

"That is like asking why a mother loves her infant. The child has done nothing to deserve the love of the parent. He has even caused her great duress in birth. But her heart is filled with a love so deep that nothing the child does could possibly cause the mother to stop loving him." Mary paused for a moment then said, "That is how God loves every one of his children."

The young man considered each word that she said. He remembered something he had not thought about in many years. It was the memory of his own mother just prior to giving birth to his sister Polly. She was sitting in her favorite chair, reading from her Bible to him. He was just seven years old at the time. She told him how much God loved him and encouraged him to give his heart to the Lord.

Tears began to well in Daniel's eyes.

After a long pause, he said, "I shall contemplate what you have said."

At that moment, Sarah woke up, her voice trembling.

"Mary," she cried. The child was shuddering painfully, chills ravaging her body.

The older sister climbed onto the bed and picked up Sarah in her arms. She held her closely, trying to warm the shivering child.

Daniel got up from his chair quickly. He grabbed some quilts off the bed and wrapped them securely around Sarah. As he did so, his arm found its way across Mary's shoulders. They looked at each other so closely that she could sense the warmth of his breath upon her cheeks. Her heart began to quicken. She could barely breathe.

"Thank you, Daniel," she said.

"I hope this helps to warm her," he said awkwardly. He reluctantly stood up and moved away from the two sisters.

"It shall," she said, holding Sarah closely. How she wished that his arms had stayed upon her shoulders, even just a moment longer.

He walked with a limp to the chair across the room and watched the pair. Mary was rocking Sarah in her arms and humming the melody from "Aylesbury" to comfort the child.

The wind was beginning to howl. Daniel looked at the supply of wood near the fireplace to be sure there was enough to provide warmth through this snowstorm. By the sound of the gale outdoors, this would be a powerful blizzard.

***

Three days had passed, with Mary tending to her ailing sister. Sarah was becoming worried about their mother, who was still not home from the birthing.

"I am sure that Mother will be home as soon as this terrible storm ends," Mary said. "She will be safe indoors with Missus Stearns and her family."

But Mary was concerned as well. She knew that their mother would not take any risks in this weather. But her long absence from home and this unending winter storm were worrisome.

Daniel did his best to distract the Thomsen sisters from becoming fearful. He read to them and told ridiculous jokes that made them giggle. Daniel smiled warmly every time he saw Mary laugh.

The young woman was grateful for Daniel's presence. She did not know how she would have managed taking care of Sarah without his help.

Because of the storm, he had strung a rope from the farmhouse to the barn so that he could find his way each day to do the milking. He brought in fresh supplies of wood for the fire several times a day. He even killed one of the chickens in the barn when Mary had expressed a desire to make some broth for the ill child.

Stretched across the bed in exhaustion on that third night of Sarah's illness, Mary's heart lifted as she envisioned the sight of Daniel covered in snow and chicken feathers, holding up his prized kill. She dreamily remembered his sweet grin as he handed her the precious offering.

Had his hand lingered on hers a moment longer than necessary? She smiled at the possibility. So consumed were her thoughts about Daniel that she barely noticed the aching in her limbs.

I must be especially tired from all the extra chores, she thought, as she drifted off to sleep.

When Mary awoke before dawn on that fourth day, something was not right.

Her head was throbbing so hard that she felt it would burst. She had thrown off her quilts during the night but was still covered in sweat. Her shift clung to her damp skin. When she tried to stand, she felt dizzy and nauseated. Her first thoughts were of Sarah.

Mary tried to get up to make tea for the child, but she could not walk straight. She nearly fell. Pain ravaged her body and she craved something to drink.

"Daniel," she whispered, barely able to swallow. She tried to call his name again, but all that emerged was an unintelligible croaking sound.

Mary held on to furniture and then steadied herself against the wall as her bare feet struggled to find the way to Daniel's room. She leaned on the door and tried to call his name again. The fevered woman began to panic. She wondered if she even had the strength to open his wooden door. But she knew that she must find the resolve. She threw her last ounce of energy into grabbing the door handle and pushed as hard as she could.

She fell headlong onto the floor. She was so dizzy she did not hear Daniel awaken or see him leaning over her, saying her name. The ringing in her head was obscuring all other sensations.

Daniel had awakened with a start. He was not sure what the sound was outside his door. When it opened suddenly and he saw Mary fall to the floor, fear gripped at his heart.

Throwing off his quilts, he hurried toward Mary. She was mumbling something but her words were not coherent.

"Mary! Mary!" he cried, but she did not respond. He tried not to panic as he picked her up in his arms and carried her to her bed. The fevered woman was covered with perspiration and her cheeks were flaming red. Intense heat radiated from her.

"Snow," he said to himself, trying to keep his thoughts focused. "I need to get some snow."

He opened the door of the farmhouse and was assaulted by the frenzied storm outdoors. The cold air whipped at the soldier as he stooped over to grab some of the newly fallen white flakes. His warm hands turned suddenly frigid in the short time it took him to collect the snow.

"Blasted, horrible weather," he said angrily as he squinted against the winter onslaught. It took all his strength to shut the door forcefully against the wind when he returned indoors.

Sarah had awakened in the meantime and sat up in bed. Her fever had finally broken and her color had returned to its normal tone. She was still very weak from the influenza. When the girl saw her sister in a fevered state, she began to cry.

"Mr. Lowe, what is wrong with Mary?' she asked.

Daniel looked at the young child and forced himself to be calm.

"Your sister is just a little fevered—that is all. I shall cool her down with some snow," he said.

He tenderly rubbed the snow-wrapped cloth across Mary's forehead and brushed her hair back from her face with his fingers. The young woman's eyes occasionally opened, but she did not appear to be awake. Mostly she kept her eyes closed and appeared to be in a fitful state.

The soldier massaged the cool cloth across the insides of her arms, as he had seen Mary do for Sarah. He stared at Mary's lean limbs in his large hands.

Recalling how she had helped him walk to the wigwam so many weeks ago, he wondered in awe at how such a frail-looking young woman could possibly have borne his weight to bring him to shelter. His hands smoothed across her forearms where Josiah Grant had once left his mark upon her skin. The bruises were gone now but the memory of that event rekindled his outrage. Daniel was beside himself with worry. He had never felt as helpless or fearful as he did at this moment.

How can this be happening?

Only last night she had been laughing and teasing him about his "triumphant hunting catch." He could still see her radiant smile as she took the small chicken he had slaughtered and plucked it for the soup.

Sarah's small voice broke into his anxious musings.

"Shall we pray for her, Mr. Lowe?" she asked.

Daniel looked at the girl and rubbed the hair away from his forehead.

"Yes, little miss," he said. "I think that would be an excellent thing to do. But let us get you back in your side of the bed. You are still not recovered yourself."

He laid the cold cloth back on Mary's forehead, then helped Sarah back under the quilts on the far side of the bed.

When Sarah was comfortably under the covers, she closed her eyes and folded her hands. She was waiting for him to say a prayer.

Daniel paused awkwardly and said, "Perhaps you could say the prayer, little miss—just the way your mother likes to say it." He did not feel worthy of making requests to the heavenly realm, but he saw no reason to tell Sarah this.

Why would God answer a prayer from someone such as me?

"Dear Heavenly Father," Sarah began in her small voice, "please make my sister well. She has always been a good sister and always loved her family. Please, Dear Lord, do not take her from us." Sarah's lips began to tremble. "I would miss her greatly. In the name of your Son, Jesus Christ, Amen."

Sarah opened her eyes and looked at Daniel in surprise.

"You are crying, Mr. Lowe."

The young man quickly wiped away the tears from his face.

"It was a beautiful prayer, little miss. Now, let us try to rest. I shall bring you some broth shortly."

What am I doing? What am I supposed to do?

The difficulty of the situation was beginning to reveal itself. He realized that he did not know what else to do for Mary's fever.

"Do you know what kind of tea Mary was making for you when you were ill?" he asked the younger sister.

"I am not sure. But there is a book over by the medicinals that Mary and my mother use sometimes," Sarah said, pointing to the cabinet across the room.

Daniel walked over to the pine cupboard and looked at the numerous bottles marked with such names as "Linseed," "P. Bark," "Parsley," and "Plantain Leaf." He was confused by the numerous selections. Then he found the book that Sarah was referring to.

"*Every Man His Own Doctor,*" he said out loud as he opened the small edition that described a variety of ailments and what could be done to provide care.

He found the page entitled "Fever" and was horrified to see instructions to "bleed 20 ounces, without loss of time." Daniel's breath caught in his throat.

Bleed Mary?

He had seen it done in the camps for fevered soldiers, but the thought of bleeding his young friend caused him great distress. But the book had said "without loss of time" and Daniel's fear was causing him to waste precious moments.

The soldier found a knife and quickly prepared for the procedure. His hands were trembling, which made it difficult to prepare for the bleeding without dropping the bowl and cloth that he would use. When he had gathered all the necessary supplies, he looked at Mary resting fitfully on the pillow. His resolve disappeared immediately as he grappled with the idea of letting blood from his sweet friend. He turned away from looking at her face and picked up her limp arm. His hands were shaking.

What if I cut her too deeply?

As he struggled to calm himself, sweat began to pour off his forehead onto her arm. He wiped away the perspiration, which was blinding his view. He was finally ready to make the incision on her arm and held the knife against her smooth skin. Just then he heard Sarah yell.

"Stop! Mr. Lowe," she cried. "Mother does not let out the blood. She says it is too dangerous and many die from it."

Daniel looked gratefully at the frightened child and breathed a deep sigh. He gently laid Mary's arm down on the quilt and looked at Sarah.

"Thank you, little miss. I did not want to do a bleeding. I was following the instructions in your mother's book but I am so relieved that you stopped me."

"Mother says the doctors are wrong to bleed. She says that plants are the right way to help a body heal. That is why she uses so many teas."

"I shall remember that," Daniel said. "Let me put these things away and I shall get you some broth."

Daniel was overwhelmed with relief but shuddered at what he had nearly done. He busied himself with ladling the broth for Sarah and tried to put the troubling thoughts out of his mind.

When Sarah was finished with the soup that Mary had made the previous day, the young girl's eyes grew heavy. When Daniel tucked her back into bed, Sarah looked up at him.

"Do you think that God heard my prayer for Mary, Mr. Lowe?"

"Yes, little miss. I am certain that he did," he said, reassuring her with a smile.

The girl yawned. It was still morning, but Sarah was as tired as if it were bedtime. The fever had taken a toll.

"Good night, Mr. Lowe."

"Good night, little miss."

By the time Daniel returned to the other side of the bed to tend to Mary, young Sarah was already fast asleep.

Mary was beginning to shiver now and Daniel placed extra quilts from the bed upon her. He went to the fireplace and added more logs to encourage the flames to send out more heat. Despite the increasing temperature in the room, Mary was shuddering uncontrollably from chills that racked her body. The woman's reddened eyes opened up and she recognized her friend.

"Daniel," she said with a low, raspy voice. "I am so cold." She could barely get the words out. Her body was at the mercy of the influenza.

The young soldier picked her up, quilts and all, and carried her to the chair by the fire. He held her closely and Mary clung to him as though her very life depended on the warmth emanating from his body.

Daniel gently stroked her head, hoping that the touch would bring her comfort. Soon he perceived the tension in her body lessen as the fitful chills ceased. He could feel her hand rest gently on his chest, and he covered her fingers with his. Her head relaxed and fit snugly into the notch of his neck.

For a short while, the illness seemed to relent and Daniel took momentary relief in the consolation of his friend. But the comfort was only temporary as the fever soon returned. This time, it raged with even greater fury.

Daniel placed Mary back in the bed. He tried to cover her with a quilt but she kept kicking it away. Her cheeks were bright red and she was sweating profusely. He spoke to her, not sure if she could hear him.

"Mary, I must get more snow to cool you," he said, panic rising in his voice.

He faced the treacherous outdoors once again and brought in a basin filled with the frozen liquid. He resumed his attempts to cool her from the persistent fever, applying the snow-filled cloth on her forehead, then on her arms and neck, and then back to her forehead again.

The frantic young man sat down on the cold floor next to her bed and rested his head on the edge of the quilts. He was utterly exhausted. He would close his eyes only for a moment, he thought, but sleep overtook the fatigued soldier.

Sometime later, Sarah's urgent voice finally stirred him from his slumber.

"Mr. Lowe," she said, sitting straight up in bed. "Mary is calling Asa's name. I am frightened."

Daniel got up as quickly as his wounded leg would allow him. Mary's eyes were open, but she was staring at nothing in particular. He leaned in closer to Mary's lips and heard her whisper Asa's name.

"Mary! Mary, please wake up." He grabbed at the linens in the basin only to find that the snow had long since melted.

"You fool," he berated himself. "How could you let yourself sleep?"

He rushed out to the snowdrifts a third time and brought in a heaping basin-full. Mary was still staring in a trancelike state, her fever making her cheeks as red and hot as the flames in the hearth.

Daniel scooped large handfuls of snow onto a cloth and held the snow directly onto her skin. She gasped at the sensation, as he moved the ice from one part of her body to another. He lifted her arms up and wrapped them around his shoulders as he put more snow on the back of her neck in an attempt to halt the fever's progress. The sudden change of temperature on her neck seemed to rouse Mary's consciousness, but it did not awaken her; she appeared to be in a dream.

"Do not go," she whispered, her voice strained and low. Daniel had laid her head back on the pillow and he had to lean closely to her to discern her words.

"What is it, Mary?"

Tears began to form in the woman's eyes as she stared at the ceiling.

"Daniel," she whispered again, "do not leave."

"I am here, Mary. I have not gone."

He stroked her face. She closed her eyes and went back into a fitful slumber.

Daniel sat on the edge of her bed and wept. He was overwhelmed with sadness and fear.

What if Mary dies?

He could not bear the thought of losing her. He never had such affection for a woman before and he was in despair that she might slip away from him. He was doing everything that he could, yet it did not seem to be enough.

Filled with hopelessness, Daniel sought the only source he could think to turn to for help. He began to pray.

"Dear God," the soldier sobbed, "I know I've no right to ask anything of you, but I ask this for Mary. I ask that you would heal her of this infirmity and bring her back to us. We need her." He paused before continuing his prayer.

"I need her," he said softly. He bowed his head and stayed there quietly for a long time.

***

The next two days were a blur of activity. Daniel brought tea and broth to Sarah, more snow to cool Mary's fever, and more wood for the fire. He made sure that the cow was milked each day and that the food over the fire was stirred frequently.

And he prayed.

On the morning of the third day, Daniel's head was in his usual sleeping position on the edge of the bed while he sat on the floor next to Mary. As dawn broke, he finally heard what he had been waiting and hoping for—the voice of the woman he loved.

"Daniel," Mary whispered. She weakly touched his face with her hand, feeling the scraggly beard, which he had not shaved since her illness began.

"Daniel," she said again.

The soldier's eyes opened wide and he grabbed at her hand. He kissed her palm several times and held her hand against his face. Tears of relief filled his eyes and his voice was thick with emotion.

"I have missed you," he said.

"Daniel. I thought you had gone away," Mary said, and she began to cry.

Squeezing her hands with both of his, he kissed them again.

"I am here," he said in a whisper. "I have not gone away."

"Please," Mary said still crying. "Do not leave me."

He gently kissed her forehead and looked at Mary tenderly.

"As long as you need me, I shall not leave you. That is my promise."

Chapter Fourteen

Healings

For the first time in a week, the sun rose brightly with no hint of a storm.

When Daniel looked out the window, the reflection of the light on nearly three feet of fresh snow was blinding and energizing.

"Look at all the snow," Sarah said excitedly. She touched the layer of ice on the inside of the window. "May I go out and play in it, Mr. Lowe?"

"I think you had best stay in a bit longer, little miss, until you are no longer coughing." He filled a bowl of gruel for Sarah and placed it on the table for her to eat.

"Thank you kindly, Mr. Lowe." She glanced over at her sleeping sister in the bed. "Do you think that Mary would like any?"

"I think I shall make her some slippery elm tea, instead," he said. He remembered how soothing that brew had been when he was so very ill not long ago.

Daniel went over to the cupboard of herbs and spices and found the bottle of elm bark. He crushed a small amount and placed it in a pewter mug, then crushed a little cinnamon bark into the cup for flavor, just as he remembered Mary doing for him. After making sure the water from the kettle was not too hot, he poured some into the cup. He brought the tea over to her bedside and pulled a chair up close. He placed his hand on Mary's shoulder and gently squeezed. He would have preferred to let her sleep, but he knew that she desperately needed sustenance.

"Mary, I've made you some tea."

The young woman slowly opened her eyes, squinting against the bright light shining through the windowpanes. She held her head as if in pain. Daniel immediately went to the source of discomfort, closing the curtains to dim the light.

"Thank you, Daniel," she said, her eyes still closed.

Mary's face was very pale—not even a hint of color in her cheeks. She moved her arms with great effort as though there were heavy weights attached to each limb. She tried to move her head and shoulders to sit up for the tea, but had little strength for the effort. She let her head fall back to the pillow, then opened her eyes in dismay.

"How long have I been ill?"

"Three days," Daniel replied. "Let me help you sit up."

He wrapped his strong arms around her shoulders and easily pulled the woman to an upright position against the pillows. The movement made her dizzy, and she had to close her eyes while she adjusted to the new arrangement.

When she was able to open them again, she looked fearfully at Daniel.

"Where is my mother?" she asked. The effort of the question obviously taxed her and caused her to cough deeply.

"I am sure that she is safe at the Stearns' home. No one would dare venture out in such a storm. She is probably enjoying cradling that new baby even as we speak."

Mary tried to smile.

"I hope you are right," she said.

Sarah hurried over to Mary's bedside and hugged her tightly.

"I prayed for you, Mary. I was so afraid when you would not wake up." Even at the age of six, Sarah already knew the seriousness of illness. Death at any age was a common occurrence in the colonies.

Mary touched her sister's face.

"Thank you, Sarah. God heard your prayer."

"Our prayer," Sarah corrected her. "Mr. Lowe prayed for you, too."

"You did?" she asked, sounding surprised. "Thank you, Daniel." Mary stared at him with affection and gratitude in her eyes.

Daniel looked down at the drink in his hand. He was self-conscious about this revelation and he struggled to find the right words.

"I think the shepherd heard our prayers," he finally said. Then, changing the subject, "You must drink this tea, Mary."

Sarah released her sister from her embrace and returned to her bowl of gruel at the table. Daniel held the mug to Mary's lips and she took a sip. She closed her eyes as the sweet flavor covered her dry tongue. She anxiously took the cup a second time and swallowed several gulps.

"That is all for now, Daniel. I am so grateful to you ... for everything." She winced at the lingering pains in her legs and back and coughed hard before speaking again. "I feel as if I've been battered about."

"You must rest, Mary. Sarah and I will see to the needs of the farm," Daniel said.

He gently took her hand and she returned his touch. They held their gaze into each other's eyes for a long while. No words were spoken, but they both knew their friendship had grown more deeply in these past few days. He smoothed her disheveled hair gently back from her face with his free hand.

"I must sally to the barn," he finally said. "I am sure that Susannah is quite irritated with my tardiness. And I am quite certain that she is anxious to have you return to the milking. I know she prefers your touch."

He smiled at Mary as he stood up and released her hand.

The woman watched him grab the coat and milk bucket, and go out the door to the barn. Shivering from the freezing air that wafted her way from the cold outdoors, she pulled the quilts up around her shoulders as Sarah returned to her sister's bedside.

"Mary," the girl began, "I heard Mr. Lowe praying for you in the darkness when he thought I was asleep."

"You did?" Mary said.

"Yes," Sarah said. "And then he started to cry."

Mary was so moved by her sister's words that tears welled in her own eyes.

"Thank you, Sarah," she said, embracing her sister. "Thank you for telling me."

Mary released her, and the child returned to a book that she had started to read. The older sister closed her eyes and drifted into a deep sleep. When she awoke much later, the sun coming through the windowpanes had dimmed. Daniel was reading in the chair next to her bed. When he saw her awaken, he hurriedly put the book on the floor and smiled.

"Let me bring you some gruel," he said to her.

"Just a small bowl, please," Mary said. "What have you been reading?" she asked, trying to see the words on the book lying on the floor.

"*Pilgrim's Progress*," Daniel said. "I am nearly finished."

Mary stared after him as he ladled the corn gruel into the bowl for her. He brought the steaming porridge to her bedside.

"Be careful, it is quite warm," he cautioned.

She smiled at him and took the wooden bowl.

"The warmth feels good on my hands. Thank you," she said. She stared down at the volume on the floor. "What do you think of Asa's book?"

Daniel paused to consider his answer.

"It is an amazing allegory, Mary. But I wanted to ask you about something that Asa wrote in the margins on one of the pages."

He opened the large book to page thirty-four and noted Asa's handwriting. The script was not the youthful markings found on the inside cover when he first opened the volume. This inscription was written just three years prior, dated January 29, 1775.

"What does this mean?" he asked Mary. Since she was holding the warm bowl, he read it out loud to her: "On this day, Asa Thomsen released the burden of sin upon his back and obtained mercy and favor from his Lord Jesus Christ."

Daniel looked at her with questioning eyes. Mary placed the bowl upon her lap and wiped the tears away from her eyes.

"That must be the part in the book where Christian goes to the cross of Christ and the Lord releases him of the oppressive load upon his back—the burden of sin we all carry. I remember the day Asa told me that he had surrendered his will to Christ. His eyes shone more brightly than ever." Mary looked out the window as the tears continued to flow.

"I am sorry to have brought up such a painful memory, Mary."

"No, I am crying tears of relief, because I know that Asa is with God. Of course I miss him so very much. But I know he is safe with Jesus."

The soldier was quiet for several moments.

"Surrendering to the enemy is not a pleasant affair. But I know that God is not my adversary." He looked down at his hands, folded as if in prayer. "I think that I need to spend some time with the shepherd."

He slowly got up from his chair and looked at Mary. He touched her hand gently and squeezed it.

"I shall be back in a short while," he said.

Mary watched him go into his room and close the door.

She wept more tears of relief and joy, for she knew that Daniel was answering the knock at the door of his heart.

Daniel's eyes would shine more brightly with the Savior's love as the heavy burden he had carried for so long on his back finally rolled away.

Chapter Fifteen

Motherhood

With the assistance of a neighbor and his horse, Widow Thomsen finally came home two days later.

"Thank you kindly, Mister Eaton," the widow said as she slid off the large brown animal. "Can I repay you with a cup of warm cider, sir?"

"No thank you, Widow Thomsen," Mr. Eaton replied. "It is kind of you to offer but I have much work to do at home feeding my livestock. Take care now, ma'am."

The gray-haired man tipped his hat to the woman and his eyes crinkled when he smiled. She returned the friendly grin as he rode back home, his horse plowing slowly but expertly through the snow.

Widow Thomsen hurried inside, anxious to check on her daughters. When she opened the door she saw Sarah setting out bowls for a meal. Daniel was stirring the food over the fire.

"Mother, you are home!" Sarah said excitedly, throwing her arms around the woman's waist.

The mother hugged her younger daughter. "Where is Mary?"

Daniel greeted the widow but avoided making eye contact. He knew all too well that he had already broken his promise to the woman concerning Mary, and he was not anxious for a confrontation.

"She has been gravely ill, ma'am," the young man said, pausing as he served up the warm soup. "Mary is recovering, but she had Sarah and myself quite concerned."

The widow moved quickly over to the bed and stared intently at her older daughter. Mary was sound asleep in the bed.

"Good Lord, Mr. Lowe. How long has she been ill?"

"Several days, ma'am, but she is eating some now and seems to be doing well." In addition to reassuring her, Daniel also hoped he might change her mind about the couple's mutual affection.

Mary's eyes opened and she smiled.

"You are finally home, Mother," she said weakly. She reached out to the woman at her bedside. Widow Thomsen hugged her for a long while, then looked at her pale daughter. Mary was nearly as white as the linen sheets.

"Thank the Lord you are recovering," the widow said, nearly in tears. She looked up at Daniel gratefully. "And thank you, Mr. Lowe, for taking good care of my Mary. When I left here more than a week ago, it was only Sarah that weighed on my heart. I never imagined that both my daughters would be in such need of my prayers."

Daniel glanced at the widow briefly and gave a smile while stirring the soup over the fire.

"Mr. Lowe never left her side, Mother," Sarah said. "He was just like a doctor."

"I hardly think that my skills in medicine would be sought after by most," he said wryly. "I did the best that I could, but my endeavors were sometimes pathetic. I was quite out of my element."

The widow looked at him curiously.

"Well, you obviously were successful in helping her to recover and I am beholden to you, Mr. Lowe," she said.

"We prayed for her, Mother. Mr. Lowe and I did," Sarah said.

Widow Thomsen seemed as surprised at this piece of news as Mary had been. It was the first time that she was aware of Daniel acknowledging his Maker.

"God is always the best healer, is he not?" she asked.

"Yes, ma'am. He is," Daniel said.

"Let me help serve up these victuals. It seems as if you are due for some relief, sir," she said.

"I shall gladly hand over the ladle to you, Widow Thomsen." In jest, he bowed formally.

"Thank you, sir," she said laughing.

Daniel limped over to Mary at her bedside.

"And may I bring you some fine victuals from the Thomsen hearth, miss?" he asked.

Mary's face lit up.

"Why yes, sir, if you would be so kind," she said in the same mock formal tone. They both laughed as he brought her a bowlful of the warm soup.

Widow Thomsen's smile faded slowly as she heard this playful interaction between the two. She turned in time to see Daniel briefly take one of Mary's hands as he passed the bowl into her other. She noted the look of affection on Mary's face toward the man. The widow quickly turned back toward the fire, her brow furrowed.

"Oh dear," Widow Thomsen whispered to herself.

***

The next morning brought more cold air but sunshine instead of storms. "At least it is not snowing," Widow Thomsen sighed as she glanced at the rays streaming through the curtains.

She pulled herself out from under the quilts to start her workday. While she was grateful to be back home and grateful that her daughters were well, her thoughts were fraught with concern about Mary and Daniel. She looked over at her two sleeping daughters. The mother moved carefully so she would not awaken them as she grabbed the milk bucket. But before heading for the barn, she decided to check the embers in Daniel's fireplace. The widow lifted two large logs and carried them into his room without knocking. She shivered from the cold air as she placed the logs on the dying fire. While stoking the ashes, she noticed that Daniel had fallen asleep reading the Bible.

The woman glanced at the passages from the Book of James where his fingers were laying.

"'Blessed is the man that endureth temptation, for when he is tried, he shall receive the crown of life...'" she whispered. She looked at the young man peacefully sleeping.

"Keep enduring that temptation, Mr. Lowe," she said to herself. "Keep working on that crown."

She sighed deeply as she left the room and closed the door.

The mother checked on her sleeping offspring once more before heading out the front door of the farmhouse.

As she opened the door to the barn, Widow Thomsen greeted the cow as though she were visiting an old friend.

"Well now, Susannah. How have you been doing while I've been away?" The cow looked over at her and mooed its reply.

"Yes, I feel the same way," the widow said. She pulled the milking stool over next to the bovine and sat down wearily.

"So Susannah, you have been tended to by our Mr. Lowe these days. And what do you think of the gentleman?" The cow was eating her hay and ignoring the widow's voice.

"I suppose he is a fine enough man but ... we barely know him. He is just a stranger." The widow paused and looked up at the animal. "You are a mother—would you let your daughter take up with an unfamiliar bull that suddenly showed up in your pasture one day? I should say not."

The widow kept up the rhythmic motions on the cow's teats, producing great streams of fresh milk.

"But I shall tell you something more, Susannah. He is no ordinary suitor. No, this man is a soldier of the King. The enemy. And he's making eyes at my daughter."

She paused thoughtfully for a moment.

"And she is making eyes at him." She gave a deep sigh before resuming the milking.

"I do wish my husband James were here."

Susannah continued eating while the widow reminisced.

"I shall never forget when I met my husband. I offered him some cool water at the barn raising. I confess I'd been eyeing him from a distance. He looked at me, sweat streaming off his forehead, and his handsome green eyes looked into mine." Widow Thomsen sighed again. "I knew when I saw those eyes that James Thomsen was the only man for me."

For a few moments the only sound in the barn was the splash of the milk into the bucket.

"I do not object to Mr. Lowe himself, Susannah. He has taken care of my daughters better than most men would. But there are no secrets in this village, and soon everyone would know the truth about Daniel

Lowe. At the very least, they would run him and my daughter out of town. Mary and Daniel would have to move far away, perhaps even to Halifax, where the Tories have fled. I might never see Mary again. And if the townspeople were cruel..." Tears pushed past the brim of the widow's eyes. "I have already lost a child ... could I bear the hurt of losing another for a man that she thinks she loves?"

She paused in the milking long enough to consider this.

"But what if she really does love him? No amount of interference from her mother could change her heart. And without Mr. Lowe, my Mary might not even have survived." She stopped for a moment, furrowing her eyebrows.

"Now," she said pointedly, "the man is praying and reading the Bible. Is this supposed to sway my feelings on the matter?"

She stood up from the milking stool, her chore complete. She looked up to the rafters of the barn and closed her eyes.

"Dear Heavenly Father," she prayed, "this turmoil is far beyond my ability to discern any possible solution. But Lord, you have designed the heavens and the earth—surely you have the answer to this plight. Help me, Lord, to trust in your creative resolution. Amen."

The widow started to carry the full bucket toward the house, but paused for another moment to look heavenward.

"And please, Dear Lord, keep Daniel reading the Bible—especially those verses about temptation."

Chapter Sixteen

Longings

"Hold still, Daniel," Mary said, her voice filled with annoyance.

She was standing upon a chair with the soldier in front of her. He was growing impatient, as he had work to do on the door lock. He had been trying on this new shirt that Mary was sewing for him for several days. The constant fittings were becoming tiresome.

"Ouch! You have stuck another pin in my shoulder!"

Mary knew she was working quickly but it was already February. She needed to complete this shirt before spring—before Daniel would be outdoors, where visitors would see him. The more the clothes looked like they had been tailored for him, the less suspicious he would appear.

"It would be easier to avoid sticking you if you would not move so," she said.

"But my leg, Mary," said Daniel, feigning discomfort from his war injury.

She put her hand on his shoulder and said with worry in her voice, "Are you in pain, Daniel?"

He turned and grinned at her.

"No, but it was worth the lie to hear the tenderness in your voice."

Mary was doubly annoyed now and threw her hands into the air.

"I surrender. We are finished for today."

She shook her head in exasperation and started to climb down from the chair. Before she could get very far, Daniel lifted her in his arms and swung her to the floor in front of him.

"That was the best part of the shirt fitting right there," he said teasingly, flashing the grin that always took her breath away.

"Daniel, let me go," she whispered, nodding toward Sarah. Mary did not want her little sister filling their mother in on her close encounters with Daniel.

The recovering soldier reluctantly released her, but he continued holding her with his eyes. She returned to the hand sewing in one of the chairs near the fire.

The young farmwoman never tired of new linen. Woven from flax grown in their fields, this material took well over a year to process from the time of its planting until it was ready for sewing. Linen fresh from its sun bleaching on the grass was a valuable commodity. Mary stroked the precious fabric before resuming her careful stitching.

"I shall complete this shirt despite your wily behavior, Daniel Lowe," she said.

She tried to look stern, but her sparkling eyes gave her away. She could never stay annoyed with him for long.

He looked at her with delight again. He returned to his chore of repairing the wooden brace used to bar the Thomsen door. He had noticed weeks ago that its hardware was ill fitting and the wood swollen. Anyone, friend or foe, could enter their home as they pleased. So far, the visitors had all been welcome. Daniel had found tools that served the purpose for fixing the faulty device.

As he was returning to his task, Widow Thomsen unexpectedly arrived home from a neighbor's labor and delivery. The midwife had only been gone for a few hours.

"That was a fast birthing, Mother," Mary said.

The older woman rubbed her cold hands together.

"Yes, it was one of the fastest that I have attended. Sometimes it works quickly when it is not the first—and this child was number seven."

"Seven?" Sarah said in wonder. "What a great many babies! Was it a boy or a girl?" Sarah asked, as usual wanting to know the details.

"It was a boy, a big healthy one at that. Started eating right away. Quite the sturdy little patriot," the widow said with a satisfied nod. "I just stayed long enough to make sure all was going to remain well with Missus Burk, and long enough to catch up on some news."

"What news, Mother?" Sarah asked.

News in this isolated community was always anxiously received. The farms in the village of Deer Run were so far away from the cities that reports from the Congress and the war front were always delayed. Neighbors depended upon each other to carry information from one home to the next. It was not uncommon for "current" reports to sometimes be weeks or even months old.

"Well, let us see," Widow Thomsen said as she took off her cape. The midwife sat wearily in a chair that was opposite Mary's near the fire. "Oh, that warmth is so good on my feet."

Her two daughters looked at their mother expectantly.

"Yes? Go on, Mother," Mary said, trying not to be impatient. She had already fixed some tea for her mother and set the warm cup into her cold fingers. Daniel was listening in as well. He was curious to hear news of the war, although he sometimes preferred to forget about the military conflict just miles away.

"We have a new name for our country," the widow finally declared proudly. "The Congress has decided to call us the 'United States of America.'"

"The United States of America," Mary repeated. "Then we are to be called … 'Americans'?"

"That is correct, Mary. For the first time we are not just a separated group of colonies looking out for our individual interests. We are a nation."

Widow Thomsen sighed in awe. The entire group pondered the ramifications of such a pronouncement. Daniel was especially speechless. The colonies were now declaring themselves a separate country from England! Never before had settlements in the New World done so, and this left him with mixed feelings that he did not have the words to express. The strangest part about his thoughts was the unexpected *hope* for this new nation. A perception that this was the way it should be. He was baffled by his own reflections on the matter.

"So what other news did Missus Burk have for you, Mother?" Mary asked, anxious for news about the American soldiers.

"She said that our army is taking shelter at Valley Forge through this miserable winter. The snow and cold there has been even more treacherous than here in Massachusetts," the widow said.

"Where is Valley Forge?" the older daughter asked.

"In Pennsylvania," Widow Thomsen said. "Not too far from Philadelphia. It has been a dreadful winter there. Many of our troops have died of disease and starvation. But that General Washington—he has stayed right there beside his men encouraging them to stay the course." Widow Thomsen always spoke highly of General Washington. She greatly admired his commitment to the troops and to the fledgling nation.

"Missus Burk also brought out a letter from her son, Robert," the widow said, looking at her older daughter. "He has been asking about you, Mary. He speaks fondly of you and hopes to visit when he returns from the war camp." The widow sipped at her tea and hummed a hymn under her breath.

Mary stared angrily at her mother.

"I am sure I do not know what you are talking about, Mother. Robert and I have not been friends for many years now."

"Ah, well, war has a way of tugging on one's heartstrings for the people we hold most dear," the widow said. She stretched out her feet before the hearth.

Mary glanced at Daniel and saw the anger in his eyes. She did not know how to refute her mother's insinuations. How would she explain this entire conversation about her childhood friend?

"I think I shall work out in the barn for awhile," Daniel said. His voice was as frigid as the air outside. He hurriedly pulled on the deerskin jacket and shut the door behind himself. He stalked off toward the barn, limping as he went.

Mary gave her mother an icy stare.

"What exactly was that all about, Mother?" Mary asked angrily.

"I was just repeating the information from Missus Burk's letter—that is all, Mary," she said with feigned innocence.

"That is not all you were doing, Mother," Mary said with growing rage. "You have made every attempt to dissuade me from setting my heart upon Daniel Lowe. And now you have made me appear to be a flirtatious woman who would throw a man's feelings into the mire. I am not that kind of woman, and you know that."

Widow Thomsen stared at her older daughter, drawing her lips into a thin line.

"I am merely watching out for your best interests, dear. I do not want you to be hurt."

"*You* are hurting me, Mother. My heart longs for Daniel and you are treading upon my deepest affections. Please, do not make me choose my allegiance between Daniel or you."

Mary stared intently at her mother. She grabbed her cape and followed Daniel to the barn, slamming the door as she went. Her cheeks were burning with anger.

How could my Mother be so hurtful? she thought in disbelief.

Widow Thomsen stared after Mary, completely speechless. Sarah, who had been staring at the two women throughout this heated conversation, broke the silence.

"I think that Mr. Lowe is smitten with her beauty."

***

Mary's face was red with indignation as she approached the barn door. When she opened it she could see Daniel taking out his frustration by planing the wooden bar from the door lock. He glanced up at her only briefly.

"So, is there any more news about lonely soldiers awaiting your embrace at their homecoming?" Daniel asked sarcastically. There was fire in his deep-set eyes.

The young woman's face was red with embarrassment.

"Daniel, I have no one away at war that I am longing for," she said. "Please believe me."

"Your mother does not appear to believe so."

Mary looked down at the hay-strewn floor and moved the straw with one foot.

"Please do not be angry with my mother," she said. "I am furious enough with her for the both of us." She looked up as his eyes met hers.

"Well it is quite obvious that she does not approve of me taking an interest in her daughter." He continued planing the piece of wood with rapid and forceful thrusts of his arms, then stopped suddenly. "And just who is this Robert Burk person that she was talking about? Another soldier who wanted you to wait for him, like James' friend did?"

"No, Daniel, nothing like that. Robert and I were friends when I was thirteen or fourteen. I have not seen him except at Sabbath meetings in many years," she said, her eyes pleading for him to believe her.

His demeanor began to soften slightly.

"And I suppose this soldier has some special memory from age fourteen that is still in his thoughts?" he asked with a hint of lingering annoyance.

"Well," Mary said, flirtatiously hugging herself with her cape, "I do remember him kissing me once secretly behind the meetinghouse." She stared innocently up at the rafters of the barn, waiting for Daniel's reaction. She did not have to wait long.

Daniel stopped his work as his face fell.

"He kissed you?" he asked, crestfallen.

"On the cheek, Daniel," Mary said, laughing. "I was only fourteen. If I remember right, I went home and washed my face."

The young man set the planing tool down on the wood and walked over toward Mary. He came up close, held gently but firmly onto her arms, and stared deeply into her eyes.

"So," he said, his voice thick with emotion, "is this how he kissed you?"

He leaned toward the young woman and touched her cheek lightly with his lips.

Mary's eyes widened and her breathing quickened. She looked up at him and said, "Actually, it was this cheek." She pointed to the opposite side of her face.

He leaned even closer and kissed that cheek slowly and tenderly.

"Like that?" he whispered, his lips right next to her ear.

Her heart was racing now and she could barely speak.

"No," she whispered hoarsely. "Your kiss is much sweeter."

This time Daniel leaned in towards her lips. He met them gently with his at first. As she eagerly returned his tender kiss, his became more inflamed with passion. Mary was breathless when he pulled away and she saw the earnest look in his eyes.

"I have been longing to do that since we first met," he said.

He held her close, and she could feel his trembling hands squeezing her shoulders as she rested her head against his chest. She looked up at Daniel as he held her face and caressed her cheeks. His eyes were filled with love and … something more. They were filled with hope—hope for a future with Mary.

As they embraced and kissed once more, Daniel prayed fervently that, despite the war and the widow's objections, his hope would one day be fulfilled.

Chapter Seventeen

Questions

Daniel heard the front door close. It was just before dusk in early March of 1778 and Widow Thomsen was returning from a neighbor's home where she had been on a medical visit. The soldier had been in his room reading the Bible. It was the final light of yet another cold day that offered no hint of spring. The weather only added to the somber mood of the Thomsen house. Everyone was worried about the illness of the Beal baby. By the look on the older woman's face, Mary knew the news was not good.

"How is Richard's little brother?" Sarah asked hopefully.

Her mother looked at the eager face of her young daughter. She sat wearily in the chair by the fire.

"Come here, Sarah," the widow said sadly.

"He is all right, is he not? He is such a sweet baby," she said, climbing into her mother's lap.

Her mother took a deep breath and spoke slowly.

"Sarah, God has seen fit to bring young Adam home with him to heaven."

Sarah looked at the widow with a quizzical expression.

"I do not understand, Mother," she said. The young girl glanced at Mary, who was stirring the pot of soup over the fire. She noticed that Mary had put her hand over her mouth. Tears were beginning to roll down her sister's cheeks.

"Young Adam has passed away, child. I stayed with his mother long enough to comfort her and lay out the child in fresh clothing."

The widow said these words with great difficulty. She knew the sadness this would bring her young daughter. Sarah had been with her when Adam was born. She had held and rocked him, admiring his beautiful face and hands. The impact of his short life would leave a deep mark upon her heart.

"No, Mother. This cannot be. Why?"

She began to sob—great loud wails that could be heard throughout the house. Mary could not bear this painful news. She wanted to escape from this terrible sorrow. The young woman grabbed the milk bucket and her cape and raced outdoors toward the barn, covering her mouth to stifle her sobbing.

Daniel came out of his room at the commotion. He saw Sarah and Widow Thomsen's deep distress and looked for Mary. She was nowhere to be seen, so he assumed that she was the one who had gone out the door just a moment ago. He grabbed a coat and hurried toward the barn.

When he entered the chilly building, he could not see Mary but heard her crying over near Susannah.

He walked over toward the hay-filled stall and gently put his hand upon her shoulder. She was clutching a wooden post with a grip that turned her knuckles white.

"What has happened, Mary?" he asked.

When she was unable to stop sobbing, he put his arms around her shoulders and held her closely.

After a few moments she pulled her head from his chest and spoke through her tears.

"The Beal baby has died. He was so young and full of life not two weeks ago. The child's father is away at war and will not even know about his son's passing." Mary looked up at Daniel with reddened eyes as he wiped the tears off of her cheeks. "It seems as if even when there is hope for new life, it gets taken away. Will death always triumph over hope?"

She rested her head back upon Daniel and clung to him with desperate hands. Without lifting her head, she added, "And will this dreadful cold never end?"

Both stood in silence, letting her tears slowly subside.

"I was just reading about hope," he finally said. "And about difficult times. Something about glorying in tribulations because they lead to patience and patience to experience. The experience then leads to hope which makes us not ashamed, because the love of God is shed in our hearts."

He looked tenderly at Mary.

"I am so sorry about the baby. It must be so painful to lose one's child," he said.

Mary pulled away from his chest once again.

"Yes," she said flatly. She was beginning to feel numb. It was a familiar sensation that overcame her when sadness overwhelmed her spirit.

Daniel lifted her chin slightly so that he could look into her eyes.

"When I was reading in the Book of Romans about tribulations leading to hope, my thoughts were consumed with the memories of the last several months. My injury and then escape, your rescue and nursing care, my healing, your sickness—so much has happened that has been such hardship. And yet there is still hope, just like the words say."

Mary listened in thoughtful silence. When she did not say anything, the young man continued.

"I am so very grateful for all that you have done for me. I never could have survived without your assistance and I shall be forever beholden to you."

So that is the reason he is saying this to me, Mary thought. *He wants to thank me before he leaves.*

Her mother had warned her this would happen. He may have shared a kiss along the way, but apparently it was no more than mere gratitude for saving his life. She chided herself for putting more stock into his affectionate manner.

Mary drew away from his embrace and looked up at him.

"You need not thank me further, Daniel and you are not beholden to me." She took a step backward. "I suppose that you are planning on leaving when spring arrives. I suppose you are bidding me an early farewell?"

Daniel's expression looked wounded and confused.

"Bidding you farewell? I am trying to express my deepest regard for you."

He moved toward her once again and held both her arms gently but earnestly. He tried to calm his voice.

"I fear I am not making myself clear. I know that I am far more adept in the ways of war than of love."

He now had her full attention and he nervously moistened his dry lips.

"Mary, you have captured my heart completely and I am a willing prisoner of your affection."

Daniel was trembling. His eyes were wide with apprehension about Mary's possible response. He bravely continued on, more fearful of her eyes than of an entire column of cannons on the battlefield.

"When you walk into a room, I cannot take my eyes from you. You have made me laugh and you have moved me to tears. You have been my true friend and I wish for you to be my true love." He gently touched her cheeks with his moist hands. "I do not know all the answers to our uncertain future. But I do know one thing." The young soldier swallowed hard. His voice was barely more than a whisper. "I do not wish to have a future without you by my side. Please Mary, will you be my wife forevermore?"

There was a look of total surrender in Daniel's eyes as he waited nervously for the answer to his question.

Mary gazed at the soldier for a moment before slowly touching the cleft in his chin. She smiled softly and reached up with both of her hands to draw his face toward hers. She kissed him tenderly on his lips and she felt him respond in kind.

The kiss continued as their embrace became impassioned. Her heart fairly burst from her chest as her blood raced through her veins. When she finally drew away, Daniel started to kiss her neck. His warm lips made her tremble with each encounter.

"I love you, Mary," he said in between his caresses. "From the first time I saw you, I have loved you."

"I love you so much Daniel," she said in a whisper.

He suddenly stopped kissing her and looked at her strangely.

"You never answered my question," he said.

She looked at him and gently touched his face.

"Yes," she whispered into his ear. "Yes. I shall be your wife, Daniel Lowe. I shall be your wife forevermore."

Chapter Eighteen

Prudence

Spring had not truly arrived each year at the Thomsen farm until Great Aunt Prudence came on the scene. Prudence was a formidable woman, with a wide face and tightly wound hair beneath a too-tight cap.

"It is a wonder that her head does not ache from the constriction," Widow Thomsen had once said of her aunt. But Prudence always insisted that it was the only way to keep her hair neatly confined. The cap, in addition to an unpleasant smelling pomade, kept every lock in perfect order. No one ever had the courage to ask the woman what the source of the oily substance was.

Aunt Prudence had never been married. She had long ago had the opportunity when she was engaged to a merchant in the town of Bridgewater. But the woman's commanding presence could be intimidating. Before the planned wedding could take place, the slightly built groom-to-be closed up his shop and disappeared. He was never heard from again.

"I think she frightens men away with her imperious attitude," Widow Thomsen had said. Mary could well imagine.

Despite her overbearing demeanor, Prudence had a good heart when it came to helping others. And ever since Mary's father had died, Prudence came faithfully every spring and fall to bring two of her servants to help with planting and harvesting.

"What is a successful farm without the strength of men?" Prudence had said matter-of-factly.

The great aunt had a very profitable farm that she managed well. She was the sole heir of her father's land and was very adept at finances and agriculture. Her independence as a farmer was secure as long as she remained single.

"If I had married that no-good Mr. Crowell, I should never have had such freedom," she had once said, referring to her absconded fiancé.

As Prudence approached the Thomsen farm earlier than expected that April morning, Mary hastened to the barn to warn Daniel. She berated herself that she had not thought to caution him of her aunt's impending visit.

"Daniel, Aunt Prudence is here," she said, out of breath from running. "She is not someone who will keep her silence. You must hide or you will face her interrogation."

The young man had been sharpening the tools to prepare for planting. He was confused by her caution. The former soldier had discussed his introduction to the townsfolk with the two Thomsen women. They would explain that Daniel was wounded in the war and was helping out on the farm in exchange for food and shelter. He was not expecting to be further secluded. But Daniel could hear the earnest tone in Mary's voice, and he knew that he should heed her advice.

"Where do you want me to hide?" he asked, setting the hoe down against the barn wall.

"Under the hay. Quickly!" As Mary threw large piles of hay over him, she said, "I feel like Rahab hiding the spies," referring to a story about Joshua in the Bible.

Daniel looked at her with feigned shock.

"Mary! Was not Rahab a harlot?" He looked at her with a grin partially covered with straw.

Mary glanced at him with exasperation. "You have a very selective memory from the Bible, Daniel Lowe," she said, trying not to grin.

"I must say, it is quite shocking that my future wife should compare herself with a woman of such dubious occupation," Daniel teased her.

Mary rolled her eyes at him and threw one last pile of straw over his face.

"Hush before my aunt hears you," she said in a whisper.

The young woman left the barn and walked toward Aunt Prudence, who was approaching on horseback. The visitor was accompanied by two servants driving a wagon filled with supplies.

Future wife, Mary thought with a smile emerging on her face. Yes, she would soon be Daniel's wife.

But there was one obstacle that overshadowed Mary's joy—Daniel still had to speak to her mother. It was a conversation that Mary had begged him to put off until spring, but the season was now upon them and she would have to allow him to approach Widow Thomsen to ask for her blessing.

But the young farmwoman had already made a firm decision. Should her mother reject Daniel's request, Mary would elope with him. As difficult as leaving her home would be, Mary could not imagine the pain of losing this man that held her heart. She prayed desperately that her mother would consent to the marriage.

"Hellooo, Miss Mary," Aunt Prudence hollered. The stout woman waved vigorously at the young woman approaching the party of travelers.

"Welcome, Aunt Prudence," Mary said, immediately noticing the tight cap upon her aunt's head. "And how are you this fine April day?"

"Well enough, my dear," said Prudence in her loud, brash manner. "I have brought my servants Jubo and Gibb to help out with the spring planting."

Mary approached the two men managing the reins of the horses drawing the wagon.

"Welcome, sirs. We are grateful for your help. And how are your wife and family, Jubo?" Mary had known this man and his family since she was quite young. Gibb had only been with Aunt Prudence a short time.

"They are doing well, Miss Mary," Jubo said. "My wife says to thank you for the blanket you made last year for our newest baby."

"You are most welcome, Jubo. I hope the baby is doing well."

Widow Thomsen and Sarah came out of the farmhouse and approached the three visitors from Bridgewater. The young girl was far more subdued than usual. Sarah had likely received strict instructions from their mother about not divulging Daniel's presence, Mary thought with relief. Her little sister's enthusiastic chatter could reveal too much information to their always-inquisitive relative.

Aunt Prudence heaved her generous girth off the saddle of Dash, her large brown mare. The overburdened animal seemed to exhale in relief.

Poor Dash, Mary thought, gently stroking the animal's nose.

"May I take Dash into the barn and feed her?" Mary asked her great aunt. The animal gently nuzzled the farmwoman's hand. The horse was familiar with Mary's generous offerings of hay and apples.

"Yes, of course," Prudence said. She turned to the two servants and raised her voice in a stern command. "Jubo, Gibb. Unload these supplies and carry what's needed to the fields."

The two men began the work of lifting and unloading the crates and barrels. Aunt Prudence had brought new tools as well as a fresh catch of salted ocean cod. The fish were a welcome luxury this far inland.

"Here is a barrel full of fine cod for your table, Ruth," said Prudence to the widow.

"Thank you, Aunt Prudence," she said, looking at the crate of cod. "You know how much I miss the ocean bounty."

"Miss Mary," Aunt Prudence called loudly after her great niece. "Make Dash at home in one of your stalls. He is going to be staying here with you. Your mother needs his swift legs to deliver those babes, especially in the cold of winter."

Widow Thomsen's jaw dropped. "Aunt Prudence, I could not accept such a gift," the midwife stammered.

"You are doing Dash a favor," Aunt Prudence said. "She is not getting any younger and I am not getting any leaner. She will live a longer life underneath your smaller frame, I am sure." Aunt Prudence gave the widow a smile that said the discussion was finished.

"Thank you, Aunt," said Widow Thomsen.

Aunt Prudence carefully scrutinized Mary as she led the horse toward the barn. The older woman tilted her head and furrowed her generous brow. Her mouth frowned in displeasure.

"Speaking of small frames, your Mary seems to need a few extra pounds upon her bones," Aunt Prudence said.

Before Widow Thomsen could intervene, the resolute aunt marched toward Mary with long, forceful strides. "Miss Mary," her aunt called out with a voice that could rival the tenor of musket fire.

The young farmwoman flinched at the command. She paused in her steps as she neared the open door of the barn.

"Yes, Aunt Prudence?" she answered dutifully.

Prudence took stock of Mary's figure.

"You seem to have some potentially fine flanks and hindquarters for child bearing, my dear. But perhaps a few extra spoonfuls at each meal would serve you well," the horsewoman said with a critical eye. "When those lads come home from the war, they will wish to court the women with ample figures to feed their babes."

Mary's face turned crimson with embarrassment. Had her aunt realized there was a gentleman within hearing distance, naturally she would not have spoken so frankly. But Mary knew that Daniel was nearby and she was mortified. The situation was even more humiliating due to the older woman's annoying habit of discussing one's physical appearance as if she were livestock.

"I shall keep that in mind, Aunt Prudence," said Mary, her face getting hotter by the moment.

"Well then, I shall see you back at the house," Prudence said. She strode back to the farmhouse with the same forceful steps with which she had approached Mary. If she had noticed Mary's intense embarrassment, Aunt Prudence never acknowledged it.

Daniel watched through a small opening in the hay as Mary slowly led Dash to the stall next to Susannah's. He immediately recognized Mary's discomfort, and as much as he wanted to laugh at Prudence's amusing advice, he thought better of it. When he heard the door to the farmhouse close behind the visitor, Daniel moved the hay away from his face.

"Is it safe to come out yet?" he asked Mary.

She looked over at him, her face still a bright red.

"You heard, did you not?" she said without smiling.

Daniel stood up, his linen shirt and breeches covered with bits of hay. He walked over to the object of his affection and put his arms around her.

"I think you are perfect."

"I am mortified," she said, not daring to look at his face.

"Look at me, Mary," he said, lifting her chin upward. "If you were as large as your Aunt Prudence, I would be fearful you might injure me."

Mary could not help but giggle, imagining such a scenario. Daniel could always find the humor in any situation.

"Mary," Daniel said, touching her hair and caressing her cheeks, "you awaken deep feelings of desire within me." He tenderly kissed her lips and drew her closer. "I cannot wait until we are married."

His look of passion nearly made her forget that there were visitors nearby.

"I had best go inside before I lose myself in your kisses," she said.

Mary released herself from Daniel's embrace and walked back toward the farmhouse. She looked back at him for one last glance.

Daniel stared after her and took a deep breath. He slowly exhaled, trying desperately not to think about her flanks and hindquarters.

When Mary opened the door to the farmhouse she was still trying to recover from the sweetness of Daniel's kiss. Her ears were suddenly assaulted by the resonant voice of Aunt Prudence. The visitor was discussing the Revolution, marriage, and patriotic responsibilities.

"It is the duty of every citizen to do everything possible to promote our revolutionary cause," Prudence said emphatically, her hand swinging up and down like a hammer. Her other hand was holding the tankard of cider and rum that she had requested from her niece, Widow Thomsen.

The visiting relative looked up at Mary.

"Ah, yes, just the person we were discussing. Have a seat, miss."

The widow looked at her daughter as if to apologize for the impending verbal onslaught. Aunt Prudence took a long swig of her drink and then a deep breath before starting.

"So, Miss Mary, I was telling your mother that it is the duty of every young woman in these colonies to marry and replenish the supply of citizens that have been lost in the war."

"Duty? Replenish the supply of citizens?" Mary asked, her eyes widening with the declaration.

"Yes, miss. How else will these United States of America flourish without its citizens being fruitful and multiplying?" Aunt Prudence asked. She took another long swallow of brew.

"Well," Mary began thoughtfully, "I am sure that will happen naturally as young people fall in love. Do you not think so, Aunt Prudence?"

Aunt Prudence's eyes narrowed and the imposing woman leaned forward in her chair.

"Love?" the woman said, aghast. "I am not discussing love. I am talking about the duty of every patriot. If a farmer needs more livestock in the field, he just brings in a few stud animals and lets nature take its course."

Mary was speechless for a moment but finally found her voice.

"But Aunt Prudence, we are more than animals. We are humans with a need to love. Marriage is a gift from God," she said bravely.

Aunt Prudence rolled her eyes.

"If we wait for every citizen to 'fall in love,' we shall run out of time to replenish the American population. And leave it to the Thomsens to dwell upon God and love. I tell you, there is more to life than following the 'Good Book,' as you call it."

"I disagree, Aunt," Widow Thomsen spoke up. "There is much wisdom to be gleaned from reading the Bible. And marriage should be based on love as well as suitability." She looked at her older daughter, who stared at her mother gratefully.

Her aunt was not to be dissuaded from her intended goal.

"So it is love you are after, is it?" Aunt Prudence asked her niece. "Are you telling me there are no men in your town suitable to provide a caring home for you, Mary?"

Sarah tried to answer the question but was immediately interrupted by Widow Thomsen, who firmly squeezed the girl's arm. She knew full well her younger daughter would be volunteering Daniel for the role of husband for Mary. Sarah was frustrated by the interruption. She folded her arms tightly and pouted.

"Most of the young men are away at war," the widow explained.

"Well, what about the older widow men?" Aunt Prudence suggested helpfully. "I'm sure they would appreciate the fine withers of a strong girl like Mary."

There it was again—another comparison to equine anatomy. Mary looked pleadingly at her mother.

"I am sure that Mary will set her eyes on a proper husband who will sire many children for the sake of America, Aunt Prudence," Widow Thomsen said, hoping to sidetrack the woman's barrage of suggestions. Aunt Prudence was not so easily disarmed.

"So, Mary, is there a young man who you have set your heart upon who could help you in this patriotic cause?" she asked.

Mary's face blushed and she was afraid that her demeanor would invite more pointed inquiries. Sarah again tried to make a suggestion, but she was once again halted by her mother's firm grip upon her arm. When the widow looked over at Mary, her older daughter's discomfort brought a look of sympathy from the mother. Widow Thomsen turned resolutely toward her aunt.

"I think that Mary will use good judgment in whom she chooses to father her children," her mother said. "There are several men who are suitable and would be more than willing to offer their help as patriots."

"Good!" Aunt Prudence said, finally seeming satisfied. The great aunt raised her tankard of drink for a toast.

"To mother's milk for the Revolution!" She took one last swig and belched heartily. "Well, I must start my journey back to Bridgewater before I lose the light of day. I shall return in a few weeks to collect my servants."

The sizeable woman stood up and straightened out her rumpled clothing. As she started for the door, no one asked her the obvious question about her safety traveling alone. Everyone knew that no one would dare harass Aunt Prudence—not even someone as brave as General Washington.

While standing in the doorway watching their mother say farewell to Aunt Prudence, Sarah tugged on her older sister's arm.

"Mary," she whispered. "Why did you not tell Aunt Prudence about Daniel? He loves you and would make many fine babies for the cause." Sarah had a wounded look upon her face because no one had listened to her ideas.

Mary bent down towards her sister and hugged the girl.

"I think you have a fine suggestion, Sarah. It was just not the right time to tell Aunt Prudence."

The young woman watched her aunt drive off in the wagon and wondered when it would be the right time. She prayed that soon there would be no more need to keep so many secrets.

Chapter Nineteen

Decisions

Daniel watched as Mary leaned over the slightly greening gray spikes of lavender. The leaves were just starting to awaken on this sunny April morning. It was a reminder that, at long last, winter was finally over.

"My favorite plants are coming back again," Mary said with excitement.

It had been two days now since Aunt Prudence had returned to her farm in Bridgewater. Spring planting was well underway, with Jubo and Gibb tilling the soil in the flax field.

Mary breathed in deeply of the fresh air, which carried the scent of warm earth and sun-drenched grass. The straw bonnet that shielded her from the bright sun shifted slightly. Her fingers quickly redid the ribbon into a tighter bow. She moved on toward the field, which had been readied for the corn seed. A pouch of kernels was hanging over her shoulder and she toted a tall planting stick. The bottom of the tool was formed into a point, which allowed the seeds easy access into the soil. She prepared to show Daniel how to start the field of corn, pumpkins, and beans that grew together in rows.

Daniel was looking forward to spending the day outdoors. It had been a wearisome winter of cold and snow, and the sun felt like a balm on his skin—skin that had spent more than enough hours shivering through the long bitter months. Now, in this new season, he especially relished the thought of a day working alone with Mary.

"You take the stick to poke the hole in the mound and then drop a seed corn inside," she explained. "After each corn seed has been put in the ground, we will plant pumpkin seeds and beans that will grow around the stalks. We learned this from the Indians."

"Why is there such a large mound of dirt around each spot for the corn plant?" Daniel asked.

"The Indians say it represents fertility—like the belly of a woman with child," she said. She suddenly became self-conscious and looked away.

"I see," he said bemusedly.

The couple continued on with the task, moving up and down the long rows.

At first, Daniel felt awkward with this unfamiliar task, but he quickly caught on to the maneuver. Soon, he was right across from Mary on the adjacent row.

"So you have caught up with me," she said.

"I will do whatever it takes to be close to you, Mary Thomsen," he said.

Mary grew more serious, and paused.

"Daniel, I think it is time to speak with my mother."

Daniel put one last seed into the ground and returned her gaze.

"I know," he said soberly. He looked at the pale green leaves just beginning to emerge on the maple trees at the edge of the field. After a moment he turned back toward her. "And what if she says no?"

Mary took a deep breath. She looked straight at him and said with resolve, "Then I shall go away with you."

Daniel was taken aback by her reply.

"You would leave with me if I have to go?" he said incredulously. "But your life is here. I have nothing to offer you."

Mary set the stick down and came next to him. She took his hand.

"My life is with you." Her lips began to tremble. "I know that this would not be easy. But Daniel, I cannot let you go without me." Fresh tears washed over her face.

Daniel reached out to her and held her closely to himself without speaking a word.

He did not know what to say. How could he convince Mary—the woman that he loved more than life—to stay behind if her mother refused them permission to marry?

But Mary had always been taken care of by her family. How could he provide a home for her when he had no skills other than being a military man? And would she resent him if he failed to be a proper husband? He shuddered at the thought.

Somehow, he would have to convince Widow Thomsen that he would make her daughter an acceptable husband—a suitable American husband. Somehow, he must make her understand how much he loved her daughter.

He hoped and prayed that that would be enough.

Daniel finally broke the silence.

"I shall speak with your mother as soon as I find the right opportunity. I shall speak with her by tomorrow."

Mary shivered. "All right," she said. Then she looked up at him with deep affection. "I love you Daniel."

Daniel picked up both of Mary's hands and kissed them tenderly.

"I love you more than I have ever loved another person," Daniel said, working his jaw hard to control his emotions. He let her hands go with regret and they both returned to their task.

The day went by slowly. The weight of this decision lay heavily on both of their hearts.

When the sun began to set on the horizon, Daniel brought the tools back into the barn. He noticed that Jubo and Gibb were staring into the toolbox. They had been intending to place some of the hoes and spades into the wooden storage when they came upon an unexpected find.

Daniel immediately knew what it was—his red coat, which Mary had found in the woods last fall. She had stored it in the toolbox for safekeeping. In the ensuing months, it had long been forgotten. Now it was discovered by two strangers, whom he did not know if he could trust with this secret.

Daniel looked at both men with fear and trepidation. Jubo and Gibb looked at each other and then back at Daniel. They had been told that Daniel had been wounded in the war. But now they would know which side he had been fighting for.

146

Gibb spoke excitedly to Jubo in his native African tongue. Jubo responded in the same language, which was completely foreign to Daniel. The two servants spoke loudly and with excited hand gestures for several moments.

The British soldier's breathing quickened and he mentally devised a plan. He knew that if they shared this information with Prudence, she would turn him over to the rebels without hesitation. His adrenaline was causing his heart to race and it was difficult to concentrate on a reasonable course of action because he now had so much to lose. If he left the farm, that would mean leaving Mary. He could never take her with him if he were being sought by the Continentals.

Just when he thought all was lost, Jubo began to speak to him in English. His words were simple but powerful.

"Miss Mary has much feeling for you, Mr. Lowe," he said. "If you are her friend, then you are our friend too."

Daniel was speechless. He looked at the two men with deep gratitude and did something he had never done before to a man from Africa. He held out his hand in friendship.

"Thank you," he said, grasping Jubo's fingers with relief.

The two men returned the gesture and then went about their work as if nothing had happened.

After Mary brought out supper to the three men and they had all eaten until they were full, she gathered the bowls and turned to Daniel.

"Tomorrow?" she asked Daniel with hope in her eyes.

"Tomorrow," Daniel answered and touched his fingers to his lips as a sign of his love to her. She touched her own fingers to her lips as well and returned to the house.

The soldier settled into his new sleeping area in one of the barn stalls. With the arrival of the warmer weather, Widow Thomsen had suggested that it was time for him to sleep in the outer building with the other workers. He knew without her saying so that this was a way for the widow to keep him at a further distance from Mary.

He hoped to shorten that distance after speaking with her mother tomorrow.

Chapter Twenty

Intruder

Daniel was restless and he did not know why.

The long day of planting should have been sufficient reason alone to put him into a deep slumber. But his rest was disrupted when Widow Thomsen was called away for a birth at a neighbor's. Daniel had helped saddle Dash for the midwife and watched her ride away down the dirt road toward her patient's home. He hoped that she would not be delayed too long. He did not want anything to interrupt his plan to speak to her the next day about Mary.

Even when he lay back down, however, sleep still escaped him. He tossed about under his blanket and his eyes opened wide when he heard an owl in one of the nearby trees. Occasionally, he felt the hair on the back of his neck stand up. He listened intently but heard no obvious signs of danger.

Probably just nervous about speaking with the widow, he thought. He took in a deep breath and tried to relax.

***

Before she rode off on Dash, Widow Thomsen had cautioned Mary to set the bar that locked the door. The young woman checked it once more before settling in for the night.

Both of the Thomsen girls were in their night shifts, ready to retire from a long day of work. Mary was tempted to open one of the windows to let in the balmy night air, but she thought better of it.

It will probably get too chilly later on, she thought.

Mary tilted her head to one side while plaiting her waist-length hair into a single braid. Before blowing out the candles for the night, she noticed a reddened spot on her foot from walking down the longs rows of corn earlier that day. She sleepily made a salve from the slippery elm bark and rubbed it over the abrasion.

Sarah was in a giddy mood, which was a sharp contrast to her sister's fatigue. The younger sister, enlivened by the spring weather, chatted with excitement about seeing her friends at church meeting on Sunday, which was still two days away. The warm season always brought out the mischievous spirit in the girl and this April was no different.

"Settle down, Sarah," Mary chided her gently. "It's way past your bedtime and morning will be here before you know it."

Sarah was repeatedly tossing her cloth doll up in the air and catching it. One time she threw it too high and it fell on the floor out of sight. She climbed down on the floor to look for it.

There was a gentle knock on the door.

What did Mother forget this time? Mary wondered.

As she opened the door, instead of seeing a friendly face, she was confronted by a large man wearing a red coat. The intruder looked with an evil intent at Mary and pushed her down to the floor. The look in his eyes was unlike any that Mary had seen before. It frightened the trembling woman to her very core.

The man's hair hung in greasy strands down onto his shoulders. His uniform was filthy and the smell of the man was nauseating.

Mary could barely breathe, much less scream. She slowly crawled backwards to get away from this frightening apparition. She pulled herself up by the bedpost and moved away from the British soldier, who was eyeing her like a wild animal encircling his prey.

"Well now, lovely lady. Your husband gone to war, is he?" the man sneered. "Gettin' a bit lonely are ya? I could take care of that."

The stranger began to pull his filthy shirt out of his breeches and unbutton his waistcoat. Mary's breathing quickened. Nausea overwhelmed her and then she began to feel faint.

"I've been known to satisfy a lady or two," he said. "Just wait 'til you experience the pleasure, ma'am."

Despite her anxiety, Mary had a moment of clear thinking. She remembered something her brother James had told her before he left for war. At the time, she had not wanted to listen to his words—they were both embarrassing and fearful to the young woman. But James had insisted.

"Listen to me, Mary," James had said. "In case anyone tries to attack you, you have your best defense by kicking him between his legs. If you cannot use your legs, use your knees or hands. And be harsh about it, not gentle. It may give you enough time to get away."

She wished desperately that her older brother were here. But even though he wasn't, his words guided her actions.

As the man narrowed the distance between them, she decided her knees were the best choice for defending herself. Using all the strength she could muster, Mary thrust her upper leg into the man's groin and the intruder bent over in pain. As she sped past him, he grabbed at her shift and pulled her back next to his body, more determined than ever to carry out his intentions.

Mary scratched at his face, but he grabbed both of her arms and held them down.

Sarah was watching this horrifying scenario unfold from under the bed. Without thinking, the child waited for the moment when the intruder had his back to her. Then she fled out the door, running as fast as her small legs could carry her.

***

Daniel heard a noise that sounded like the door of the house opening. He had fixed the lock weeks ago but maybe the spring rains had swollen the wood. Perhaps the bar no longer fit.

I'd better check on it, he thought wearily. He was exhausted but still on edge.

As Daniel walked towards the front door, he saw a small figure running quickly toward him.

"Sarah?" he said with alarm. He had never seen such a look of terror on the child's face. She was sobbing and pointing toward the house.

"That man … that man," was all she could say. Her eyes were wide with fright.

Daniel's heart began to pound.

"Go to the barn. Stay with Jubo," he ordered as he ran toward the house.

Though he still had a pronounced limp, Daniel raced frantically to the front door without faltering. What he saw in the house chilled his blood. The man had Mary pressed against the wall with his entire body. He was trying to tear off her shift and she was fighting him with every ounce of her strength.

Daniel lunged toward the intruder, grabbed him around the neck, and pulled him off of Mary. The enraged young man swung at the stranger with powerful fists. Daniel's shoulder-length hair came undone from the ties and his face was covered in sweat.

The intruder was now bleeding from his mouth. After being punched with several precise blows, he suddenly realized he was not facing an ordinary colonial farmer. This defender was a trained military man. The attacker shoved the infuriated man away and pulled out a knife from a sheath hidden beneath his coat

"Daniel!" Mary screamed.

The terrible nightmare continued as the intruder swung his knife at Daniel. One of the thrusts of the weapon connected with flesh, leaving a bloodied mark on the defender's cheek.

While feeling the warm blood running down his face, Daniel looked around frantically for anything he could use as a weapon. When he saw the Thomsen's butter churn near the fireplace, he knew he had found his opportunity. He lunged for the long wooden handle and spun around, smashing it against the intruder's ear. The man dropped his knife on the floor as he cried out.

Mary ran to get the knife and the enraged intruder slapped her hard across her mouth.

"You bloody trull," the attacker screamed at the panic-stricken woman.

Daniel was infuriated. He grabbed the knife from the floor and with a firm thrust of his arm, set it deeply into the man's neck. Just as suddenly as the attacker had made his frightening assault, he now slid to the floor without further motion.

For a moment, Mary's fitful breathing was the only sound. Daniel made sure that the man was dead before looking over at her. What he saw made his heart wrench.

She was staring at the floor, one cheek red and swollen, struggling to cover herself with her torn shift. Daniel ran over to her and placed one of the quilts from the bed around her bare shoulders. He did not speak but put his arms gently around her. As she clung to him, she glanced up and saw that the intruder was sitting upright against the far wall.

"Daniel, he is still here!" she screamed.

"Mary, it's all right. He is dead."

Daniel kissed her head and wrapped his arms protectively around her. He gently smoothed her disheveled hair away from her face. His hands were trembling. He finally was able to get the words out that he feared saying.

"Did he ... did he harm you?" he asked, forcing back angry sobs.

"No," she said, trying to get the words out in between her own tears. "He tried, but he did not. Daniel..." She wept as if she would never stop.

She looked up suddenly with alarm in her eyes.

"Where is Sarah?" she screamed.

"She is safe with Gibb, Miss Mary," Jubo said from the doorway. Daniel looked up and saw that the man was crying silently.

"Thank you, Jubo," Daniel said, his voice shaking.

The night's event made his heart race with fear. He was not unused to fighting, but he had never before fought to protect the woman he loved and he was deeply shaken.

Mary touched Daniel's cheek tenderly. "You are hurt," she said.

Daniel hugged her close to himself, afraid to let her go.

Just then they all heard the sound of a horse's hooves. His adrenaline still running high, Daniel stood up and placed himself in front of Mary to protect her.

"It is Widow Thomsen," Jubo said to the frightened group.

The door to her home was wide open and the widow saw Jubo outlined by the pulsating light of the hearth inside. She approached the doorway.

"Jubo?" she said. "What has happened here?" Then she saw Mary and Daniel and assumed the worst—that Daniel had taken advantage of the widow's absence.

"I never should have left you two here, Daniel Lowe," she yelled. She started for her musket but then saw the dead intruder propped up against the wall. "Good Lord," she cried. Her eyes were wide with horror. She realized the truth about the terrifying scene that had just played out in her home.

"Daniel, I am so very sorry," she sobbed.

Then she looked at her daughter, bruised and frightened.

"Mary," she barely whispered. She wrapped both of her arms around her daughter's shoulders as if trying to protect her from further injury. But for tonight, the harm had already been done.

"Let us get this pathetic creature out of here," Daniel said.

He and Jubo carried the body out of the house. They laid it outside, where Sarah could not see it when she returned. Jubo ran to get Gibb, who brought the frightened child to her mother. Widow Thomsen clung tightly to both of her daughters, rocking them slowly as they all sat quivering on the edge of the bed.

"We will take this man to the river, Mr. Lowe," Jubo said. "The water will carry him away and no one will know where he was killed."

Daniel looked gratefully at his new friend.

"Thank you, Jubo."

Daniel fought the tears that were welling in his eyes. He turned back toward the open door of the house and saw Mary and Sarah clinging to their mother. They were all crying for what they had lost tonight—the naive belief that perhaps danger would never come right to their own door.

The young soldier saw a glint of metal lying on the ground outside of the house. It was the intruder's firelock, which he had set down before breaking in.

The man was a deserter, Daniel thought in disgust. All the prisoners of war with the British Army had been forced to give up their arms along the banks of the Hudson River. This rogue left his regiment still armed, long before the surrender. How many other women had he terrorized from New York to Deer Run? The thought made Daniel sick to his stomach.

The young man picked up the Brown Bess musket and sat down just outside the front door with the weapon at the ready. He would make sure there would be no more intruders this night.

Chapter Twenty-one

Trauma

Daniel had not slept for a moment all night, as his mind wrestled with the terror of the previous evening.

What if I had ignored the sound of the door opening and delayed getting up? What if Sarah had not made her escape when she did? What if Mary had not fought back? What if...? Daniel had to stop the whirlwind of panic rushing through his mind. His heart raced with fear every time he allowed these alarming questions to run free.

The truth was that Mary was alive. God had protected her from the intruder carrying out his wicked intentions.

Despite this realization, all of them were greatly traumatized in their hearts by this malevolent encounter. And Daniel and Mary both bore physical pain from it as well.

The door to the farmhouse opened up and Widow Thomsen came out with the milk bucket in hand. Her eyes were as fatigued and swollen as Daniel's.

"Let me get that for you," Daniel said, reaching for the wooden pail. "Perhaps you should stay with Mary."

The widow looked at him, her manner subdued.

"Thank you, Daniel," she said as she handed him the bucket.

Widow Thomsen watched the weary man place the Brown Bess against the outer wall of the house. It seemed clear where the musket had come from. The look on her face revealed her repulsion at the previous owner.

"We should keep that inside by the bed in your room," the widow called out to Daniel.

He turned back to look at her and gave her a questioning look. "Inside?"

She looked up at him, shielding her eyes from the early morning sun.

"Yes," the widow said. "The barn is too far away."

The exhausted mother went back into the farmhouse and the young soldier stared after her for a moment before heading back to the barn.

Daniel's wounded leg ached sorely this morning, made worse by the night's struggle. He winced with each step, making his way slowly to the outer building. Jubo was already awake and setting up the supplies for the day's planting. He looked at Daniel and noted his red and bleary eyes.

"How are you, Mr. Lowe?" Jubo asked.

"I am grateful we are all alive, Jubo," Daniel replied. He looked squarely at his new friend. "And I am grateful to you, sir, for your help last night." Daniel fought back the tears once again as he began to milk Susannah.

"Is Miss Mary all right, sir?" Jubo asked. He was obviously distraught.

"I hope so, Jubo. I have not seen her yet today."

He resumed the rhythmic pulling at the cow's teats for a moment and then stopped.

Daniel looked down at the straw-covered floor and said, "I thought I was finished with killing when I left this war." He rubbed at his eyes and smoothed the hair back from his head.

"Killing a man is never a good thing, Mr. Lowe," Jubo said. "But sometimes it is a necessary thing."

Daniel was silent for a moment.

"Please call me Daniel, sir," he said.

Jubo looked at him and smiled.

"Yes, Mr. Daniel."

Gibb and Jubo headed out toward the field to start their day's work. Daniel had just finished the milking when he heard the voice of a child. It was the same neighbor that had come last evening with the false alarm. The young boy raced up to the house and called for the midwife. Widow Thomsen opened the door and was greeted by the frantic youngster.

"Please, Widow Thomsen, we truly need you right away this time. My mother asks you to come with haste!"

"I shall come directly, Amos," the midwife said.

Daniel set the bucket down in Susannah's stall and went over to saddle Dash for Widow Thomsen. The woman came in a moment later, her supplies in a pouch that she carried over her shoulder.

"Thank you Daniel for preparing the horse," the midwife said. "I have barely finished helping Mary this morning—she is so distraught and too bruised to even brush out her hair without great pain. Can you stay with her while I am gone? I fear for her well-being."

Daniel had never heard the widow so anguished. The young man swallowed with difficulty and said, "Of course." He felt despair over the widow's description of Mary.

"Widow Thomsen …" he began, then hesitated. "I know this is probably the worst possible time, but I have promised your daughter that I would speak to you today."

The widow stopped in her frantic preparations and looked at Daniel, her eyes full of understanding.

"About declaring your love for her, Daniel?" she asked.

Daniel swallowed nervously. "Yes … I love your daughter, ma'am, and I am asking you for your blessing."

Widow Thomsen stepped off the horse block used to reach the saddle and faced the tall young man. The midwife looked weary and somehow much older this morning.

"God and I had a long conversation last night," she began. "Actually, it was a one-sided conversation—he spoke to my heart and I listened. I have judged you unfairly from the start, Daniel. All I have been able to see is your red uniform rather than your good heart and your integrity. Mary has seen you quite clearly. She has known you to be a good man and she loves you deeply. And if it were not for you … if it were not for you, I might not even have a daughter." She quickly wiped away the tears that began falling down her cheeks. After a moment, she said, "And so, Daniel, I will defend you and your reputation to the most ardent colonial patriot. And yes, you have my blessing. I only ask that you go slowly with Mary as she recovers from her wounds. The bruises will heal faster than her heart."

Widow Thomsen climbed up onto the sidesaddle with ease and looked down at Daniel.

"And I thank you, sir, for saving my daughter."

With that, the widow prodded Dash into a fast canter so that the new babe would not be born before she could get there.

Sarah came running out of the house after her mother.

"Do not leave me here, Mother," the child cried.

The woman halted her horse and made a quick decision.

"Daniel," she called, "please help Sarah up onto the saddle with me."

Daniel limped as quickly as he could to the child and lifted her up onto the horse in front of her mother.

"Tell Mary we will be back as soon as the child is safely birthed." With that the two riders set off down the dirt road.

He stared after them until they were out of sight. He should have been relieved and elated at hearing Widow Thomsen's words of blessing. But her words had come with a price. Daniel feared that Mary's heart would be deeply wounded by the events of last night.

***

The young man slowly opened the door to the farmhouse and walked inside. Mary looked like a frightened child suddenly alarmed by the sound.

"It is I, Mary," Daniel said softly. When she saw who it was, her expression relaxed.

Her mother had helped her clean up and Mary was now dressed in a clean shift. Daniel noticed the fresh scent of lavender in the room, no doubt meant to eliminate the horrible stench of the intruder. Mary's left cheek was swollen and dark purple from the stranger's cruel blow. The young woman huddled on the edge of the bed in silence, hugging herself with a woolen shawl.

Daniel walked over to her and sat beside her on the edge of the bed. He went to take her hand and noticed that she was holding a brush. He remembered her mother saying that she was in too much pain to brush out her hair. Her long locks that flowed to her waist were disheveled and matted.

"May I brush your hair for you?" he asked.

She looked at him with mild surprise. Her eyes were moist and filled with despair. She slowly handed him her hairbrush. He began at the lower edge of her locks, gently brushing each section and slowly unraveling the twisted strands.

"I used to brush my sister Polly's hair," Daniel said, breaking the silence. "She would sometimes get upset because the servants were too busy to do her hair carefully. They would pull too hard and make her cry. She would plead for me to take over the task because I took more time to unravel the strands. Our mother was long gone by then." Daniel's eyes became moist thinking about these losses in his life.

Mary began to relax. Daniel's voice was soothing to her spirit. By the time the brush had reached the crown of her head, she was closing her eyes, the tension falling from her face.

Daniel smoothed her soft locks with his hand. "There. Your hair is lovely."

When he put the brush down, Mary turned to look at him. She noticed the dried blood on his right cheek, a reminder of his encounter with the intruder's knife. She touched his face, which made him wince. She furrowed her brow and stood up, walking to the medicine cabinet. When she returned, she cleaned off the blood and applied slippery elm to the long but shallow knife wound.

Daniel took her hand and kissed her palm slowly.

"Thank you, Mary. I'd quite forgotten it was there."

Mary looked at him with a deep pain filling her eyes. "I should not have opened the door," she said finally, her lips trembling and the tears flowing.

"What?"

She took a deep breath in between her sobs.

"The door," she said. "It was locked and I thought it was my mother returning. I should not have opened it." Her tears spilled forth like a river flowing over a burdened dam. Daniel looked at her with tenderness.

"You did not know, Mary. How could you know? This was not your fault."

He held her closely and let her sobs slowly subside. When she was finished crying, he looked at her and wiped her tears with his linen shirtsleeve.

"Come sit with me, Mary," he said. He led her to the chair by the fire. It was the same chair that he had held her in when she had been so ill with the influenza. It was the same place of comfort when she could not get warm. He sat on the wooden seat and held out his arms to her. She gingerly crawled onto his lap and curled up in his arms.

"Rest your head on my shoulder," he whispered. She found the familiar notch in his neck that seemed as if it were made just for her. She placed her hand on his chest. He once again covered her long fingers with his large hand.

Without lifting her head, she spoke for the first time without crying.

"I love you, Daniel."

The young man struggled to contain his own emotions as he answered her in kind.

"I love you too, Mary."

The exhausted couple closed their eyes and rested for the first time since last night.

Daniel was finally able to relax. He knew deep in his heart that Mary would one day be able to put aside the horror of the intruder's heartless touch. She would instead remember the tender embrace of the man who loved her.

Chapter Twenty-two

Friends

It took weeks for the purple mark on Mary's cheek to fade, but the terror from that night continued to plague Mary. Daniel could see it in her eyes every time he walked through the front door unexpectedly.

Sarah, too, had been deeply afraid ever since that night. She had become far more nervous about letting Widow Thomsen out of her sight. Her mother was patient with these fears, letting her daughters recover slowly and offering each of them ample love and attention. Daniel watched the widow take extra pains to allow them time to recover. She let them join in with the chores as much as they were able. The young man realized that he could learn much from the widow's long suffering.

"I have faith that with time, God will bring healing," she said to Daniel.

It had been over three weeks now since the dreadful incident and the widow wanted to return to some sense of normalcy. So on a bright sunny morning in early May, she surprised everyone with an unexpected question.

"Who wishes to go to the meetinghouse today for Sabbath services?" she asked.

The Thomsen daughters looked at each other and then back at their mother. They, too, were anxious for life as it once was.

Mary knew that it would never be completely the same. She would now carry with her the memory of coming face-to-face with evil. But

161

Mary desperately wanted to put this incident behind her. What better place to do it than at church, where she could worship God and be surrounded by friends?

"I shall go—if Daniel can come as well," Mary said, looking over at her intended.

It was just after dawn, and Daniel had come out of his room only a moment before. He still had the partially open eyes of someone just awakening.

"The meetinghouse?" he said, suddenly alert but with apprehension in his tone. "Would this be imprudent of me?"

Widow Thomsen looked at him with understanding. "There will be more conjectures made about you if you do not come as a part of our family," she said to allay his fears. "Besides, Mary has just completed your new waistcoat and you will be dressed quite smartly for worship."

"Waistcoat?" Daniel said in surprise. "I was not fitted for such a piece of attire."

He stared at Mary with a questioning look. A shy smile emerged on Mary's face.

"I used your old one from when you first arrived here. It guided my sewing. I worked on it when you were out in the fields every day." Mary went to the wooden chest of drawers where she had been hiding it.

"Do you like it?" she asked, holding up the vest.

Daniel looked at the richly dyed garment of blue linen that she had painstakingly pieced together each day. Each stitch was evenly placed, each button gleaned from his old waistcoat carefully covered with the same blue material to match the fine garment. He looked at it with admiration.

"This is as splendid a piece as any I have owned," he said with gratitude.

Mary smiled with relief.

"Why do you not try it on?"

Daniel carefully slipped both of his arms into the holes and buttoned the indigo-dyed vest. The fit was perfect, and very flattering to Daniel's appearance. He had never looked more handsome to his future wife.

"Perhaps you should not wear this to the meetinghouse today," Mary said teasingly.

Daniel's face fell. "Why not? It is a perfect fit and exceedingly well done."

"Because, Daniel Lowe, other young ladies may set their eyes upon you when they see how handsome you look in this waistcoat," Mary said.

It was the first time she had spoken to him in a playful manner since the incident. Daniel grinned, walked over to her, and kissed her gently on her cheek, not caring that her mother and sister were present.

"I only have eyes for you, Mary Thomsen," he said. Widow Thomsen and Sarah looked at each other, enjoying the moment.

Mary blushed but was grateful that at last she and Daniel could show affection for one another in front of her mother. She only wished that the fear in her heart would leave for good. Her recollections of Daniel's tender moments of endearment brought tears to her eyes. In her prayers, she pleaded earnestly that God would remove the memory of the intruder. She longed to set the time for her wedding to Daniel but did not want to be fearful of his embrace on her wedding night.

Thankfully, she couldn't have asked for a more patient man than her future husband. He gave her the time that she needed to recover, and his devotion was obvious and constant. This made her love him all the more.

The family hurried through the morning chores so that they would arrive at the meetinghouse early. Mary and her mother both knew that there would be much curiosity about Daniel, and they wanted to address the issue prior to the worship. The Thomsens did not wish to distract everyone's attention from the service while the townsfolk speculated about his presence.

***

Everyone from Deer Run posed the same questions. "This is Mr. Lowe from up North—in New York, I believe," Widow Thomsen said to each curious congregant. "Yes, he was injured in the war. Yes, he has been helping us out at the farm with our work and we are so grateful for his assistance."

There were a few raised eyebrows among the congregation. After all, Daniel Lowe was a complete stranger to them, and in such a small village strangers were usually seen as a threat. But the townsfolk knew

163

the Thomsens well. They had been a respected family in the community for many years and there was no cause to mistrust any friend of the family.

When they finally settled into their pew, the Thomsens and Daniel breathed a collective sigh of relief. All that is except Sarah, who still did not know the details about Daniel's origin. The young girl was oblivious to the tension the rest of the family was feeling. She was just grateful to be back at church with all of her friends.

As the singing of one of Isaac Watts' hymns began, Mary smiled. It was the same song that Sarah had requested last winter when the young girl was ill. Mary and Sarah glanced at each other, both recalling the soothing lyrics. This was the song that had inspired both admiration from Daniel and a discussion about the shepherd who guards his flock. Mary glanced at Daniel and noticed he was looking at her. The couple smiled as they remembered the special moment.

Reverend Phillips began his sermon; today's topic was forgiveness of our enemies. The subject had been a struggle for many colonists as the war waged on between the King's army and General Washington's. With the onset of warmer weather, the battles would likely increase, and all the residents were feeling the tension. As Mary scanned the faces of each congregant she read fear in their eyes. Missus Burke wiped a tear off her cheek and Missus Stearns struggled to maintain her composure. Nearly everyone fretted for a loved one at war and Mary knew they were each wondering if their family member would be the next casualty.

She looked down at her hands and wondered about James.

Lord, please protect my older brother, Mary prayed in her heart.

When she looked up from her prayer of supplication, her thoughts were suddenly distracted by what she perceived as a completely different kind of threat—the persistent glances of the Howard sisters looking straight at Daniel.

Buxom and brash, Hettie and Matilda Howard had an "interesting reputation," as Widow Thomsen would say. They had much to offer a man's desire and were not afraid to flaunt it. Even in so sacred a setting, they seemed more interested in earthly desires than heavenly ones. Mary wished she could discreetly offer each a kerchief to cover her endowments—not that either would accept such assistance in the cause of modesty.

The two sisters whispered back and forth and giggled, casting several glances towards Daniel. He did not appear to notice the two young women. Instead, he listened intently to the preaching. Mary tried to focus on the reverend's words as well, but she could not ignore the lascivious young women.

In exasperation, Mary shifted her position on the pew closer to Daniel. This caught Daniel's attention as her leg was slightly touching his own. He looked over at Mary in mild surprise but seemed pleased. He carefully touched her finger with one of his own, which made Mary smile. She circumspectly stroked one of her fingers across the back of his hand, which made him both grin and shift his weight on the pew.

Daniel's occasional glances warmed Mary's heart, and she soon forgot about the Howard sisters. She could not wait to be alone with him later. When the sermon was finished, the congregation paused for a time of eating. Since the weather was warm, many had brought blankets to place on the lawn of the meetinghouse. The Thomsens had brought simple fare of cheeses, breads, and dried fruit, and they all ate vigorously.

"Why does going to church make one so hungry?" Sarah asked. The ravenous group nodded in agreement.

When every last bite of their meal was consumed, Mary's friend Hannah White walked over and greeted all of them warmly.

"It is so good to see you, Mary. And Widow Thomsen and Sarah. You are all looking well," Hannah said. The young woman was twenty years of age, with light hair and kind blue eyes. Her soft manner of speaking occasionally made it difficult to hear her words. Mary suspected that her overbearing father was the source of Hannah's shyness.

Mary stood up and hugged her dear friend.

"You look very well also," she said with a warm smile. "Hannah, I would like you to meet Mr. Daniel Lowe. Daniel, this is Miss Hannah White. Her father is one of the Selectman from our town."

"It is so good to meet you, Mr. Lowe," Hannah said.

"It is my pleasure to meet you, Miss White," Daniel answered, rising to his feet.

"May I speak to you in private, Hannah?" Mary asked.

"Of course, Mary," she replied with a questioning look on her face.

The two young women stepped aside and spoke in private. It was obvious to anyone watching them that their conversation involved happy news. The long-time friends hugged and then returned to the group awaiting them.

"Sir, you know that you have won the heart of the most sought after young woman in Deer Run, do you not?" Hannah said, keeping her voice low so as not to alert others nearby.

Daniel grinned and responded quietly.

"I do not deserve such a treasure as Miss Mary Thomsen. But she has agreed to my request to become my wife, and I am a most fortunate man."

Mary's countenance glowed brightly at his words, and her cheeks grew warm.

"I think it is my friend that feels fortunate," Hannah said with a smile. Then her expression turned sober. "Mary, have you heard news of your brother James?"

Mary's face grew serious.

"No, Hannah. We have heard nothing," Mary said sadly. "He may have tried to write but his letters can be intercepted. I assume you have received no correspondence as well?"

"Nothing," Hannah said, fighting back the tears. "Every day I await the post rider and every day there is no word from him." She paused for a moment to build her resolve. "But I shall continue to wait for him, as he asked me to before he left."

Mary touched her friend's hand. "I know he will come back to you, Hannah—to all of us."

Hannah gave a brave smile to her friend and bid them all farewell before returning to her father.

Mr. Myles Eaton approached the group. The robust widower with the hearty laugh grinned at Widow Thomsen and tipped his tri-cornered hat. His success in raising fine livestock was well known in the community and he generously helped out many who were in need. But his spirit of giving seemed especially focused on one particular neighbor—the widow, Ruth Thomsen.

"Would tomorrow be a good day to bring those little piggies over to your farm, Widow Thomsen?" the farmer asked. "They're a fine lot this year, ma'am."

"Why yes, Mr. Eaton, tomorrow would be an excellent day. We shall have the enclosure ready for them. I thank you, sir."

He tipped his tricornered hat once again.

"After a bit then, ma'am," he said, walking back to his large horse, the same animal that had trudged through the snow last winter to carry Widow Thomsen home after the blizzard. Winter was a distant memory today as they sat in the balmy breeze that carried the scents of lilacs and apple blossoms through the air.

After everyone had had a chance to rest, the congregation returned to the meetinghouse for afternoon service. Mary walked closely to Daniel, steering him clear of the Howard sisters whenever it seemed they might approach.

The preaching resumed for several more hours. Mary noticed many in the sedate group struggling to keep their eyes open. When their attempts failed, one of the ushers would faithfully bring the long pole with the squirrel's tail on the end to tickle the nose of the dreamer. The sight of this always made Mary laugh. Daniel found the practice quite amusing as well. They locked eyes and grinned at one another.

When the church meeting was finally over, the sleepy congregation slowly made their way out of the wooden building. The Thomsens were in somewhat of a hurry this afternoon as Aunt Prudence would be arriving at any time. She was coming to pick up Jubo and Gibb and bring them back to Bridgewater. The Thomsens bid farewell to their friends at church, explaining their need to hurry home.

Mary and Daniel walked together, followed by Widow Thomsen and Sarah. The mile-long hike was mostly uphill, and they walked as briskly as they could. They arrived home just in time for Aunt Prudence's arrival. This would be the woman's first time meeting Daniel, and Mary did not know what to expect from her aunt. She did not have long to wait for the answer.

"Your intended?" Aunt Prudence said with obvious delight. "So you have taken my advice! Good lass!"

While Daniel shook Jubo's hand and then Gibb's, Aunt Prudence sized up Mary's future husband. Prudence leaned over to her great niece and whispered something in Mary's ear. The young woman's eyes opened wide and her face turned bright red.

"Aunt Prudence!" she said, aghast.

The older woman smiled and continued to stare at Daniel as the wagon pulled out of the farmyard. Daniel waved good-bye to her as she drove off. He looked at Mary with a confused expression.

"What did she whisper to you?" he asked, feeling a bit uneasy.

Mary glanced briefly at him and then looked away.

"Nothing that I shall ever share with you," she said. She walked toward the house with her eyes looking downward. Daniel stood there, wondering why he felt like livestock at an auction.

***

The next morning, Widow Thomsen hastened to get through the morning chores. She was in a hurry to prepare the pigpen and Mr. Eaton was expected at any time.

"I can clean the pen, Widow Thomsen," Daniel offered.

Mary looked at him and shook her head. He did not have any experience with the foul-smelling chore.

"I had best help you, Daniel," she said.

The couple walked out toward the field behind the barn. The enclosure was as far from the house as it could be placed but still close enough to easily tend the little piglets.

"Why is the pen so far out back?" Daniel asked.

Mary looked at him and stifled a laugh. "You have obviously never smelled a pigpen before, Daniel Lowe," she said.

"It has been quite some time," he answered. "By the way Mary Thomsen, why were you tempting me at church yesterday? I was trying to concentrate on the reverend's words and you were doing your best to distract me."

She took hold of his arm. "I was doing my best to distract you from the glances of two sets of ladies' eyes."

"And I missed that? Were they pretty?" he teased her, grinning broadly.

"Daniel, you are incorrigible," she said in mock distress.

"And you," he said taking her in his arms, "are far too beautiful for me to be tempted by any other woman."

"And you," Mary said, "will be judged by your Maker for speaking such lies."

Daniel grew serious. "But I am not lying," he said in a whisper. He drew her close to himself and for the first time since her encounter with the intruder, Daniel tenderly kissed Mary's lips. She did not pull away but reveled in the gentle touch that she remembered well. Daniel's kiss became more impassioned, but he could feel Mary's arms becoming tense. He immediately stopped, seeing fear flash across her face. Silently, he cursed the intruder.

Mary began to tremble. "I am sorry, Daniel," she said, tears welling in her eyes.

Daniel held her closely. "You have nothing to apologize for," he said. "There are times when I wish I could kill him all over again. And yet, I know that is wrong and I pray that God will forgive my unforgiving heart."

"You are a gift to me, Daniel Lowe. And I know that soon, I shall be able to forget that man's touch—because I long so for yours."

They held each other for several moments before resuming their task. The two had no sooner finished cleaning out the pen than Mr. Eaton's wagon came down the road. They could hear the squeals of the little animals coming from the crate in the back. Widow Thomsen and Sarah came outdoors to greet the man and his noisy cargo.

"Look at them, Mother," Sarah said excitedly. "Can we name them?"

The widow and Mr. Eaton looked at each other. Their faces seemed to envision the child's pet being turned into Sunday sausage.

"Probably not the best idea, miss," Mr. Eaton replied.

Sarah, Widow Thomsen, and Mary each picked up one of the squirming piglets and laughed at their active antics. They each placed a piglet over their left shoulder, much as they would a human baby, and carried them out to the pen. The two men stared after the women with the "infants" over their shoulders.

"Some hideous-looking babies on those ladies' shoulders, eh?" Mr. Eaton jested. "Looks like Queen Charlotte's brood."

Daniel tried not to laugh but nodded in assent. He and his fellow soldiers in the camp had often discussed the plain look of their country's queen.

"You have a quick wit, Mr. Eaton," Daniel said.

Mr. Eaton continued to stare at the ladies.

"Now that's a handsome woman," he said, staring at Widow Thomsen.

Daniel looked at Mary.

"Yes, she is, sir," he said with admiration.

Mr. Eaton looked at him and slapped his shoulder in jest.

"I was talking about the widow, Mr. Lowe," he said.

Daniel's face became confused.

"Widow Thomsen?" he asked.

"You young lads cannot imagine the beauty us old men see in a woman like her, can ya?"

"So ... you are setting your eyes on Mary's mother?" Daniel asked incredulously. "Are you married, sir?"

"Was. Been widowed some years now. Looking out for your lady's mother, are ya? Good lad," Mr. Eaton said. Then he added, "These long winters get mighty cold, sir, if ya know what I mean."

Daniel did not know how to respond. He was completely bewildered by this conversation. There was much that his young mind was trying to comprehend.

Mr. Eaton became serious.

"So I understand you have set your heart on Miss Thomsen. She is a fine young woman," he said.

"Yes, sir," Daniel replied. He smiled as he looked up at the field where Mary, her mother, and her sister were laughing at the piglets.

"You've been at war, Mr. Lowe," Mr. Eaton said. "To be blunt, sir, I hope you have not brought home any peculiar diseases from the ladies in the camps. Wouldn't want to see Mary getting hurt now, would we?"

Daniel looked at Mr. Eaton squarely. "I have not, sir. I stayed away from the trulls and doxies. It's not that I was not tempted, but I saw enough of my friends suffering from one night's pleasure that it did not seem worth the cost."

Mr. Eaton paused for a long moment to look at the ground. He stared downward for so long that Daniel began to get nervous.

Have I said something to give myself away? Trulls and doxies! he lamented to himself. *You are a fool, Daniel Lowe. Your own words have given you away.*

The former British soldier tried not to panic, but he felt a sweat beginning on his brow. When Mr. Eaton finally looked up he put his hand on Daniel's shoulder.

"Widow Thomsen told me how you took care of Mary when she suffered from the grippe last winter," Mr. Eaton said. "You're a good man, Mr. Lowe." The farmer started to unload the hay that he had brought for Widow Thomsen's horse and cow. "I figure the way to a woman's heart is through the stomach of her livestock," Mr. Eaton said with a laugh.

He paused in his work and looked again at Daniel. He noticed the look of terror on the young man's face and placed his hand on his shoulder in a fatherly manner.

"Any friend of Widow Thomsen's is a friend of mine as well," he said. "Any secrets you may have, lad, are safe with me."

Chapter Twenty-three

Freedom

Mr. Eaton became a regular guest in the Thomsen home that summer.

The widower lived all alone now. His youngest daughter had married the previous winter and the loss made him feel the absence of his wife even more. He felt the loneliest at the evening meal, he had confided to Widow Thomsen one day. She was more than willing to oblige him with the hospitality of a hearty dinner several times a week.

"It is the least I can do for the man in return for all he does for our family," the widow said, explaining Mr. Eaton's increasing presence at the Thomsen table to Mary.

Still, Mary wondered about this turn of events. She asked Daniel what he thought about it when they were walking towards the town square. They were going to the second anniversary celebration of the Declaration of Independence. It was early evening and the mosquitoes were having a feast on the young couple. The two were trying desperately to avoid being bitten. Daniel thought about Mary's question before replying.

"I think Mr. Eaton is quite fond of your mother," he said, swatting at yet another insect. He tried to keep his voice low, since the widow and Sarah were not too far behind.

Mary seemed startled. "Fond?" she repeated with surprise, then remembered to keep her voice low as well. "How can that be? My mother is far too old for such affection, do you not think?"

"I think," Daniel said slowly, "that your mother and Mr. Eaton are free to decide if they want to become friends—or even develop a deep affection for one another."

The young woman became silent as she pondered his words. The thought of her mother setting her eyes on another man was disquieting, not to mention unexpected, but she knew that Daniel was right. Both her mother and Mr. Eaton were widowed and they were certainly free to pursue one another. However, it would take Mary some time to get used to this idea.

As the group of four approached the festivities, they saw the object of their discussion approaching.

"Good day, Mr. Eaton," Widow Thomsen said brightly. Mary wondered if her mother was always this animated around the older man. The widow's cheeks even seemed a deeper shade of red when she looked at him.

"It's a good day when we can celebrate the freedom of this new country of ours," Mr. Eaton said happily.

The whole town of Deer Run had come out for the celebration. Daniel was curious but nervous about participating. His past still weighed heavily upon him, an anxiety that only Mary and her mother could understand. The heat was inducing volumes of sweat from everyone, Daniel most of all.

"Are you all right, Daniel?" Mary asked, noticing the strain on his face.

"Is my anxiousness that obvious? Perhaps I had best practice looking relaxed."

Mary took his arm. Her demeanor and touch calmed the young soldier. He limped beside her amongst the townsfolk who were lifting up their ale tankards and singing loudly about freedom from "bloody King George."

Several of the men in the town were setting up wood for the bonfires. These would be kindled in celebration of the United States of America declaring its liberty. The fires would be lit simultaneously right after the reading of the Declaration of Independence by Selectman Jonathan Grant.

Children were running everywhere. Some of them were playing "Ring around the Rosie" around the village liberty pole. Most villages in Massachusetts as well as other colonies had set up these wooden poles in prominent positions in the center of town. They were a silent declaration of their support for the troops fighting in battle and their own wish for freedom from England. A ribbon was attached to the pole for each Minuteman from Deer Run. Asa Thomsen's ribbon was now a black one.

Since most of the younger men were off at war, there were not the usual sporting events included in the festivities. Instead, clusters of older men and young teenagers stood around discussing the affairs of this struggling nation. When they saw Daniel approaching arm-in-arm with Mary, they drew him in to the conversation.

"So, Mr. Lowe," said one gent with long, thinning hair as he pulled the young man into the group, "what is your take on the French getting involved in helping out our troops? Those bloody frogs were the enemy not so many years ago, and now we're lookin' to fight side-by-side with 'em."

The villager wiped the sweat off of his forehead while awaiting an answer. Daniel tried not to appear surprised, for he had not yet heard of this alliance with France. He weighed his words carefully before replying.

"I think that, in the course of time and various circumstances, those who were once our enemies can just as quickly become our friends. Much to everyone's surprise," Daniel said, trying to hide his anxiety from these patriots. All the men in the group stared at him while they pondered his words.

The silence was abruptly broken by another gentleman with thick gray hair and a tankard of ale. The liquid spirits kept spilling every time the excitable man spoke.

"See," he said, "I told you it could work."

Everyone began to talk at once and Daniel felt Mary's arm encouraging him away. She understood that this was not a comfortable setting with so many strangers, and he with so much to hide.

"Ah, that Miss Thomsen already has her hooks in you, Mr. Lowe," the men teased him as they left the group. Daniel looked back at the group of men and smiled.

When he turned around again he breathed deeply and whispered, "Thank you." Mary squeezed his arm gently. "You are a rock of strength to me," he said.

"We can go back to the farm, Daniel," Mary said. "We can make up a plausible excuse."

"No, I shall be all right. This is something I must do if I am to be a part of your life here," he said.

She stared at him affectionately. "I hope you know how deeply I love you, Daniel Lowe," she said. She wished she could kiss him right here in the midst of the town gathering.

"If you keep talking that way, Miss Thomsen, I shall have to kiss you passionately right here in front of this whole town," he said under his breath, only half teasingly.

The town bell rang out for the first of thirteen times, each ring representing an American colony. She and Daniel watched as a group of thirteen men with muskets fired toward an empty field. Each gun was loaded and shot thirteen times as a salute to the new nation.

It was late in the day, so everyone began to gather outside the meetinghouse for the reading of the Declaration of Independence. It was a somber moment filled with emotion as the words of Thomas Jefferson were read by a veteran of the French and Indian War. The reader was Selectman Grant. When Daniel heard the man's name announced by Reverend Phillips, he looked over at Mary inquisitively. Mary looked at him and nodded.

"Yes," she said, "that is Josiah's father."

The older man was similar in appearance to Josiah, but the resemblance ended there, as the father had a more humble demeanor in both his countenance and his speech. He read the Declaration with a clear, audible tone, obviously moved by the passion underlying the text. It was easy to understand why Mr. Grant had been chosen to do the reading.

"When in the course of human events it becomes necessary for one people to dissolve the political bands which have connected them with another and to assume among the powers of the earth, the separate and equal station to which the Laws of Nature and of Nature's God entitle them, a decent respect to the opinions of mankind requires that they should declare the causes which impel them to a separation.

"We hold these truths to be self-evident, that all men are created equal, that they are endowed by their Creator with certain unalienable Rights, that among these are Life, Liberty and the Pursuit of Happiness. That to secure these rights, Governments are instituted among men, deriving their just powers from the consent of the governed. That whenever any Form of Government becomes destructive of these ends, it is the Right of the People to alter or abolish it, and to institute new Government…"

The speaker continued with the words that listed the "long train of abuses" King George had levied against the colonies.

Daniel appeared in awe of the words. He had never heard this document read before or seen it in print. The colonists' message of outrage and their fervor to obtain justice for the people of America seemed to awaken his understanding of the Revolution.

Sunset was upon them, and despite the dimming light, Mary noticed the tears on Daniel's face. She did not fully grasp their meaning, but she placed her arm around his waist and rested her head against his shoulder. His spirit had clearly been moved by the whole event. He put his arm around her shoulders and she could feel him trembling.

Mr. Grant slowly and fervently read the final line to the audience of listeners: "And for the support of this Declaration," he read, "with a firm reliance on the protection of Divine Providence, we mutually pledge to each other our Lives, our Fortunes, and our Sacred Honor."

Selectman Grant rolled up the parchment and slowly walked off of the meetinghouse steps.

There was not a dry face in the group of onlookers who stood in silence. The mood was so somber that none of them was of a mind to move. Everyone knew what this document had already cost, and they all knew that they were not yet finished paying the price of this Revolution. Many had already paid with their lives.

All at once, one of the town leaders shouted out, "Light the bonfires!" The flames were lit in the three piles of wood simultaneously. It was a splendid sight, as the glow from the fires glimmered across the tear-stained faces in the crowd. The whole town stood watching the flames for several moments in silence.

Gradually, hushed conversations began in a few small groups while other townsfolk slowly began their walk home. The Thomsens were in this latter group, somberly heading back toward the farm. Mr. Eaton approached Widow Thomsen and offered to drive them all back to the farm on his wagon. Sarah was beginning to fall asleep, leaning against her mother, and the widow gladly accepted the ride.

Mary spoke up. "I think Daniel and I will walk back, Mr. Eaton, but thank you for your kind offer." She wanted some time alone with her young man. She was anxious to talk with him about the days' events. Mr. Eaton gave an understanding smile to the young couple.

"Don't get lost on the way," he said teasingly.

When the wagon pulled out of sight ahead of them, Mary looked at Daniel.

"You look troubled," she said.

The young man stopped walking for a moment. Now that they were out of sight of the townspeople, he took her in his arms and kissed her deeply. She responded in kind and they held each other for a long while. When they resumed walking, Daniel finally spoke.

"For the first time today, I've begun to understand this Revolution. Not just in my mind but in my heart as well. It both excites me and grieves me, as I feel as if everything I have been doing for the past few years has been for naught." He paused briefly. "The arrogance of the King had become my arrogance. I have been a part of hurting innocent people, forcing them to submit to the Crown."

His words caught in his throat.

"It was wrong. I was wrong," he said.

Mary paused in mid-step and took his face in both of her hands.

"You thought you were doing the right thing," she said, staring into his eyes. "I know you Daniel. You are a man who would choose the honorable way."

He put his arms around her waist.

"But it was not always honorable," he said. "I can still hear those words read from the Declaration: 'sent hither swarms of Officers to harass our people and eat out their substance.' I was one of those officers, swarming like a hornet, following the King's orders." He paused, struggling to contain his emotions. "It was unforgivable."

He looked off in the distance down the hill, observing the lighted bonfires still glowing dimly in the darkness.

"Nothing is unforgivable in the eyes of God," Mary said. She gently held his face to look at hers.

"But can you forgive me for my part in this war?"

"Yes, Daniel. You do not need my forgiveness. But if you are asking for it, yes, I forgive you."

She stood on her tiptoes and kissed him. He held onto her as never before and wept for so much that he had lost, and for all that he had gained but did not deserve. They embraced in silence, and then just as silently, resumed the walk up the hill toward the farm.

Mr. Eaton had already passed them on the way back down the hill. He waved to them both in his friendly manner, winking at Daniel as he drove by. When they reached the farmyard, Daniel noticed the outdoor fire from earlier that day. The widow and Mary had been doing washing in the huge kettle over those flames and there were still a few embers glowing in the darkness.

"Please wait here," said Daniel. He walked over to the barn and after a few moments walked out with something in his hands. As he drew closer to her, Mary could see what the object was—his red coat of the King's army.

Daniel walked over to the glowing coals. He took one last look at the stained scarlet wool and placed it firmly on the fire. The young soldier drew Mary away from the heat. As the fibers fed the embers, it quickly ignited in a rupture of energy that made Mary gasp. Placing his arm around her, they watched the uniform disintegrate into ashes and molten metal. The deed was done.

Mary turned and looked up at Daniel. The two kissed with a passion that encompassed so many thoughts and emotions. The couple's embrace had never lingered for so long and Mary's heart was racing as never before. She could feel Daniel holding her closer than he had ever done and she had a sudden and surprising realization. Not only was she no longer filled with fear about the touch of the intruder, but she did not want this kiss to stop.

In a moment of clear thinking, she pushed Daniel away. His lips were moist and his eyes heavy. He stared at her as he tried to catch his breath.

"You are no longer afraid of me," he said.

"I am only afraid that I will not stop," she said, trembling. She took a step away from him.

"Can we marry soon, then—so we do not need to stop?"

"Yes," she said. "The sooner the better."

Chapter Twenty-four

United

"I don't know what she sees in that face, Daniel Lowe," the young man said to himself as he studied his reflection in a small mirror. "You look quite the ragged bloke to me."

It was July 28, the day of the wedding. The soldier had spent little time perusing his appearance in the last few months. As he stood in the barn observing his reflection, he was once again disconcerted to see the long red scar on his right cheek. It was a permanent reminder of the intruder's knife. But the young man also had an older look about him—lines etched in his skin that reflected the last two years of pain and struggle. Anyone might have easily mistaken him for a man several years older than his twenty-three years of age.

As he shaved away the last remnants of facial bristle, he went too close to his skin, causing a small cut.

"Blasted razor," he said angrily. "That will help your appearance."

He wiped away the blood as best he could and started to put on his white linen shirt. He realized how nervous he was as his fingers began to tremble while buttoning up the garment.

For the first time in many months, Daniel was thinking about his father back home in England. Here Daniel was about to be wed, yet his parent had no idea that the event was taking place. There were so many things he would have liked to ask his father, but communicating during the war was too much of a risk.

"So how is the future husband doing this morning?" The voice of Mr. Eaton broke into the young man's thoughts. Daniel turned to look at him. "I see you've been wrestling with an angry razor there," the older man said.

"I am all thumbs this morning," Daniel said, still trying to finish up the last of his shirt buttons.

"A bit shaky there, lad?" Mr. Eaton said, patting Daniel on the shoulder. "You'll be fine. No regrets about this wedding?"

Daniel looked at the man in surprise. "Regrets about marrying Mary? Good Lord, no. I still cannot believe she will have me. Just look at me," he said, pointing to his scar. "And that is not the worst of the lot. My leg wound is hideously scarred—I hope it does not frighten her."

Mr. Eaton stared at Daniel.

"If you think Mary Thomsen would be terrified by a mere scar on a leg, then you do not know your future wife. She is made of much hardier stock than you know, lad. Besides, I've seen the way Mary looks at you. I've never seen her look at another lad like that before. You're a lucky man, Daniel Lowe."

The young groom beamed. He took his blue waistcoat off of a hook on the wall and slipped his arms through the sleeve holes. He turned toward Mr. Eaton. "May I talk to you—man to man, that is?"

"Aye, be happy to," Mr. Eaton said. He was touched by the close friendship that was developing between the two men. "Never got to have a weddin' talk with a young man before. Had all girls, we did—seven of 'em!"

Daniel's eyes widened.

"Seven lasses?"

"Yep," Mr. Eaton said. "Got 'em all married off now. Lots of grand babies, too."

"You must be very proud." Daniel hesitated for a moment and took a deep breath. "So ... were you and Missus Eaton ... happy?"

"You mean under the quilts?" Mr. Eaton laughed. "Aye, very happy. And those seven daughters? They didn't all start out in this world as *my* idea, if you know what I mean," the older man said, patting him heartily on the shoulder.

Daniel smiled nervously. Mr. Eaton regarded the young man with a look of sympathy.

"I remember my own weddin' day these many years ago, lad." He put his arm in a fatherly gesture around Daniel's shoulders. "Come. Take a walk with me."

***

The two men were in a deep conversation in the distance when Mary looked out the window from the farmhouse.

"I wonder what Daniel and Mr. Eaton are doing?" she asked. "You don't suppose Daniel has changed his mind and Mr. Eaton is trying to talk him in to staying, do you?" Mary asked. She clutched a lace cap and twisted it nervously back and forth in her hands. It was the cap that she would be wearing for the ceremony.

"That is not likely, dear," Widow Thomsen said. She shook her head in exasperation. "Mary, you will ruin that lace if you keep twisting it like that. And please sit back down and let me finish your hair."

The bride-to-be was wearing the same indigo-dyed dress that her mother had worn on her wedding day. It was made of a soft linen fabric that felt cool and comfortable on this extraordinarily warm summer morning. The lace kerchief that fitted at the neckline matched the cap that would complete her attire. Mary kept pacing the small room that was to be hers and Daniels. She had waited so long for this day. Now she was desperately afraid that something would interfere with the wedding.

"Once and for all, Mary, please sit down!" the widow said, growing impatient with her daughter's fidgeting. The young woman finally resigned herself to sitting still and placed herself on the edge of the bed. She sat at an angle so her mother could reach her hair. "Where are the blue and green quilts, Mary?" Widow Thomsen asked, looking down at the bed that the couple would soon share.

Mary turned to her Mother with a mischievous smile.

"It is a surprise—for Daniel," she said.

It was obviously a private surprise, as Mary offered no further explanation. Widow Thomsen did not press for details. She understood that Mary was becoming a married woman. There would be some things the daughter would not want to share with her.

"Mother, I am a little nervous." Mary turned around as the last hairpin was placed. "Weren't you at all ... fearful?"

The widow smiled in sympathy, remembering her own wedding day.

"I was terrified," she admitted, "but I was so in love with your father, the fears slowly melted away." Widow Thomsen swept a piece of Mary's hair that had loosened from its pin back into its position. "Your father was a gentle man and ... I think he was as nervous as I was."

"But ... what if I do not please him?" Mary asked. "What if he is not happy with me?"

Widow Thomsen put her arm around her daughter. "Let us have a talk," the widow said.

***

The wedding was a simple event with very few guests. Mr. Eaton was there, of course, encouraging Daniel with an occasional smile. Hannah White had come at Mary's request, holding the bouquet of lavender flowers and roses for Mary while she and Daniel said their vows.

The bride and groom's eyes were locked upon each other as they promised to love and cherish one another through sickness and health. Reverend Phillips officiated the ceremony. He grinned broadly at the nervous couple as he read the words that would unite them as husband and wife.

Widow Thomsen and Sarah wore their best linen dresses. The mother fought back tears at the sight of her daughter becoming a married woman. Mary would always be her daughter, but now she would be, first and foremost, someone's wife.

As Daniel took Mary's hands, he noticed that hers were as moist as his own. He looked at her long fingers remembering the first time he had laid eyes upon them back in the woods. It seemed so very long ago. So much had occurred since then. But he could still remember the feel of her fingers smoothing away the sores on his hands and her gentle touch offering him comfort.

Mary also glanced down at Daniel's hands holding hers. She thought of his comforting touch when she had been so ill. She recalled his protective grip on her after the assault by the intruder. These were the hands that had held her, loved her, cared for her.

They both looked at each other's eyes as they completed their vows. Their words affirmed in front of this small gathering that the couple had decided, no matter what, that their love would endure. They would not allow anything in this world to tear them apart. No war, no set of ideals, no government would ever come between them.

"I now declare that you, Daniel, and you, Mary, are married in the eyes of God and according to the laws of the Commonwealth of Massachusetts," Reverend Phillips concluded. He looked over at Daniel. "You may now kiss your wife."

The new groom paused only briefly before leaning down to his eager wife with trembling lips. Mary's were trembling as well, but she warmly returned the kiss.

This is really happening, she thought. *We are truly husband and wife.* The realization filled her with a sense of joy that she could hardly describe.

The hugs and handshakes of congratulations began. Wine was poured for all, except for Sarah, who had turned seven in June. She was given some cider instead. Mr. Eaton continued to pat Daniel on the back, giving him an occasional mischievous wink. Hannah, though clearly happy, occasionally wiped away an errant tear from her eye. Sarah was dancing around the room, asking for another piece of the spicy wedding cake that Widow Thomsen had made.

But Daniel and Mary only had eyes for each other. When they felt they had lingered an appropriate amount of time with the guests, the young couple looked at each other and slipped out the door.

Widow Thomsen was sitting across from the reverend. She was discussing Daniel's plans to build a log cabin on the road to Deer Run. It was a section of the Thomsen farm that she was deeding over to the couple as a wedding gift.

"I was just telling Mary ... Mary?" Widow Thomsen began looking around the room for the new bride. The reverend's back was to the window and the widow was relieved, because at that same instant she saw Daniel and Mary running off into the woods. The widow's eyes widened at the sight and her face turned red. This prompted the reverend to follow her gaze toward the window.

Before he could see the couple escaping amongst the trees, she gently grabbed his arm and said, "More wine, Reverend Phillips?"

***

Daniel and Mary were out of breath from running and laughing. When he knew they were out of sight of the farmhouse, Daniel pulled on her arm to stop her. He drew her close to himself and started kissing and embracing her more freely than he ever had before.

Breathless, Mary pushed against his chest.

"Wait," she said laughing.

Daniel was crestfallen. "Wait?" he said in confusion. "Why?"

"I have a surprise for you. Meet me at the wigwam," she said. Mary backed away from her husband a few steps and pulled off her lace cap. She then untied the kerchief at the neckline of her bodice, removed it, and threw it playfully at Daniel. She smiled flirtatiously and then ran off into the woods.

"You are a cruel wife," Daniel called after her as he struggled to keep up with his new bride. His leg was aching and he had to slow down his pace. This gave Mary the advantage of arriving there several moments ahead of him.

When the young husband finally came to the familiar bark enclosure, he slowly opened the door. What he saw made his heart stir.

Mary had set up their first marriage bed. She had placed piles of fresh hay on the ground—hay that she had carried one armload at a time from the Thomsen farm. On top of the straw, she had laid two clean quilts. A flask of wine was lying next to the quilts and bouquets of lavender flowers were everywhere, filling the wigwam with their sweet aroma.

The young bride had taken out every pin from her hair. Her waist-length locks enveloped her shoulders, which were covered only with her thin linen night shift.

Daniel could barely breathe as he began to fumble with the buttons on his waistcoat.

Mary saw he was having difficulty and said shyly, "Let me help." She carefully undid each button that she had lovingly sewn. She touched his chest and looked up at her groom.

"Welcome home, my husband," she whispered softly to him.

He leaned over to kiss her and then turned to close the door of the wigwam.

Chapter Twenty-five

Letters

Dawn was breaking that late August morning when Daniel awoke. The window was open, allowing a soft breeze to cool down the humid air. In the distant woods, Daniel heard the mournful cooing of a pheasant looking for its mate. Susannah gave a gentle bellow in the barn as if to hurry up the hands that would milk her and Dash whinnied, anxious to start her day before the August heat set in. The smell of the maturing crops in the field wafted through the open window, competing with the aroma of lavender water that was the scent of the woman lying next to him in bed. He nuzzled in closer to the back of her neck and kissed her skin and hair.

Mary stirred slightly but did not yet awaken. Daniel held her closely, still marveling at the circumstances that had brought them together at such a time and place. On occasion, he rubbed his eyes to make sure he had not just imagined that Mary was his wife.

Daniel caressed her skin and kissed her again on her shoulder. She started to move slightly and opened her eyes sleepily.

"Happy birthday, Mary," Daniel said in hushed tones so as not to awaken Widow Thomsen and Sarah in the next room.

Mary smiled dreamily and turned to face her husband.

"Thank you, Daniel," she said. He leaned over his young wife and kissed her on her lips. As the kiss became more passionate, they heard Widow Thomsen close the front door on her way to milk Susannah.

The young husband looked mischievously at Mary. He threw the quilts over them both and enveloped her in his arms.

***

When the couple emerged from their room, Sarah was still asleep but Widow Thomsen was just getting back from feeding the livestock and milking Susannah.

"It's going to be another hot day, I am afraid," the widow said, wiping the perspiration from her forehead. Widow Thomsen suddenly stopped her morning activities and grinned at her older daughter

"Happy birthday, Mary," she said, giving her a hug. "Twenty years of age. It does not seem possible." The widow always struggled to hold back sentimental tears on any of her children's birthdays, and today was no exception.

"Thank you, Mother," Mary said.

"Yes, Mother Thomsen, thank you for having Mary," Daniel said, giving his wife a hug too. "I cannot imagine my life without her."

"Nor can I imagine life without you," Mary said, kissing him slowly on the lips before returning to the hearth to stir the gruel.

Sarah was now sitting up in bed rubbing her eyes and yawning.

"Happy birthday," she said to her older sister. "When do we get to eat your cake?"

"Later," Widow Thomsen said, "after we have our supper. Hannah is coming to join us."

Hannah White had shared Mary's birthday dinner with the family every year for as long as the Thomsens could remember. It had been at Mary's fifteenth birthday when James first began to notice Hannah as someone who was more than just Mary's childhood friend. James was seventeen then and could not take his eyes off the young farm girl. His obvious stares of appreciation for Hannah's beauty finally forced Widow Thomsen to send him out to do some chores.

"Mother, do you remember when James tripped and fell?" Mary said, laughing at the memory. "He was so taken with Hannah at my fifteenth birthday party that he completely missed the step outside to go and milk Susannah. Poor James turned so red in the face! It was all Hannah could do not to burst out laughing!"

Widow Thomsen chuckled at the recollection.

It is good to see Mother smile so, Mary thought.

"How come I do not remember that?" Sarah asked, feeling left out of the party spirit.

"Because, little miss, you were only two," Daniel said. "If it makes you feel better, I do not remember the occasion either."

"Daniel and I do not remember it," Sarah said, proudly. The young girl delighted in the fact that she could now call him by his Christian name. But she had told her brother-in-law that he could still call her "little miss." She declared that that was his special name for her and no one else could call her that. Sarah and Daniel looked at each other with what appeared to be smugness. Mary rolled her eyes at the two but grinned in amusement. She was so grateful that her husband fit in so well with her family, as if he had been a part of them all along. And now that he was a part of her, she felt complete.

"Let us get the chores done before the heat sets in," Widow Thomsen said, fanning herself with a towel.

Daniel drank a large tankard of cider before heading out to the field of flax. No other crop on this farm took as much time or effort as this one did. The new farmer had already been hard at work for several days using the large wooden flax brake that separated the woody fibers. It was a strenuous job that required heavy muscle and tenacity, and in this heat, a strong constitution.

The young man had become quite adept at using the tool, pounding the blades repeatedly to break down the fibers, which were then spun and woven into processed strands. These would eventually become linen. It was an industry that required much patience and perseverance.

This particular step of the process had to be done in clear, sunny weather. In order for the fibers to separate, they had to be absolutely dry. The uncomfortable heat increased Daniel's thirst, which compelled him to take frequent breaks to drink water. By noon, the exhausted young farmer had to stop for several hours.

As he walked back toward the farmhouse covered with dirt and sweat, he saw Mary finishing up in the vegetable garden. She was carrying a basketful of turnips and sweet potatoes that she would store in the cold root cellar. Mary's face lit up at the sight of her husband.

Even covered in grime he is still the most handsome man, she thought.

They both stopped at the basin on the log near the front door. The couple used the bayberry soap and water to wash their faces and hands. The water was still dripping off Daniel's chin when he leaned over and kissed her wet face.

"May I kiss you twenty times today in honor of your twentieth birthday?" Daniel asked her with a wide grin.

"Why so few?" Mary asked in mock displeasure.

"Well then, I had best get started since you require so many," he teased.

They were still laughing when they went in to the farmhouse to eat their noon meal. Their mouths watered at the smell of cooked vegetables from the garden, cheese, salt pork, and more cider. They all ate heartily, then rested in their chairs around the table.

"So, Mother Thomsen," Daniel said, "tell me about when Mary was born."

Widow Thomsen got a faraway look on her face as she recalled the events of that day.

"It was a wonderful day and a sad one as well," the widow began.

"Sad?" Mary said in surprise. "You have never told me that."

"Well, it was mostly happy because you were born, Mary. A strong and beautiful child—you made my heart melt when I laid eyes on you," the widow said. "But the sad part was your father was not there to see you, and he could not come for several days."

"Why have you never told me this before?" Mary said in amazement.

"I suppose because I always just dwelt on the happier side of the memory," her mother said. "It all started when family came to visit from Bridgewater. We had a lovely time seeing them, of course, but one of the young ones was not feeling too well. After they left we received a letter from a post rider that said the ill child had smallpox and we should take measures to contain the contagion. It was not four days later that your brother James came down with the illness. He was but two years old."

Mary was stunned with this news.

"What happened?" the daughter asked.

"Your father had to send me away because I was with child—I was carrying you, Mary. Your father took care of little James and made arrangements hastily for some friends to take me to stay with Widow

Baxter, the midwife in Williamston. I stayed with her for two weeks before you were born." The widow wiped at a tear as she recalled the difficult separation. "I had to write your father a letter to tell him he had a beautiful daughter."

Everyone was silent, imagining the young mother's loneliness. The widow continued. "But little James recovered well and no one else came down with the dreaded pox. When your father was finally able to come to Williamston, he looked at you, Mary, with his handsome green eyes and said, 'Welcome, my sweet daughter.'"

Everyone listening to the story had eyes brimming with tears.

"I miss Father," Mary said, wiping away the wetness from her cheeks.

Daniel took her hand. "So that is where you got those beautiful eyes," he said softly. Mary gazed with affection at her husband.

"Well, then," Widow Thomsen said hurriedly as she wiped away her own tears, "this day is not getting any longer." She stood up from her chair and began to pick up the bowls.

Daniel and Mary began to clean up from the meal and then retired for some rest from the heat and work. The young couple lay down in their bed and fell into a deep slumber with Mary nestled against Daniel.

When Mary awoke hours later, she was by herself in the bed. She arose sleepily from the quilts and came in to the main room.

"Where is Daniel?" she asked her mother. Widow Thomsen was preparing the cake for the evening's birthday celebration.

"He is in the barn working on something," the widow answered her. "I think it is a surprise for you."

"I wonder what it could be?" she said, trying to imagine what Daniel was up to.

"Hannah is here," Sarah said excitedly as she saw the young visitor walking down the dirt road toward the farmhouse. Hannah was carrying a large basket with some fresh cherries and green apples from her orchard, but the young woman was carrying something far more valuable than produce. She was bearing letters from James—one for the whole family and one just for Mary, for her birthday.

"James asked me to hold on to these until Mary's birthday," Hannah explained to the widow. "I hope you do not mind waiting these extra few days for word from him?"

Widow Thomsen trembled as she held the pages.

"No, of course not," the widow said. "I am just so relieved he is well."

They all sat down to hear the news from the oldest Thomsen child, gone to war now for over two years. The widow began to read:

My dearest Mother and Sisters,

Words cannot convey how much I miss you. I pray for you every day as I know that I am in your prayers as well. I trust that the Lord is watching over you, as He has been so faithful in doing for me.

This war seems as if it goes on forever. We have been fighting southward from you. I cannot disclose the location where we are, but I can tell you that our troops continue on with great fervor and excellence of endeavor.

General Washington continues as always to be an inspiring leader, even rallying our troops when others (that is Major General Lee) had our men in complete disarray. I must confess to our troops giving a hearty cheer when, due to Lee's inept leadership, Gen. Washington was inspired to set off a volley of oaths at the man. (I know you will think this offensive Mother—please forgive me this small pleasure).

The heat has been unbearable causing the loss of nearly one hundred of our soldiers. It seems that if is not agonizingly cold in our battles, then it is insufferably hot. Disease continues to plague us in the camps.

But I will not belabor these difficulties. I am certain that you are bearing your own arduous endeavors just trying to survive.

I hope to obtain leave to see all of you within the next year. I have enclosed a separate letter for Mary since I know it is soon time for her twentieth birthday. And of course, a private correspondence for Hannah.

With my earnest hope and prayers for seeing you all soon.

Your loving son and brother,

James

Widow Thomsen set the letter down in her lap and wept. Hannah, Mary, and Sarah all gathered round her in an embrace, fresh tears on their faces. Daniel walked in from the barn and saw the distraught group.

"What has happened?" he asked, fearing the worst.

Mary looked up at her husband. "We finally received news from James. He is well, but we have been so fearful for his safety that we are crying with relief," she explained.

He looked visibly relieved. "I am grateful that he is well."

"Let us get the cake ready," Widow Thomsen said, quickly rising from her chair. She busied herself with food preparations. "There is comfort for me in staying occupied," she said as she set out the plates for the dessert.

They were soon in a festive mood, celebrating the first twenty years of Mary's life. This was an especially memorable birthday for Mary, as it was her first as a married woman. She seemed unable to keep her eyes off her new husband, the main source of her joy on this happy occasion. She still had to pinch herself at times to be sure that she was not dreaming.

After the birthday song was sung and the cake served, Daniel presented Mary with the surprise he had been working on. In secret, Mr. Eaton had been teaching Daniel the skill of whittling. The new husband had decided upon the shape of a deer. It would decorate the base of Mary's distaff, a tall wooden piece that untangled the fibers of flax for spinning. Daniel had inscribed their initials "D. L." and "M. L." with a carved heart in between on the body of the deer.

Mary held the gift in her hand as if it were the most precious possession in the world, worth far more than gold.

"Thank you, Daniel," she whispered. Her heart overflowed with love for this man. "Thank you, so much." She put her arms around him and held him tightly.

Hannah was smiling but became teary-eyed. "Well," she said, "it is time I went back home. Father will be looking for me before dark."

The young woman stood up and everyone bid her farewell. Mary thanked her for coming and the two long-time friends hugged warmly.

It was after Mary and Daniel had retired to their room for the night when Mary finally had a chance to read the letter James had written just for her.

Dear Mary,

So you are now a young woman of twenty. It is difficult to believe that my little sister is so grown up. I wish so that I could be there to make sure that you are well and that only young men of good character are pursuing you.

Ever since I was little, I have felt a strong urge to protect you. If there was danger involved, I wanted to be the first to stand between you and whatever the threat was. Unfortunately, my desire to protect you and the rest of the family necessitates me being so far away, as the threat is far wider and greater than a mere mean-spirited bully from a village.

The danger is our Mother country, who has abandoned her infant colonies and denied them her maternal sustenance. I will be so eternally grateful when this new country of ours has left the birth nest and flown to freedom. Then we can rest in the loving arms of liberty. Be well, my dear sister, and know that I am fighting for you on this your birthday.

Your loving brother,

James

Then there was a postscript added. "Be assured of the necessity of staying away from Josiah Grant."

I already surmised the need for that, Mary mused. *And now, dear brother, I am a married woman. But you would not know that.*

Mary gave a deep sigh. She looked up and saw her husband looking at her, patiently waiting for her to finish reading.

"Please come to bed with me," he said in a whisper. He held out his arms to her and she happily complied with his request.

Chapter Twenty-six

Expectations

Mary looked pale and weak as she walked in the front door of the farmhouse.

"I do not feel well," she said to her mother. Her voice was shaking and her eyes opened wide. She hurried in to her bedroom just in time to vomit into the basin.

It was a late September morning and the young wife had picked through her gruel at breakfast. Her usual hearty appetite was suddenly dulled. Mary lay down on the bed breathing in spurts and looking whiter by the moment. She tried to open her eyes, but the room kept spinning so she closed them tightly.

She felt her mother place a cool cloth on her forehead. After several moments the tumultuous sensation in her stomach began to ebb and Mary bravely opened her eyes.

"I do not know what happened," the young woman said. "I was just bending to get the sweet potatoes from the ground and my head started to spin. I thought I would vomit right there, but after a few seconds the feeling stopped—for a moment anyway. When I did not feel much better, I decided I had best come inside out of the sun."

Sarah came into the room with a look of concern on her face.

"Are you ill, Mary?" she asked.

"I shall be fine, Sarah. I am just so very tired today."

"Sarah, please go in and stir the vegetables. Then set the tableboard for our supper, dear," the widow said.

Sarah still had a furrowed brow. "Please get well, Mary," the child said as she dutifully left the room.

Mary smiled weakly and closed her eyes again. "I do not think I can eat anything," she said to her mother. "I am still feeling quite queasy."

"It will not hurt you to miss a meal or two. Just try to eat a few bites every day, several times a day," the widow instructed.

Mary looked at her mother quizzically. "I do not understand what you are saying, Mother. Every day? I am sure I just ate something disagreeable to my digestion. I shall be recovered by tomorrow," she said with certainty.

"You will certainly recover," Widow Thomsen said. "In about nine months or so."

The young wife opened her eyes as widely as possible. She sat up too quickly, bringing on the nauseating sensation again. She was forced to lie back down.

"Nine months?" she said, aghast. "But we have only just been married two months. What will Daniel think? What if he is disappointed?" she asked. Fear gripped at her thoughts as she mused over Daniel's reaction.

Widow Thomsen gave a small smile.

"I am sure Daniel is aware that this can happen. Why would he be so surprised—or even disappointed? Give the man a chance. Most fathers get used to the idea, whether they thought it would happen or not."

"But ... are you sure ... that I am with child?" Mary asked in disbelief.

"Have you been in the manner of a woman recently?" the mother asked her directly.

"Well, no ... I suppose I was not even paying attention to that. I have not been in that manner since Daniel and I were married," she said. Mary's lips began to tremble and tears welled in her eyes as the reality of the situation became clear. "It is not that I do not wish for a child. I just do not know how Daniel will respond."

Widow Thomsen gave her daughter a hug. "You will both be fine parents," the widow encouraged her, then kissed her daughter on the top of the head. She turned toward the doorway of the room when she heard the front door unlatch. "There's the young father, now," she whispered to Mary. "Do not wait too long before you tell him."

The widow stood up from sitting on the edge of the bed just as Daniel appeared in the doorway. His face fell with concern when he saw his wife lying on the bed.

"What is wrong, Mary?" he said, sitting on the edge of the bed. He took her hand and kissed it, looking even more anxious as he noticed her pale complexion.

"I shall be fine," Mary responded in her bravest voice. "I think I was in the sun too long, that is all."

"May I get you something that will bring you relief?" he asked, feeling helpless. He tenderly smoothed her damp hair back from her face.

"No, I think I shall just rest for a bit," she said. Mary's eyelids were becoming so heavy that she was forced to close them. She fell into a deep slumber and Daniel reluctantly went out to eat his dinner. He checked on his wife again after he was finished with his meal but found her still sleeping peacefully. He brushed his lips across her forehead and resumed the afternoon fieldwork.

The young woman slept the rest of the day and did not awaken until she heard her husband come in from work. He immediately went to check on Mary.

"I cannot believe I slept all afternoon," she said as he appeared in the doorway. She sat up gingerly in their bed and took several slow breaths so that the nauseating feeling would not return. She was grateful that it did not.

Daniel approached her, concern still in his eyes. "I have been thinking, Mary. I have been keeping you awake too much at night," he said to her with guilt in his voice. "I am so very sorry. Please forgive me. You work so hard all day and then—"

"Daniel," she said, stopping his false conclusions short. She gently touched his lips and stroked his cheek. "I love being with you. I love loving you," she whispered. They kissed tenderly and he held her tightly.

"I do not want you to be ill because of me," he said.

"I am not ill because of you," she said. "In fact, I am quite hungry now. Let us see what my mother has fixed for evening meal."

Widow Thomsen could tell by the conversation at the table that Mary had not told Daniel about the baby. Her older daughter's appetite had returned and she ate a hearty portion of gruel as well as sausage and vegetables. Now that everything appeared normal once again, Daniel became relaxed and put his fears about her health to rest. Mary, however, could not close her eyes after the candles were extinguished that night.

How will I tell Daniel? she thought, fighting back tears.

The next day was Sunday and everyone was in a hurry at the Thomsen house. Chores needed to be done early so they could attend service at the meetinghouse.

Once again, Mary picked away at her morning gruel, only managing to swallow a few bites. But she did not want to miss this day of worship and visiting with her friends, especially Hannah. There was much she wanted to share with her good friend today.

The family began the mile-long trek to the center of town. The walk was far easier on the way to the village, since it was downhill. Mary bravely marched next to her husband making every effort to keep up with his long strides. Downhill walking was always easier for Daniel with his leg wound. His war injury, however, still caused him to limp.

They strode past the blacksmith, who was working on some new horseshoes for a soldier's mount.

I wonder if the sheriff will chide the smithy for working on a Sunday? she mused with concern. She hoped the magistrate would understand the needs of a soldier during war.

The young wife managed to maintain her composure until she and Daniel rounded the bend to the meetinghouse. There, affixed to the outside wall of the structure were three wolf heads. They had been recently hung following a bounty-induced hunt. The horrific sight startled Mary. The long fangs jutted out from the open jaws and dried blood covered the fur. The worst part of the macabre scene was the stench.

That familiar sick feeling gripped at Mary. She was terrified that she was going to vomit right in front of Daniel as well as the entire inhabitants of Deer Run. She released Daniel's arm and scurried behind the meetinghouse building just as the waves of nausea overtook her.

Hannah had been standing just a few feet away and ran to help. Mary was gasping for air as the retching slowly ebbed. Hannah handed Mary a kerchief to wipe her mouth.

"When will your child be birthed?" Hannah asked, a smile spreading on her face.

Mary looked at her friend who knew her so well. "Early May, I think," she said, sitting down on a log lest her shaking legs give out.

Daniel hurried around the edge of the building with fear in his eyes. "Mary!" he said, his voice frantic with concern.

"I shall leave you two alone," Hannah said. She rejoined her father, who was entering the meetinghouse.

Daniel sat next to her on the log and put his arm around her. "Does not your mother have any medicinals that can help you?" he said, his anxiety growing by the minute.

Mary fought back a smile and tried to appear serious. "She says that there is no medicine that can cure my condition."

Her husband appeared distraught.

The church congregation began singing a hymn. The plaintive melody coming through the open window seemed to add to Daniel's emotions as he bowed in silent prayer.

Mary saw the look of fear on his face and knew she could no longer leave him in misery. She drew his strong jaw to face her.

"Daniel," Mary said. "I am with child." She smoothed her fingers across the cheek of the man who held her heart.

The look on Daniel's face went from fear to confusion, to relief and then joy all in a single moment. He hugged her tightly and then released her.

"How long have you known?"

She looked down and bit her lip. "I must confess I have wondered for several days now, but I knew it in my heart yesterday when I became so ill," she said. "Are you disappointed?" she asked anxiously.

Daniel was confused. "Disappointed? Why would you think I would be?"

She turned away from his intent gaze. "We have been married such a short time ... I did not know how you would feel," she answered.

It was Daniel's turn to bring her face toward his. "Mary, our love has made this child. God has sent him ... or her to us because we became one. This child is a gift. You are a gift to me," he said earnestly, kissing her tenderly.

She held on to him tightly and they embraced silently for a long while. Daniel was careful to not let Mary see even a hint of fear in his eyes. He could not have been happier about the baby, but he nevertheless felt apprehensive about the birthing that she would endure months from now. It was during his own mother's last childbirth that he had lost the first woman in his life. He was terrified of now losing the most important woman in his life, his beloved wife.

He kissed Mary again and tried to put his fears to rest.

Chapter Twenty-seven

Return

What started out as a simple discussion between Widow Thomsen and Daniel soon turned into a disagreement. She felt that women should continue to work as much as possible when they were with child. Daniel believed that this was a delicate time for a woman and that she should be treated with gentleness and indulgence. They finally settled on a compromise after they both reasoned that neither extreme would likely benefit mother or child.

But Mary had her own ideas about the pregnancy. As long as she was not vomiting or completely exhausted, she wanted to keep active, even working in the garden and milking the cow.

"There is nothing worrisome about pulling a few weeds, Daniel," she explained to her husband. "I have been doing such work since I was able to walk."

"She's got a point there, young man," Mr. Eaton said. He was visiting on a late September evening, sharing some baked pumpkin with milk. The dish was a favorite of the Thomsen family for many years. "She'll know if she's doin' too much, lad. Mrs. Eaton always did," he said.

Widow Thomsen had a pensive look on her face.

"Perhaps if I had worked a bit less strenuously on the farm, I would have more children that survived," she said.

Mary looked with sympathy at her mother, knowing that her parent had endured the loss of two children before they were born.

"Perhaps you were right, Daniel, in wanting to allow Mary more rest," the widow added.

And rest her daughter seemed to need—the widow had never seen her daughter so fatigued. So when Mary awoke the next day looking pale and haggard, Daniel and Widow Thomsen agreed this was to be her day to sleep. The new mother did not have the energy to argue. She simply turned around and went back to her quilted bed.

"I'll be back at the flax field today, Mother Thomsen. Please call me if you or Mary need anything," Daniel said, taking a final drink from his tankard of cider. "Just one more day should finish the job."

Daniel headed for the barn to retrieve the hetchel, a three-foot long wooden plank that had sixty sharp iron teeth fixed to the center of the board. These five-inch-long metal combs separated the strands of flax into fibers suitable for spinning. Once Daniel was finished with the hetcheling today, the flax would be ready to hand over to the women. It had been difficult and tedious work, but Daniel was satisfied with his labors, which were nearly complete.

There was just a hint of autumn in the air. Daniel welcomed the relief from the heat, as he was able to move more quickly at his task. These warm summers in America were an adjustment for an Englishman more accustomed to less sunshine and abundant rain. Still, he was beginning to adapt to this new land and home, and he looked forward to felling the trees on the land deeded to the young couple on their wedding day.

Daniel envisioned he and Mary in their own log cabin raising their family. His heart was filled with emotion as he thought about their first child already forming inside of his wife. He recalled the description he had read in the Psalms: "Fearfully and wonderfully made." The realization caused him to pause in his labors and thank the Lord who had instilled life into this child.

And he also thanked God, as he had on numerous occasions, for the gift of his wife.

Just thinking about Mary still caused his heart to stir. His initial assessment when he first met her nearly a year ago still held true—she had completely disarmed his emotions. Long before he had met this young colonial woman and before the many months of disillusionment and defeat, Daniel Lowe had been a dedicated lieutenant in the King's army. He had been loyal to the Crown, an expert marksman and fighter.

Settling down with a British wife had been somewhere in the young man's future, he thought, but war was his skill and conquering opposing armies his goal.

That is, until Mary Thomsen conquered his heart. He knew when he met her that he would never be the same. And he knew when he met the shepherd of his soul that he would be refined into the man God wanted him to be. He had surrendered to them both and he had no regrets.

As he contemplated these changes in his life, a lone figure coming down the dirt road caught his attention. He did not recognize the man, but he recognized the familiar deerskin uniform of the Continental forces. When the figure came closer, Daniel greeted the man with caution.

"May I help you, sir?" Daniel asked the stranger.

"Just lookin' to see Miss Mary Thomsen," the man said, "not that it's any of your concern, sir."

He may not have recognized the face, but Daniel would never forget that voice. He had heard it from the bed where he had been recovering from his wound nearly a year ago. That voice belonged to Josiah Grant.

"I do believe that you are referring to Missus Daniel Lowe, sir," Daniel said, glaring at the man. "She is my wife."

The words struck the Continental soldier like a physical blow. He stopped short in his brisk walk toward the farmhouse.

"Your wife? That cannot be. She was waitin' for me," Josiah said, his eyes widening in anger and disbelief.

"That is obviously not true, sir."

"Everyone in town knows that is true," Josiah said, his voice rising with rage, his face turning a bright shade of red.

"Then why is it that no one in Deer Run objected to our marriage? The announcement was posted at the meetinghouse for three Sundays, sir," the young husband said.

Daniel kept seeing in his mind the bruises that this man had inflicted upon his wife's arms so very long ago, the thought of which still enraged him.

Josiah tried to form an objection to Daniel's logic, but the words caught in his throat.

"Good day, sir," Daniel snapped.

The young husband knew that he was finished working the flax today. He needed to return to the farmhouse and cool off from his anger. Daniel picked up the long hetchel and turned to walk back to the house.

Rage filled Josiah as he stared after the man who he believed stole Mary's heart. He would not so quickly give this stranger the triumph in love.

"You were not the first with her you know," Josiah said in a lewd tone.

Daniel stopped in his tracks, his back to the man. His heart was racing with fury. From the corner of his eye, he viewed the sharp metal prongs pointing upward on the hetchel sitting on his shoulder.

It would be so easy to impale this liar on those spikes and be done with the man, Daniel thought to himself. In the same moment he repented of this murderous thought.

But the object of Daniel's hatred was not finished with his lies just yet.

"So tell me, Mr. Lowe, is her skin still so soft under the quilts?" The soldier could get no further in his slander. In a swift and studied maneuver, Daniel spun the hetchel over his arm and forcefully plied the wooden end of the tool into Josiah's jaw. The spurned suitor landed with a thud on the ground. The stunned soldier could only stare at Daniel in disbelief and moan from the severe impact.

"Get your lying tongue out of here. And do not ever set foot near my wife or I shall kill you," Daniel said, his heart racing in his chest.

Daniel watched Josiah slowly get up and walk back down the road toward his father's home. He waited until the unwelcome guest was out of sight before turning around to go back to the farmhouse.

Josiah held his jaw as he walked home in defeat. Then a look of realization grew on his countenance.

"That lying swine is no patriot," he muttered to himself. "I've seen those moves a time or two in battle."

An evil smile began to grow on Josiah's swollen face as he surmised the obvious.

"Miss Mary Thomsen has married a Redcoat." The jilted suitor smirked with satisfaction. "We'll just see how soon we can make her a widow."

Josiah hurried down the road to his father's house. His pace quickened as he began to hatch his plot.

Daniel could feel the heat of anger boiling in his face as he returned the hetchel to the barn. He started to throw the wooden tool at the wall but something stopped him—an inner voice that urged him to plead for God's help in overcoming this fury. He submitted to the silent appeal in his heart and sat down on the hay. He held his head and prayed for God to forgive him for this hatred toward Josiah, and for his desire to kill the man.

Then he began to pray for protection for his wife. He sensed a danger here that he could not put words to. He did not know what else to do but give this fear to God. When he finished with these supplications, he slowly got up from sitting on the hay and walked somberly back to the farmhouse.

Widow Thomsen was starting to spin the flax on her wheel in preparation for weaving the fine threads into linen. She saw the strained look on Daniel's countenance and paused in her work. She placed a finger to her lips and pointed to the couple's bedroom, indicating that Mary was still asleep. Sarah was outside weeding in the vegetable garden so the two adults were free to speak.

"What weighs on your heart, Daniel?" the widow asked.

Daniel leaned against the warm hearth that was burning steadily and looked at the flames. He turned towards the widow and gave a hushed reply.

"Josiah Grant has returned."

The widow's mouth opened in surprise and anger.

"What did he want?" she asked, her voice filled with indignation.

"He was looking for 'Miss Thomsen,'" Daniel said, shaking his head at the gall of the man. "After what he did ... I cannot believe he has the unmitigated nerve to return here."

"What did you tell him, Daniel?"

"I told him that Mary and I were married. He said that was impossible, that Mary was waiting for him. He said ... some other words ... and I hit him."

For a brief moment, Widow Thomsen looked pleased that Daniel had injured the man, but her smile just as quickly disappeared.

"Do you think he will come back?" she asked.

Daniel stared at the fire again. "I do not know," he said wearily. He turned to sit on the chair by the hearth and rubbed his head slowly.

"Why do you not take the remainder of the day to rest, Daniel. You can finish the hetcheling tomorrow."

"I thank you, but no. I must complete the task. I am much calmer now and the work will consume my energies so that my thoughts do not overwhelm me," he said. He stood up from his chair and took a drink of cider. "I am well," he said, trying to put the widow's mind at ease.

Daniel went out the front door and headed back to the barn to retrieve the tool.

Widow Thomsen stared at the strands of flax waiting to be spun. A look of apprehension filled her eyes. Fighting the panic rising within her spirit, she sought out the One Who she knew she could cast all of her fears upon.

"Dear Lord," she whispered in prayer, "protect us all."

Chapter Twenty-eight

Revenge

Jonathan Grant stared at his son in disbelief.

"You must be mad, Josiah. Mary Thomsen's husband is no Redcoat. I've seen the man about the village myself."

The angry father took a long gulp of rum, poured to celebrate his son's return but now a means to dull his growing anxiety.

"It's true, Father," Josiah said with visible rage. He took another hearty swallow of the spirits. Some of the brew dripped down the side of his mouth and he wiped it off with the sleeve of his deerskin coat. "I saw the man fighting like a King's soldier myself. No one in our regiment can fight like that. He spun that hetchel so fast over his arm I did not even see it comin'. And you can see what he did with it." Josiah pointed to his swollen and reddened jaw.

"The man could have done far worse damage to you than he did. A hetchel can be deadly," Jonathan said, eyeing his son. "I don't suppose you did anything to set him off?"

"I did nothin'!" Josiah yelled, averting his eyes from his father. The younger man paced across the room, spilling some of his rum as he went. "And his fine, mannerly speech—it's a dead giveaway. He's a Lobster, to be sure!"

"This would not have anything to do with your feelings for Missus Lowe?" his father asked. "Please tell me this is not about revenge."

Josiah's back was to his father and his shoulders bristled. He spun around and faced the man.

"I am a soldier of the Continental Army, Father. Do not accuse me of having a personal vendetta against a soldier of the King!" He set his empty tankard of rum down on the wooden table with force and glared at his father. "So are you a true patriot, Father? Are you going to defend our town from this spy?"

Jonathan scrutinized his only son, who had become such a disappointment to him. "I regret that I was gone too long fighting in the French War, Josiah. You did not even know me when I returned," Jonathan said.

Josiah stared at his father in confusion. "What are you saying, Father. What does this have to do with a British spy right in our midst? Have you taken leave of your senses?" he asked angrily.

"Your mother ... your mother coddled you so while I was away. She thought you could do no wrong, but I could see your lying ways. If the war taught me one thing, Josiah, it taught me to recognize a liar and a cheat when I saw one." He stared at his handsome son. "Your fine features cannot hide your evil heart. And what you are proposing has the stench of evil through and through. I will not bring such charges against the man. And I will not be a part of this hanging." He finished his rum and placed his head in both hands as he looked down at the table.

Josiah glared with hatred at his father and wiped the sweat off of his reddened face.

"Then I shall find others who will," he said with disgust. The soldier walked out of the house and slammed the door. He headed for the home of another of the town's leaders. On the way there, he stopped walking for a moment and held his head.

"This wretched sunlight. I need some ale for this pain. Or a few camp women to ease my discomfort." He stood for a moment under the shade of a maple tree and rubbed his temples. "Those females—they only remind me of Mary. I'll feel like a new man when her bloody Redcoat is dead and in the ground. Then my pain will turn to pleasure." He resumed his walk down the road, more determined than ever to get rid of Daniel Lowe.

***

Josiah approached the house of Selectman Caleb White. Hannah answered the knock on the door and was startled to see the soldier.

"Josiah, how good to see you," she said.

He pushed past her into the house. "Your father here?" he asked tersely, looking around for the selectman. He sneezed and wiped his nose off with his sleeve.

"He is outside, working on some muskets," Hannah said. The young woman appeared confused by the purpose of this visit. She was also hoping to get news about James, but Josiah pushed past her once again to go find her father. She went to the doorway and saw the soldier approach her father. Then the private began to rage about the presence of a British spy right in their own village. When she heard the name Daniel Lowe, she gasped and went to the window. She was able to hear their conversation without being seen by the two men.

"I tell you that man is a Redcoat, a spy," Josiah was shouting. He was fairly spitting in her father's face with rage. She noticed the soldier's reddened countenance and the sweat pouring from his brow despite the cool September weather.

Her father was listening intently.

"Do not believe him, Father," Hannah spoke under her breath, her heart beginning to race.

"All right," her father said. "We shall gather as many men with muskets as we can. We'll assemble at the meetinghouse tonight at midnight. We can take him from the Thomsen farm and bring him back to the village. We'll not allow a bloody Redcoat to remain in our midst. The big oak tree will serve for the hanging."

Josiah tipped his tricornered hat at Mr. White and strutted off in satisfaction. When her father came in, Hannah stared at him in horror.

"Please, do not do this terrible thing, Father," she pleaded with him. Her eyes were filling up with tears.

"Do not interfere, daughter. If Mary's husband is a British spy then he deserves to die," her father said coldly. "And do not attempt to warn your friend."

"But, Father," she entreated him passionately. "Mary is with child."

"That cannot be helped. Justice must be done and I am responsible for the safekeeping of the citizens here," Caleb White said. "I shall begin to gather the townsfolk. And you ... you are confined to this house."

He walked out the door and locked it from the outside. The frightened daughter covered her mouth as hot tears flowed down her cheeks. She knew that if she tried to escape from her home to warn Mary, she would pay the price with a beating from her father. But she knew she had to do something.

"Gracious Father in Heaven," Hannah prayed. "Show me what to do. Please protect Daniel from this evil."

Once her tears had subsided, she began to piece together a plan. Standing up, she found an empty basket used to collect fruit in their orchard. She filled the basket with red apples and one green one. Hannah grabbed a piece of paper and wrote a short note that she attached with a hairpin to the bottom of the green apple. The young woman went to an open window that faced the road and waited. She knew that the boys would soon be getting out of school and she peered down the path looking for the first child. It seemed an interminable wait, but her patience was soon rewarded. It was red-haired Richard Beal, Sarah Thomsen's friend.

"I say, Richard," Hannah called out to the boy from the window. The confused child looked around and Hannah called his name again. He finally saw the source of the greeting and waved.

"Hello, Miss White," he yelled in a friendly manner.

"Richard, can you take something to Missus Lowe for me over at the Thomsen farm?" she said as calmly as possible.

The child's face brightened at the thought of an excuse to see his friend, Sarah.

"Certainly, Miss White," he said. The child walked over to the window and Hannah handed him the basket.

"I want my friend Missus Lowe to have some fresh apples from my orchard, Richard." In spite of her calm manner, her heart was in her throat. "You may eat one of the red ones yourself."

"Thank you, Miss White," the boy said. He grabbed the piece of fruit and eagerly took a huge bite.

"And Richard—this is most important—please tell Missus Lowe that the green one is especially tasty. She will want to eat that one first," Hannah said, trying to control the trembling in her voice.

"All right, Miss White. I shall tell her." He started to walk away but then turned back toward the window. "The green one, right?" he asked, somewhat perplexed.

"Yes, Richard, the green one," she said, almost breaking down in tears.

The preoccupied child did not seem to notice her distress, and he walked down the road happily. Hannah watched the innocent dispatcher head for the Thomsen farm. Only then did she allow herself to weep.

"Dear Lord above, please protect my friends from harm," she prayed.

Chapter Twenty-nine

Terror

Mary had just awakened from her afternoon rest and was excited to show something to Daniel.

The young wife walked out into the late afternoon sunshine. She breathed in deeply of the cool fall air and noticed the woods in the distance. The leaves on the trees were richly imbued with hues of red and gold. Mary always loved this time of year, but this season seemed especially glorious for another reason. She was carrying her first child.

She heard Daniel in the barn returning the tools from working in the field. She knew her husband would likely be finished with the flax today and was relieved that he would soon be finished this tedious task. Although he did not complain, the young wife knew the strain this chore was on her husband's war injury. She often noticed him rubbing the muscles on his left leg after a long day in the field. Mary worried about the stress this was putting on his already-injured limb.

As she walked into the barn, Daniel looked up in surprise.

"I thought you were resting," he said, putting down the tools. He walked over to her and gently put his arms around her waist. "Are you feeling all right?" he said, smoothing a wayward lock of hair from her forehead. Her cheeks were a brighter pink from the pregnancy.

"I am well. I want to show you something," she said shyly. She took Daniel's large hand and placed it on her belly. "There. Has the baby not grown?"

Daniel actually did feel a slightly rounded swelling. He looked at her in amazement.

"Already?" he asked her. "I did not think we would notice him—or her—just yet."

"Neither did I," she said, grinning, "but when I awoke, I placed my hand over him and there he was. Our baby."

Daniel held her closely. This child was becoming more real to them both all the time. Their tender embrace was interrupted by the voice of Sarah shouting out from the garden.

"Richard! Richard Beal!" The excited seven-year-old was jumping up and down and waving.

"Richard?" Mary said. "I wonder why he is here?"

"He probably could not wait for Sabbath day to visit with her," Daniel said. He was amused by Richard's flirtation with young Sarah.

"I had best go see if his mother needs anything. Perhaps someone in their home is ill," Mary said. She walked out toward the farmhouse where the two youngsters were.

"Good day, Miss ... I mean Missus Lowe," Richard said. "Miss White has asked me to bring you these apples to eat."

"Hannah? How thoughtful of her," Mary said, bewildered by the unexpected gift.

I wonder why she did not bring them herself.

"Thank you, Richard. And how was school today?"

"It was quite exhilarating, Missus Lowe," Richard said.

Mary smothered a smile. Richard always loved to try out new words from his spelling lessons at every opportunity. "Exhilarating" must have been one of his recent assignments.

"I wish I could go to school," Sarah said, folding her arms and pouting. "Williamston has a summer school for girls. Why cannot Deer Run have a girls' school?"

"We hope to have one soon, Sarah," Mary said. "In the meantime, keep up your lessons at home. I am sure you will find Mother's teaching 'exhilarating' as well."

"Well, I had best get home before my mother wonders where I have been," Richard said. The boy remained standing there, clearly having no desire to leave.

"We are very grateful to you for this special gift you have delivered, Richard. Do come again soon. By the way, would you like one of these apples? I am sure you must be hungry," Mary said.

"Miss White has already offered me one," Richard said. "But thank you kindly."

With gentlemanly grace, he bowed first to Mary, then to Sarah. The younger sister giggled at the gesture.

The boy turned to go back home when he remembered Hannah's message for Mary.

"Missus Lowe," he called back to her, "Miss White says that the green one is especially tasty. She says you should eat it first."

"All right, Richard," she called back to the boy. As she watched him go back down the road, a look of confusion crossed her eyes.

Hannah knows the red ones are my favorite. And why did she only put one green one in the basket?

Mary walked inside the farmhouse and Sarah returned to weeding the garden and gathering vegetables. Widow Thomsen was still at work spinning the flax from the abundant crop.

"That is odd," Mary said, a puzzled expression on her face.

"What is odd, Mary?" Widow Thomsen said.

"These apples from Hannah. She sent them with Richard instead of bringing them herself. And then she said I should eat the green one first."

Mary picked up the green apple and only then noticed there was a note attached to the bottom.

"What's this?"

"What is it?" the widow asked getting up from her spinning wheel and walking toward Mary.

Mary's face turned white as she read the words on the note from Hannah. They sent terror through her heart.

"No!" Mary cried, covering her mouth with her hands and dropping the note to the floor.

Widow Thomsen picked it up and read the frightening message: "They are coming for Daniel tonight. He must hide."

The young wife sat down on the floor and began to shake uncontrollably. Her throat tightened with fear. "Get Daniel," she whispered. Widow Thomsen ran out to the barn as quickly as she could. Within moments, Daniel was at his wife's side.

"Mary what is it?" he asked, alarm in his voice. She could not speak, but handed him the note from Hannah. The color drained from Daniel's face as he read the ominous message. The young couple looked at each other, paralyzed with fear. Then Mary began to sob uncontrollably and Daniel held her in his arms, shaking nearly as much as she was.

All of their joy was suddenly threatened by an unseen enemy. Mary was at a loss to understand this horrible turn of events, but Daniel knew exactly who the source of this terror was. He had encountered the man earlier today. It was Josiah Grant, bent on revenge.

Daniel tried to gather his wits about him. He needed to be brave for his wife. "Mary, listen," he said cupping her chin in his hands. His expression struggled to be stalwart when he saw the pain on her face. "You must be strong. I shall hide in the wigwam until dawn. Then I will go through the woods back toward New York. I shall send for you when it is safe."

"Daniel, take my horse," Widow Thomsen offered. Daniel noticed the fear on her face as well.

"I cannot ride that well," Daniel admitted. "They would likely overtake me. My safest course is to go on foot. I know the way."

"Please take me with you, Daniel," Mary sobbed.

"I cannot," Daniel whispered. "If they catch me then you will be endangered as well. And so will our child."

They held each other again. This time they were afraid to let go, afraid that this could be their last embrace.

"Daniel, you must hasten," Widow Thomsen said, her voice trembling. "Evening draws near. I shall pack you some food and drink." She was already gathering supplies and putting them in a leather pouch.

He helped Mary to her feet.

"Please, take care of our child," he said. Mary threw her arms around his neck and would not let go. Daniel finally released himself from her desperate grip. He kissed her with heartbreaking passion. Then he turned away from his wife and walked toward the door.

"Daniel," Mary called to him, sobbing, her hand over her chest. "You are the song in my heart."

The young husband looked at his wife with so much pain in his eyes that Widow Thomsen was forced to look away.

"Why Lord?" she prayed under her breath. The widow's plea to heaven went unanswered. When she turned back around, Daniel was gone.

Mary was inconsolable. Widow Thomsen held her daughter as if she were a small child. But it had been far easier to soothe away the pains of childhood heartache then it was to alleviate the deep despair her daughter was suffering from today.

Sarah walked into the house looking confused. When she saw how upset Mary was, she started to cry as well.

"What is happening?" Sarah asked.

Widow Thomsen drew her younger daughter toward herself and the three of them held each other and wept. It was not long before they heard someone on horseback approach the farmhouse. They all looked up in fear.

"Stay here, daughters," Widow Thomsen said. She took down her late husband's musket from the wall and made sure that the powder and ball were at the ready. She opened the door and breathed a sigh of relief when she saw a friendly face.

"Mr. Eaton!" she said. The widow broke down in tears and rested the weapon at her side.

"Caught wind of the village rumor," he said, dismounting his horse with a grave expression upon his face. "Thought you could use a friend—and a firearm," he said holding up his musket.

"Yes," Widow Thomsen said through her tears. "We could use both."

Chapter Thirty

Intervention

The sun was dropping below the horizon when Daniel reached the wigwam.

Even though he knew where it was located, he still had difficulty finding the entrance. The vines were abundant this fall and the clustered leaves served as camouflage over the structure. It took several frantic attempts on Daniel's part to locate the door in the midst of the entwined reddened leaves. The young man opened the precariously hinged door—barely hanging together with a stiff leather strap—and walked into the dim interior.

He was once again consumed with the scent of lavender. Mary had left this private hideaway intact since their wedding day, and it had often served as an oasis for their love. Today, however, he felt desperately alone. The reminders of the affection he had shared with his wife now filled him with despair. He wondered if they would ever be together again.

Daniel sat down on one of the quilts remembering their first time together, on their wedding day. He would never forget Mary smoothing her hands across the wretched scar on his thigh. She had looked at him with tenderness and spoken words that he would always treasure: "This shall always remind me of how we were brought together."

Daniel's eyes stung with tears at the memory of their passion that day. He closed his eyes and held his head.

"Dear God," he whispered in prayer, "please bring us back together again."

He did not have a Bible with him but he remembered the words that he had recently read in Psalms. They consumed his present thoughts: "In thee, O Lord, do I put my trust; let me never be put to confusion. Deliver me in thy righteousness, and cause me to escape; incline thine ear unto me, and save me."

These words had been written so long ago by the young King David while fleeing from a man bent on killing him. The verses took on an aura of reality for Daniel.

And then he began to wonder.

How many others in Deer Run will follow Josiah's urging? How many other townspeople will turn on me?

Then an even more frightening thought occurred to the young husband.

What if they turn on Mary?

Daniel had forgotten to remind his wife that she should deny any knowledge about his past. But even if she did, would they believe her?

Surely they must.

Fear still gripped at his heart. He had seen too many mobs get out of control with misplaced fervor.

"Oh, God," Daniel prayed once again, as he had pleaded with him earlier that day. "Please protect my wife."

*** *

Myles Eaton stood guard outside the front door of the Thomsen farmhouse, his eyes fixed to the road where the men intent upon hanging Daniel Lowe would soon come. He glanced over at the musket sticking out of the side-room window, the room where Mary and Daniel usually slept. Widow Thomsen had her firearm at the ready and she knew well how to use it. It had been nearly two hours since everyone's lives were upended by the ominous note. Few words had been spoken since, but tension was written on everyone's faces.

Mr. Eaton finally broke the silence.

"How's Missus Lowe doin'?" he asked.

The widow tried to keep her voice calm, but Mr. Eaton could hear its trembling pitch.

"She's lying on Daniel's pillow in my bed, hugging her sister. Sarah finally went to sleep but Mary is still crying." Then she added, "Mary says the scent of Daniel on his pillow brings her comfort."

"Aye, I understand," Mr. Eaton replied. The robust farmer recalled his own memories of despair after his wife died. "I remember takin' my wife's shawl to bed with me after she passed on." He looked over at Ruth. "I never shared that with anyone before."

Widow Thomsen looked over at her friend with compassion.

"I feel pleased that you would entrust me with your sad memories, Mr. Eaton."

Myles Eaton nodded in acknowledgment. No words were spoken for several moments. Widow Thomsen was the first to break the silence.

"So when do you suppose Josiah and the others will come?" she asked.

"Hard tellin', Widow Thomsen."

They both startled at the sound of a wolf howling in the distance. They tried to relax when they realized the source of the plaintive noise, but the tension never fully abated, lingering in the air as surely as the early fall breeze.

"Have I told you how grateful I am for your help, Myles?" Widow Thomsen said after several minutes. Mr. Eaton looked over at the distraught mother struggling to hold back her tears.

"Aye, Ruth Thomsen, you have told me you were grateful. But you do not need to thank me. It is just what I do for my friends."

Mr. Eaton could not see the slight smile that brought a glimmer of joy to the widow's tear-stained face. It was the first time they had called each other by their Christian names.

***

Several of the armed men who gathered on horseback at the meetinghouse were carrying torches. They were awaiting their patriotic leader and beginning to get impatient.

"So where is Josiah?" one gray-haired man asked Caleb White, who was obviously annoyed as well. "The man spreads the word about this Redcoat and now we're all waitin' on the instigator. I thought he was leadin' the group?"

Most of the dozen men gathered for the lynching were over the age of fifty. Many had sons serving in the war of Revolution, but most in the village were too old or infirm to carry their own muskets on the battlefront. They were forced to defend their new nation on the home front, and they were more than willing participants in carrying out justice. But none of them wanted to lead this particular crusade, especially since Josiah seemed to have enough youthful fighting spirit to carry out that task himself. The townsfolk were ready to follow him at this midnight hour—if only he were here.

"Let's ride over to the Grant place," Mr. White said. "Maybe something has delayed the man." He wanted to get this hanging done as quickly as possible; no sense in delaying the inevitable.

They rode slowly over the half-mile distance to the home of Josiah and his father. There was a new moon that evening that shed little light and the lynch mob feared injuring one of their horses on the rough terrain.

"I wish Josiah had chosen a night with a full moon," Selectman White mumbled to himself.

When the group arrived at the Grant home, it was strangely quiet. The group of men all thought Josiah's horse would be at the ready. Wouldn't he be preparing to rouse their patriotic fervor in bringing justice to their village and their new country? The mob sat in their leather saddles looking at each other with confusion.

"I'll go see where he is," Caleb White finally said.

Dismounting from his large brown mare, he walked up to the door and knocked. Instead of Josiah answering, Jonathan Grant opened the door. He had a look in his eyes that was filled with fear and anger. The distraught father held a wet cloth in his hand and a basin of water.

"Lookin' for your 'captain,' are you?" Jonathan asked in disgust. "Well, there he is, gentleman," he said, pointing to the bed where his son lay.

Caleb White walked over to the young man lying on the drenched sheets and gasped. The selectman drew back from the bed, for the sight of the stricken soldier filled him with horror and dread. Even in the dim candlelight, he could see the hundreds of raised, red marks all over Josiah's face, arms, and legs. These pustules revealed a frightening truth.

Smallpox.

"You'd best be on your way, Mr. White," Jonathan Grant said.

The terrified man did not need to be convinced. He exited the front door as fast as his legs could run. Caleb White looked up at the men on horseback, his face strained with apprehension.

"There is smallpox here. Everyone that was with Josiah Grant needs to be confined to their homes lest we have an epidemic," he said.

The blood drained from the men's faces. The subdued mob rapidly made their way back to their separate homes. There would be no further talk of a hanging this night. All the men were aware of the terror of smallpox, and all of them knew that this deadly plague could decimate the town of Deer Run.

Chapter Thirty-one

Enemies

The pounding of a solitary set of hooves stirred Myles Eaton and Widow Thomsen to alarm.

They readied their muskets to fire at whatever danger was approaching. Their moist fingers gripped the triggers, their nerves on edge in this dark of night just before dawn.

They breathed a sigh of relief when they realized that the rider was not Josiah Grant. It was his father, Jonathan.

"Widow Thomsen," Jonathan pleaded with the woman. He shifted in his saddle. "Please help me. My son is dreadfully ill. It's the pox."

The widow and Mr. Eaton audibly gasped at the news.

"Are you certain?" the widow asked in horror.

"As sure as I've been of anything," Jonathan said, nervously fingering the horse's reins. "I've seen it plenty in the last war. The whole town is in quarantine."

Widow Thomsen placed her musket down. She went to the main room to get some medicine for the man's son, moving silently so as to not awaken her two daughters. Mary and Sarah were finally asleep in the large bed. The midwife gathered some hyssop leaves to make a tea for Josiah's fever. She also gathered a large portion of the inner bark of several trees, including sumac, pine, and Spanish oak. These would induce vomiting, which was recommended in the physician's guide. The patient would also require old, clean linens to soothe his sores, the widow reasoned.

Moving automatically in response to the request for help, it was a moment before a realization dawned on her.

"I cannot go to help Josiah," she whispered. "I could bring back this dreaded disease to my whole family. I cannot risk this. I will not risk it … but I know someone who could do this—if he is willing to go."

After writing out directions for the use of the powders and leaves, she walked outside with the supplies. She handed them in a pouch to Jonathan Grant, who was waiting anxiously on his horse.

"Mr. Grant, it is impossible for me to attend to your son. My daughter is with child and I cannot take the chance on bringing this contagion into my home. However, there is someone that I know who has survived the pox. With your permission—and his—I shall send him to attend to your son, and to you in the event that you become ill."

Jonathan Grant looked at the widow and swallowed hard. Smallpox had not reached the village of Deer Run in many years. The only possible nurse would likely be a stranger from elsewhere. Perhaps someone that his son despised. "And who would that be, ma'am?"

Widow Thomsen took a deep breath.

"It is my daughter's husband, Daniel Lowe," she said firmly.

The father paused only briefly before giving the only answer he could.

"Yes, of course, Widow Thomsen," he said. "If he is willing, I would be grateful for his help. I thank you, ma'am, for your gracious spirit."

He tipped his tricornered hat to the woman and rode back to his home and his stricken son.

Myles Eaton turned to the widow with a questioning look.

"Are you sure you want to ask Daniel to do this? After what Josiah has been up to?" he asked.

"It is Daniel's choice to help the man or not," she said, "but if Daniel shows himself to be a loyal help to the people of Deer Run at such a critical time, how can they deny his allegiance to the citizens of America?"

Mr. Eaton had no answer for the woman. There was a truth in what she said.

"But are you sure Daniel will be willing to help his enemy?" he asked.

"That will be between him and God," she said.

The woman went in to her house and picked up her Bible before heading off to the wigwam.

"I shall return directly, Myles. Please guard my family while they are sleeping," she said.

"I shall, Ruth," he said.

The widow walked down the long path toward the old structure in the woods. She wondered how the aged wigwam had lasted through the years despite so many storms. The leaves of fall were just beginning their annual descent from the branches. There was a thin carpet of gold and red on the path leading through the dense trees.

Widow Thomsen arrived just before dawn. Daniel was putting his food pouch over his shoulder when he heard her footsteps. He hid behind the crude hinge of the door and stood prepared to fight. When he saw it was his mother-in-law, he sighed with relief.

"Is Mary well?" he asked.

"She was sleeping when I left, Daniel. Mr. Eaton is guarding the house, musket in hand," the widow informed him.

A feeling of gratitude overtook Daniel. Then he wondered what had transpired during the night.

"What about the people from the town? Did they come? Did Josiah come?"

"The only one who came was Josiah's father. Jonathan Grant brought some news. An unexpected report," she said, then paused. "Josiah has the smallpox."

Daniel looked baffled at the news, then relieved.

"So he is not coming?" he asked. He took in a deep breath for the first time since receiving the note from Hannah.

The widow continued, "I understand your relief, Daniel, but this will be short lived. Once he is well—if he recovers—and once the rest of the town is deemed clear of infection, the mob will come again."

The young husband regarded the woman somberly.

"You are right of course. I must think this through," he said. He sat on the dirt floor of the wigwam and put his hands on his temples.

"I have an idea," she said, "that might change the town's belief in your loyalty to the colonies once and for all." Daniel looked at her questioningly. "I know that you have survived the pox and likely will never get it again," she said. "If you go and take care of the victims in the village—starting with Josiah—it will make them see you for who you really are, a loyal and caring American."

"Nurse Josiah Grant through this illness?" Daniel said, horrified. "Do you honestly think that I could tend to his needs? He is my sworn enemy! Do you know what he has done? Do you know what he has said?"

Daniel was enraged. The young man was no longer sitting on the ground but had risen to his feet and was pacing angrily.

"I can well imagine," the widow answered. She waited for Daniel to calm down before speaking again. "You know, Daniel, when Mary first came and told me about you, I felt the same way. I was so filled with hatred towards you, towards all the King's soldiers, that I could not imagine helping my enemy."

Daniel looked at her, his face still reddened with anger. He remembered the unexpected turn the widow had taken, even helping to bring him back to her own home.

"Why did you help me, Mother Thomsen?" he asked, still amazed at the change of heart she had shown by her actions. "I never really understood your explanation."

"It was God speaking to my heart, Daniel—through his words in the Bible. I read about tending to the needs of my enemy and helping those being led away to death," she said. Tears stung at her eyes at the memory. "There are many words," she continued, "about loving your enemy, doing good to them that hate you, blessing them that curse you, and praying for them which despitefully use you."

"I do not think that I can do that, Mother Thomsen."

"None of us can do that, without the power of God to help us," she said. She placed her hand on his arm. "Would you like me to leave you alone to think about it, Daniel?"

He covered his eyes tightly with his soil-encrusted hands.

"Yes. I need to contemplate this. And I need to pray," he said, looking down at the dirt floor of the wigwam.

"And I shall pray for wisdom for you, Daniel," she said, her eyes full of compassion. She placed her Bible on the quilts. "Here is my book of wisdom, if you care to consult it."

The woman walked out the door and left her son-in-law alone. Daniel sat down on the makeshift bed once again and struggled in his spirit. He did not want to do this thing, but he wanted to do the right thing, the honorable thing in God's eyes. He kept fighting away the vision in his mind of the bruises Josiah had left on Mary's arms and the memory of the horrible things the man had said to her and about her.

Then Daniel thought about the ramifications of Widow Thomsen's forgiveness. While the woman had desperately struggled with her feelings to make the right decision, her final choice had had a profound impact. It had brought him health to his body, healing to his soul, and, ultimately, love to his life. He could not deny the powerful changes that her resolve had birthed.

Can I make the same choice to smother my hatred and forgive? he wondered.

"Oh, God," he prayed in anguish. "Help me to do the right thing. Help me to do your will."

He sat there for several moments before he heard the familiar creak of the dry hinge on the wigwam door. He looked up and saw the face of the woman he loved. Mary's eyes were swollen from crying and her long hair was disheveled. She had just awakened and was still wearing her night shift. Her feet were bare and she had covered herself with a shawl for warmth. Despite her unkempt appearance, she was the most beautiful sight to Daniel.

"Mother told me what she said to you," Mary said, trembling. "Are you really going over to Josiah Grant's to tend to his illness?"

Daniel looked up at her.

"Yes," he said. The young husband reached his arm up towards his wife.

Mary sat next to him, putting her arms around his waist.

"But what if you get the smallpox from him," Mary pleaded, tears coming down her cheeks.

"That will likely not happen, Mary. I have been around many in the camps who had the pox and I have never become ill. You know that I had it as a child," he reminded her. He gently laid her head on his shoulder and stroked her hair.

"I know, but Daniel … you will be gone for so long," she said. "It will be weeks before it is safe to come back and not carry the contagion with you. I cannot bear the thought of being without you. Especially now," she said, placing one hand on her growing belly.

Daniel touched her cheek with his fingers, wiping away her tears.

"Mary, this is my only chance to show everyone that I am one of you—a loyal American. They will not believe me otherwise. Besides," he added, "this is what I feel I must do. Deep in my spirit, I know this is right."

He looked at her, remembering when they had first met nearly a year ago.

"I need to do good to my enemy," he whispered in her ear. "Just as you did for me."

His lips met hers and he drew her down onto the quilts. They both clung to one another in a desperate passion. The couple shared their love once more before the separation that they both dreaded.

Chapter Thirty-two

Smallpox

Daniel and Mr. Eaton sat on their horses looking down the hill at the Grant home.

"Are you sure you want to do this thing?" Myles Eaton asked his friend.

"Want to?" Daniel said with a wry smile. "I do not think that is quite the word for it. Feel compelled to, yes, but my desire is to turn Dash around, right here and now, and return to my wife."

The young husband stared with trepidation at the house that harbored not only disease but hatred—hatred that was directed right at himself. He fought the urge to escape this confrontation and prayed for a firm resolve to complete this mission of mercy. The young man slid off the bare back of Dash and handed the reins to Mr. Eaton. With no saddle for a man's use at the Thomsen farm, Daniel had been forced to ride in an unfamiliar manner.

Myles Eaton looked at his friend one last time and tipped his hat.

"You're a far better Christian than I," he said.

"I think not, sir," Daniel said. "Just a Christian who is hopeful for peace in my heart. And desperate for safekeeping for my family. Not better than you, sir."

He started to walk away to the Grant house when he remembered something important.

"Mr. Eaton, can you please watch out for Mary while I am gone?" he asked his friend.

"I shall check in on her every day, lad. Do not worry about your wife—she is in good hands."

Daniel bowed to his friend gratefully and walked with determination toward the log house with the wood smoke drifting skyward from the chimney.

That warm hearth is probably the only inviting thing that I will experience in this visit, the young man thought ruefully. He limped toward the front door and knocked twice. After what seemed like an interminable wait, Jonathan Grant answered. He had been at his son's bedside, holding the basin under Josiah's chin to catch the volumes of vomit coming from the patient, a result of the potent elixir of tree roots Widow Thomsen had prescribed. The effect of the harsh potion was both immediate and merciless.

When the father finally opened the door, he was still holding the pan of vomit in one hand. Daniel nearly lost all resolve to stay when the stench of the basin's contents reached his nostrils.

"Come in, lad," Mr. Grant said. Daniel took a deep breath and walked inside the cabin. He fought away the urge to spew the gruel that Mary had served him that morning.

The entire cabin was filled with the smells of a single man's world. Ever since Josiah's mother had passed away the previous year, Jonathan had, for a time, done his best to keep up with the cleaning. But the disheartened and grieving husband had lost the will to keep up the effort. Filthy clothes and linens were in piles everywhere and food-encrusted utensils and bowls were stacked on the tableboard. The stench of disease only added to the foul aroma that filled the small cabin. The only welcoming smell was the smoke from the heavy oak log burning in the long fireplace.

Jonathan looked down at the basin in his hand and then noticed the look on Daniel's face.

"Let me dump this outside," the father said.

He walked out the door and threw the contents on the ground. He grabbed a bucket of water from the well and poured some into the bowl. The exhausted man swished it around a bit before throwing that on the ground as well.

"There, that's done."

The father walked back inside and saw Josiah glaring at Daniel.

"You will make Mr. Lowe welcome here, Josiah," he said tersely. "He has come to help."

Josiah lay weakly on his bed. The only energy in his entire being was in his eyes, which were intense with hatred for the visitor. Daniel looked at the weakened man and was suddenly filled with pity. The pox were everywhere, almost making the man unrecognizable. One sore blended into another on his face, distorting his features and making it difficult for the man to move his lips or open his eyes. He was pathetic in his illness, yet still consumed with loathing for the man who had come to bring mercy. Josiah was even more filled with rancor now that Daniel could observe him in such an unsightly state.

The waves of nausea from the emetic were beginning to take hold of Josiah again. Jonathan had gone outside to stir the linens in the large washing kettle. This prompted Daniel to grab the basin and hold it under Josiah's mouth while the patient expelled the contents of his stomach.

When he was finished puking, Josiah looked up with fresh rage in his eyes. He grabbed the basin and flung the putrid contents all over Daniel's clothing. Josiah gave a self-satisfied smirk as he weakly settled back onto his bed. Daniel was repulsed. He wanted to grab the ungrateful pox-covered man by the throat, but something stopped him from carrying out his vengeful thoughts. Instead, he turned around and walked toward the front door, praying for self-control.

Jonathan was in the doorway and had witnessed his son's disgraceful behavior. He glared at the patient in the bed.

"I'm certain that my son has some clean clothes for you, Mr. Lowe," he said without looking at the visitor. He continued to frown at his grown child while taking out fresh clothing from the chest of drawers. "Let's take those clothes of yours out to the lye soap, Mr. Lowe," he said.

The two men walked out towards the large laundry kettle in the yard. Jonathan also brought over a bucket of fresh water and bar soap for Daniel to wash the vomit off of his skin. Daniel gingerly unbuttoned the linen shirt that Mary had so lovingly stitched for him last winter, feeling a fresh wave of fury at the memory of Mary's skilled fingers as they worked so carefully to make this piece of clothing.

How dare Josiah dump something so foul and odious on her work? As Daniel was seething with regret that he had ever decided to come here, Jonathan interrupted his thoughts.

"My son's actions were unforgivable, Mr. Lowe," the father lamented. "I hardly know what to say."

Jonathan placed each piece of soiled clothing into the large steaming kettle as Daniel undressed.

The young husband paused in his angry musings long enough to look with compassion upon this saddened veteran. He remembered that Jonathan Grant had been the inspiring reader of the Declaration of Independence at the Fourth of July celebration. He was now astonished at the difference in demeanor between this father and son.

"I am certain that this illness is adding to Josiah's difficult behavior," Daniel said. "His fever appears to be affecting his judgment."

"That is kind of you to say, sir. I think we both know that it is more than smallpox that influences Josiah's disposition."

Daniel picked up the bar of soap and hurriedly washed up. He was shirtless and wet, and the chill of the late September air was causing him to shiver. Despite his discomfort, Daniel was pleased to wash away all evidence of Josiah's insult. After Daniel had removed all the soiled clothing, he hurriedly dressed himself in Josiah's simple attire. The sleeves were not quite long enough, but they would do. They were clean.

"Thank you for the clothing, sir," Daniel said.

The older man stirred the contents of the kettle filled with lye soap and water. It was obvious he had other things than cleaning on his mind.

"I should have been a better father to Josiah," Jonathan began sadly, wiping at his face with the back of one hand. "I was so happy to see him and his mother when I returned from the war that I didn't want to appear too harsh about his behavior, but I should have been more diligent. He was so spoiled..." The man's voice drifted off.

"I am sure that none of us gets through life without regrets, sir," Daniel said.

"That is true enough, young man," the father said, "but you do not want to have too many regrets about your children. You want to know that you raised them up proper-like." He looked towards his house.

"Not undisciplined or ungrateful," he said, pointing his chin toward the structure. Jonathan looked back at the kettle for a moment then looked at Daniel. "Lowe, is it?" the older man said.

"Yes, sir," Daniel answered.

"I served under a Major William Lowe in the French War," Jonathan said, remembering scenes from long ago.

"That was my uncle, sir," the young man answered.

"He was a good man, sir. One of the King's faithful officers. Very brave on the battlefield." He paused for a moment. "Sorry loss for our troops when he was killed. A sad loss for your family as well, I am sure."

"Yes, sir," Daniel said. "I do not remember him myself but I do remember my father's sorrow when we heard of his demise."

"I see that you have a limp and a nasty scar from the war as well, Mr. Lowe," the older veteran said.

He looked at this young man who had been accused of being a spy. Yet what Jonathan saw was not an enemy soldier but rather the conscientious and brave man of character that he always wished his own son had been. Tears stung at the older man's eyes.

"I am sure you were very brave and honorable in war, just like your uncle was," Jonathan said.

Daniel looked down at the ground and then met the man's eyes. "I hope so, sir," he said.

"Well then, Mr. Lowe, I have not even asked you how your wife is doing."

"She is quite well. Thank you, sir," said Daniel, brightening at the mention of Mary.

"I am sure you will have a fine family to be proud of one day."

"Well, as a matter of fact, our first child should come in the spring," Daniel said proudly.

"That is fine news, sir, indeed," he said, patting Daniel on the shoulder.

Josiah Grant lay in bed inside the house, but he could hear the conversation between the two men outdoors. He had heard every word. And when he heard that Mary was expecting Daniel Lowe's child, salty tears burned like fire on the open sores around his eyes.

***

The scourge of the pox continued for several days. Daniel tried to assist Josiah with cold cloths for his fever, but the angry patient just grabbed the linens out of Daniel's hands.

"I can do it myself," Josiah said.

Daniel refused to respond to this unruly behavior. He just continued making soups for the patient and cleaning the soiled linens and clothing. He made the hyssop tea that Widow Thomsen had sent over and placed the tankard by Josiah's bedside. Daniel knew that the resentful patient would only drink the brew after he walked away. Josiah's pride would not allow him to appear grateful in any manner. The pox-ridden patient did his best to provoke Daniel with his vindictive behavior. But no matter how hateful his actions were, Josiah could not arouse the response he hoped for. He was frustrated and perplexed.

On the fifth day of Josiah's illness, the situation took an ominous turn when Jonathan began to complain of a throbbing headache. Daniel noted the flaming redness in the man's cheeks and was forced to acknowledge the obvious—Josiah's father was the next victim of this dreaded illness.

"Of all the times there was pox in the camps, I never became ill," Jonathan said weakly, his face covered with sweat. "Why now?"

"I know not, sir. But I shall take care of you as well," Daniel said sadly. He had grown fond of this older gentleman in the last few days and prayed that the man had the strength to recover. Daniel was filled with dread. The emetic concoction that would bring on the violent vomiting was difficult enough for a younger man to endure. It could be devastating for an older man like Jonathan Grant.

The drink brought about the desired result, but it did not alleviate the symptoms of disease. Instead, the fevers became worse. Each day, Daniel attempted to cool down the man with fresh water from the well, but the illness continued to rage.

In the middle of the night on the fifth day of Jonathan's illness, the older man's breathing began to change. A strange rattling emerged from Jonathan's chest and he was unable to speak. Daniel had heard this sound before. He knew the end would soon be near. Daniel walked slowly over to Josiah's bedside and looked down at the recovering soldier.

Josiah's pox were just beginning to dry out. Several of the scabs were still clinging to his beard as they slowly fell away from his face, leaving behind their telltale craters in his skin.

"Your father is not doing well, Josiah," Daniel said, wiping the sweat off of his own forehead with the back of his hand.

"I have brought this illness upon my father," the man's son said with trembling lips. He weakly rose from his bed and walked over to his parent's bedside. Daniel watched Josiah's face contort with indescribable pain as he looked at his dying parent.

Whatever the son wishes to say to him is best left between the two, thought Daniel.

The young husband walked outside and closed the door. He moved away from the house and looked up at the stars on this clear and cool October evening. He breathed in deeply, grateful for the refreshing it brought to his body and spirit.

As Daniel stood there in the quiet, he was overwhelmed with homesickness. But this time it was not the desire for his family in England. He longed to be home with Mary, to hold her in his arms and feel her vitality. Tears stung at his eyes as he wondered how his wife was faring. With the village quarantine, it was impossible to send letters to her for fear that even the paper he touched might transmit the illness to Mary. His feelings of emptiness were soon interrupted by the sobs of Josiah at his father's bedside.

Daniel knew that Jonathan Grant would never again recite the Declaration of Independence at a Fourth of July celebration. That thought filled him with immeasurable sadness.

***

He was just completing the burial of Jonathan Grant when Daniel heard someone shouting at him from a distance.

"Daniel!" It was the voice of Widow Thomsen, standing up on the hillside, the same bluff that he and Myles Eaton had stood upon nearly two weeks prior.

"Mother Thomsen! How is Mary?"

"She is well, Daniel. But the White family has come down with the smallpox. Can you take the medicinals over there?" the widow asked.

Daniel's heart sank. He had been hoping to wait another week for Josiah to completely recover before he would feel secure in not bringing the smallpox back home. But this news would mean delaying his return even longer. The man was overwhelmed with fatigue and anxious to see his wife. But he knew there was an even greater concern. Smallpox at the White home had great significance for his family. Hannah White was Mary's best friend. This young victim of the pox had also promised to wait for Mary's brother James, who was away at war.

Mary must be beside herself with worry, Daniel thought.

"Yes, of course," he said.

Widow Thomsen noted the freshly mounded grave that Daniel was standing near as he held a shovel.

"Who has died, Daniel?" she asked, fighting back tears of despair. The danger of the pox was suddenly more real to the woman than it had been a few hours ago.

"Jonathan Grant," Daniel said. Then he added, "Josiah is recovering."

Widow Thomsen placed her hand over her quivering lips.

"I see," she said. "How are you, Daniel? Mary wanted to ask you herself but I would not let her come. I knew she would not be able to keep herself from running to you."

Daniel had to smile at the woman's words. He knew that he would not have been able to resist holding Mary in his arms either.

"Tell her I am well, Mother Thomsen. And tell her," he stopped and swallowed, "tell her how much I miss her."

"I shall, Daniel," she said. "And thank you for what you are doing. You have never been braver on the battlefield."

The widow turned and disappeared into the woods leading to the Thomsen farm.

Battlefield, indeed, Daniel thought. He had never been in such a fight before that did not involve muskets and bayonets. He felt wounded and weary but definitely not defeated. The most effective weapon, he had come to realize, can often be the "sword of the Spirit, which is the word of God."

***

As he followed the directions given by Josiah Grant to the White's home, Daniel thought about the last few weeks with both sadness and satisfaction. Sadness at the passing of Jonathan Grant and satisfaction at the final words that Josiah had said to him before Daniel departed from the Grant home.

"Please tell your wife I am sorry," Josiah had said.

It had taken losing the friendship of Mary Thomsen, a close call with death, and now the passing of his father for Josiah to realize that his love had been self-seeking and without honor. It was a recognition that had come far too late.

Daniel had stared at the broken man covered with unsightly pock marks and felt pity for one who had lost so much.

"I shall tell her," he had said as he shook the man's hand.

But as the home of Selectman White appeared in the distance, Daniel was filled with renewed apprehension. He now had to prepare to face the village leader, who was ready to send him to the gallows. The young man steeled himself for this next skirmish and prayed for victory.

No one answered the young man's knock at the door. Unsure of what to do, Daniel opened the front door.

"I say, Mr. White? Miss White?" he called.

No one answered. Daniel was perplexed but eager to find them. When he did, it was a most disturbing sight. Mr. White was in a severe fever in his bed, barely able to recognize Daniel. His words were unintelligible. Hannah fared not much better, although she recognized Daniel and tried to smile.

"Thank you for coming, Daniel," she said. Her breathing was labored and her face was as red as Mary's had been when she had the influenza.

Hannah and her father required Daniel's prompt intervention. He immediately prepared the tree root concoction that encouraged the dreadful vomiting. Although the patients were barely able to swallow, the little they consumed produced the desired result. Daniel would just finish assisting with one patient before the one in the next room needed his assistance. By the time the emesis treatments were complete, Daniel was exhausted.

The dreaded pustules had already broken out all over their faces and limbs. Daniel hoped that the delay in his arrival had not cost them their health. All he could do now was apply cool water for their fever, bring them hyssop tea to drink, and pray.

***

Three days later, Daniel was making a fresh batch of chicken broth in the large hearth when he heard Hannah's voice calling his name. He appeared in her doorway and was relieved to see that her fever had finally resolved.

"You are looking much better, Miss White," he said.

"I am feeling better. I cannot thank you enough for helping us Mr. Lowe." Weakly she added, "I heard how you helped out at the Grant home. You are very brave."

"Not so brave, really," he said.

"Mary thinks you are the bravest man she has ever met," Hannah said. "And the handsomest."

"I am afraid my wife must suffer from an affliction of her sight," Daniel said. In a more serious tone he added, "I honestly do not know what she sees in me."

"May I tell you something, Mr. Lowe?" Hannah asked weakly.

"Yes, of course, Miss White," Daniel said. He looked intently at his patient.

"I have known your wife since we were small children. She was always the one who attracted the glances of the village lads intent upon winning her heart. But none of them ever won her affections the way you have. Mary was looking for a very special partner in life—and she has found her perfect consort in you. I have never seen her love another as she loves you."

Daniel's eyes filled with tears at her words.

"I am sorry, Mr. Lowe. I did not mean to inflict pain upon you with these words," she said.

"It is not pain, Miss White. It is just that … I miss Mary so, and your words remind me of the joy that she brings to me, even when I cannot be with her."

"I so hope that you can be with her soon," she said.

"As do I," Daniel said in a whisper.

237

***

It had been nearly three weeks with no further outbreaks of the disease. The residents of Deer Run were cautiously beginning to venture out of doors, and Daniel soon thought that it was safe to return home without the threat of carrying smallpox with him. After thoroughly cleaning his clothing with more lye soap and laying them out in the sun to dry, he carefully scrubbed himself with soap and water, paying special attention to cleaning the beard that had grown in the last few weeks. He wanted to remove any possible remnant of the illness.

He was outside the White's house preparing to finally return home when the selectman came out the front door. He was still feeling weak from the devastating disease, and he had multiple scars from the pox, which made him appear much older.

"I hear that you are going home, sir," Caleb White said.

"Yes, sir, I am," Daniel said.

Mr. White was embarrassed about the events prior to the outbreak of the illness in their community. He and Daniel had not discussed the details of that infamous night, but it was obvious how closely their lives had come to changing forever. It was a humbling realization, especially for Caleb White.

"I do not know how to thank you, sir, for saving the lives of my daughter and myself," Mr. White said, eyes cast down.

"I administered the medicinals, Mr. White, but it was God that healed you," Daniel said. "I am grateful that I was able to assist you and your daughter."

"I hear you and the Missus are expecting a child in spring," the older man said. "Perhaps you and she would like to have dinner with Hannah and myself sometime before winter sets in."

"I'd like that, sir. When you are feeling recovered, of course."

"Of course," Mr. White said.

Hannah came out of the house to bid Daniel farewell. She had fewer pock marks on her face and arms than her father did, but the evidence of the illness was there nevertheless. She was already shy, Daniel knew, and he hoped that these scars would not increase her withdrawn demeanor, especially with James.

"It should not be long before James comes home for a visit," he said encouragingly. She touched her cheeks and felt the marks beneath her fingers. A shadow of concern crossed her eyes. "He will be most anxious to see his beloved Miss White," Daniel said. He smiled and she returned the grin.

"Thank you for everything, Mr. Lowe," she said as she and her father waved good-bye.

Daniel would have run the entire way home except for the leg wound that prevented such a gait for more than a short distance. Instead, he limped along as quickly as he was able. He could barely contain his joy at finally returning to his wife.

He saw an unfamiliar child walking along the road.

"I say there, lad. Do you know the way to the Thomsen farm?" he asked the boy.

"Everyone knows the way to the Thomsen farm, sir," the child answered. "That's where the midwife lives."

"Yes, of course," Daniel said, grinning so widely his mouth was beginning to hurt. "Can you take a message for me to Missus Lowe that lives there?"

"Why yes, sir."

"Please tell Missus Lowe that her husband is coming home and to please meet him in their special place," Daniel said.

"Their special place?" he asked, scratching his head.

"Yes, lad. She will know what that means," Daniel said, hurrying down the road. "And tell her I said you can have an apple," he called back to the boy.

The child looked at him and shrugged his shoulders before heading to the Thomsen farm to deliver the message.

Chapter Thirty-three

Reunion

Mary was sitting in a chair by the fire on an early November morning, knitting a blanket for the baby. Clouds were starting to gather outdoors, dimming the light inside the farmhouse. The grayness in the room mirrored the young woman's mood.

Daniel had been gone from home for nearly six weeks now and she was fighting thoughts of despair.

When will he return? What if he has come down with the pox? What if Mr. White has decided to arrest Daniel despite being a Good Samaritan? What if I never see my husband again?

Mary fought back tears as she struggled to hide her turmoil from her mother and sister. They were only a few feet away doing a reading lesson.

The young wife looked down at the blanket that draped over her rapidly growing belly. Although she was not overly large for a pregnant woman, she was far more swollen than she or her mother thought she should be at this point. There had been a questioning look on her mother's face containing the suggestion that Mary and Daniel had given into their passions before they were married. This profoundly annoyed Mary. Although she and Daniel had both been anxious to share their affections, they had managed to delay that fulfillment until after their marriage.

Yet, despite their commitment to save their love for the wedding day, this child was growing so fast, and Mary wondered why.

Dear Lord, she prayed silently, *please do not let this child be so large I cannot deliver him.* She shuddered when she heard stories from her mother about difficult deliveries when the child was far too big. Mary tried on a daily basis to push these fears aside.

The young woman's anxious thoughts were interrupted by a small knock at the door. Widow Thomsen was in the middle of the lesson with Sarah, so Mary carefully arose from her chair and set the knitting upon it.

When she opened the door she was surprised to see young Benjamin Putney. The sweet-faced boy with the impish grin had a larger-than-usual smile on his face.

"Good day, Missus Lowe," Benjamin said, giving a formal bow to the young wife.

They must be teaching more on manners at school these days, Mary thought with amusement.

"Yes, Benjamin, how may I help you?" she asked. She had not heard that the boy's mother should be near childbirth just yet, and he seemed far too lighthearted to be reporting an illness.

"I have a message for you, Missus Lowe. From Mr. Lowe." The boy grinned wider than ever.

Mary felt her heart begin to race and her throat become dry.

"Yes?" she asked expectantly, smiling broadly as well.

Benjamin was thoroughly enjoying being the courier of happy news. The whole town was aware of the sacrifice that Daniel Lowe had made for the desperately ill in their community, and everyone was in a grateful and celebratory mood. Despite the tragic loss of Jonathan Grant, the townsfolk of Deer Run knew that they had been spared a far worse outcome. And they had Daniel to thank for his efforts.

"Mr. Lowe says that you should meet him in your special place," Benjamin said.

No sooner had the words proceeded from the boy's mouth than Mary grabbed her shawl and began to race for the wigwam. Widow Thomsen came to the door as she heard the message and yelled after Mary.

"Do not run," she cautioned her pregnant daughter.

"I shall not run. I shall just walk extremely quickly," Mary said to herself, slowing her pace slightly.

In the distance, she could faintly hear Benjamin Putney asking for an apple.

"I shall get you an apple, Benjamin," Widow Thomsen said, grinning at the happy news.

Mary hurried as fast as her rapid walk could carry her.

Was the wigwam really this far? she wondered. It seemed as if she would never close the distance to the hideaway that secluded her husband.

As she neared the bark structure, fear once again filled her mind. Daniel had not seen her in six weeks and she knew that her appearance had changed. Would he be dismayed at her growing belly? Would he still desire her?

Mary carefully opened the door to the wigwam and walked inside. Daniel turned to face her and she gasped at the appearance of the bearded man standing in front of her. Once she realized it was her husband, she smiled shyly, her heart racing in her chest.

Daniel self-consciously rubbed the bristly hair on his face.

"I did not have a razor. I apologize for my unkempt countenance," he said, regretting that he had frightened Mary with his unexpected appearance.

The young wife's eyes glistened. She gingerly walked closer to this man that she loved and stroked the hair on his cheek.

"It reminds me of when we first met—just over a year ago," she said, her voice trembling.

"When you touched my face with your hand when I was so ill, I wanted it to stay there always," he said, kissing her palm gently.

Daniel reached over to her linen cap and carefully removed it from her head. He slowly undid the pins that held her long curls in place and watched as her locks fell around her shoulders.

"When your hair stroked against my cheek, I was mesmerized by your beauty. I wanted you to tarry longer. I never wanted you to go away. But when you did, you came back again to me. You saved my life." Passion filled his voice as he remembered the committed way in which she had cared for him.

Mary touched the scar on his cheek above his beard.

"As you saved mine," she said, her voice soft and low.

"You risked everything for me," Daniel said. He placed his hand upon her firmly growing belly. "You even hid my coat as though you were with child. And now..." His voice trailed off as he gazed upon the evidence of their baby beneath her wool gown.

He looked at her face with tears in his eyes.

"You are so beautiful, Mary."

The young husband moved his hands around her lower back and drew her close to himself. He kissed his wife with deep passion and she melted in to his embrace.

He began to kiss her neck.

"Daniel, I missed you so much," she whispered, her voice quivering.

Daniel looked down at his wife and picked her up in his arms. He gently laid her down on the quilts over the hay. He tenderly embraced her, as their passion for each other obliterated all the fears and sadness of the last several weeks.

Chapter Thirty-four

Recollections

Mary and Daniel had spent most of the afternoon in the wigwam. They both knew it would likely be their last visit to this hideaway before the severe cold of winter set in, and the couple was not anxious to leave.

"I shall miss coming out here to be alone with you," Daniel said, stroking her hair as they lay next to one another on the quilt.

"I shall as well," Mary said, holding him closely. "But as long as you are by my side, it does not matter where we are." She looked up at him and kissed him tenderly. "And someday we shall have our own home where we can be quite alone."

"We will not be alone. We will have our little one," Daniel said, grinning. He kissed her slowly. "Have I told you how happy I am to be home?"

"About ten times now," she said. "But you can tell me as often as you want and I will not tire of the words. Speaking of our own home, would you like to go see our land?" She looked up at him expectantly.

"If you would like. Are you sure that would not be too long a walk for you? It is getting quite cold by the sound of the wind."

"We can put the quilts around our shoulders to keep warm," she said. "We need to take them home for the winter anyway."

The couple reluctantly got up from the bed of hay and Daniel wrapped one of the blankets around his wife. He used it to draw her close and give her one last kiss before leaving their haven.

"We must remember to come back here next year," he said, smoothing her hair away from her face. "And every year after."

They held each other for a long moment before leaving the warmth of the enclosure to face the cold outdoors. The clouds that had been slowly building through the day were starting to produce small flakes of snow, and the wind was stirring the frozen particles into a gentle dance.

"At least it is not so freezing as when I first brought you here," Mary said.

Daniel had his arm around his wife to keep her warm as they walked towards their property. It seemed ironic to him that the land he now owned encompassed the very path that he had used as his escape from the Continental guards. When their home was built, he would be able to view the road to Deer Run that he had trod upon as a prisoner of war. He hoped that his yearlong pilgrimage since that time would help remind him to never despair again. That there was always hope if he would trust in the God that spared his life and the God that had blessed him with his wife and unborn child.

The young husband looked down and squeezed his wife's shoulders. Mary looked up at Daniel.

"What?" she asked. Snowflakes were starting to land upon her hair and he brushed them gently away.

"I was just thinking about the first time I came along this path," Daniel said. "I was running for my life. I thought I was running away, but now I realize I was hastening towards something ... towards someone." He kissed the top of her head as they continued their stroll.

Mary rested her head against Daniel's shoulder and hugged his waist more tightly. "I so missed your tender touch," she said.

They walked a short distance further when Daniel stopped.

"What...?" He could not believe his eyes. Where thick rows of birch and maple trees had once stood now lay several dozen fallen timbers, leaving a large opening in the woods.

Mary looked up at him with joy.

"Several of the men from the village came by in the last week and wanted to start clearing our land for us," she said. "They asked me where you and I wanted our home built and I showed them. They have not quite finished felling the trees, but they said they would come back in early spring."

Daniel stood there in silent disbelief.

"It was all right for them to start, was it not?" Mary asked, concerned that perhaps he had wanted to begin the project himself.

"It is more than all right," he said, nearly overwhelmed. He knew by this neighborly act of kindness that he was being accepted into this community. And he knew that his past would no longer need to haunt him or cause either of them any fear.

Daniel wrapped his arms around Mary. A great weight had been lifted off his shoulders. The young couple held each other and dreamed of a peaceful future.

The wind started to pick up in intensity and Mary started to shiver.

"Let's sally to the farmhouse," Daniel said, wrapping the quilt more snugly around his wife.

"You missed seeing Jubo and Gibb while you were gone," Mary said, recalling the events of the last several weeks. "And Aunt Prudence, of course," she added, grinning.

Daniel had to smile remembering the previous visit. The great aunt had assumed that Mary had become engaged to Daniel solely due to the older woman's encouragement. She had been adamant that it was Mary's patriotic duty to bear children to replenish the colonies.

"Aunt Prudence must have been beside herself with joy that you were with child," Daniel said.

"I think she was ready to sign up our son for the Continental Army," Mary said.

He stopped and looked at Mary more seriously.

"I hope that our sons never have to face a war."

Mary touched Daniel's bearded cheeks.

"I pray that as well, Daniel," she said.

They resumed their walk in a more sober demeanor. War was still on everyone's mind as the colonial forces continued to clash with the King's army. They both wondered when this conflict would be over once and for all.

Daniel finally broke the silence.

"I have been wondering how Sarah took the news—about my past?"

He was concerned about his young sister-in-law and the friendship they had developed. He feared that the truth could jeopardize her trust in him. Mary paused before answering.

"At first, she did not believe it, but then, when she realized that you actually had been a British soldier, she was quite angry. She cried much over it."

Mary paused in their walk, noticing the look of distress on Daniel's face. She put her arms around her husband's waist.

"And then one day she woke up and said, 'I do not care who my brother used to fight for. He is now an American and he is my brother.'"

Mary held Daniel close and he returned the embrace.

"Thank you, Mary," he finally said.

"For what?"

"For believing in me when no one else would," he said.

"Well that was easy," she teased. "You quite swept me off my feet with your passionate glances. I could not resist you."

"So you could not resist my filthy clothing, wretched wound, and scraggly beard?"

She kissed him gently.

"It was your eyes that won my heart, Daniel Lowe," she said.

She shivered again from the wind, and Daniel encouraged them to quicken the pace. "I forgot to tell you that Mr. Eaton brought over some fresh lamb's wool for the baby," Mary said as they continued their hike back to the farmhouse. "I spun it into the softest yarn and I am making him a blanket." Mary always referred to their unborn child as a boy.

"Mr. Eaton is a true friend," Daniel said, remembering how the man had helped the family so many times in the last months.

"Do you know that he came over every day while you were gone?" Mary asked. She was still amazed at the frequency of the neighbor's visits.

"I am not surprised," he said, recalling the man's promise back at the Grant house.

The couple was nearing the Thomsen home and Mary tried to tidy her appearance some before entering the house. Daniel looked at her and couldn't keep from laughing. Their clothes and hair were completely covered with bits of hay from the wigwam.

As Daniel picked a piece of straw out of Mary's hair, he grinned mischievously.

"Do you suppose your mother will know where we have been?"

Chapter Thirty-five

Meetings

The deep cold of winter set in with ferocity, forcing the residents of Deer Run to stay indoors as much as possible.

A brief thaw in mid-December, however, allowed everyone to attend Sabbath services at the village meetinghouse. It would be a welcome relief for the housebound townspeople, perhaps their last chance to visit with friends before the inevitable snows would arrive.

As Mary dressed in her woolen gown for the occasion, she slowly smoothed the soft fabric tightly over her large belly. Her baby was now growing at an alarming rate, and the young mother knew that eager tongues would likely wag concerning the timing of the conception. Tears stung at her eyes as she anticipated the unfair gossip.

Daniel walked over to her, still buttoning his waistcoat.

"What is troubling you, Mary?" he said, tenderly embracing her waist.

"You know what everyone will think, Daniel," she said, fighting back the tears. "I am far too large to be ready to give birth in early May. At least, that is what they will intimate with their glances."

"Mary, look at me," Daniel said, pulling her chin up. "You and I know that this child started after we said our vows. Do not fear their glances. It does not matter what the townspeople say. We know the truth." He tenderly put his large hands across her belly.

"You and I know the truth, Daniel. But even Mother looks at me in wonder as she sees how much this child has grown. I confess, I am at a loss to explain it," she said, starting to cry. Mary's emotions were very fragile these days, and Daniel did his best to not say anything that would make her cry.

"If you do not want to go today, I shall stay home with you," he said.

"Why? Are you ashamed of how I look?" she said, crying even more.

"No! Of course not," he said hurriedly. He held her as she wept uncontrollably. He had learned that sometimes it was better to just comfort her rather than say something she might misconstrue.

When she was finished crying, she stood back from him.

"I shall go to the meetinghouse and sit proudly, knowing I have done nothing wrong," she said with resolve.

"There's my strong Mary," he said, kissing her.

She washed off the tears from her face and set her cap over her pinned up hair.

"There," she said. "I am ready."

Mary and Daniel walked out of their room and saw that Widow Thomsen and Sarah were already waiting for them.

"Would you like to ride on Dash to the meetinghouse, Mary?" her mother asked.

"No, I think the walk will do me good," she answered with a slight smile.

Sarah was openly staring at Mary's belly with wide eyes. The thin wool garment seemed to accentuate the size of the growing baby. Widow Thomsen saw the young girl's gaze and placed her hands on the girl's shoulders.

"Let's be off then, Sarah," she said, hurrying the child along. "We will discuss these long gazes at an appropriate time later," she whispered to the curious girl.

The women all donned their woolen capes and Daniel put on the deerskin coat over his waistcoat. Mary was still in the midst of sewing him a woolen coat, but it was not yet complete.

The air was chilly but refreshing and revived Mary's spirits, and the family was soon chatting and laughing the entire length of the walk to the village. It would be Daniel's first visit to the meetinghouse since the outbreak of smallpox and he was unsure of the reception he would receive. It was not long before he realized that the townsfolk of Deer Run were awaiting his return with open hearts.

"Welcome back, Mr. Lowe," a gray-haired gent exclaimed, shaking his hand with fervor.

"Thank you, sir," Daniel said, smiling cautiously.

Myles Eaton approached the family with a wide grin.

"Good to see you back in town, Daniel," he said, putting his arm around the young man's shoulders.

As the group walked toward the wooden building, Selectman White turned towards the family to greet them.

"Hello, Mr. Lowe," the man said, shaking Daniel's hand warmly.

The young man took note of the deep scars on the man's hands and face from the disease that had nearly taken his life. Daniel smiled as though he had not noticed any change.

"Hello to you, sir," Daniel said. "I am glad to see you are well."

"Thanks to you, I am," Mr. White said humbly. "I am indebted to you, sir."

Daniel bowed to the selectman and turned slightly to see that Mary and Hannah White were embracing. The long-time friends had not seen each other since Hannah's illness, and Mary's friend was chattering excitedly about how wonderful she looked.

Bless you, Hannah, Daniel thought with relief.

Although this survivor of smallpox still had several visible scars, Hannah had been spared from serious disfigurement. Unfortunately for Josiah Grant, the same could not be said about him. The numerous pox had left insidious craters over his entire body. The previously handsome young soldier had lost his prideful swagger, now replaced by the slumped shoulders of a broken man.

Josiah had seen Daniel and Mary approach the door to the meetinghouse far too late to avoid the inevitable greeting. The scarred soldier was forced to engage the couple in conversation. Mary was startled at the appearance of Josiah. Although she knew he had been ill, she was not prepared for this metamorphosis.

"Good day, Josiah," she said nervously.

Josiah's gaze was drawn automatically to the young woman's large belly, and it was with obvious pain that he looked at her face. Daniel put

Elaine Marie Cooper

his arm around his wife's waist and drew her close to himself protectively. The move did not go unnoticed by the unsuccessful suitor.

"Good day, Daniel. Mary," he said nervously, tipping his tricornered hat far too quickly.

"Good day, Josiah," Daniel said, still holding his wife closely. "I am glad you are recovered from your illness." His words were sincere, but Daniel was always guarded when it came to Josiah Grant.

"Yes, thanks to you, sir," Josiah said, casting his eyes downward.

"So what are your plans, sir?" Daniel asked.

"I leave tomorrow to return to camp," Josiah said, wiping the hair off his forehead nervously. "I've closed the house up in the meantime. Don't know when I'll return."

He glanced briefly at Mary's eyes with a pained look.

"There's nothin' for me here."

Mary paused nervously. She was grateful for Daniel's firm grip, as she felt frightened and weak. This was her first encounter with Josiah since the incident so long ago and she trembled with the memory.

"I shall pray for your safety, Josiah," Mary said more calmly than she felt.

"Thank you, Mary," he said, tears starting to sting his eyes. He tipped his hat again and hurried inside the building.

"Let's go sit down," Daniel said.

She nodded in assent and the two made their way to their pew.

No sooner had Mary taken her seat than she noticed the Howard sisters looking at her and whispering to one another. They were counting on their fingers, apparently trying to determine the number of months that Mary and Daniel had been man and wife.

They probably cannot count without using their fingers, she thought angrily.

Daniel noticed the Howard sisters' obvious insult and he glared at them. He took Mary's hand and squeezed it gently, giving her a reassuring smile.

The singing was soon underway, and the soothing lyrics from the Psalms were a comforting respite for Mary. They helped her focus on God's encouragement amidst the many storms in her life.

***

Mary was not feeling well after the morning service, and Widow Thomsen hurried over to Mr. Eaton. "Myles," she said in earnest, "would you be so kind as to drive Mary home on your wagon?"

Mr. Eaton could see the concern in his friend's eyes. "What troubles you, Ruth?" He whispered so as not to attract glances in their direction.

"I am worried about her, Myles. Something is amiss but I cannot explain my fears. And now she is feeling ill and I feel I must take her home as soon as possible."

"I'll get my wagon ready with haste and take you both home. Do not fear, Ruth. She and this child are in God's hands." Mr. Eaton discreetly gave her hand a reassuring squeeze.

"Thank you, Myles," she said, gratitude in her voice. Widow Thomsen walked hurriedly back to her family. "Mary, Mr. Eaton has offered to take us home."

"Thank you, Mother," Mary said, her face paler than normal.

"May I stay for the afternoon service, Mother?" Sarah asked anxiously.

Mary hated to be the cause of disrupting her younger sister's day. This would perhaps be Sarah's last time at the meetinghouse through the long winter ahead. And yet Mary knew that she needed her mother more than anyone else right now.

"Daniel, would you be willing to stay with Sarah for the afternoon? My mother can look after me," she said.

"Of course I can stay with Sarah," he said agreeably, although he was reluctant to leave Mary's side. "We shall have a grand picnic together."

"Thank you, Daniel," Sarah said gratefully.

In one respect, the young man was thankful for this opportunity to spend some time speaking with the seven-year-old child. He had noted a slight change in her demeanor towards him since he had returned from the White's home. He suspected that, although she loved him as her brother, she still struggled in her mind with Daniel's past. He hoped that Sarah could resolve in her mind that he had once been an enemy soldier. The opportunity to speak about the situation finally afforded itself on their walk home later that afternoon.

They walked mostly in silence, and Daniel noted that Sarah was definitely not her usually talkative self.

"So how did you enjoy the afternoon service, little miss?" Daniel asked.

"Fine," she replied.

"Fine? That is all you have to say to me?" Daniel said, trying to appear lighthearted. "We used to have such jolly conversations, little miss."

"That was before…" She stopped herself from speaking further.

"Before you knew I had been a King's soldier?" he asked her, daring to put words to her unspoken thoughts.

"You lied to me, Daniel," she said with anger. "You said you were injured in the war!"

"That was not a lie. I was injured in the war," he said. They paused on the road home to the Thomsen farm.

"But you did not tell me you were a Redcoat, Daniel!"

"And what would you have done if I had told you that I was?"

"I do not know, but it was not right that you made me think you were one of us."

Her childish words stung at his heart. He looked off into the distance at the clouds that threatened to bring measurable snow.

Sarah realized immediately that her words had been cruel. She did not wish to hurt him, but she had felt betrayed ever since she realized the truth about his past.

"I am sorry, Daniel," she said sadly. "I know that you are an American now." She paused. "Why did you become a King's soldier?"

Daniel looked at his young sister-in-law.

"Where I come from that is what second sons do," he said.

"Second sons? So you have an older brother?" she asked inquisitively.

"Yes," he replied. "His name is William and he inherited the family home."

"I see," she said. "And why did you have to come here to fight our people?"

"I was told to, little miss," he said, remembering the day he received his orders. "I did not have a choice."

Sarah pondered all these revelations for a moment. She gently took his hand.

"I am sorry I was so angry with you, Daniel. I did not understand," she said, looking up.

"It's all right, little miss. Many things in life are difficult to understand."

"I am glad that you were told to come here," she said, "because now you are my brother."

"I am grateful as well," he said.

The two walked hand-in-hand up the hill toward home.

***

When Daniel and Sarah arrived home, the young husband inquired about his wife's well being.

"She is fine, Daniel," Widow Thomsen reassured him. "It was a very difficult time for her at the meetinghouse, what with seeing Josiah Grant and all."

Daniel always had to resist the urge to bristle at the name. "Yes, I know," he said, his jaw working to restrain his emotions. "Is Mary asleep?"

"I know she is resting but I do not think she is asleep," the widow answered.

"I will see how she is faring," he said. He went to their bedroom and closed the door.

"Daniel?" Mary said, sitting up in bed.

"Please do not get up, Mary. How are you?" he asked, kissing her cheek and sitting next to her on the bed.

"Better, thank you," she replied, lying back down on her pillow. "I am very tired, that is all."

Daniel lay down next to her and wrapped his arms around her. Mary gasped and grabbed at her belly.

"What is it?" Daniel asked in alarm.

"He's moving," she said, laughing. "A great deal."

She placed Daniel's hand on her belly so that he could feel their child. He waited but felt nothing.

"Every time I put my hand on you, the child stops moving," he said, disappointed.

"Well, he is an active little one. He must be a boy," Mary said. Then she started to laugh. "That's exactly what I said to that soldier last year when I was hiding your coat."

"What soldier?" he asked curiously.

"I never told you?" she asked. "It was when I wrapped your red coat in my petticoat and pretended to be with child. A soldier came by on horseback and I said I was out walking for my health."

Daniel looked at her in complete surprise and concern.

"You never told me this," he said. "I did not realize that you were so endangered."

"I was safe, Daniel," she reassured him. "But my bundle in the petticoat slipped at one point and I nearly gave birth to your coat right in front of the soldier."

She was amused. Her husband was not.

"You could have been arrested," he said, horrified.

"Daniel, I did not mean to cause you distress. I was just remembering what I had said to the soldier: 'Active little one. Must be a boy.' I am sorry that this frightened you."

"You continue to amaze me, Mary Thomsen," he said, smiling and kissing her hand.

"Excuse me, sir," she said with mock disdain. "That is Mary Lowe, if you please. I am a married woman."

He placed his hand upon her belly.

"Well that is a fortunate thing considering your condition, Missus Lowe," he teased her.

When he said these words in jest, he felt a forceful kick against his hand. The surprised look on his face made Mary burst out laughing.

"Mr. Lowe, please meet your son. He is trying to shake your hand."

Chapter Thirty-six

Patriot

The young soldier pressed forward with resolve, walking down the spring-dampened dirt road.

His blue uniform was covered with mud and the powdery residue of musket fire. The facing on his coat, which used to be white, was now a dingy gray. An occasional stain of old blood added more color than was intended for this Continental uniform. The only purposeful scarlet was the single epaulette on his right shoulder, signifying a rank of sergeant.

As he drew closer to his destination, his gait quickened, as did his anticipation. He had been away at war the better part of three years, but James Thomsen was finally coming home. As he approached the family farm that late-March afternoon, the weary man wondered how much had changed since his last visit. That previous journey had been the most painful of his life. His mission that sweltering summer day was to return the lifeless body of his younger brother Asa, who was then buried in the family plot next to their father. James shivered at the memory. He desperately hoped that this short respite from war would prove a far happier visit.

The first to notice the soldier was Widow Thomsen. She was leaving the barn with a fresh bucket of milk when she first spotted the figure in the distance. She did not recognize the uniform, but she would have known that long dark-blonde hair and the familiar stride of her son anywhere.

James was home at last.

The soldier saw his mother running toward him with tears streaming down her cheeks. He grinned widely, his green eyes dancing. They embraced silently in a mutual grip of relief and joy.

Widow Thomsen reluctantly released her son and touched his face.

"You are well?" she asked through flowing tears.

"I am, Mother," he said. As he held her tightly, his youthful expression made him look far younger than his twenty-three years.

"This uniform, it is new?" the widow asked him as she touched the graying lapel.

James looked down at his apparel. "Not exactly new. It was issued to me several months ago. I am now a sergeant."

Widow Thomsen touched his face and for the first time noticed lines around her son's eyes. A few scars here and there revealed that he had been in harm's way more than once.

"Your father would be so proud," she said, her lips quivering again. "Come to the house. There is much news to tell you."

As they headed down the road, the door of the house opened and Daniel walked outside.

"Who is that?" James asked his mother. He stared at the stranger with suspicion.

"That is part of the news, James—" She started to explain but her son interrupted her.

"That man is not from Deer Run, Mother," James said, eyeing the stranger.

Something about the man's features sparked an ominous recognition in James' mind. At first he could not place the familiar face, but it only took a moment for Sergeant Thomsen to recall that moment in battle he would never forget.

From a distance, Daniel knew immediately that this Continental soldier was Mary's brother. His return had been anticipated for months now. But as he approached the man more closely, the young husband's smile began to fade. A brief flash of recognition played in Daniel's mind as well—the recollection of a soldier with blond hair and green eyes, hovering over him as he held his dying brother Oliver. The soldier held a bayonet that threatened to end Daniel's life, but the colonial had vanished in an instant without using the weapon. That merciful soldier was Mary's brother, James.

While Daniel was filled with heartfelt gratitude, his former adversary became suddenly enraged.

"You bloody Redcoat," James yelled, drawing his sword. "Did I spare your life so that you could prey upon my family? I have never stayed my bayonet in battle before. I should not have done so in Saratoga!"

James' face was red with anger as he stalked angrily toward the unarmed man.

Widow Thomsen yelled frantically at her son.

"James, stop! You do not understand!"

But it was the voice of his sister, screaming and crying from the open door, that made the furious young soldier stop in his tracks.

"James, no! He is my husband!" Mary cried hysterically.

The startled brother halted his advance and looked at the young woman in disbelief. He had to stare long and hard to comprehend the unexpected sight. It was his sister Mary, who appeared ready to give birth at any moment. The very pregnant woman slowly made her way to him with tears streaming down her face.

"He is my husband, James," she said in a whisper, her lips trembling.

The brother carefully put his arms around his sister. His fury was stopped cold but his heart still pounded in his chest. James looked over her shoulder at Daniel.

"You are her husband?" he asked in disbelief.

Daniel swallowed hard and wiped away the sweat from his brow.

"Yes," he said. Daniel's eyes were wide and his throat suddenly dry.

James held his sister tenderly a moment longer as her tears subsided. Widow Thomsen touched James' arm.

"Son, we must speak with one another. Please come with me."

She drew him aside, and the soldier released his embrace on his sister, still glaring at Daniel. James followed his mother reluctantly. He was upset and baffled by this situation.

Daniel put his arm around his wife as Widow Thomsen and James walked toward the barn.

"Mary, let us go back inside," he said. The young husband was worried that this stress could bring on the birth of their child too early.

Although labor appeared to be imminent, according to Mary the expected arrival was not for another month. However, the size of Mary's belly told Widow Thomsen that this child would be born sooner.

Mary knew that her mother believed she had become pregnant before their wedding day. While the midwife's conclusions were incorrect, Mary knew her mother would not hold this against them. Widow Thomsen had often delivered a child less than nine months after a wedding. But Mary just wished that her mother did not assume the same was true of their child.

The young couple walked back into the farmhouse. Daniel helped his wife up the step that led to the main room and led her to the chair by the fire. Although spring was on its way, the air still held a damp chill. She shuddered as much from the aggressive actions of her brother as from the cold.

"Daniel, I am so sorry about James," she said, shaking her head. "How did he know you were in the British Army?"

Her husband sat in a chair next to hers and took her hand.

"Do you remember when I told you about Oliver? How I held him as he died? A Continental soldier came with his bayonet uplifted, and I thought it was my demise?"

Mary nodded. "You closed your eyes for a moment and when you opened them, he was gone," she said, recollecting the incredible story.

Daniel took a deep breath. He was still trying to comprehend this strange turn of events. He finally spoke the words that were difficult even for him to believe.

"That soldier who spared my life was your brother James."

Mary's eyes opened wide. "James?" she said in astonishment. She sat back in the wooden chair and was silent for a moment. "Did you recognize him as well?"

"Yes," Daniel said. "As soon as I saw him I knew he was familiar. It only took a few moments to realize who he was. I envisioned his green eyes staring at me with his bayonet held high. I was just getting ready to thank him when he made the same connection between us. I realized then that he sorely regretted his mercy back in Saratoga."

Mary squeezed his hand. "Thank God that he did spare you," she said, tears welling in her eyes.

"I hope he begins to feel that way as well," he said.

The young woman shifted restlessly in the chair as she placed her hands over her enormous belly.

"This child seems far too active," she said, wincing. "He moves so much—it is exhausting."

Her husband looked at her with sympathy. "I am sorry you are suffering so," he said, rubbing her arm. And no wonder that she was. Though he would never say this to his wife, he had never before seen a pregnant woman so large. And on her slender frame, the contrast with her enlarged belly was startling.

The young husband kissed his wife and served her some warm cider in a pewter tankard. Mary had finished most of the cider when her mother, James, and Sarah all came in to the house. Sarah had been collecting eggs in the barn and had missed the initial encounter between Daniel and James. The young girl was brimming with enthusiasm over the return of her brother.

"Did you see who is home?" she asked Mary and Daniel excitedly, as she danced around the room.

The couple smiled at Sarah's joyful demeanor.

"Sarah, please put the basket of eggs down before you break them," Widow Thomsen chided. The young girl giggled and set the container down before hugging her brother once again. James briefly embraced Sarah in return before removing his tricornered hat.

The soldier meekly approached his brother-in-law with an apologetic attitude. He cast his eyes downward for a moment and fidgeted with his hat. His mother had just spoken with him at length regarding Daniel, including how the former British soldier had intervened on more than one occasion to rescue the Thomsen women.

"I am greatly humbled by the enlightening reports my mother has given me regarding your help to my family, Mr. Lowe," James said to his brother-in-law. "I beg your forgiveness for my aggression towards you upon my arrival."

"Please call me Daniel. And your response was certainly understandable." Daniel held his hand out to Mary's sibling. "Let us be friends—as well as brothers."

James' green eyes looked intently at his sister's husband. The Continental soldier still bore the hyper-vigilant edge of someone fresh off the field of battle. His demeanor was now more subdued, however, and his eyes were filled with gratitude.

After a long pause he spoke. "It appears that the Lord had me spare you for a reason. And I thank you for saving my sisters while I was gone."

James took his hand and the two men shook. Daniel noticed the strong familial resemblance between Mary and her brother. It somehow made him feel an immediate kinship with the man.

Turning his attention to Mary, James bent down near her chair and looked at her belly.

"It appears you have been occupying your time well while I have been gone, little sister," he said teasingly.

She pushed him on his shoulder. "You are always the jester, brother James," she said.

"So when is the little one due to arrive?" he asked. "It looks to be at any moment."

Mary's face grew serious.

"Not for another month or more," she said as she rubbed her swollen belly.

James' expression showed his surprise.

"Really?" he said. "I was hoping the little one might arrive while I am home on leave."

The young woman's expression became saddened.

"You have to go back soon, James? You've only just arrived. Please tarry as long as possible."

Her brother touched her arm. "I will be here for a short while—long enough to ask Hannah to be my wife," he said. "If she will have me, of course."

Mary grinned widely and teased her brother.

"I do not know, James. She may have decided you were not worth waiting for."

Daniel saw the look of consternation on James' face.

"My wife can be cruel, can she not?" Daniel said in jest. Then he reassured the concerned soldier. "Of course, Hannah has been waiting for you. She will be beside herself with joy that you are home."

James smiled in relief and pinched his sister's cheek.

"Some things never change between brothers and sisters," he said, laughing. He stood up and hugged his sister awkwardly.

"I am going to see Hannah immediately, before she decides that I am not worth the wait." He looked back at his very pregnant sister and pointed at her belly. "Do not birth that baby before I get back."

He grinned at her, put his hat back on, and walked out the front door.

"It is such great relief to have my brother home, even if it is only a short while," Mary said.

Daniel was also relieved. He was finally relaxing from the tension of James' arrival.

Widow Thomsen began setting out the evening meal. Daniel helped Mary out of her chair so that she could go over to the table. The young woman would not be able to eat a great deal, but the small amount she could manage would sustain her for a few hours—until the middle of the night, when she would awaken her husband to get her some bread and milk, which had become their nighttime ritual.

When the couple retired to their room that evening, they both lay awake in bed. Their minds were busily reflecting on the events of the day.

Daniel watched in awe at the movements of his child in Mary's belly as she lay on her back, propped up on several pillows. It was amazing to both he and Mary just how active their little one truly was.

"So what should we name our child, Mary?" Daniel asked after a long silence.

"I think we should call him Daniel," she said.

"Daniel?" The young father furrowed his brow. "How about James, after your father?" he suggested.

"We shall see," Mary said, nestling contentedly next to her husband.

"We have not discussed lasses' names," Daniel said after a moment. "I think we should call her Mary."

He kissed her on the cheek. The young wife looked up at the face of her husband and placed her hand on his cheek.

"I think a daughter should be named Polly—after your dear sister," Mary said, caressing his face.

Daniel kissed his wife's forehead and held her close.

"Thank you, Mary," he said.

They held each other in a comforting embrace. Soon she could hear the gentle snore of her husband and feel his arms relaxed in sleep.

Mary, however, was wide-awake. After trying to find a more comfortable position in the bed, she realized that her mind was far too active to rest. She picked up the Bible on her bedside table.

Perhaps reading about new mothers in God's word will soothe my anxious thoughts.

She opened the pages to the book of Genesis and read about the birth of Isaac to his mother Sarah in her old age.

"Poor woman," Mary whispered to herself. "I am grateful that I am not so old as Sarah."

Mary continued to peruse the pages until she found the passages about the delivery of Rebekah, wife of Isaac. She read about the woman's difficult pregnancy and how she had entreated God for an answer as to why there was such an uproar in her belly.

"And when her days to be delivered were fulfilled, behold, there were twins in her womb," Mary read.

The young mother paused in her reading and looked down at her enormous belly of activity. She thought for a moment.

"No, that is not possible," she said with certainty.

She placed the Bible back on the table and blew out the still glowing candle.

Chapter Thirty-seven

Travail

It had stormed heavily in Deer Run during the night, but it was sunny and clear that early April morning. The earth was starting to awaken from its long winter hibernation, and Mary felt energized by the new life in her surroundings.

She paused briefly as she did every day to check the progress of her favorite lavender plants. The gray leaves were just starting to come back as they did each spring, the gradual greening of the dormant spikes promising another year of fragrant purple flowers. Mary looked out at the cornfield ready for planting. The rows of dirt mounds were meant to simulate the belly of a pregnant woman, according to Indian lore. The young woman looked down and draped her linen gown tightly over her growing child. Mary had always thought that the piles of soil were similar to the dimensions of an actual pregnancy. Somehow, the hills in the field seemed inadequate to any comparison to her belly. She furrowed her brow.

"I think we need to add more dirt to the mounds," she said. Mary continued her waddling walk to the barn, milk bucket in hand. She entered the barn and smiled at Daniel, who was cleaning the tools for the upcoming planting. Aunt Prudence would be here any day now and everything needed to be ready for Jubo and Gibb.

"And how do you fare this morning?" Daniel asked. He looked down at the bucket she was carrying. "You're not going to milk Susannah, are you?"

"My mother says that sitting on the milking stool will help prepare me for the birth. Besides, I am feeling so energetic this morning—I could probably start planting, I feel so good," she said.

"Well that is not going to happen," Daniel said, stopping long enough to kiss Mary. "I am certain that milking Susannah is quite enough. But once you've filled the bucket, let me carry it back inside. I know that your back has been feeling the strain."

Her husband was resuming his task of cleaning the tools when Mary stopped him.

"Daniel, I have been thinking. Have you thought about writing to your father to tell him about the baby? He does not even know we are married," she said, looking at him sympathetically. She knew that her husband greatly missed his only living parent.

Daniel looked at her with sadness. "That would cause me great joy, Mary … but with the war still going on, I can not risk communicating with him just yet." He looked at his wife with tenderness. "Thank you for thinking of him. I hope that someday he will be able to meet both you and our child."

He kissed his wife tenderly and returned to his labors. Daniel had a somber look on his face.

To lighten the mood, she began to sing a lyric that she had composed for him. He loved it when Mary sang. She would occasionally write down words and then put them to music in her mind. It was a pastime that she and her brother Asa had enjoyed before he had gone off to war—before the war had silenced his music on the fife forever.

She walked over towards Susannah's stall and started to sing:

There was a lad named Daniel Lowe,
Across the sea come sailin'
He met a girl, set his heart atwirl,

Before Mary could get out the next line, a tightness seized her belly with such force that she could not speak. She gripped the wooden post in the stall, her knuckles turning white. The intensity of the contraction brought her down onto her knees and she felt a warm liquid coming out from between her legs. She knew now that this child was going to be born—and soon.

He was looking down at the tools he was oiling, smiling broadly with pleasure at the song.

"What is the next line, Mary?" he asked. When she did not answer, he looked up in surprise and saw his wife's hand clutching the post above the wooden barrier of the stall.

His face blanched. "Mary!" he yelled. He hurried over to his wife and crouched beside her, his wounded leg jutting out awkwardly.

"Daniel," she said once the pain had abated enough so that she could speak. "The baby—it's too early." Her voice was filled with fear.

"This child has decided otherwise," he replied, trying not to panic. He stood and picked her up to carry her to the house.

"I can walk, Daniel. The pain has lessened," she said. "My mother will keep me walking through much of my travail."

He reluctantly put her down but kept his arm around her as they walked cautiously back to the house. Before they reached the front door, Mary grasped her belly again, her knees bending with the force. Daniel held her up and noticed her cheeks turning a bright red with the effort of the contraction. It seemed to go on interminably, stretching the time before she was able to breathe with ease. She wearily headed back toward the farmhouse, supported by her husband's strong arms. Widow Thomsen and James were discussing the young soldier's upcoming wedding to Hannah. When they saw Daniel assisting Mary indoors, a look of distress appeared on both of their faces.

"It is time?" the widow asked.

She looked concerned but not surprised. Mary nodded in assent as yet another intense pain clenched at her belly.

"Bring her to the bedroom, Daniel," she instructed. "And please get the birthing stool from the barn, James."

James ran to the barn followed by Sarah.

"The baby is coming, James? So soon?" Sarah asked, out of breath from the excitement and the running. "I thought it was coming next month," she said as they entered the barn.

Her older brother reached up to grab the birthing stool from a hook on the wall. He also grabbed an old rag and dusted it off.

"Sometimes babies come sooner than we thought," the young soldier said. James and his mother had previously discussed their mutual belief that the baby had been conceived prior to the wedding.

James looked at the old wooden birthing stool and was impressed with its design. The slender edge of the chair allowed the woman to sit while providing an opening for the baby to be delivered.

"I remember getting this down for our mother when you were born, Sarah," James said.

"But that was a very long time ago, James. I am quite grown up now," she said. Sarah stood as tall as her short height would allow.

James tousled her hair with one hand. "Then you'd best get that hair pinned up under a cap if you are such a lady," he teased. Then he grew more serious. "But do not grow up too quickly. Having one sister marry and start a family is sufficient for now."

They both walked back to the farmhouse, one on each side of the birthing stool. Together they transported the chair that would soon witness the birth of their nephew or niece.

As they entered the house, Daniel was sitting in the chair by the fire, rubbing his head and looking distraught. This child really was birthing sooner than expected and this concerned him greatly. When he saw the birthing stool in their hands, he took it gratefully and brought it to the door of the bedroom. He knocked. Widow Thomsen opened the door, grabbed the stool, and shut the door quickly. Daniel caught a brief glimpse of his wife bending over in yet another bout of gut-wrenching pain. The frightened husband turned his back to the door, his face pale.

James looked at his brother-in-law with concern. "Perhaps you should sit back down, Daniel. You look a bit done in."

Daniel accepted his advice. Sarah approached him, concerned for the soon-to-be father as well.

"It will be all right, Daniel," she said, touching his large hand with her small one. "Would you like to pray—like we did when Mary was ill?"

Daniel looked at Sarah with gratitude. "Yes, little miss. That is what we should do," he said.

James joined the group in a prayer for Mary and her unborn baby. Daniel tried to put to rest the never-ending fear that arose in him at the memory of his mother dying in childbirth.

Dear God, please take this fear away from me, he silently entreated. When the prayers were completed, James looked up.

"I must go and get Hannah. Mary wanted her to come at this time," he said.

James left the house and went to the barn for Dash. He noticed with annoyance the lack of a man's saddle.

"I shall just have to ride bareback," he said to himself. He set the brown mare next to a partition between the stalls and used the wooden structure to boost himself onto her back. His strong legs gripped the horse's flanks for the precarious ride to Hannah White's home in the village.

Daniel continued to sit in the chair near the hearth. He tried not to flinch every time he heard his wife's moans from the bedroom. Sarah brought him some apple cider to drink.

"Thank you, little miss," he said, grateful for the liquid on his dry throat.

His young sister-in-law then brought over *Aesop's Fables* so that she could read to the anxious father. Daniel tried to pay attention to the stories but his mind constantly returned to the events taking place in the side room.

Although it seemed like hours, James soon returned with Hannah astride Dash. The young woman hurried into the house, her eyes wide with concern. Daniel nodded toward the bedroom and Hannah hurried inside. She shut the door behind her, but they were able to briefly hear Mary's groans more audibly.

James noticed the strained look on Daniel's countenance.

"Let us go work, rather than worry," James said to his brother-in-law, patting him on his shoulder. Reluctantly, the distraught husband got up.

"You will call me if Mary needs me?" Daniel asked Sarah anxiously.

"Yes, Daniel," she said. "But I think she just needs the women right now."

The two men went outdoors and Daniel breathed in deeply of the fresh air. He looked out towards the distant woods. The emerging buds promised lush greenery before long.

"This child is coming too soon," Daniel said soberly.

James stared at him for a long while.

"You mean, this really is not expected?" he asked in surprise.

Daniel stared at Mary's brother.

"No, it is not—although I understand why you ask that. I have never seen a woman so large with child before. Mary and I have both been concerned all along. But no, this baby began its life right after our wedding day," Daniel said emphatically.

After a long pause James said, "I believe you." But now he was concerned as well.

A rider came down the road toward the farmhouse and the two brothers looked over and saw that it was Mr. Eaton approaching.

"Heard there were big goings on at the Thomsen farm," Mr. Eaton said, then paused as he noted their expressions. "Why so somber, gentlemen? This is a happy occasion," he added, slapping the soon-to-be father on the back.

Daniel and James told the visitor about the baby arriving ahead of schedule and the three of them stood in deep thought, trying to ascertain what this meant for Mary and the child. Their fears worsened when Widow Thomsen came to the door, yelling for the men to come quickly.

"Daniel, something is wrong." The midwife tried to appear calm but her trembling lips betrayed her apprehension. "I need someone to get Widow Baxter, the midwife in Williamston."

James stared blankly at his mother.

"Widow Baxter?" he asked in complete surprise. "Is she not dead?"

Widow Thomsen glared at her son. "Of course she is not dead, James!"

"No, really, I thought she was. Is she not nearly a hundred?"

"She is in her eighties, but she is still able to help with a birthing. And I need her experience right now, so please hasten!" she ordered.

"Right," James said.

He ran to get Dash from the barn once again. He rode away as quickly as he could to fetch the elderly midwife, who lived three miles down the road in Williamston.

While the widow was arguing with James, Daniel had slipped into the house and went to the door of the bedroom. He opened it cautiously and saw Mary in bed crying.

"Daniel, I need to speak with you alone," his wife said in great distress.

Hannah exited the room quickly and Daniel shut the door. He hurried over to Mary and grabbed her hand.

"Daniel," Mary said gasping. "You must promise me something," she said, in between her labored breaths. Her face was dripping with sweat and as red as he had ever seen it.

"Yes, anything," he said, trying to fight back tears.

"If I do not survive this birth, I want you to tell our son that I want him to grow up to be a good man, just like his father," she said.

Daniel shook his head, unable to speak for fear that tears would begin to flow along with his words.

"And tell him that I love him," she said before another grinding pain assaulted her swollen abdomen.

Daniel watched as his wife put every ounce of her being into delivering their child. He suddenly felt an overpowering surge of hope and conviction, and he was determined to be stalwart for Mary.

When her pain abated, Daniel looked at her with tears but with strength.

"You will survive this birth," he said to her with firm but gentle resolve, "and you will tell him you love him yourself."

He kissed her with a brief but passionate kiss and released her back to the care of her mother, who had hurried back to the birthing.

Daniel walked back to the main room, wiping the tears away from his face. Myles Eaton looked at him with sympathy.

"Come on lad," he said, putting his arm around Daniel's shoulders. "Let us take a walk and clear our heads."

Chapter Thirty-eight

Midwife

It took James only twenty minutes to ride from the Thomsen's farm to Williamston. With the strain of the situation, however, it felt much longer. As the young soldier arrived at the edge of the town square, he slowed the mare to a canter. He scanned the somewhat familiar surroundings, yet could not locate the home of Widow Baxter. Seven years earlier he had come here to fetch the midwife for Sarah's birthing. But the town had grown and changed since then, and he could not fairly discern which cabin it was. His anxiety made the effort even more difficult.

"Good day, lads," he said to two young boys, who were each perhaps thirteen years of age. "Can you tell me where the midwife lives?"

"Yes, sir," they said eagerly, saluting the young sergeant. "Follow us, sir."

They ran down the road a short way and pointed to the log cabin, which James now recognized instantly.

"Thank you, lads," James said. "You are worthy young soldiers."

Like so many colonial youths, these boys were anxious to be at war, helping the cause for freedom and frustrated by the age restriction of sixteen years. James surmised correctly that they would feel proud to be helping a sergeant.

"Thank you, sir," they said in unison, looking at James and smiling. The taller lad asked him about the need for Widow Baxter.

"Is it your wife needing the midwife, sir?"

"No—my sister," James said, jumping off of Dash's back. "Can one of you lads hold the reins for me while I get the widow?"

The boys' eyes danced at the request and gave their hearty consent. They stroked Dash's nose and forehead as though she were the steed of General Washington himself. James raced to the front door and knocked loudly. He waited a moment with no response and knocked even harder.

"Maybe she did die," he whispered fearfully. At length, the slow-moving woman finally opened the door. She looked at James with her head tilted back to allow her to see him through her spectacles.

"Yes, young man, may I help you," she said with a crackly voice.

James' expression reflected his despair. Her ancient appearance seemed to support the jests of local children that Widow Baxter had likely birthed those born aboard the Mayflower over one hundred years ago. James attempted to smother the telltale signs of his growing panic.

"I am Sergeant Thomsen from Deer Run, ma'am. You are still the midwife, Widow Baxter?" James asked. He swallowed with difficulty.

"I still do some birthings, sir, that is correct," she replied, flashing a nearly toothless grin. She looked at him more carefully. "Do I know you, sir? Your face looks familiar."

"Yes, ma'am, I fetched you seven years ago for the birth of my younger sister in Deer Run," he said. "But I am here today to bring you to assist in the birthing of my other sister's child. She is in some distress and my mother needs your assistance."

The light of recognition appeared in Widow Baxter's eyes.

"Ah yes. Your mother is midwife in Deer Run—Widow Thomsen," she said, remembering her old friend that she had mentored in midwifery. "So it is your sister in distress, sir?" she asked, putting her finger to her lips as she tried to envision the young mother. "She must be the lass that was born here in my own home. You were home ill with the pox, as I recall."

"Yes, Widow Baxter, that is correct." Sweat began to form on James' brow. "If you please, ma'am, my mother is most anxious for your help. I can take you to Deer Run on horseback, but we must hasten."

The widow reached up to touch James' cheek and pat it gently.

"Do not fear, young man. I shall get my things."

Slowly, she walked over toward a cabinet and pulled down a bottle of spirits.

"Does your mother have enough wine for the new mother?" she asked.

James looked uncertain.

"I suppose she does, Widow Baxter. She is always quite prepared for these events," he said unsurely.

"Good."

The elderly woman took the lid off of the flask of spirits and took a hearty guzzle. She replaced the flask in the cupboard.

James helped the midwife get her shawl over her shoulders and practically carried the thin woman out the door. The two boys were faithfully keeping guard over Dash. The horse seemed very content with all the attention being lavished upon her. As James approached the mare with Widow Baxter, he paused to determine the safest way to get her aboard the horse's back. The experienced soldier then came up with a plan.

"If we can get cannon up a hill, surely you men can help me get the midwife up onto this steed," he said, inspiring the boys' patriotic spirit.

"Yes, sir," they said eagerly.

James brought Dash over to a sturdy maple tree with large overhanging limbs.

"Men, climb up onto these branches and I shall hand you Widow Baxter. You can then assist her in getting mounted safely onto the horse," he said.

"Aye, sir," the lads answered in unison.

The limber youths immediately clambered up the tree. Once they were in proper position on the branches, James lifted the midwife up into their waiting arms. They carefully placed the frail woman onto the horse's back as securely as they could.

"Hold on to the horse's mane whilst I climb up there to secure you further," James instructed the woman.

Widow Baxter was laughing heartily at all this activity.

"Why, I have not had that many hands of young men upon me since my courting days," she said with a chuckle.

The two boys in the tree looked at each other with raised eyebrows.

"Someone courted this shriveled woman?" one whispered to the other. The boys shared a look of amazement.

James looked at them and smiled an understanding grin. The elderly woman's poor hearing prevented her from catching their words, and she sat happily awaiting the ride to help the new mother.

"Good job, men," James said as he climbed behind Widow Baxter onto the horse's back. "I am grateful for your help. You have assisted in the safe delivery of what will be the newest patriot in the colonies. Well done!"

James saluted the boys and they returned the gesture, beaming with pride.

Holding the reins tightly, he wrapped his arms protectively around the elderly widow. To ensure safe passage for Widow Baxter, he trotted Dash at a somewhat slower pace than he had on the ride out.

It seemed so long since he had left his sister in distress. He prayed that their arrival would not be too late.

Chapter Thirty-nine

Birth

Back at the farm, James' arrival was met with both relief and consternation. They were comforted by the fact that a second midwife was now on the premises, but they were alarmed at how frail the woman appeared. Daniel and Mr. Eaton carefully assisted the woman off the mare as James lifted her down.

"Thank you for coming, Widow Baxter," Daniel said. He tried not to appear as frightened as he felt.

"You must be the young father," the woman said, grinning her toothless grin. "Let's see what we can do for your wife, sir. Show me the way."

The men gingerly assisted the woman inside and led her to the bedroom. They could hear Mary's wails of discomfort. Widow Baxter noticed the looks of concern on the men's faces.

"Why don't you gents take a walk for a bit," the elderly midwife suggested. They readily followed her advice.

Sarah was kept occupied fetching small buckets of water from the well and tending the hot water over the fire. Whenever the women inside the birthing room requested warm cloths to soothe Mary's abdomen, the young girl had them at the ready. Although she had accompanied her mother to several deliveries in the past, she had never before been to one that seemed to cause such worry. The tension in the home made her grateful for the tedious but time-consuming job.

When Widow Baxter entered the birthing room she was greeted by pained looks that quickly turned to looks of relief. Help had finally arrived.

"Thank you for coming, Widow Baxter," the younger midwife said. She was near exhaustion from trying to assist Mary. She had first tried one position for her laboring daughter, than another. It seemed that this child could not present itself to the world and Widow Thomsen was near despair.

The older woman assessed the situation closely but spoke few words. She went over to Mary and greeted the laboring woman. Mary was greatly fatigued from this travail and Widow Baxter gave her a comforting pat on the shoulder.

"Haven't seen you in some time, lass. Let me put my hands on your belly here to see what is where," she said.

The elderly woman deftly felt each portion of the huge abdomen. Although she appeared frail, the older midwife worked with a strength that came only with experience. She moved her sinewy hands all around Mary's belly.

"I see," she finally said. "It appears that they are both trying to be birthed at the same time."

The women all stared at Widow Baxter, unable to speak. Finally Hannah White broke the silence.

"Both?" she said weakly.

"You did not know there were twins?" the older midwife said, perplexed.

Widow Thomsen turned a deep shade of red. "No ... I thought ... that is ... I should have known," she stammered.

The older woman patted her shoulder.

"Do not fret, Widow Thomsen. It can be easy to miss, especially when it's your own daughter. We midwives can be fooled," she said.

A severe pain gripped at Mary's belly and she urgently felt the need to push. Widow Baxter suddenly became commander of the delivery.

"All right then. We're going to figure out just which babe is ready to come out first. They seem to be jammed like logs in a river. We need to hold one back to let the other downstream," she said.

Mary was in the midst of a bearing down pain when the older midwife ascertained which twin was approaching first and which was the log-jammer. When the urge to push ceased, Widow Baxter encouraged her troops.

"All right, ladies, let's get this brave mother onto the birthing stool."

She assisted Mary as much as she herself was able. Hannah and Widow Thomsen did most of the lifting. Mary was exhausted from hours of travail.

"Let us lean her forward some. And you, young miss, put your hands like this," she directed Hannah.

The old woman showed the younger how to put upward pressure that would slightly lift the second baby off its twin. This would allow an easier exit for the firstborn. It was a difficult maneuver to carry out, especially once the muscle contracted so tightly.

Widow Thomsen joined in the effort in lifting the baby in front upward. This would allow the baby in the back—the one struggling to be born first—to finally make its way into the world. Bent down almost to the floor, the older midwife encouraged Mary to bear down with all her might. The young woman drew upon inner resources of strength that she did not know she possessed. As she grimaced and groaned deeply, she heard Widow Baxter say triumphantly, "Here is the head!"

Mary was encouraged by the woman's words but also greatly fatigued. As the pain temporarily ceased, she rested her head upon her mother's shoulders and breathed in deeply, sweat dripping from her brow. Widow Thomsen was overwhelmed with guilt that she had failed to notice the presence of the second child. The thought of two children in her daughter's womb had never crossed her mind. And with the one child tucked behind the other, it would not always be obvious even for an experienced midwife's hands.

"Mary, I am so sorry. I did not realize there were twins. I should have known—" she started to say. There was no more time for conversation, however, as this first twin was now intent upon arriving. The laboring mother gathered her strength once again. She bore down with all her might as she gave birth to her son.

"It's a boy!" Widow Baxter shouted. Her voice carried out to the main room, where Sarah was listening at the door.

The young girl ran outdoors where the men stood waiting. The expressions on their faces were somber. They steeled themselves for whatever report came from the birthing room, be it good news or bad.

"It's a boy!" Sarah shouted to the group. She jumped up and down before returning to the house.

Daniel's mouth opened in amazement at the realization that he had become a father. A smile slowly emerged on his face. Both James and Myles Eaton slapped the new parent on his back, congratulating the relieved young man.

"I have seven daughters and you get a son on your first go 'round," Mr. Eaton said, shaking his head and grinning. "Good job, lad."

There was little time for pausing to celebrate in the birthing room, however. Unbeknownst to the men outdoors, a second birth was about to occur.

While Widow Thomsen tenderly held her firstborn grandchild, Hannah took on the role of encouraging Mary to bear down once again.

The new mother followed Hannah's instructions. Within a moment, Mary felt her second son arrive into the awaiting hands of Widow Baxter.

"It's another boy!" the midwife exclaimed loudly.

Sarah was listening again at the door to the room. Her eyes were wide with wonder.

"Two boys?" she said in disbelief.

Running out the door again—nearly tripping on the bucket this time—Sarah scurried to the men. Their conversation stopped as the excited girl approached. The look of astonishment on her face caught their attention.

"It is another boy," she said incredulously. "It is twins!"

At first, all three men stood silently, unable to comprehend this unexpected report.

"Twins?" James finally said in astonishment. "It is no wonder Mary's travail came early."

"Well done, Daniel!" Myles Eaton said, slapping him jovially on his back.

Daniel stood there, a look of utter disbelief on his face. Then he thought about all this labor that Mary had been through and his heart broke for her pain.

"Is Mary well?" he asked Sarah.

"I think so, Daniel, but I am not certain. They would not let me in."

Her brother-in-law did not wait for her answer as he raced towards the house to his new family.

Daniel stopped short of bursting through the door. He managed to knock gently despite his racing heart.

Hannah answered the knock, her face grinning widely.

"You must be patient, Daniel," she said, then closed the door in his face.

Daniel closed his eyes and put his back to the door as he slid into a sitting position on the floor. For the first time all day he was able to relax. He was so grateful that God had blessed him and Mary with not one but two sons. And he was so grateful that Mary had survived.

"Thank you," he whispered, looking up toward heaven.

Inside the birthing room, Widows Baxter and Thomsen were assisting each infant to nurse. When the eager infants latched on to their mother, Mary winced with pain.

"Will that always feel like that? Like my toes are curling from the discomfort?" Mary asked, closing her eyes tightly.

"It will get easier," both midwives said simultaneously. They looked at each other and laughed at their identical words of encouragement. As the infants settled into their eager but gentler suckle, Mary became desperate to see her husband.

"Where is Daniel?" she asked, looking with earnestness at her mother. "I want him to meet his sons."

Widow Thomsen looked down at her daughter, who was still feeding her babies.

"Why do you not wait until they are finished eating?" the widow asked, uncomfortable with a young father in the room at such a private moment.

"Do you think he has never seen his wife before?" she asked teasingly, trying to remain patient.

Widow Baxter smiled and looked at the new mother. "Most grandmothers prefer to assume their grandchildren were conceived miraculously," the older woman said mischievously. "In my time, I have delivered many a 'miracle' that began its life beneath the quilts on a cold winter's night."

Widow Baxter gave Mary a wink. Mary smiled appreciatively at the older midwife. She was grateful for her humor and for her help. Widow Thomsen rolled her eyes in defeat.

"All right then. I shall get your husband." The new grandmother gave an exasperated sigh at this breach in proper protocol.

When Mary's mother opened the door, Daniel was still leaning against it and nearly fell inside.

"I am sorry, Daniel," Widow Thomsen said, helping him to his feet. "I did not realize you were there."

The three women watched as the eager father approached his new family, and they quickly exited as a group. The young husband stood at the end of the bed and viewed the incredible sight of his wife feeding his two new sons. He was transfixed by the beauty of the scene. It brought tears to his eyes and a smile to his countenance.

"Mary," he was finally able to say with difficulty. "Two sons?" He whispered the words in disbelief.

His wife was exhausted but elated.

"Come meet them, Daniel," Mary said eagerly.

Her firstborn was finished eating and had contentedly closed his eyes with his mouth still open.

"Here is our first son. This is Daniel," she said.

She nodded towards her second born.

"This is James," she said. She laughed at the smaller twin vigorously suckling. "He has quite an appetite."

Daniel just stared at his sons. Although he spoke no words, his eyes were filled with a depth of gratitude to Mary. He was overwhelmed with a love that was deeper than any he could have imagined. He finally was able to speak.

"You are amazing," he said, looking at his wife tenderly and stroking her face. She could see his mouth beginning to tremble.

"I love you Daniel," she said, her eyes welling with tears.

Daniel gently leaned over her and kissed her tenderly.

"Thank you, Mary. Thank you for our sons," he whispered.

Mary's heart was so full of love for her husband and now for their children. The blessings of this day were only now beginning to be felt as an indescribable joy within her heart. This was a moment in her life that she would always treasure—and never forget.

"Would you like to hold young Daniel?" she asked.

The father looked uncomfortable and more than a little worried.

"I do not want to injure him."

"Just hold him behind his head. He will be safe in your arms," she said encouragingly.

He gingerly lifted up the bundle in the knitted blanket and held his firstborn in his strong hands. He looked down upon his sleeping child and tenderly kissed his face.

"Welcome, my son," he said. "Welcome to America."

Chapter Forty

Peace

Four years to the day after General Burgoyne's surrender at Saratoga in 1777, British General Cornwallis began to work out his own terms of surrender at Yorktown with General George Washington. It was four years to the day since the start of Daniel's new journey in America.

The hostilities between England and the colonies continued until February of 1783. There had been nearly eight years of war between the mother country and her colonial offspring, and with the end of the fighting came Daniel's opportunity to finally write to his father. This long-awaited attempt occurred nearly five years after Daniel and Mary had become husband and wife.

"I only hope he is still alive," Daniel said to his wife as he sent the message off with the postrider that spring.

Fortunately, Daniel—now the father of three children, with another imminent arrival—did not have to wait long for an answer. It was midsummer that year of 1783 when Mary slowly made her way to the flax field. The four-year-old twins were helping Daniel weed. The expectant mother waddled her way to see her husband while holding onto the hand of two-year-old Polly. Mary held a folded parchment in her other hand.

"Daniel!" she called excitedly.

Her husband looked up at her with a furrowed brow of concern.

"Is it time?" the husband asked anxiously, looking at his very pregnant wife.

"No," Mary said, out of breath from climbing up the slight embankment. She noticed that young Daniel and James had taken advantage of this moment when their father's back was turned to them. Instead of using their hoes to weed, they were pointing them at each other, pretending that the tools were muskets.

"Daniel! James!" she scolded the boys.

Her husband turned around toward the mischievous children.

"Cease fire, gentleman," he called out loudly. The boys hung their heads submissively and resumed their work. "It helps to have experience in the army," he said, grinning broadly. He looked down at his daughter. "And what have you been doing today, Polly?" he said, picking the young girl up. "Helping your mother?" He gave her a kiss on the cheek.

"Not exactly." Mary had her hands on her hips and she spoke with a tone of exasperation.

Polly laid her head, flowing with fine blond hair, onto her father's shoulder and pouted.

"Now Polly, you know you must mind your mother," Daniel chided the girl. "I'm sure you will do better now, yes?" Polly smiled at her father and gave him a peck on his cheek. "There's my lassie," he said. "What's this, Mary?" he asked, looking at the paper in her hand.

Mary grinned broadly at her husband as she handed him the parchment.

"A letter," she said, her cheeks glowing even brighter with the news. "From your father," she said, fighting back tears.

Daniel stared at the folded piece for a moment, his hand shaking.

"Open it, Daniel, please!" Mary pleaded with him. She was almost as anxious for this long-anticipated communication as her husband was.

He set Polly down next to her mother and opened the letter, turning away from his wife so that she could not see the emotional struggle playing across his face. He had not spoken to his father or heard from him since the day Daniel and Oliver had set sail for the colonies, and war. Daniel had had to write the excruciating news to his father about Oliver's death and then about his own disgrace as a prisoner of war.

But he was also able to tell his parent about Mary—how she had saved his life, how they had fallen in love and married, and how they had made him a grandfather.

It seemed to Mary as if Daniel would never finish reading the letter. At length, he slowly turned around and she saw that he had been weeping. Mary was heartbroken, assuming that it was a distressing report—until she saw Daniel's face brighten.

"He is coming to see us, Mary," he said, wiping the tears away. "My father thought I was dead," he said, beginning to sob.

Mary put her arms around Daniel's waist and Polly hugged his legs.

"Do not cry, Papa," the young girl said sadly.

Daniel picked up his daughter and hugged her in one arm as he held Mary with his other.

"These are happy tears, Polly." He turned to look at the twins. "Lads! Your grandsire is coming to visit you in America," he said joyfully. "Let us celebrate!"

The twins threw their tools down in excitement and ran after their parents and Polly as they went down the small embankment towards their home—the log cabin that Daniel had built on the road to Deer Run.

Across the Sea

There was a lad named Daniel Lowe
Across the sea come sailin'.
He met a girl, set his heart atwirl,
Now his love is never failin'.

"O love, now come away with me
Our love's beyond all measure.
Please be my wife and share my life,
Your love's my greatest treasure."

"I'll be your bride, dear Daniel Lowe,
My heart with yours is one.
We'll kiss until our love's fulfilled,
I'll gladly bear your son."

There was a lad named Daniel Lowe
Across the sea come sailin'.
He met a girl, set his heart atwirl,
Now his love is never failin'.

From the diary of Mary Lowe

Author's Note

As a line on the cover says, this book was inspired by real events. The story of British solder-turned-American Daniel Lowe was inspired by my real-life great-great-great-great grandfather, Daniel Prince.

Here is part of his true story:

It was likely a chilly day on that eighth of December, 1775, when twenty-year-old Daniel Prince was recruited into the British Army. Little did he know the long and treacherous journey he was about to embark upon.

He signed up with the Twenty-first Regiment of Foot, also known as the Royal North British Fusiliers. That regiment had been scouting all over Great Britain to increase their ranks. After all, it was going to take thousands of soldiers to put down the rebellion going on in those upstart American colonies.

The Twenty-first Foot was placed under General John Burgoyne. Private Daniel Prince was one of the 658 soldiers that set sail for America from Plymouth Dock, England, on April 7, 1776.

The journey across the Atlantic Ocean took nearly two months. While crossing the ocean on his way to war, Daniel turned twenty-one years of age on the first of May.

These long voyages were fraught with dangers, and recruits often died of disease along the way. The weary company arrived in the Americas on May 31.

Daniel Prince's regiment was involved in the British campaign along Lake Champlain in New York. They wintered in Canada that year before resuming the long and bitter British struggle against the colonists.

These soldiers of the King's army were quite successful for a time, even intimidating the small numbers of Americans at Ticonderoga to abandon that fort in the summer of 1777. But another enemy began to make its presence known in the Americas against the British regiments—disease.

Beset by scurvy, dysentery, malaria, and other maladies, a sizeable percentage of the troops were too ill to fight at any given time. The official British Army muster rolls for the Twenty-first Regiment in July of 1777 indicate that Daniel and at least a dozen of his fellow soldiers were "sick."

But their troubles continued. Hoped-for support from British forces, commanded by General William Howe and Colonel Barry St. Leger, did not arrive. Hunger also became a huge problem, weakening the already disease-ridden soldiers.

And then the Battle of Freeman's Farm near Saratoga occurred. The colonists had rallied many thousands of troops to hold back the British—and the King's army paid dearly. The Twenty-first Regiment was one of three British regiments hit hard at this turning point in the Revolution. Many were wounded and many killed. It is not documented that Daniel received any injuries at this time but it is certainly a possibility.

After the British surrender at Saratoga, all the surviving soldiers were marched away as prisoners of war. They were sent to Rutland, Massachusetts, more than 150 miles from Saratoga, and ordered to build a fortress of wood. This would be their prison camp for nearly a year.

Following his unexpected defeat, Burgoyne had tried to have his defeated army moved to Boston for eventual return to England. But General George Washington would have none of that plan.

The American General feared that a British attack on Boston—some 60 miles to the east of Rutland—could result in a siege that would free the imprisoned soldiers. If so, they would again turn against the colonists. In order to lessen the chances of rescue by the British, Washington decided to send Burgoyne's troops to Virginia.

One can only imagine the despair of Private Prince and his fellow soldiers at this prospect. It was now autumn of 1778. They had been gone from home for over two years and had already survived diseases, battles, and a prison camp. Now they were to move even farther from their homeland.

So as the regiments were marched down another road southward, hundreds of the troops escaped into the Massachusetts countryside. This is likely when Daniel Prince escaped.

While his exact journey is not known, we do know that by the following year he had met and married my fourth great-grandmother, Mary "Polly" Packard of the small town of Goshen, Massachusetts.

The new family settled in Williamsburg, Massachusetts, where Daniel built a log cabin. Their first child, a girl, was born in 1780. Twins Daniel Jr. and James were from Mary's third pregnancy.

I am descended from Daniel Prince Jr. The site of the log cabin where they were born is marked with a chiseled rock called the Prince Monument that is still in existence today. I have visited this site where my ancestors trod.

Daniel Prince never did return to the British Army. But he did become an American.

When I was young and first heard that one of my grandfathers had been a Redcoat during the Revolutionary War, I was somewhat embarrassed. Growing up in Massachusetts had made me proud of our country's heritage. But instead of finding zealous patriots in my bloodline, my DNA was from an enemy soldier! Calmer reasoning prevailed, however, as I thought about the reality of Daniel and Mary's tale. Living conditions in Colonial times were difficult, to say the least. It was a frightening period in our history for both Americans and the British. And in the midst of our nation struggling to be birthed, two people on opposing sides in a bloody war met and fell in love.

This story from my family's history was transformed in my thinking into an inspiring one of romance, unhindered by the politics of the day. It became, purely and simply, a love story.

And so was birthed the idea to create a fictional account of actual events. Since the story is from my imagination, I opted to change last names, the names of the communities, and many other details of the time.

However, many of the historical events such as the Thanksgiving Proclamation of the Continental Congress, Mary's background genealogy, and descriptions of the Battle at Monmouth, New Jersey, as described in James' letter, are documented facts.

The particular information on Daniel Prince's military background was discovered thanks to the diligent work of Betty Thomson, independent researcher at the National Archives, Kew, in England. Well done, Betty!

My visit to the Prince Monument was arranged courtesy of Ralmon Black, Historian at Williamsburg, Massachusetts. He trekked up into the woods with my husband, nephew, two cousins, and myself on a chilly October morning to show us the actual site where the cabin was built. I cannot express how moving a moment this was for me.

In *The Road to Deer Run*, I made every effort to stay true to the times. Descriptions of food, homes, clothing, farming, and worship practices are the result of extensive research. And, yes, even the wolf heads mounted on the outside of meeting houses occurred in the 1700s to encourage the hunting of these animals. I am grateful we do not see that today.

And I am even more relieved that our medical practices have improved. As a registered nurse, I shudder to read how some diseases were treated, often making the patient worse off than when they started.

It has been a personally inspiring experience to write this novel. While the times have changed since the eighteenth century, the same struggles of their day are our own. Forgiveness, fear, pain, illness, despair, the worry of having a family member at war, the death of a loved one—these are all the battles we contend with in the twenty-first century.

But we also share faith, laughter, love, the excitement of that first kiss, and the wonder of looking at a newborn. These are the same joys that we share with our ancestors who are so much a part of who we are.

Their journeys are interwoven with our own.

Made in the USA
Lexington, KY
17 December 2010